"Moore does a fantastic job of building worlds and characters in *Seven Forges* as we hop on board the train that is about to meet its doom."

Troubled Scribe

"Wow, that twist. In some ways I think I should have seen it coming, and I kind of did, but *Seven Forges* just lulled me into security and BAM! Craziness!"

On Starships & Dragonwings

"The story is just as epic as the cover art. I am not going to go into specifics because I don't want to give any aspects of the storyline away, but let's just say this is fantasy on the scale of Terry Brooks or Brandon Sanderson. It is that good… The book starts off with a bang, pretty much from page one, and continues on through the climax."

Shattered Ravings

"*Seven Forges* is a perfect story of political intrigue, brutal fighting, beguiling magic and assassinations. I think you can safely say that I 'quite' (read absolutely, fully, thoroughly) liked the book. The build up of Seven Forges was done in an excellent way with first a heavy emphasis on the characters and the obscure Sa'ba Taalor and later neatly shifting the focus onto another developing storyline, but still keeping the exploration of the world at the front. *Seven Forges* has the WOW factor."

The Book Plank

JAMES A MOORE

City of Wonders

SEVEN FORGES, BOOK III

ANGRY
ROBOT

ANGRY ROBOT
An imprint of Watkins Media Ltd

Lace Market House,
54-56 High Pavement,
Nottingham,
NG1 1HW
UK

angryrobotbooks.com
twitter.com/angryrobotbooks
On rocks and souls

An Angry Robot paperback original 2015
1

A catalogue record for this book is available
from the British Library.

ISBN 978 0 85766 504 1
EBook ISBN 978 0 85766 506 5

Set in Meridien by Epub Services.
Printed in the UK by 4edge Ltd.

This book is for Caroline's Ellie.
May you always know joy, little one.

This book is also dedicated to the memory of Tom Piccirilli,
gone far too soon, missed, loved and remembered.

Special thanks to my Robot Overlords for their amazing patience,
to Charles R Rutledge and Chris and Connie Golden,
Scott Goudsward, Amy Young, Paul McNamee, Jonathan Maberry,
Sara Jo West, Dan Brereton, Cliff Biggers, Allison Pang,
Linda Robertson, Matt Bechtel and Martel Sardina.

You all know why.

PROLOGUE

Teagus stared at the smoke that pointed down toward the ruins of Tyrne like an accusatory finger.

He could not seem to catch his breath.

Not a hundred feet away from him, the Empress stood in consultation with her wizard and her general. It was the general that caught his eye right then. Merros Dulver. His lip curled. Dulver was the one who'd ordered him from Tyrne.

"Etrilla." The word crept past his lips.

Etrilla, the god of the cities. Etrilla, who demanded that the priests of his faith dwell within their cities for life, as they were the eyes and soul of the city. As the head of the Church of Etrilla in Tyrne, Teagus should have been there, should have protected the city as best he could from the disaster that fell upon it.

Merros Dulver would likely claim that he had saved Teagus's life.

Blasphemy.

The man was godless.

Teagus had a god. Teagus had Etrilla, whom he had now betrayed because of Merros Dulver.

He walked toward the general even as he took in a deep breath that tasted of ashes and loss.

Merros Dulver looked around the area and forced his hands to relax. They had a powerful desire to ball into fists, but there was nothing to hit, no one to hurt.

Tyrne was gone. He needed only look toward the south and east to know that.

The winds from the Blasted Lands grew stronger and brought with them the taste of ancient ruination. Ash and grit from the great crater rose past the Edge and spilled toward the gathered forces.

For some insane reason Merros had believed, however briefly, that the men with him would be enough to protect the Empress. All that had saved her in the end was that the King in Iron turned and walked away.

Somewhere below in the Blasted Lands an army waded through the raging storm. His men would have been broken by the force of that fury. The Sa'ba Taalor were not broken. Instead they were honed by the savage winds and the endless dust storm.

One of the priests was coming toward him. Merros saw the man and read the expression on his face with ease. He was enraged and shocked and hurt by the death of Tyrne.

They all were.

Desh Krohan was speaking, trying to calm the Empress. Nachia Krous was angry. She had been challenged when they had come to parley for peace. The first of seven kings of the Sa'ba Taalor had scoffed at her, looked down upon her and then had driven his sword into the ground and murdered an entire city.

She was not merely angry. She was tortured by guilt for

every life ripped away by the roaring fire that had swallowed the Summer City.

Teagus came toward him. His demeanor was not what it had been before. He did not duck or bow or cringe. Instead he walked with purpose, his eyes locked on Merros and his wide face set in an expression of righteous rage.

"This will go poorly." Merros mumbled the words, but Desh Krohan heard them and looked his way and then toward the Elder of Etrilla.

"Do you want–" Merros cut off the wizard's words with one sharp wave of his hand.

This would be his battle alone. He had to make clear to the priests that they served the Empire, not the other way around.

Still. He did not have to enjoy the task.

"They are all dead!" Teagus's voice cracked as he came closer. His eyes were wide and teary, but his expression was not one of sorrow. It was rage and hatred that made his face an ugly mask.

One nearly delicate hand pointed a long finger toward Merros. "They are all dead! You forced me from Tyrne and Etrilla has punished us all for your arrogance!"

His teeth ground together as he listened to the accusation. "Don't start your ramblings, priest. I have enough weight to carry."

"You have the blood of *thousands* to wallow through, you swine!"

Merros looked at the man for a dozen heartbeats and Teagus matched his stare. A day earlier and the soldier would have thought the priest incapable of anything that didn't involve cringing.

"You are grieving." Merros took one step toward the priest. "For that reason I will forgive your insult. Go back to the other priests and leave me to my duties."

Teagus spat at him. A wad of phlegm soared toward his face and Merros avoided it with ease, even as he drew back his hand and stepped toward the smaller man. Teagus was short. He was not in good shape. He was older and heavier than he should have been and if the rumors were true his only real exercise came from chasing girls who were not yet women.

Merros's gloved fist slammed into the older man's face and sent him staggering backward. "We are done now."

Desh Krohan looked his way, past the shoulder of the Empress.

Merros pointed to one of his soldiers. At that precise moment he could not have guessed a name. "Lock him in chains. Let him walk behind the wagons and consider his actions."

There were some that might have considered the punishment harsh. Merros considered it a kindness as he had not drawn his sword and killed the man on the spot.

The soldier came forward and hauled the old priest to his feet. Teagus's lip was split and bled freely. The anger had faded and grief took its place. The man cried silently.

Merros understood exactly how he felt. Just the same, the man was locked in chains and made to follow the rest.

Some decisions haunt a person.

The winds below hissed and scathed the walls of the deep valley. Jost paid them no mind. They were not important. Above her the land was smooth and free of the worst of the toxic storm that forever marred the Blasted Lands. Her gods demanded that she leave her home behind and that she lead a small army, the likes of which had never been seen before.

Some armies are easy to command and some are not. Hers was not.

The beasts were not soldiers. They lived solely to kill and to eat. The Pra-Moresh were great, hulking things, larger than most predators that walked the skin of the world, and they were always desperately hungry, just as the Daxar Taalor had designed them to be.

Everything in the Taalor Valley and the surrounding lands served a purpose. Nothing was wasted, not ever.

The gods of the Seven Forges had saved her people after the Cataclysm, helping the wretched and burned, the starving and diseased to live and to thrive, and in exchange, they demanded fealty. The Sa'ba Taalor, the people of the valley, were glad to serve, grateful for the chance to prove themselves.

Three weeks earlier, as Jost was sharpening her weapons and contemplating the possible war against the people of Fellein, Wheklam spoke to her.

Wheklam was not one of her chosen gods. She followed Paedle and she followed Wrommish. They taught her well and she served them well.

There are simple rules in this world: when a god calls you to a task, only a fool questions that god's orders.

Wheklam was the God of the Sea, of Lead and of group conflicts. Not the god of armies, but the god of combat that embraced numerous opponents.

When Wheklam spoke into Jost's mind, the sound was like the crash of angry waves upon a rocky shore. Jost listened to the voice and obeyed, for that was her sacred promise to the Daxar Taalor.

As they spoke, a searing agony cut into the right side of Jost's face, from her high cheek down to her jaw, and she carefully set her sword aside and waited for the words and the pain to end.

She had been given a gift that came with a price: She had been marked as favored by the god. In exchange, Jost had but to finish one task.

When that was finished, she followed Wheklam's commands, adjusting to the Great Scar on her face and moving into the woods in the shadow of Wheklam's great mountain. For two days she walked without sleeping and carefully stalked one of the great rams that frequented the mountain.

The rams were aggressive and powerful, many of them standing nearly as tall as Jost and weighing several hundred pounds more. They were fat beasts, well fed and capable of killing a fighter without much effort.

Her fight with the ram left her bruised across her ribs, both legs and her right arm, and aching from her thigh to her neck on the left side of her body. Four deep gashes ran across her stomach, so she took the gold from her gear and asked favors of Wrommish, who let the gold sear into her flesh and stopped her death. The gods were kind that day.

When she had recovered enough, she cut the great horns from the ram and then cleaned the carcass. There was no food in the area and no heat. She ate the meat raw but set aside the entrails, as Wheklam had instructed. When her belly was full the rest of the carcass was set with the entrails.

The right horn of the ram was ideal and she set to carving it, carefully listening to the details offered by Wheklam and cutting the holes where the god demanded as she hollowed out the horn and cut away the raw flesh still attached.

When she was done and the god was pleased, Jost collected the meat of the ram, tied the horn to her belt with a slice of hide stretched and braided into a proper band, and then headed away from the valley.

She walked, as she had not yet earned a chance to hunt and capture a mount.

The storms outside the valley were as powerful as ever and the winds scoured her and carried the scent of the carcass she hauled behind her.

The meat did not rot. The Daxar Taalor did not want it to rot. She ate what she had to in order to survive. The rest she pulled along in her wake as a ship might haul along a fishing net.

Jost had never been on a boat. She had never spoken to Wheklam before the god spoke to her. It was not a matter of disrespect; so much as the situation had never arisen before. Many of the people she'd met when she was in Fellein would have been surprised by the notion of a god speaking to a person, but Jost and her people knew better.

The gods spoke. The Sa'ba Taalor listened and learned and obeyed.

At the end of her long journey Jost reached the great wall of the divide between the Blasted Lands and the Fellein Empire.

By the time she reached her destination, the vast armies of the Sa'ba Taalor were on the move, following the commands of Tarag Paedori, Chosen of Truska-Pren and the King in Iron. All of the kings ruled their kingdoms, but at this time, in this place, they also obeyed Tarag Paedori, as the Daxar Taalor willed it.

She did not know where the armies of the Sa'ba Taalor were moving. That was not her place. She had been told by a god to kill a ram, carve one of the horns in just the right way and drag the great carcass behind her to the area called the Edge by the people of Fellein.

Jost listened to Wheklam and was told to bathe herself in

the remains of the ram and scale the great wall of stone. She cut the hide from the carcass and wrapped it around her body, soaking in the viscera. She was not shamed or repulsed by the feeling. Jost was Sa'ba Taalor, and it was not the first time she had bathed herself in the blood of her victims, intentionally or no.

There were no paths. The stone had been scoured by endless winds and storms for a thousand years and the surface was often as smooth as the ice that coated it. That was not important. The gods made demands and she obeyed. That was the way of the world.

So she scaled the Edge and she did not fall to her death though there were a few close calls.

Far below her the carcass she had carried still waited, the offal from the great thing covering her body. She slipped free of her cloak of bloodied hide and dropped it on the ground. The skin was still covered in the blood and remains that she had smeared it with. Perhaps the winds should have washed the scent away, but the gods have their ways.

When Jost was done stripping off the hide of the ram she untied the horn that she had carried throughout her journey. Wheklam told her what to do and she obeyed, blowing through the great horn, though she heard no noise come from it. She heard no noise, but she felt the vibrations of the sound that escaped. The note was too high for her to hear, and so powerful that most of her body shivered with the ringing that touched her flesh.

Far below, deep in the Blasted Lands, that single note carried, traveling farther than should have been possible over the roaring winds and endless ice storm that covered the land.

Thus was her army summoned.

Jost did not wait around for them to come, but instead rose

from her seat on the rough, flat lands of the Wellish Steppes – where once, long ago, her people had fought the Overlords and weakened their enemies greatly before being driven away – and headed for the distant shadows on the horizon. She was not done traveling. She had a trail to mark and she intended to do just that.

The ram's hide still bled heavily, far more than should have been possible. She knew that, but did not question it. The Daxar Taalor performed miracles every day. This was merely one more among the many she had witnessed in her life.

The trail she left behind was bloody and refused to dry.

Jost walked many miles before she reached the forest and the great trees that marked it as unique. Massive oak trees and great willows, hardwoods that she had never seen in her life, as she had never seen so very many trees in one place. Once in the forest she found a vine, green and fat and hard as stone, which rose from the ground into the trees themselves, and she carefully placed her feet and started walking the path the vine offered to her. The ram's skin bled freely behind her and painted the vine as red as a setting sun.

Wheklam told her that she had done well and commanded her to follow a path he offered to her deeper into the woods.

Being a faithful servant, she obeyed without question.

ONE

Trecharch lived. That was more than could be said for most kingdoms.

The walls in Trecharch were made of wood that was thick, very solid and very much alive. The trees of the region were walls, homes and barriers against enemies. No one had ever successfully invaded Trecharch in the time of the Fellein Empire, though, in the past, a few had foolishly tried.

The trees at the center of the Great Green – as the area was often called by the poets and scribes – were monumental. They towered higher than should have seemed possible. Most of them were well over a thousand years of age, and joined to the outer levels of the forest by the Mother-Vine that connected all of the Sentinels, the hardest and heartiest of the monolithic hardwoods.

If the people of Trecharch could be said to worship any deities, they would be the Mother-Vine and the Walking Trees.

The Walking Trees were all of the vast Sentinels in the area. Though they did not move far, they did move, and their motion was part of the reason that the people were safe. On several occasions through their long history, the Sentinels had moved themselves across the ground and blocked passages that might have let attackers past their natural barriers.

The Mother-Vine was a tapestry woven across the area: a vine as thick as a fat man's waist that wrapped around tree trunks, spiraling out between the Sentinels, sometimes at the level of the ground and sometimes hundreds of feet above. In the latter case the people of Trecharch often built guide lines and rope railings, making bridges to move from one tree to the next, allowing them to look at all of their land from above and from the level of the ground.

Not surprisingly, the guards from Trecharch were adept archers.

"It should be warmer by now." Deltrea's voice was edging toward petulant. The woman hated working the higher levels, where she could not so easily find a man to flirt with.

Cullen, already in a mood because of the endless, pissing drizzle, pressed her lips together rather than start another argument with the other sentry. They were friends and they worked together well, but the miserable weather and the stench coming from the Blasted Lands had put them both in foul moods. Best to keep a silent tongue when dread whispered in the mind that something was wrong.

In her guts, Cullen knew that something dark was going to happen. She tried to deny it with her head, but her innards knew better.

Only days earlier Tyrne had died in flames. The city was gone and it hadn't taken long to know it. The birds all left the forest at the same time, rising above the woods and heading east. One bird makes a whisper. A thousand make a sigh. All the birds at once make for screaming nerves.

Within a day the feathered denizens had returned as if nothing had happened, but the omen had been noticed by one and all.

Scarcely half an hour earlier, the birds rose up again, a cloud of different colors against a backdrop of dark storm front. They had not returned. Cullen's guts said it was trouble. She tended to listen when her body told her things. She knew people who had not and they had paid the ultimate price for their arrogance.

"Winter is stubborn this year, that's all." Cullen made dismissive noises that even she did not believe. She stood at her post, looking out toward the distant Blasted Lands and admiring the amazing view offered by their position on the far edge of the Trecharch Forest, near the top of Old Root, the last of the Sentinels before the trees rose only a hundred feet at the highest levels.

The filthy air from the Blasted Lands had been creeping into the area since Tyrne had become a burning mountain, and the Edge no longer seemed capable of holding back the dark winds that had always been locked away in the past.

"I think it's more than that." Deltrea shook her head. "Lurne says…" Just that quickly Cullen tuned the other woman out. Once she spoke of Lurne, her sometimes lover, the talk inevitably went to how much he wanted to rut with her. Lurne was a pig. Rutting was his constant desire.

Sometimes she envied Deltrea her freedom when it came to mating. Sometimes she did not. There had been men in the past. A few of them had been demanding. Two of their bodies were lost in the woods and would never be found. She pushed that thought away.

She wasn't quite sure what at first, but something caught her attention. A motion, perhaps, or a sound. Maybe, she hoped, it was the damned birds coming back, signaling that all was well.

Before the eruption in Tyrne no one had truly considered

the possibility of a disaster reaching into Trecharch. Since then, however, the guards were stationed in twice as many places and they were doubled.

Deltrea was still going on about her man, which sometimes seemed the only thing the woman ever wanted to talk about. "Lurne can't help himself. As soon as we're together and the curtains are closed, he's ready to couple."

Cullen, who had seen Lurne and knew the man was hardly a stallion, was about to make a rude comment when the sounds came to her.

Distant, soft, echoing up from far below, the sounds of laughter and weeping came together. Children mumbled, adults cried: a constant gathering of noises that should not have been together in a cold and lonely forest.

She held up one hand and Deltrea stopped talking immediately. Gossip was a fine thing, but work came before pleasure when one was guarding the area.

"What is it?" Deltrea leaned closer, and craned her head in an effort to hear better.

"Noises. Too many noises."

To prove her point the sounds grew louder, a cacophony of moans and sighs and broken sobs, now mingling with insane cackles.

Deltrea looked her way. "Is that a Pra-Moresh?" Her voice rose to a higher pitch, evidence of her shock at the notion.

Cullen frowned. "More than one, I'd think." The great beasts didn't usually come this far north, but it had happened on a few occasions. When she was a child she'd seen the carcass of one hauled out for everyone to see. The thick teeth, the long claws, and the sheer size of the brute had focused her nightmares for a few weeks afterward.

In the distance, at the very edge of the forest, she saw

movement and shook her head. She should not have been able to see movement there. They were far enough away that anything she saw should have barely been noticeable.

Without bothering to consider the consequences if she were mistaken, Cullen reached for her horn and sounded the alarm. The note was low and deep, and for a moment it consumed all other sounds.

Deltrea stared at her with a querulous expression: to call everyone to arms was a serious action. Likely the other woman thought she was acting irrationally. That hardly mattered. There were Pra-Moresh in the area, several if her eyes weren't playing tricks.

Within seven seconds the next horn sounded further into the territory and after that the sound echoed again and again from different stations.

For a moment she wondered if she had made a mistake.

Then the sounds of screams reached her ears from the edge of the forest and Cullen was glad she'd made the call.

Prill was not a coward, but he saw the demons and he ran.

They were nightmares made flesh and there were dozens of them. They came toward Western Point from the edge of the Blasted Lands and the Wellish Steppes, and they came en masse, a wave of fur and claws that cackled and sobbed as it moved forward.

There had been a few noises, enough to make him look in that direction, but when the horn sounded from Old Root, the Pra-Moresh treated it as a summons and came with a vengeance.

Prill was the guard at the edge of the territory and he took one look and thought only of his family in the small town. Merra had to be warned. The children had to be collected and all of them had to make it to the forest proper and the closest Sentinel. Old Root was a distance off, but they could make it if they were fast. The great trees were nearly impervious, surely enough to hold off the claws of even the Pra-Moresh.

Behind him the unholy tides rolled in; great, shambling bodies with teeth and claws and eyes that seemed too large to be real.

Borrogun had been standing next to him and grabbed his spear, prepared to fight the things. Prill ran.

He felt no shame, not even when he heard his fellow guard's screams. Not even when the growls and laughter swallowed the guard's desperate cries for help.

Not but a thousand feet to the proper edge of the Western Point. Once past the clearing he would be able to get to safety and help everyone.

Prill's horn bounced at his hip, as completely forgotten as the spear he'd dropped and the short sword slapping against his other flank.

Perhaps if he had remembered either of them he could have made a difference to the outcome. Instead Prill ran, and in so doing, sealed the fate of all the people he knew in Western Point. No alarm was sounded save the screams of Borrugun, who was too distant for his cries to carry that far.

Prill did not scream. He never had a chance to. The powerful teeth of the Pra-Moresh slammed down on the back of his head and ended his life and any attempt to warn his loved ones.

Some people should not be guards.

The Western Point was called by that name as a formality. There were no proper barriers. The town was small, and served mostly as a guidepost. Travelers coming to Trecharch from the Wellish Steppes would easily get lost in the vast forest if they didn't know the proper routes. For a few coins a good number of the local youth would work as guides. Naturally there were some in the small town who made a profit in the process. Some of the finest wood carvers in Fellein lived in Western Point. From trinkets to fine and elegant furniture, the locals managed to sell their wares and in a few cases were well sought after for additional work.

Prill would have been the first to admit that the skills in the area dealt more with carving wood than with carving flesh. Still, a proper alarm might have made a difference. Though the predators came fast, and though they made noise, there might have been a chance.

The Pra-Moresh moved into the town and feasted as they seldom had before. There had never been a time when the beasts roamed in so large a pack. There had never been a time when they found so very much to feed on.

The people in Western Point were barely aware that they were being attacked before it was over. The only positive note was that they screamed a great deal and in their deaths they warned the rest of their people.

The Pra-Moresh came into the territory in a rush, pushing through the trees and attacking anything that was on the same level as they were. Livestock died quickly. Cattle and geese and swine all tried to escape the lumbering monsters, but there simply was nowhere for them to go in their pens. The birds that had not been pinioned had already made good their escapes, but the larger animals found themselves the victims of the insatiable hunger of the monsters.

Had there only been one, or even a dozen, it was possible that most of the animals would have been saved, but the numbers were much larger, more than could be counted in the sudden chaos of their attacks.

Cullen stood at her position on the Mother-Vine and readied her bow.

Both she and Deltrea had moved much closer to the ground and both had a large supply of arrows. Should those fail them, there were also short spears. If the spears did not do the job, they were ready with swords.

They were not alone. Their fellows stood at the ready, in different locations and on different trees. The young, the frail and those with babies in their bellies were hidden in the Sentinel trees. Everyone else would fight. That was the way in Trecharch: those that could, did. Those that couldn't, prayed.

The Mother-Vine provided.

Cullen was only thirty feet off the ground, standing on the Mother-Vine and holding her place. Fear fluttered in her guts, but that was to be expected. It wasn't every day one faced a childhood nightmare.

The first of the Pra-Moresh came into the area, muzzle and arms covered in gore. It giggled like a happy child and screeched like a wounded cat as it moved forward. Her arrow was true and sank into the left eye of the monster all the way to the fletching.

The beast let out a shriek of pain and shook its head before falling backward and smashing into the ground. It shit itself as it died.

She allowed herself half a heartbeat of celebration, but that faded when four more of the things came forward, drawn by the sound.

The demons attacked the trees, shaking them, clawing the thick bark, and in a few cases trying to climb higher. Cullen trembled inside but calmed herself and grabbed more arrows. Her aim was good but not perfect. She fired and missed, fired and struck one of the damned things in its back, and fired again, not bothering to see where the arrow struck before she reached for more.

The Pra-Moresh could not reach as high as her position. Try though they did, the beasts were, ultimately, just large beasts and not very bright. She felt a thrill as her arrows rained down, some wounding and others killing. A second of the monsters fell, and then a third. The fourth proved a better climber; Deltrea stood above it and aimed half a dozen arrows into the beast's face before it fell back and sought easier food elsewhere. Still more of them came, pushing between the trees and seeking more meat to cram into their mouths. A few fell on their own dead and ripped into the fresh kills with no regard for their fallen brethren. Meat was meat and they were always ravenous.

All around Cullen the archers worked their bows and those without bows grabbed spears and took careful aim. The Pra-Moresh kept coming, some stopping to feast, others moving through the hail of missiles and continuing on, deeper into the Great Green and the center of the Mother-Vine's domain. More guards were waiting there. She did not let herself worry about the ones that got past her. There were other considerations. There were more nightmares still coming.

Cullen wished she could have climbed higher, could have seen for certain how many of the things were there, because there seemed to be an endless tide of them washing through the forest floor below.

Sometimes it's best not to know.

The sounds of laughter, of sobbing fear, and wailing sorrow filled the air as the Pra-Moresh continued on their odd exodus from the Blasted Lands. She had seen them and sounded the alarm but she had never guessed there could be so many.

Her arms ached and before she knew what was happening the last of her arrows was gone.

She was not the only one. Most of the archers had used up their supplies yet still the damned things came out of the woods and into the area where she lived. The air was heavy with the stench of blood and other bodily fluids. The only blessing they had at that moment was that most of the Pra-Moresh didn't seem capable of scaling the Sentinels.

She had four spears. Cullen grabbed the first of them and looked down at the gradually dwindling stream of nightmares.

Next to her Deltrea called out, "Save them, Cullen. Tremm says there might be more of them coming. Let these pass and we'll gather more supplies."

Tremm was an ass. A little mead in his system and he tried to grope any female within range, but he was also one of the commanders. She might have argued but her arms ached and her belly still felt cold and shaky.

Down below the last of the migrating things lumbered past.

"How in the name of the gods could there be more of these things?"

Something roared in the distance. Not the maddening noises of the Pra-Moresh with their endless mimicry of human sounds, but a full-on sound like a short bark of thunder.

The sound was unsettling by its own right but where it came from was far worse.

Cullen and Deltrea looked toward the sky and the strand of the Mother-Vine made tiny by distance.

"At arms!" Deltrea screamed, her voice breaking harshly. "We are attacked from above!"

The arrow that took her life came from a height that made

the archer look tiny. The point jammed through the top of Deltrea's skull and rammed into the Sentinel behind her with enough force to leave her standing even after her legs failed and she should have fallen to the ground.

Cullen ducked around the side of the tree as quickly as she could when she saw the arrow falling from the sky. The black rain came down and sent several others to their deaths. Those less fortunate lived through the impacts, the missiles hitting with enough force to punch through bone and meat alike.

Not far away, Tremm screamed in pain, his bicep shattered by the impact of the weapon that forced him to drop his horn before he could call another alarm.

Grit rained down from above, and Cullen squinted against it, looking toward the Sentinel above her and gasping as she saw the shape sliding down the vast side of the tree.

Thick claws hooked into the bark and slowed what should have been a high-speed descent. The form was enormous, and worse still there was another shape atop it. With fifteen or so feet to go the shape that was mounted, hanging half free from the dropping mass, let go and fell toward her, with a sound that might have been a scream or possibly a laugh.

She wanted to move, but shock froze her body.

It was a man falling toward her. His weight tapped against the Sentinel and he skidded a bit, his descent not slowed so much as directed.

Landing on her body was what slowed him.

His boots drove into her side as she tried to get away. The pain was a powerful thing and she staggered backward, bouncing against the Sentinel before dropping from the bridge where she'd watched the Pra-Moresh feast and die. As her body had possibly slowed the stranger's descent, the corpse of a great, stinking predator slowed hers. It would be a lie to say her landing was cushioned.

She'd been raised in the woods of Trecharch. Her father had taught her to climb and how best to fall. She had managed a hundred falls without hurting herself too severely, but this? This was not a fall so much as a hard push at the earth below.

The world flipped around several times before she slammed into the bloodied remains of the beast. A bone snapped loudly. She could not tell if it was hers, or the monster's. Either way Cullen felt the world fade away in a gray wash that covered her senses completely.

For a moment, perhaps longer, there was blessed silence and then the screams came to her. People, her people, were crying out. Metal sang as it clashed against metal and warmth washed over her, wet and sticky and reeking of blood strongly enough for her to notice it past the stench of the dead thing beneath her.

Pain came back to visit her and Cullen groaned, the noise lost in the sounds of combat. She had never heard combat before, not really. She had heard instructors yelling commands as she and the others practiced their swordsmanship or worked the bows, improving their strength and their accuracy. This was different. This was cacophony, madness and screams and the sounds of people falling to their deaths. Somewhere up above another roar came her way and a man screamed. The sound was cut short, fading into a gurgling cough.

She looked up to see the demon that had slid down the tree running along the Mother-Vine and swatting at people, knocking them through the air to rain down around her, most of them, dead before they hit the ground. Not far away the shadow of a person danced across the Mother-Vine in the opposite direction, sweeping a sword around it in a flurry of activity. Wherever that metal tongue licked flesh it tasted blood.

Both the rider and the mount had eyes that blazed like candle flames.

Cullen tried to sit up and reach for her sword and the gray claimed her a second time, sweeping her into darkness.

The Walking Trees walked.

For over three hundred years the great Sentinels had moved themselves occasionally, but never very far and not as one unit. There had simply been no need. No one had invaded the Trecharch in all that time and the Sentinels had simply stood their ground, never needing to offer a unified front. Now and again for whatever reason a tree might think wise, this or that of the monoliths had cracked the ground and shuffled a few inches or even a foot or two, and then settled again. It was a noise that was unique to Trecharch, a sound impossible to ignore, and one that caused a certain level of panic when it was first encountered by anyone who had ever seen a towering tree fall to the ground. Wood creaked and sighed and moaned as it moved.

Now the Sentinels moved, shifting and sliding through solid ground, breaking stones and well-packed soil alike as they drew closer together and closed the gaps between trees.

Four of the great Pra-Moresh, the very stuff of nightmares for more people than could be easily counted, were crushed in an instant. Bones shattered, bodies pulped and blood fell down to feed the roots of the Sentinels.

Close to the level of the ground the barrier formed by the Sentinels was a dense wall that could not be easily ignored. Squirrels might squeeze between the Walking Trees, but nothing much larger would manage the feat.

Higher in the air was a different tale. The Mother-Vine was set in her ways and while she offered a little yield, she did not easily change her shape.

The Sa'ba Taalor took advantage of that.

Glo'Hosht walked the Mother-Vine with grace, and brought death along for companionship.

How many prayers can be said in the dark? Medba did not know, but he said more of them and tried to find a limit.

Old Root surrounded them and most of the people around him were calm, save a few of the children who were scared and uncertain how to act in the hidden chamber that the Sentinel provided.

When he was younger, he'd asked his father about the chamber, wanting to know how it was that the cavernous area could exist without killing the Walking Tree.

"Mother-Vine feeds the Sentinels and provides," his father had said. "That is her way." He'd thought as a young lad that the place was carved into the great tree. It was only later that he learned the hidden places locked away within the trees grew naturally.

The Mother-Vine provides. The words were true all his life but now he feared otherwise.

The sounds from outside the great tree were horrid. There were roars and screams and then, possibly worst of all, there was silence.

He had lived over seventy years in the world, and Medba was not afraid of much, but the silence left his senses stretched, and every noise, every breath of air that moved across his skin was a reason to wonder what would happen next.

The air inside the chamber was heavy. Too many bodies crushed into the area. There was air to breathe, but it grew as humid and hot as the worst part of the summer in the chamber.

Babies and little ones fidgeted and then one started crying, a sputtering, frustrated noise, and others followed suit.

The Mother-Vine provides, but damn, the sounds would surely draw someone to them if they did not abate.

A great rapping struck against the wall behind him and continued on, moving slowly along the edge of the wood, a notice to all inside that someone had found them.

His stomach clenched.

Not far away a boy hollered into the darkness, "We're here!" His voice was panicked. Like as not he thought whoever heard them was there to save them from the darkness. Somebody slapped the child hard, a loud report that cut off the boy's screams and replaced them with shocked sobs.

Through the walls of their shelter a voice spoke in a language that made no sense. The voice echoed impossibly.

A moment later the hidden door of the chamber shook violently. Several blows hit the thick wood and then the impossible happened. The wooden barrier, strong as any shield ever made, broke under the repeated impacts.

This time when the boy screamed, several other voices joined in.

Medba rose on shaky legs and held his weight for a moment with his arm as well as his legs while he leaned against the rounded wall. The wood was warm and soft to his touch, nowhere near as harsh as he knew the outer bark of the tree to be. Inside the nurturing shelter. Outside the wall of protection.

And then the outside found its way in. The blow was

enough to split the protection of the door completely and flinders of the remains bounced throughout the interior.

For one moment there was light from outside, and then the forms moving in blocked it.

Medba was not a fighter, but he saw the weapons and knew them for what they were. The first ones in carried axes and hammers. The others might have carried different weapons, but that hardly mattered.

The first through the door looked down at the woman near his feet and swept his hammer around. Medba knew the girl, young, too young to be with child, but her belly was heavy just the same. The head of the hammer was stronger than the head of the woman. She died quickly. That was the last mercy the invaders showed.

Further into the forest the Pra-Moresh stalked, seeking and often finding tender prey.

Alarms were sounded and soldiers gathered.

Carnage followed, and then retribution.

And higher in the trees, the Sa'ba Taalor walked, ignoring the violence below. Glo'Hosht walked among them, silent, lost in shadows, and at the appropriate spots the King in Mercury whispered orders to those who followed.

This practice lasted well into the night, only ending when the king met up with Jost, who had marked the path with blood.

The king looked at her face and smiled. "You have been blessed, again."

Jost lowered her head in respect, the still bleeding ram's hide at her feet, slowly dripping its blood across the Mother-Vine and down a tree below.

"Wheklam has been kind to me." She shook her head

and her voice trailed off in wonder. "I had never spoken to Wheklam before."

"It is a time of change, Jost. Wheklam has made demands and you have obeyed, as you should. I think Wheklam is not yet done with you, but for now you are done with this task. Now it is my turn to strike for the Daxar Taalor."

She turned her head and listened to the wind, even as a king spoke to her. Paedle talked now, and Glo'Hosht's voice mirrored the god's. "Go now. Move carefully and find your way south and east. Swech waits in the City of Wonders and might yet need your help."

Jost smiled at the thought of the older woman. Swech had trained her and worked with her on many occasions.

"I find I miss her as well." The king looked toward the ground and a skirmish started below them. The Sa'ba Taalor on the ground were not followers of Paedle. They obeyed a different king. They fought a different battle but the same war.

Their weapons were bloodied and efficient. And loud. So very loud.

Glo'Hosht preferred silent weapons.

The junction of three different roots spread out before the king.

"Here, I think," said Glo'Hosht.

Jost stepped back, letting the king strike where she had been standing.

The long needle-like dagger struck deep, and punctured the tough outer layers of the Mother-Vine.

Jost did not know what the fluid that spilled into that wound would do. She only knew it would serve the Daxar Taalor. That was enough.

She nodded once more to her King in Mercury and then

slipped away, climbing carefully down the thick trunk of the tree nearest to her and after she touched the ground she turned to the south and the east.

She had a long ways to travel. There would likely be many obstacles.

TWO

Canhoon spread before them, a vast place that looked enough like Tyrne to unsettle for a moment.

Well, parts looked like Tyrne, or rather looked like Tyrne had looked, before it was destroyed. Desh Krohan walked beside the wagon where his Sisters traveled and stared at the city.

Canhoon consisted of two cities, really. The first was Old Canhoon, with the older buildings, structures that had survived centuries and empires alike. Old Canhoon had been the capital of the Fellein Empire since it was founded, and even then it had been ancient.

There were structures there that had fallen, burned, been destroyed and then had been reformed from the very land, growing from the ruins of what went before. The roads were cobblestone and the statues of luminaries past graced the rooftops of a number of the buildings, looking out over the city like guardians.

Once, centuries ago, the Silent Army had moved through the city as it lay in ruins. Desh Krohan and his brethren had summoned them and though the stone soldiers had saved Canhoon the cost had been monumental. There were not enough of the wizards left these days to ever attempt that feat again.

To look at the sprawling affair as it stood now, one had to squint just so to see Old Canhoon at the very heart of the vast expanse. Well, no, but it sometimes seemed that way. The buildings at the center were all of a similar color and age. Once past the Mid-Wall, which had been the outer barrier around the city when Desh was younger, there was less organization, less... majesty. The newer structures were not as grand, though they were certainly functional enough.

The Jeurgis River cut across the new city and ran around the heart of Old Canhoon, a vast moat that was connected to the rest of the city by six bridges built of heavy stone and designed to withstand the weight of an army with ease.

Desh Krohan, the wizard who had been advisor to generations of the Empire's leaders, looked to where one of the bridges spanned the water and shook his head. "Might well have to block those."

"You are already planning the defenses of the city?" Merros Dulver's voice came from his left and the sorcerer looked over and up. Dulver was currently riding on a rather magnificent charger. It was very nearly a requirement of being a general of the Imperial forces. He was also resplendent in a uniform that Desh knew the man disliked intensely.

For almost two days Merros had not spoken, focusing instead on the journey to Canhoon and on protecting the Empress from harm. He was also torturing himself for every life lost in Tyrne, as if he could possibly have prevented them.

That was one advantage of being several hundred years old: Desh Krohan could allow himself a little more callousness of nature than most. He had long since accepted that he could not possibly save everyone. At least that was what he told himself with surprising regularity.

Merros looked his way with a disapproving frown. "I believe the defense of the city falls under my jurisdiction these days."

"Indeed it does, but as First Advisor I'm allowed to make suggestions." He managed a smile for the man. The comments were meant as a jest and he took them in the proper spirit.

"I'm fairly certain if you were a pauper on the street you'd still be stating your suggestions."

"Wisdom often comes from those with the least to lose, Merros."

"You think so?"

"Well, if not wisdom then certainly truth. If you've nothing to lose you've nothing to fear losing."

Merros looked like he was ready to get into a proper debate about that. The discussion was delayed when a courier rode up to him, winded from a long ride, and handed the general a rolled scroll bearing a regimental seal.

Desh walked closer, looking on as Merros broke the wax and then opened the document, reading quickly.

"What is it?"

"The Sa'ba Taalor have wasted no time, Desh. They're attacking Trecharch."

"Trecharch? Why in the name of the gods would they attack there? The forest is nearly impenetrable."

Merros held the paper out to him. "Apparently not."

The message was coded. "I can't read this."

The general nodded, fully aware of that fact. "You study magic. I study military codes. Of course you can't read it. The information is grim. We shouldn't speak of this until we're in the city proper."

"Tell me this much, have they reached Orrander's Tower?"

"No. They haven't even reached the Norhaun yet."

"Then why are you so grim?" The general's mood was somber indeed, especially since the Sa'ba Taalor hadn't even made it to the river that fed most of Trecharch. "It sounds like they've barely managed entry into the woods."

Merros waved the note again and then shoved it into his jacket's inner pocket. "Because they're destroying everything, Desh. They're not just attacking, they're ruining everything they go past. It says here that the Mother-Vine is wounded."

Desh leaned his head back and considered the implications.

"Desh, they're doing something to the Mother-Vine that's *killing it* as they go."

He pulled muscles in his neck when he turned his head so sharply.

"What?"

"They're killing the Mother-Vine."

Just that quickly the bearer of bad news was out of the sorcerer's mind. "Sisters! To me!"

It was seldom that he summoned the Sisters with a command. They responded to the urgency in his voice, moving from the wagon where they rode, like children called by their mother.

Tataya, Goriah and Pella walked quickly to keep pace with him, barely even acknowledging the general. Pella's dark hair flowed freely. Tataya had her heavy red hair tied in a thick braid. Goriah's face was almost completely hidden by her hood and no sign of her golden hair was visible.

"Pella, I need you. It's urgent that you get to Orrander's Tower. The grayskins are on the march and they head for the source of the Mother-Vine. They are killing her. Do you understand me?"

Pella nodded and moved, running forward and then lifting

from the ground. It was seldom that any of the Sisters actively displayed their abilities and there was a reason for that. Merros Dulver nearly fell from his saddle as the woman rose into the air, her cloak changing shape, pulling into her body even as she became something else. "Gods!"

"Goriah, my dear, I need you to reach the Norhaun River before the Sa'ba Taalor make it there. They need to be warned and the river needs to be defended. Do not be seen by the Sa'ba Taalor. Do not engage them. Just make their lives more difficult."

Goriah did not change shape. Instead she lifted high above them, at a speed that should have been impossible, and then tore across the sky, her hood falling back, revealing the hair she had hidden away.

For the second time Merros Dulver stared with wide eyes, shocked by the display. In all the time he had known the women they had never used their powers in his presence. He stared after the tiny spot that was Goriah until she vanished into the clouds.

When he opened his mouth to speak, Desh shook his head. "They're sorcerers and shapeshifters, General. They're not my consorts, they're my peers."

"I never... They've never..."

He could see the poor bastard trying to work out what had just happened before his eyes. Like a child seeing a thunderstorm for the first time, he was a bit stunned. He would recover.

"I know. Now is the time to set aside a bit of caution. They do what they must." Desh shook his head. "We have to delay the Sa'ba Taalor long enough for your response, after all."

"My response?"

"We're attacked. We are at war. You have troops to move."

Merros blushed slightly, his expression angry.

"Forgive me, Merros. I don't challenge your right to lead. I'm just stating the obvious. We have been caught in a dangerous situation, but we need to move troops to deal with the Sa'ba Taalor in Trecharch, before they can push in any further. I also know you've a great deal on your mind and, to be fair, you've just seen more than you have ever seen before of what me and mine can do. It can unsettle at the best of times."

"Nothing to forgive, Desh." It was gracious of the man to say so. He hadn't meant to offend, but sometimes he forgot himself.

"Tataya, keep contact with the Sisters. Let me know what they see and what they suggest."

"Of course, Desh." Merros studied her for a few seconds, eyes narrowed, and finally relaxed when she looked his way, smiled, and continued walking toward Old Canhoon and the palace.

As the caravan moved on, Desh headed for Nachia Krous's wagon. He knocked quickly and expected one of her ladies-in-waiting to let him in. Instead it was the Empress herself that called him.

The wagon seated half a dozen with plenty of room to spare. Currently there was one occupant. "Where are your ladies-in-waiting?" Desh asked.

Her eyes regarded him for a long moment in silence, while he looked her over in return. Nachia was dressed, as she often was, in riding clothes. Her hair was pulled back in a functional tail, her clothes were disheveled and he could tell she'd worn them to bed. Overall she looked as stately and regal as a street urchin.

"Don't start on me, Desh!"

"I merely asked where your ladies-in-waiting are. I would hardly call that 'starting on you'."

She eyed him with as much suspicion as Merros had used when looking at Tataya.

"Oh, please, Nachia, calm down. I'm not here to scold you about your wardrobe or kicking out your ladies-in-waiting again. I'm here to tell you Trecharch has been attacked and to suggest a war council meeting when we reach the palace."

She actually relaxed. "How many people would attend this war council of yours?"

"You, me, Merros, Tataya, and a few others as we see necessary. And the head of the City Guard."

"So let's meet here and now. You can give our decisions to the head of the watch."

"If that's your preference."

"Find the people you need, Desh." She waved him away. "And give me ten minutes to change into something cleaner."

Desh lowered his head in a minor bow as he departed. "As you wish, Majesty."

Finding Merros and Tataya was easy. "Merros, we meet in fifteen minutes in the Empress's coach."

Merros nodded. "Who else should we gather?"

"Find one of the faithful to join us. Not all of them, just one. I can only handle them glaring at each other for so long. Bring someone to take notes for you. We're going to be very busy." Merros nodded and spurred his charger forward.

Behind them the Blasted Lands was a memory. To their south, the Summer Palace and Tyrne were ashes. Ahead of them the greatest city in the Empire sprawled out in organized patterns of roads and buildings and defensive walls. Unlike Tyrne the barriers were in far better shape and the City Guard were trained in combat and capable of working to defend the city from enemies within and without.

The Sooth had warned of Tyrne's destruction and while

some died, it could have been much worse.

Looking to the Southern Road that ran alongside the Jeurgis River, shapes moved slowly along the visible paved stretch. All he could see were pedestrians, horsemen and a few wagons. The road itself was buried under moving flesh. Vast numbers of refugees, thousands and thousands, were moving toward the City of Wonders right now, he suspected.

"We're going to be very crowded when we get there." He did not need to visit with the Sooth to know he was right on that one.

Swech wore her hood drawn down and squinted against the breeze from the Jeurgis River. She cut a slice of pabba fruit – possibly the most amazing fruit that the gods had ever created – and sucked the juices from the succulent flesh before chewing and swallowing.

The Empress and her retinue were coming back. She could see them as they marched across the bridge and into Canhoon. They did not look happy. They had no reason for joy.

A day away, the clouds of ash rose higher into the air and belched lightning bright enough to be seen at night in the City of Wonders. She'd moved along the rooftops the night before and watched, mesmerized by the pyrotechnic displays.

She had grown used to her borrowed body. It fit her now. Vigorous hours of exercise and stretching had made her feel, if not at home, then at least comfortable in the other woman's body.

Since coming to Canhoon she had been busy. Several scrapes and nicks had left their marks on her forearms and legs. Her clothes had taken the worst of it, of course. Good leathers could prevent a great deal of discomfort.

There were some, like Tuskandru, who would have teased her about the lack of scars her new body had, but she would have easily countered with the notion that borrowed flesh didn't count and that fresh scars would make it harder for her to hide in the masses around her. She had to fit in. That was her duty.

The man who came to her seemed to simply materialize, walking out of the air toward her. That marked him as surely as the four quick hand gestures he made.

She nodded her head and offered him a wedge of her fruit. He took it without hesitation and chewed, smiling. Handsome, but a bit young.

"You are Swech." It wasn't a question.

She nodded. "Have you a name?"

"I am Kallider. I walk in Paedle's wake."

She nodded. "I was told to expect you. Do you know why we meet?"

They had met before, she suspected. There were others who had thrown themselves into the heart of Wrommish's forge and taken new shapes at the end of a fiery journey. She had not looked at them for long. People were people, and she had been aware of them, but she had also been in the presence of her king and her god and they took precedence.

"I am to serve you. Should you call, I will answer." Kallider's answer was exactly as it should have been, direct.

She spoke in the tongue of her people, softly to avoid being heard as more than a murmur in the crowd. And there was a crowd, indeed, for most had not seen the Empress or her pet wizard and wanted to know who ruled them.

Merros Dulver rode past and she made herself look away, much as she wanted to stare. Strange that he should generate such feelings, but then, he had already made her show mercy on one occasion, had he not?

"For now be nearby if I need you. I will find a reason for you to be near."

He nodded his head.

"Kallider?"

"Yes, Swech?"

"Do not speak my name again. Not in this land. I am wanted here."

"As you wish." A moment later he was gone and she lowered her head as the Empress rode past.

There were four blades in easy reach. She could have killed the young woman without any trouble at all.

That was not what the gods wanted. For now the Daxar Taalor preferred the Empress be alive and to that end Swech let the ruler of Fellein pass.

A moment later her reason for waiting in this spot and at this time came past. The man was heavyset and sweating heavily despite the relatively mild weather. He looked around with narrowed, suspicious eyes. Waiting for an attack.

The thin dart scraped across the back of his neck and he swatted at the irritation, scowling. A great number of insects swarmed the area and the winds had died for the moment.

Insects were known to bite.

He carried on for almost a hundred paces before he collapsed. Swech looked in his direction only because of the noises made by the people around him. She knew he was dead. She had killed him, after all.

While the people around him called for some form of assistance, or stole from the fat corpse in the case of one street child, Swech put the last of her Pabba fruit wedges in her mouth and sucked at the sweet juices.

The gods asked that she kill and so she did. She did not have to know why. The gods knew. That was enough.

THREE

The air was colder as they scaled the side of Wheklam. There was little to hold on to and the rich veins of lead that ran through the mountain guaranteed that there would be few interruptions. Nothing grew at this height and according to Delil the lead was poisonous to the plants that might have been growing at this height in any event.

Andover Lashk did not question the girl. He had learned to have faith in her words.

He did not speak much as he climbed. Instead he focused on the task ahead of him. Delil was moving alongside him, his only constant companion since he had reached the Taalor Valley.

Down below the valley was rich with life. A thick forest of trees grew, and from a distance they were a beautiful, amazing sight. However, from up close they had been a hellish nightmare of thorns and odd creatures that lived among the twisted, gnarled branches. He could count seventeen bite marks on his left arm alone. Those were interspersed with a few dozen scratches from thorns and claws alike.

The discomfort was minor.

He looked to his left and saw Delil looking back his way,

her face uncovered, her mouths smiling.

"Another hour, Andover, and you will meet with another of the Daxar Taalor."

"Where are all the people?" He knew the answer but asked anyway.

"They have moved on. Wheklam is the God of Lead and the Sea. They have taken their ships into the waters."

"Have you ever been on one of their ships?" He had never so much as seen the ocean, though he had heard it was an impressive sight.

"No." She shook her head and wiped at the sweat on her brow. The weather was colder, yes, but the work of climbing was hot. "I am not close with Wheklam. I will be meeting with the god as well."

Andover frowned at that. Not because he did not like her company – he most certainly did – but because of what he had been told before. "I thought every person faced the Daxar Taalor alone."

Delil laughed. It was not a mocking sound, but one of simple surprise. "You have met two of the Daxar Taalor, Andover. Have you not yet realized that they are gods? If a thousand walked before Wheklam at the same time, in the same place, the god could make certain that each faced their destinies alone."

Andover thought long on that and then nodded.

"What happens if someone does not meet a god's approval, Delil? What happens if Wheklam finds me... unsatisfactory?"

Delil looked at him for a long time, her eyes moving over his face as if trying to memorize him. The night before, after they had climbed free of the forest and helped patch each other's wounds as best they could, they had rutted under the stars. They had been together twice before but this time

felt different, felt more like they belonged together. He had
come to understand the ways in which her body moved,
another mystery at least partially solved, and the feelings had
been glorious.

Watching her as she climbed, he forced himself not to
be distracted by those memories. As lovely as they were,
dwelling on their past or on possible futures would likely lead
to his death along the slope.

"You met my brother, Ventdril. Do you remember him?"

"Yes." He could hardly forget the man. Another of the
Sa'ba Taalor that made him feel like a boy not yet old enough
to shave. The man was enormous and swung his sister like
she weighed as much as a toddler.

"My brother was judged unworthy by the Daxar Taalor.
The reasons are his to discuss, but perhaps he will share them
in time." She shrugged. "Possibly he acted in a cowardly
fashion. Just as likely he disobeyed the gods. Whatever the
reason, they broke him."

"Broke him?"

"The Daxar Taalor offer us many chances, Andover. They
can be very forgiving, but they are not merciful. Mercy does
not make us stronger. So when my brother offended the gods
one time too many, they broke him. They bent his body into
a new shape; they took his mind and bent that, too. And
they took from him all possibility that he could be seen as a
Sa'ba Taalor.

"I saw him when he was punished." She shook her head.
"It was a just punishment. The Daxar Taalor are not like us.
They do not make mistakes. They found him weak and broke
him, the better for him to find his flaws. The better for him
to find his way back. Sometimes the Broken return to us.
Sometimes they die."

She sighed and looked his way, smiling again. "Ventdril passed the tests set before him. He has earned the name Unbroken and been taken back into his people. He is strong and he is stronger than before."

"So if you disappoint the Daxar Taalor, they ruin you?"

"No. They offer punishments to learn from. There are other punishments as well."

"Like what?"

"The mounts."

"I don't understand."

"The mounts that some people ride are Sa'ba Taalor. Or they were. They are the ones who will not learn."

"What do you mean?"

"If a person will not learn or cannot learn it is because of pride or a stubbornness. The Broken are punished because they have committed great crimes in the eyes of the gods. The mounts are different. They either will not learn or must be taught a harder lesson than most. They are changed and made to serve while they contemplate their actions."

Andover was shocked. "Those great monsters are your people?"

"No. They were and they might be again. But they are being taught important lessons by the gods."

Andover looked at the ground close to his face and nodded, trying to grasp the implications of what she said.

"Andover!"

He looked toward Delil as she called and watched her arm point upward. There was an obstacle, something different on the slope. Something different, large, and moving.

"What is that?" he asked, but the answer did not matter. It had a shape not at all human. It was coming for them. That was all that mattered.

"That is a Broken. Prepare yourself. They are mad beasts."

The two of them were half-prone on the mountainside, but the angle meant they were almost standing. The slope of the mountain was rough, and while his feet were aimed toward the ground far below, his knees and his hands alike were carrying most of his weight.

In order to fight the damned thing he would have to risk falling to his death.

There would be no running from the slavering thing coming at him.

The creature had a face, but it was uneven, as if someone had taken a sculpture shattered on the ground and reassembled it using mud and clay from the river. Most of the body was equally off-kilter, but much worse. The torso was stretched and too long. The limbs were functional enough, but none of them came close to matching and there seemed to be a few too many.

While he was contemplating the approaching enemy, Delil reached into her garb and pulled out one of the long, deadly daggers she had sheathed on her body. He heard the sound of her exhaling and then saw the blade cut through the air on its way to her target.

The dagger cut the gray flesh of the thing, slicing into the oddly sinuous neck of the monster and stopping its forward charge.

One malformed hand reached for the dagger and fumbled it free of the wound. The blood flow from that cut immediately increased and the thing looked toward Delil with murder in its bulging eyes.

The sound it made was a war cry, a bellow for Ordna. Andover recognized the name of the Bronze God, though he knew almost nothing of what the deity demanded of its followers. Whatever the case, apparently the nightmare in front of him had failed the god.

And now the Broken sought a way to right that wrong.

The misshapen thing charged again, dropping to all fours, as the slope of Wheklam grew more extreme.

Delil was ready. Andover prayed that he was.

His left hand held tight to the side of the mountain, fingers clutching for purchase. His right reached around to slip his great hammer from where he held it.

And the hammer fell away, lost from his grip in an instant as the Broken pounced and smashed into him with its full weight.

Andover grunted and let go of the mountain, not by choice but because he was thrown free of the surface. Gravity and his enemy's weight did the rest. For a sickening moment he was falling backward through the air. Broad, warped fists pummeled into him and did their best to break his body, but his furs took a great deal of the impact.

There was no time to think. Had there been that sort of luxury, he'd have surely screamed himself to death. Instead Andover reached out with his iron hands and caught the flesh of his enemy, hooking his metallic fingers into the gray folds of scarred, stretched skin and doing his best to rip into the muscles underneath. There was no conscious thought, only a need to kill his enemy before the favor could be returned.

The world rolled in a half circle and Andover felt his body turning. He could make no claim of having chosen to move his body but it moved just the same, and a moment later the gods themselves smiled down on him as both he and the beast landed against Wheklam's surface, skidding and scraping as they bounced twice.

How far had they fallen? He did not know. He only knew that he was fortunate enough to be on top when they crashed into the ground.

Something in the body under him broke; the warped face opened a bloodied mouth and shrieked in pain. The folds of skin he held so tightly in his grip did not slip, but instead split, and he felt his fingers slide through the ruined hide of the thing and clutch into meat and gristle.

Then they were sliding again, falling further down the slope, rolling apart from each other as his fingers pulled free of their prize.

Drask Silver Hand, Delil and Bromt had told him how to take a blow and how to recover from falling down. They'd explained the principles and then they had thrown him again and again until he learned.

Those torturous encounters as they wandered slowly through the Blasted Lands very likely saved his life.

The ground blurred as he fell and bounced and ricocheted off rocks and deep cuts in the face of the mountain, and through it, he let himself roll and absorb the blows over the least vulnerable parts of his body.

So he was beaten senseless by the rocks and not killed by them.

The thing he'd been fighting was not as lucky. A rock met with its face and came out the victor. Parts of the face were stuck to the rock. The rest of the Broken rolled away and flopped lifelessly against the slope of Wheklam.

Andover stood up slowly and checked himself. Nothing was broken.

Far above, roughly at the same height he'd been at before falling, Delil waved to him.

He carefully nodded his head and looked her way. It was a long climb and he had a ways to go.

He did not find his hammer on the way up.

•••

Depending on the day and the whim of the Daxar Taalor, the Mounds could be as close as a week away from the Seven Forges, or could take a lifetime to find.

It had not been much more than a week for Drask Silver Hand as he rode his mount, Brackka, to the forbidden territory.

A lifetime of rules still rolled in his head as he violated the orders of his gods in order to obey them. None were ever allowed to enter the Mounds. None dared explore them. That had been the truth for as long as he had been alive, and yet he now crouched on the edge of a massive stone structure covered in ice and looked down into a faintly lit tunnel that descended well below the ground and into the very heart of the forbidden.

What the gods demand must be done. That, too, was the simple truth of the matter. Ydramil, the God in Silver, made demands. Drask obeyed all of the gods, but as his chosen deity, he listened even more carefully when Ydramil spoke.

Ydramil was sometimes called the God of Reflection and demanded a certain level of calm from his warriors. Drask would never have said it himself, but more than one of the Sa'ba Taalor had commented on his dedication to the god's demands. It was rare for him to lose his temper. In comparison to some his patience was a truly staggering achievement.

He waited in the raging winds of the Blasted Lands, a growing storm – a Ta-Wren, a Cutting Wind, to be sure – until he knew that his prey had moved on, and then, finally, he descended into the darkness below.

The people of the Fellein had advantages. They were greater in numbers. They had not, however, spent lifetimes adapting to the Blasted Lands.

Drask slipped easily down the rope his prey had left behind; his silver hand holding his weight with ease and resisting any possible rope burns.

When he landed in the dust of endless ages, he did so softly, despite his size.

Drask was not the largest of the Sa'ba Taalor; still, he knew, he towered over the foreigners.

None of that mattered as he slipped lower into the tunnel, listening for the sounds of the people ahead of him, their footprints obvious in the narrow passage.

The tunnel was not for traveling. It was little more than a path that hot gasses had once used to escape the destruction of Korwa, the great seat of the First Empire.

The ground was uneven and often rounded, making walking upright nearly impossible. One had to move with feet far from the base of the tunnel, often crouching and leaning on the wall for support in order to move forward.

Drask was not bothered by this. Great Ydramil believed that reflection was best learned by overcoming diversity, and adapting. Countless times in his life he had crawled over, under or through the obstacles placed before him by the gods in an effort to train him.

Up ahead of him, not far away, he could hear the Fellein as they stumbled, fell, cursed and barked at each other, impatient to reach their destination, even though they surely had no more idea than he did as to where it was they were going.

Behind him, above him, the air caught the opening they had all used to descend and sent a whining note tumbling down the way they had come.

Drask stood perfectly still and listened to the sounds of the people ahead of him.

"What is that?" A man's voice. He sounded nervous. He had every reason to be nervous. Any place forbidden by gods must surely be a cause of anxiety.

The female – he was almost certain it was Tega, the student of Desh Krohan, the sorcerer, a cause of some trepidation – spoke softly, but he heard her well enough. "It's the wind. The sound started a moment before the winds behind us picked up."

"Aye. Makes sense." A different male.

They continued on and Drask observed his surroundings. The walls cast a pale light. He had thought at first it might come from lichen growing along the walls, but there was no lichen. Nothing seemed to grow here, though he had seen some of the atrocities that came from the Mounds. No, the pale luminescence came from crystals in the walls. The light would be useless in the Blasted Lands proper, where perpetual twilight and endless storms would have muted them to nothing, but here, in the calm of the labyrinthine tunnels, a patient soul could use the light to guide the way.

As has been stated before, among his people Drask was known for his uncanny patience.

He followed, and he listened.

Tolpen Hart spat as he crouched low to the ground and studied the tracks in front of them.

"Hard to say."

Tega looked at the hunter and shook her head.

Nolan looked too, and sighed. "We know it isn't a deer, man. You only have to look at the size of the print."

"Yes, Nolan." Tolpen looked at him and scowled. "But is it one track or a dozen crossing over each other? I can't tell without more light."

Nolan bit back an angry remark. The man was right. He was simply growing impatient. The world he knew was somewhere above him. Here, down in these maddening depths, there was only dirt, rock and glowing stones that hurt his eyes if he looked at them for too long.

He had not signed up for the Imperial Army to walk where the ground was above him. It felt too much like being buried in a grave. That notion alone was enough to make his skin shiver. Bodies should be burned, not buried. It wasn't natural.

Nolan pushed the thought away. He had signed on to the army because it was his duty. He had been chosen for this particular mission because the Empress herself thought him worthy. His father would have surely taken him outside and cleared his mind of any notions of what he was supposed to do in the Imperial Guard. His was a position of great honor and he would do well to remember it.

"We've torches." Vonders Orly was, in Nolan's opinion, the only reason the sorry lot of them were still alive. The man's family had sought fortunes in the Blasted Lands for years, and had located enough baubles and treasures to live a life of ease. There were few in the Fellein Empire who could have predicted what would happen when they started their quest to examine the Mounds, but Orly was the one who warned them against the worst of the storms and saved them from foolish errors again and again.

"We do," Tega agreed. "But if we use them, what might we attract to us?" The passage they were moving through had slowly opened up until the light from the crystals faded into a haze. They could see scant inches in front of their faces and the gloom was not something they were adjusting to. It was simply there, a palpable darkness that swallowed their vision.

"We have to take our chances," Tolpen said. "We can't see anything without more light."

It took Nolan three tries before the torch lit properly. He slid his flint away and made sure it was secure. If he had learned anything at all in the Blasted Lands it was that warmth was a commodity. When he left here, if he left here, he had every intention of moving to a place where the winters were mild.

The torch took a few moments to catch properly, spitting fitfully and smoking before the flame blazed. During that time Nolan looked away from the fire to let his eyes adjust. The light revealed much more than he'd expected.

The area widened out a great deal from the narrow passage they'd been in initially, but that did not mean it was an open area. There were obstacles everywhere.

Warped remains of what had once been were everywhere. Vonders let out a strangled sound that might have been joy or fear. The scavenger and his family had looked for years and could have continued on for decades and never have found the level of treasures that surrounded them. Nolan had never much cared for sparkling treasures, though he knew why so many did. Still, he took in a deep breath and let it out slowly as he marveled. Columns of what had possibly been buildings before the Cataclysm stood impossibly tall and faded away into darkness. Some were upright and others tilted precariously. He looked at one of the closest and wondered how it was that they had not been crushed beneath the weight. The surface was nearly smooth, and parts of it were translucent. Striations of color ran through the entire thing and though he could not see them clearly – for which he thanked the gods – there seemed to be the remains of people frozen in the clear areas, like flies in tree sap.

Nolan March walked closer to the column, which was fifty feet or more in width, and tried to make out the features of what looked like a burnt man holding a small child in his arms. The tower was too murky. Still, his stomach twisted at the thought and his heart raced. How long had that poor wretch been frozen within the depths of the crystal? Was he dead, or did he suffer some eternal half-sleep?

Not far away Tega made a noise in her throat that was more whimper than sigh, and stepped further into the depths as if to escape the sight revealed by Nolan's torch. He could not blame her for seeking the darkness, but he had to follow her.

The light went with him and revealed even more.

The pillars of ruination rose into the darkness above them, thrusting in different directions and in some cases sagging until they touched the ground. There were places where they would surely have to climb over columns of the burnt and broken remains of what the empress and her pet sorcerer told him was likely Korwa.

How could they know? How could anyone know, for certain, what it was they looked at?

Before he could catch up with Tega, Tolpen Hart stepped in front of him and blocked his path. The man had one hand held out toward Nolan and was facing away, looking down.

"Wait. Don't move yet." The hunter stared at the soft, sandy ground ahead of him, and Nolan followed suit, frowning.

There were more tracks. He could clearly see where Tega's footsteps had passed a moment before, but under that, a deeper tread marred the ground. If it was a paw print, the paw was immense, larger than a great shield like those the Lancers used when charging their enemies. Several deep punctures dug the sand around it. Nolan was not as skilled at tracking as Tolpen, but he understood that the indentations were likely from claws.

Tega spoke, her voice carrying through the vast area and echoing into a dozen whispers. "We have a long trek ahead of us, I think."

Nolan frowned and walked toward her, carefully stepping

into unmarked sand. The torch went with him, but he suspected it cast enough light to let Tolpen see what he needed to see.

Tega stood still, looking at the darkness ahead of her. As before, the darkness was not complete.

This time the illumination was better, and clearly defined what lay ahead of them.

Past a forest of broken, twisted columns like those already surrounding them, Nolan could see the cause of Tega's words. There was a long, deep chasm ahead and it seemed to fall for hundreds of feet at least.

Deep in that chasm, below more ruination and ancient debris, he could see a light source brighter than the torch.

The light moved, crawling like ants seen at a distance.

"Is it alive?" He did not look to Tega as he spoke.

"I think we must find out, yes?"

Damn. "Yes. I expect we must."

And was there an easy path to follow? Well lit and gently sloping down to this distant nest of moving lights?

No. Instead there was darkness and cliffs and gigantic paw prints.

Not at all why he had joined the Imperial Army.

FOUR

Captain Callan sat on a three-legged chair and looked at his ship through drink-blurred eyes.

There was a lot that needed doing and he had the spare coin to let him do most of it.

The boat was a good one, fast and true, but very large and in need of minor repairs and a bit of clean up. It was okay for a boat to look poor, but not okay for the boat to suffer for those looks.. The holds were currently empty and he hated that part. Empty holds did not make money.

On the other hand, he had a commission to consider. He'd been paid handsomely for finding the Brellar and negotiating with them. The red-haired woman, Tataya, had seen to his financial needs and promised him more work. Being as he was mostly honest, he'd taken her where she wanted to go and not been foolish enough to try anything like selling her to the highest bidder. Knowing she worked with a sorcerer helped keep him honest, he supposed, but he wasn't much for slavers anyway.

Still, the Brellar were an interesting lot. Had he made a poor choice in negotiations it likely would have cost him his ship and very possibly his head. Instead he was wealthy enough that he could settle in Canhoon if he was inclined and live a comfortable life of idle days and drunken nights.

Instead he looked at his poor, battered boat and nodded his head. The repairs would start in the morning. Nothing too substantial, a board here, a nail there but if she was going to remain seaworthy the work had to be done and paid for.

He had been drinking. He was not blind drunk, nor in any true danger of it.

Still, he started when he heard the voice coming from his left.

"Captain Callan?"

He looked at the man for moment.

Dressed in finery, but definitely local. He had a plain face and a soft manner. He was unremarkable, but Callan had no doubt that was because he chose to be.

"If you are looking for Captain Callan, you've found him. What can I do for you?"

"My name is Losla Foster and I have a need for a good, fast ship. I have heard you have one for hire."

Callan looked his way more carefully. His clothes were fashionable. More importantly, they were clean and needed no mending. That spoke to a certain degree of money.

Money, it should be noted, was always one of Callan's weaknesses, along with a beautiful woman. And food. Wine, of course. Truly, he had to admit, he was a man with many weaknesses.

"What did you need shipped, and to where?"

"I have a group of men who need to enter the city. They do not wish to be seen."

He raised an eyebrow. "Men who need to not be seen are often a costly cargo."

"They are. I know this."

The small sack the man dropped on the table next to his wine landed with a deep, lovely thump. Gold, Callan knew, sounded different than copper or silver when it rattled. That was the rattle of gold. He'd have known it anywhere.

"That is one half of your payment. The rest upon delivery."

"Agreed." Callan did not care what men he was carrying. He was a man with scruples, yes, but they were not very strong and easily purchased.

Later, he would regret that fact about himself.

The land was lush, ripe and green.

Trees rose as high as mountains here, it seemed, and Tusk admired their strength, their beauty. There was power in this place. He could feel it in the ground beneath him and in the trees around him. This was the land where the Fellein held sway without fear of conquest for as long as there had been a Fellein Empire.

The only threat they had ever known that was worthy were the Wellish Overlords and though few knew it, the Sa'ba Taalor had handled that matter a long time back and buried the undying bastards deep in the ground. He wondered what stories the Fellein told themselves to explain why the Overlords had gone away.

It was an idle consideration and one he brushed aside as a man might cast away a gnat.

The great forest of Trecharch had been a part of the Empire since it had been founded on the remains of Korwa. The land ahead of them sloped gently into a valley where three separate rivers ran from the north and flowed toward the great trees in the center. Around those trees, between them, and in some cases built against them, great stone edifices rose in pale imitation of the trees themselves. There were people there, great numbers of them. This was Norhaun, according to the maps they had been given. It was the seat of power in the entire area. At the center, rising like a sapling splitting from one of the great trees, was a castle that took Tusk's breath away.

Orrander's Tower rose toward the skies and would have been impressive in any other setting. Here it seemed small, a pale shadow of the monolithic trees that surrounded it and sheltered it. The trees themselves were almost as great as the Seven Forges in height. They were ancient before the Forges rose from the ground and they continued on.

"Stastha!" He did not look away from the incredible vista as he called for one of his most trusted aides. Instead he savored the view.

Stastha rode forward, her dark furred mount, Loarhun, moving with smooth grace. Stastha's face could not be seen under the great horned helmet she sported, but her eyes glimmered with silvery light as she looked at him.

"Yes, my king?"

She already knew what he would say. They had discussed the matter repeatedly as they moved across the Blasted Lands and traveled over the Wellish Steppes on their way to this place, cutting a bloody path through the people of Trecharch on their way.

"Burn it. All of it. Nothing survives us!"

She did not raise her horn to sound the alarm. Instead she offered a simple battle cry that all with them would understand. "Durhallem!"

"Durhallem!" A hundred voices mirrored the call, and then the armies of the Wounder moved forward, riding into the valley to destroy all that crossed their paths.

Far above them, moving through the trees of the Trecharch,

the other warriors moved in silence. They would continue their own ways and follow their own god. Tusk knew their plans and agreed with them.

Brodem roared under him and the other mounts added their own cries to arms. He and his cavalry charged into the heavy woods, moving across the established paths.

They had already learned the hard way why the trees were said to walk. The Sa'ba Taalor above them had already crippled many of the trees by weakening the great vine that wrapped around the mightiest of the hardwoods.

Somewhere ahead of him Glo'Hosht moved silently through the trees and killed them in passing. He could see the great vine, the damage done to it. That was the King in Mercury's sacred order. The Mother-Vine would die at the king's hand.

Tuskandru suppressed the faintest of shivers. Glo'Hosht was a deadly enemy to have. Tusk would fight anyone, anything that he had to fight in order to survive. The King in Mercury would kill just as easily, without ever touching an opponent.

He pushed the thought aside. This was a time for combat and glory. Glo'Hosht had made certain the traps of the area remained empty of Sa'ba Taalor. Tusk would see to the rest.

Brodem rode faster and Tusk felt himself grin, felt his blood surge. The axe in his left hand was well balanced and sharp enough to manage most any target he struck. The chain in his other hand would handle anything that came his way.

Up ahead he could see buildings and people. Just as importantly, they could see him.

"Durhallem!" He called out his god's name in joy. It was time at last to fight.

The chain rattled and sang as it cut the air. The blades at the end of the long links found flesh and cut that, too. The man who had been posted to guard against attacks died a moment later, a look of shock on his face as the flayed remains of his neck rained blood across his chest.

Sometimes the gods were kind.

She dreamed of her father. When she had been a child he used to walk with her along the Mother-Vine and show her the wonders of Trecharch. She had fished the different rivers, climbed every imaginable type of tree, and learned how to forage the woods when it seemed there was no food to be found.

She missed the old man. His smile, his gentle ways, and the smell of his pipe smoke. He had carved a hundred pipes in his time and given them away more often than sold them. She considered his whittling blades among her most prized possessions.

Cullen opened her eyes and looked at the world around her. The air stank of wood smoke and offal. She turned her head to the side and stifled a cough, barely suppressing the need. Moving hurt her neck, her shoulders, and her back.

People moved around her, and they spoke a language unknown to her ears.

She looked to her left, then to her right and carefully assessed the situation.

There were people, yes, but there were not many. While she watched a gathering of children – they had to be children as the corpses they were near seemed gigantic in comparison – dragged the body of Tremm from where he'd fallen and pulled his weight toward a wagon. Several bodies were already on the open cart. Whatever the bodies carried or wore was left with them.

The children wore hides and leathers and each and every

one of them sported weapons. Some carried swords, most sported clubs or axes.

One of the children – possibly as old as ten years, but she had her doubts – spoke in their tongue and gestured at the wagon. It was full. There was no way around that fact.

Just the same, an older one, closer to adulthood, argued back.

While she watched the younger of the two delivered a brutal open-handed blow across the older one's face and sent the boy rocking on his heels. He started to respond and the younger one drew two daggers from sheaths at his hips. Cullen thought they were male. She couldn't truly tell; they were at that age. Her father used to say that all children are beautiful until they grow up. Looking on these children, that statement made sense. They were androgynous.

They were also vicious. The fight happened quickly and ended with the young one drawing a deep cut across the older one's abdomen. Around them the other children looked on and did nothing to help until the fight was finished. The older sat down while two more tended to the wounds, called to do so by the victor. Two more grabbed at the wagon. It was designed to be pulled by hand, and though the children were young, they were impressively strong and wrestled the weight of the wagon and its cargo with ease.

While they were all distracted, Cullen rolled to her hands and knees and carefully looked around. For the moment no one was watching her. She moved as quietly as she could, wincing, because the pain in her neck was moving through most of her muscles, sliding between two of the trees and getting distance from the invaders. Children or not, they were in better shape that she was at the moment, and they had weapons.

She would fix that just as soon as she could, but for the moment she had to understand her surroundings and what had happened.

When she was properly hidden from easy sight, Cullen stopped and took stock further. The scent of smoke was still prevalent.

To the west she saw why. They were burning the great forest. So far only a few of the younger trees, but she could see more of them – more children! – adding fuel to the fires they had already set. The winds from the Blasted Lands only aided them in their actions. The flames were already too high for her to consider putting them out.

As she watched, one of the trees that had been a landmark in her life begin to burn. The bark had already been smoldering but now it caught ablaze. Tongues of fire licked greedily at the heavy bark, blackening the wood and dancing higher.

Cullen looked up, her eyes trying to orient on the familiar, and felt a cold wind sigh through her body.

Above her the Mother-Vine was gray and lifeless. The leaves had wilted and fallen away; the tendrils that should have held onto the trees around the great vine were withered and tucked in close to the main trunk of the vine.

The Mother-Vine was dead here, or so close to death that it hardly mattered.

What she saw simply could not be. Her mouth was dry and breathing seemed an impossibility. That last was probably because of the smoke that was thickening even as she looked around.

Cullen crouched for a moment, cursing silently and wishing that Deltrea were alive to talk of rutting and boredom. Her eyes stung with unshed tears that eased the burning just the same.

She looked around carefully once more, making sure she was not observed. She had no weapons left. If she were going to arm herself, it would be by taking from one of the children.

They were moving around her. It was only a matter of time before she ran across one or more of them. Not twenty feet away she could hear the tiny terror that had won the earlier fight bellowing at the others in that devil tongue that hurt her ears.

She risked a look around the side of the tree that she was using for shelter and saw one of the children looking directly at her.

The recognition was immediate and Cullen clenched her jaw. If the whelp cried out or called an alarm...

Instead the child – no more than twelve at the oldest, or an absolute runt – started in her direction with a smile that would have scared a Pra-Moresh.

There were no words, just motion.

The girl reached inside her loose blouse – the shirt opening enough to reveal that she fought a female – and came out with a long dagger. The blade was curved and serrated. The hilt of the thing had spikes running over the hand guard and Cullen wondered for half a heartbeat how the girl carried the damned thing without cutting herself to ribbons.

From a distance she thought the smoke was distorting her sight, but closer up she realized the child had pale gray skin.

Her stomach dropped again.

One of the demons from the Blasted lands. No matter the age, she had to assume the bitch was dangerous.

It was a good assumption. Without speaking a word the girl came in low and fast, holding one hand to ward off any possible blows and carrying the dagger with deadly intent.

Cullen did not try pleading. There was no time for anything

but action. The girl came in fast and feinted.

Cullen moved in closer still, remembering her training and getting inside the range of the dagger. The girl stepped back to compensate and Cullen stepped in again, bringing her elbow around and slamming it into her younger opponent's sternum with all her strength.

Full-grown men who'd been foolish enough to try their luck with her had been dropped by the maneuver. Cullen was stronger than she looked and faster, too.

The girl grunted, grinned and attacked, driving the blade up toward Cullen's innards. She backed away fast and narrowly avoided losing her insides.

No delays on the other side. The girl charged forward, the weaponless hand landing a powerful blow on Cullen's temple. She saw black stars for a second and fell back.

The trees saved her. Cullen fell over a thick root and landed on her ass. Even as she was falling she saw the blade cut across where her throat should have been. The little bitch meant business.

From her prone position Cullen kicked out and slammed her heel into the inside of the girl's thigh. The move worked, and knocked her enemy from her feet. She was mean, she was tough but she was still a child. Cullen was twice her weight and that alone saved her.

The girl fell and caught herself on her hand. While she was trying to get her balance, Cullen slammed her heel into the girl's jaw and neck. She felt the bones break. The child died instantly.

Her body ached everywhere. She'd fallen from a tree and landed on a monster. She was alive, but most of her body felt bruised.

Still, she was alive. Lucky, lucky.

There was no hesitation. She stole the girl's dagger. A quick search found several more weapons. A long, thin club made of metal, with a weighted end and a leather grip, and two smaller blades. She took all of them.

And then she ran away from the children, away from the fire, and toward Norhaun. There was no time to contemplate pain. She had to do what she could to get ahead of the invaders and warn the rest of her people.

The ground was uneven and the pathways were littered with the bodies of her people and, occasionally, with a dead Pra-Moresh. She saw no bodies from the enemy. They had brought monsters with them to soften up the Trecharch and it had worked well.

Cullen did not cry. She did not wallow in her grief. She focused on what mattered instead. The dead were dead. The living still had a chance.

A great peal of thunder shook the world and a moment later rains came from the east, washing through the canopy of leaves above. She thanked the gods for the good fortune of unseasonal storms.

The Norhaun River ran placidly across the land, cutting a deep path. Centuries of runoff from the north had allowed a deep ravine and several small waterfalls made certain the area had a pristine beauty.

Goriah looked at the river and the bridges across it and shook her head. The bridges, like the rest of the area, were nearly invisible. The Mother-Vine provides. The thick vine ran across the distance in several locations and the people of the area had used that to their advantage, carefully manipulating offshoots of the vine to use as guiderails along the way. Wherever possible they had avoided adding anything more than ropes or occasional platforms where the Mother-Vine sagged too heavily to allow easy access.

Here the vines were still healthy. To the west she could see the smoke, the growing blaze. The fires were getting stronger.

Goriah considered the environment carefully and settled herself against a tree limb almost a hundred feet from the floor of the heavily wooded area.

Decades of study and careful evaluation went into her decisions. Most people would have seen nothing out of the ordinary unless they were looking toward the skies far above.

The storms of the Blasted Lands were dark, dry and cold. The storm she summoned was just as violent, it had to be, but it was vibrant with water and warmer than the air around her.

When the rains came they were hard, and the winds blew the waters to the west, aiming at extinguishing the growing blaze and saving Trecharch from the flames.

Eyes closed, she felt the world around her and allowed herself a very small victorious smile.

The rains were harsh, but they were doing their work and the fires were faltering in the distance. There was still an invading force to consider but there was hope that the great forest could be spared.

Satisfied that the rains would do their work, Goriah rose from where she had rested and looked toward the bridges of the Mother-Vine. They were the only way across the Norhaun for a hundred miles or more. If she worked quickly she might be able to prevent the enemy from using the bridges to reach the great city.

Hurting the Mother-Vine was not what she wanted, but if she had to, she would. Sometimes a limb must be removed to save the body.

Still, it was a very large move to make and Desh would

want to know before she ruined the bridges.

Once more she closed her eyes and prepared to reach across the distance to speak with the greatest of the sorcerers.

And in that moment, Glo'Hosht drove the blade through her skull and ended her life.

Pella fell. Had she been in flight she would surely have fallen to her death. Instead she merely crashed to her knees, skinning them both, and never even noticing.

The pain was immense. A needle through her eyes and deep into her brain. She felt her Sister die.

Deep within the confines of Orrander's Tower, where she waited to speak with Queen Parlu, Pella fell to the ground and into a deep, restless darkness.

The storms were violent and sent shivers through the trees themselves.

The Sa'ba Taalor noticed, but did not stay their path. In comparison to the Blasted Lands the storms were only a minor inconvenience.

Tusk looked at the tower ahead and reached for his horn. It was a massive tower, the thing he had seen in the distance. True to his earlier thoughts it grew alongside a tree that was as tall as a mountain. He could not hope to understand the size of the tree until he was upon it.

No. He frowned and looked a second time. Not a tree at all. This was the Mother-Vine. He had seen the many strands of the great thing as it sprawled across the land. The vines ran everywhere. They had actually crossed thick strands of the vine as they moved over the river that cut through the valley.

The map called it the Mother-Vine and Durhallem had spoken to him of the great serpentine thing. His god claimed that many of the people in the area nearly thought of the Mother-Vine as a god as well.

He patted Brodem's neck and his mount slowed his pace. Mount and rider alike surveyed the area. There were soldiers ahead. Not as many as he had expected, but still they were there and they were likely very well trained. They had to protect not only their queen, but also their god.

That thought amused him.

"Why are you smiling, Tusk?" Stastha's voice came from his left.

He looked to her and winked. "In that tower is a 'queen.'" He frowned for a moment. Not because he was sad, but merely confused by the cultural differences. "For some reason they call their kings by that name when they have breasts. In any event, I must go meet this queen and kill her."

"And that makes you smile?"

Tusk nodded. "Yes, but I smile for a different reason. This queen, she is the protector of the Mother-Vine. That is the god of these people. It is all around us." He gestured and she looked, nodding.

"Yes." She paused a moment. "And?"

"If she must protect her god, either she is a very powerful warrior, or her god is very weak."

Stastha looked at him for a moment and then threw her head back, laughing so hard she could barely breathe.

Tusk looked around again to make sure that no one was waiting to kill them in the trees. One could never be too careful.

When his second had finished her fit he swatted her affectionately on the shoulder. "We go our separate ways now. You should kill everyone you encounter. All of them."

"And you, Tuskandru?" Her eyes blazed under her helmet.

The great horns were intact, but the helm itself was bloodied and dented.

"Durhallem has told me to kill this 'queen' and then, apparently I am to slay a god."

"What blade does one use to slay a god, Tuskandru?" She shook her head. To be fair the Mother-Vine was very large. He wasn't so sure his axe would do much damage.

He grinned again and urged Brodem forward. The great mount let out a roar of impatience and prepared for running.

Just as the beast started moving, Tusk gave Stastha his answer, "It might take more than one!"

As he rode, Stastha sounded her horn. The armies of Durhallem moved again, riding through the forests of Trecharch on their way to introduce new deities to the region.

Cullen did not have a horse, nor did she have a great beast like the invaders rode. She only had her feet and they were sore and the legs attached to them were weak and felt ruined.

Still, one does what one must. Her father had always said that to her when she was growing and her mother had nodded her agreement. Good people the both of them and as much as she missed them she was glad they were dead. They'd have been ruined by the burning of the forest they'd both loved so dearly.

She moved along the pathways that most would never have seen and cursed the fact that no one had ever thought to lay traps along the main routes to prevent invaders.

When she came to the bridge over the river there was no choice but to run it. She dared not walk. The longer she was on the bridge the greater the chance that she would be spotted by the invaders and she dreaded that notion. Though she had fought for her life, Cullen could not overlook the fact that she had killed a child. The swelling above her eye where the girl had nearly cracked her skull open helped a bit, but guilt still cut at her conscience.

After she crossed the bridge it was back to moving, running, doing all she could to reach Orrander's Tower though she knew she would be too late.

The bodies she found told her that much. The forest hid little from the ground. The trails were evident and even the less traveled ones were visible if you knew where to look.

The invaders knew how to look and they were thorough. Willist was ruined. Every house, every structure, even the Sanctuaries within the trees, all were broken open and gutted. The people inside dragged out and cut down like fresh kill at a slaughterhouse.

The ground was saturated with blood and the runoff from the rains were stained with varying shades of red.

Cullen did not have time to consider the deaths. In truth she suspected her mind might have broken. She was running toward the danger instead of away from it.

There was no possibility that she could reach Orrander's Tower before the attack and even if she did there was nothing that she could do against the invaders by herself.

Still, she had to try.

So she ran when she could and walked the rest of the time. Along the way she gathered a good bow and some arrows. Weapons she knew how to use properly.

No denying it; a time to kill was upon her. She might die and soon, but she'd take as many as she could with her into the dark.

FIVE

The differences between the Summer Palace and the Winter Palace were negligible. Had anyone placed a schematic for one over the other they would have been hard pressed to tell them apart. There were differences in the furniture, to be sure, but not much beyond that.

That meant Desh Krohan felt like he was coming home when he walked into his private chambers. The bed was the same. The walls were very close. There were fewer distractions.

A war was going on to the north. He hated that. He wanted peace in his world. That was what he had always wanted and what he had strived to achieve over the centuries. Save for a few skirmishes, he had been successful for the last few generations.

Now that had changed and there was nothing to be done about it.

He founds Tataya in his chambers.

"Goriah is dead."

Desh nodded his head. "I felt it, too. I am so very sorry, my dear." There was nothing else to be said, really. Much as he wanted to take his revenge against the Sa'ba Taalor, he was not prepared for that yet. There was too much to do, too many depended on him.

Tataya closed her eyes and leaned back until her face was pointed toward the heavens. "I feel her death, Desh. It's echoing through my head."

"You are Sisters. Of course it echoes. It will continue for some time yet." He walked closer and placed a hand on her shoulder. "Is Pella safe?"

"For the moment. She stirs. She was so close when it happened. I'm watching over her. If anyone comes for her, I will act."

"How do they fare in Trecharch?"

"You already know, Desh."

"I am close to you, all of you, but your connection is greater than mine of necessity. If I felt all that you do, I would not be able to do what I must."

He closed his eyes as well, and reached out with his mind, using Tataya as a connection point to find Goriah's corpse with greater ease. "Don't move, Tataya. I'm bringing her back."

Hundreds of miles away the body of his Sister moved, and then rose into the air. Her corpse had been gathered with others, but it was of little consequence. He moved it just the same, taking her from the mountainous pile of the dead and carrying her aloft.

Any who had seen him would have thought he was merely resting his head. Only Tataya understood the strain of moving Goriah from so great a distance. Few would have been capable.

Few had ever been as powerful as Desh Krohan.

"Will you kill their king for this, Desh?"

He did not answer immediately. Several minutes passed before he finally opened his eyes and looked to Tataya. Her eyes were still closed. Her hair fell in a crimson cascade and her face, as lovely as ever, was as pale as marble.

"I may yet. But as you know there is always a price. Even bringing Goriah back is a strain."

"I am grateful. Thank you for bringing her to me." Tataya's voice was distant, dreamy. Goriah's journey had only started, but Tataya knew the course her Sister would take.

"How could I not? I loved her as I love you and Pella." He swallowed back the tears. "How could I not?"

"How will this end, Desh?" Tataya opened her eyes and stared at him.

He made himself look back as he answered. "I do not know. I wish I did." He kept to himself that he felt the entire situation would grow far worse before it was resolved. In the past he could have done so much more.

Merros Dulver's new home was a short distance from the palace. Short enough that he walked, rather than ride his horse. That did not stop him from going a bit out of his way to find the house of Dretta March.

Her new domicile looked nothing like the last she had lived in, save that it was a house and surrounded by a strong stone wall. The gardens were better tended and smaller, though he knew she had not been living there long enough to manage much by way of gardening. There was a small orchard on the estate and the trees were blooming.

It was near those trees that Dretta waited for him at a stone table with benches rather than chairs.

"You've taken your time in finding me." She looked at him with her dark eyes and he tried not to get lost in their depths.

"Yes, well, there's the war to take care of."

Dretta nodded. "You've not managed to get yourself killed. I was worried along those lines."

It was meant as a jest and he knew it, but considering how her husband had died, it was a bit too fresh a wound for either of them to find the situation amusing. Still, he managed a small smile for her.

"I've decided I've too much to do to allow any form of death for a while."

"For the best, really. Who else will run things?"

"Desh Krohan, the First Advisor, very likely has a hundred more waiting in the ranks."

"It's his job, yes? To handle such affairs for the Empress?" There was something about the way she said those words that he found particularly amusing.

"Have you met the man? I believe he takes his duties rather seriously."

"One should when running an empire."

"Don't let him hear you say that. He'd likely deny it and then appoint you to run the palace, or possibly the Imperial Navy."

Dretta knew his situation well enough to appreciate the comment. He'd been a captain less than a year ago, and retired before that. Now he found himself in charge of the Imperial Army and he dreaded it. The responsibilities seemed endless. It was these brief visits with the widow of his best friend and second-in-command that left him feeling anchored enough to continue in his new duties.

Dretta smiled and pushed a plate full of fruit and cheese in his direction. The cheeses were varied and the fruit was fresh and ripe. She'd brewed a potent tea – one she favored from the north, where winters were colder and a hot drink was nearly a necessity – and he sipped at it happily. He had acquired a taste for the stuff.

"There are many newcomers entering the city every day." Her tone was conversational.

"There are indeed. I have no idea where we will put them. I know the Empress has ordered a great number of the older properties converted to accommodate them, but there are still more coming from, well, from everywhere. The refugees from Tyrne and Roathes, and I expect we'll have more coming from Trecharch before long."

"How goes the fight for Trecharch?"

"I've only just sent troops. They won't reach the area for days yet, but the fighting has moved on." He shook his head. "They're brutal, the Sa'ba Taalor."

"They aren't that many in number are they?"

Merros bit back a hysterical laugh. "I'd hoped that was the case, but after meeting with their King in Iron, I don't think I was right in my assessments."

Dretta continued to study him and he wasn't certain it was a sensation he liked. She had a very direct stare and he was never sure whether or not she found him up to the standards she demanded in her world.

Just to let himself recover from her eyes, he ate a slice of apple and a sharp hard cheese he couldn't identify. He barely tasted them.

"There are a lot more of them than I first thought, Dretta, and they're savage. I can't explain that well enough. I have seen them in combat and I don't know many soldiers who would have a chance against them."

"You've been training them, yes?"

"Yes, of course. But the training doesn't happen quickly and our enemies have spent their *entire lives* preparing for this." He shook his head. "I have soldiers trained with swords and I have lancers and I have archers. But they have different weapons. Things I've never even imagined before."

"So you intend to surrender?" The look she threw his way

made clear she was scolding him for his doubts.

"Of course not."

"That is good. Wollis would approve."

"With a thousand like Wollis I feel I would have a chance." He picked at a cluster of grapes. "He could train anyone. He could use almost any weapon."

"So find them. Out there, among your soldiers. Find the ones like him and make them count."

"You always make it sound easy."

"There is no easy, Merros Dulver. There is only what must be done."

She smiled at him then, and the possibility that he might actually accomplish some of his goals seemed more achievable for the moment. He tried to memorize that smile for when he was alone and she was not there to remind him of possibilities.

They came before her on the throne.

The throne room in Canhoon was nearly cavernous. Most of the rooms in the Winter Palace were mirrors of the ones that had stood in Tyrne, but not so the room where the Empress held court. The ceiling was over fifty feet in height, with great marble columns supporting the entire affair. The walls were adorned with the coat of arms for every royal family in the whole of the Fellein Empire, including a few that were nearly lost in obscurity. "Nearly" because, Nachia had no doubt, Desh Krohan could likely quote the entire history of each and every one of those families, no matter how obscure or ancient.

Before this day there had been a few who did not bother to deal with the new Empress. They sent emissaries if they responded at all. Now? Now was different. Tyrne had been destroyed. It wasn't a collection of islands out in the sea that had gone. It wasn't a gathering of savages living in huts along the shoreline of the fishing villages who had been annihilated. It was Tyrne, the Summer City, that had been leveled.

They knew Tyrne. They cared that Tyrne was gone. Tyrne mattered in their eyes and so when the Empress demanded the presence of the royal families of the Empire, this time they listened.

Now, Trecharch was falling. It was not gone yet, of course, but in less than two days the fighting had spread through the greatest forest in the Empire and the sadistic enemy was actually burning everything they could.

Nachia Krous, Empress of the Fellein Empire, was not in a good mood.

She'd hoped, prayed, that the parley between her empire and the Sa'ba Taalor would go well. That they might come to an accord and end their skirmish before it became a war.

Not because she wanted it to end. That wasn't the case at all. She wanted to find the bitch who'd killed her cousin and flay the flesh from her diseased, gray hide in thin strips. She wanted to kill any and all who had taken her cousin's life, no matter how minor their part in the decision.

She would have accepted peace just the same, because as the ruler of the Empire it was her duty to seek the best possible solution for her people.

Now the families she had asked to attend before suddenly found they had time for dealing with the upstart Empress and discovered that the peace they had all assumed would always last was crumbling away.

Part of her enjoyed the notion, just because of the looks on their faces.

Next to her, to the left side of her throne, Merros Dulver looked on, his face as hard as stone. There were few people she knew who could grow so cold in an instant.

To her right, Desh Krohan was currently not in his place. That made her nervous. He'd planned to be here for this assembly.

There were many faces in the gathering ahead of her that were familiar, but the unknown outweighed those she knew by a substantial margin. Unlike her cousin Pathra, the former Emperor, she had traveled all of the Empire at one time or another, but many of the places she'd visited had been over half her lifetime ago, and she had seen so many faces between that recognition was a challenge. Desh knew them all, of course. That was why she wanted him here.

Still, the people before her were growing restless and irritated.

Merros leaned over and spoke softly. She knew without having to consider it that no one but she was close enough to hear his words.

"Let them wait a bit longer, milady." He had an amused tone that belied the expression on his face. "Let them understand that you are in command and that they must answer to you. Look at each of them in the eyes, find the ones you like the least and stare hardest at them. Should they look away before you do, you will always have them at a disadvantage."

He waited three seconds exactly and then spoke again. "Of course, you already know that. It is merely a suggestion on my part."

"One that is appreciated," she said, while her eyes skewered Prince Torrain of Louron, whose father had not appeared and who failed to make apologies for that situation. Also, when she was much younger, Torrain had pulled her hair and gotten away with it. She still wasn't sure if she intended to hold a grudge.

For one moment Torrain looked haughty. Then he looked away, nervously worrying his lower lip. She hoped he was remembering the hairpulling incident and how he'd run to his mother for protection when it happened.

Her eyes moved to Queen Lanaie, who was her guest on an extended basis for the present. She wasn't quite sure how to handle that matter. Lanaie was the queen of Roathes. The problem was that Roathes was only a name on a map now. Most of Lanaie's people were either dead, living in Canhoon, or trying to find a place to live inside the city.

They had been among the first victims of the Sa'ba Taalor.

Her brother Brolley had affection for the girl. Then again, most men did. She was exotic, attractive and chesty. A combination that made most men and a good number of women look twice. That she was also nice only added complications.

Lanaie looked to her and smiled softly. Nachia knew she was worried about her people. That was, undoubtedly, one of the reasons she was here. She wished more assistance than had already been given. Roathes had a history of asking for help and offering remarkably little in return.

Of course, she was still a queen and had every right to be here. Just as importantly, there were others who understood that her status as a queen made her a perfect target for marriage proposals. That included Nachia's uncle, Laister, who had already expressed his desire to marry Queen Lanaie. So far Lanaie had made no response. Nachia needed to make certain it stayed that way.

Her eyes went to her brother, Brolley, who was still recovering from his escape from Tyrne. He had planned to stay in the palace until she returned. He would have, too, had Merros not ordered the palace cleared and had his soldiers take him from the castle by force.

She reminded herself to thank Merros for that again. She had already done so on several occasions, but there was simply no way she could properly convey her gratitude.

Brolley looked toward Lanaie and his eyes cast over the rest of the crowd. They were important people. Because of their status, even he had to remember to behave.

No, that was unfair. He had learned his lesson on diplomacy already. She just tended to be harder on her brother. Somebody had to watch out for him and if she did not, who would? Laister? Not very likely.

As Nachia pondered, Desh Krohan came into the chamber from the far side, moving through the gathered crowd which parted before him.

She knew Desh Krohan, had known him since she was a toddler, had sat on his knee when she was much younger, had seen him at countless functions, had wept on his shoulder when her parents died.

That was a man.

Desh Krohan, the First Advisor and best-known sorcerer in the Empire, was a different figure to behold. As he moved through the room in his hooded cloak, the people around him backed away, suddenly aware of exactly how much power he wielded.

That was, of course, exactly why he wore the robe now and why he came into the room from the far side. He wanted all present to remember how striking a figure he could be, because that way, when he stood at her right side, they would remember how powerful the Empress of the Fellein Empire was.

He was doing her a favor. He was reminding them that she was in charge.

When Desh settled at her side, his great cloak continued to shift in the still air and the great cowl hid his face. He was a sinister presence.

Had she not known the man so very well, she might have been intimidated herself.

Nachia nodded her head, acknowledging the sorcerer, and then spoke. "We are at war. As an empire, we are at war."

The emotions on the faces before her varied little. There was anger. There was fear. There was regret. The longer she looked, the more she saw of the fear.

"General Dulver can give you the details. He has studied the maps and can tell all of you what he needs from you."

"What he needs from us?" The voice was sharp and tinged with desperation. Nachia saw the speaker and was moderately surprised. Kordon Neiller was the king of Goltha, decidedly one of the largest and most powerful of the Twelve Kingdoms. Goltha was both the name of the city that grew near Lake Gerhaim, and the kingdom that sprang from the same. Gerhaim was massive and all rivers ran to the lake in their time. Kordon Neiller was her distant cousin. He was also one of the best of the allies of the Imperial Throne.

Nachia smiled at him and the man melted just a bit. They had been friendly for all the time they'd known each other. Kordon was her senior by fifteen years. He had been crowned when he was twelve and had ruled well.

"We are at war, Kordon. No one wants this. No one. But it is what it must be." She waved a hand and Merros stepped forward, looking resplendent in his uniform.

"The Imperial Army needs more soldiers. We will, of course, hire as we need to from the mercenary ranks, but that's not the same thing. In the last few decades several countries have not enforced the laws of the Empire as well as they could when it comes to training soldiers. The time for allowing young adults to stay on the farm or tend to the family must now come to an end."

Were there guilty faces? No, but there was guilt aplenty. The royal families were merely better at hiding their sins.

Merros continued, "It is requested by the throne that all present provide the appropriate numbers to the ranks of the Imperial Army."

"And what numbers do you deem appropriate, General Dulver?" The question came from Theorio Krous. The man was Nachia's relative in name, but only just. He was also the King of Morwhen far to the east. Morwhen was well known for the soldiers they trained. They were often among the elite. According to Merros, if all of the kingdoms trained soldiers as well as Morwhen, there might have been less to fear from the Sa'ba Taalor.

Theorio himself was a heavyset man, well muscled and dressed in black armor. He did not wear uniforms. He always wore, at the very least, leather armor, such as he sported currently.

Nachia lowered her head briefly, a sign of respect, and then looked him in the eyes. In comparison to the King in Iron, Theorio Krous was not an intimidating man.

Merros spoke again, answering the question. "The ledgers of the Imperial Army are very thorough. Numbers matching those offered by each of the Twelve Kingdoms one century ago are expected."

The gathered families murmured and mumbled on that one. Most of the kingdoms had fallen far short of the appropriate numbers of conscripted soldiers over the last few decades. Most still offered up numbers, but few enforced the laws of conscription as they were supposed to.

Theorio Krous smiled. "You will have double that number from Morwhen."

Merros offered a formal bow. "You have my thanks and the gratitude of the Empire, Majesty."

The man looked at Merros and smiled. It was the sort of smile she expected from a member of the Sa'ba Taalor: a promise of bloodshed and joy in the shedding.

Perhaps Merros was right.

The crowd continued to mutter among themselves until Merros brought up Trecharch and the war going on there.

When it came to bad news, it seemed everyone was ready to pay attention.

Merros and Desh walked through the inner garden, in an area officially set aside solely for the Empress. They had access, of course, though being there had once been punishable by death.

Merros spoke softly just the same, his eyes looking around constantly. "You and your Sisters. You've shown in the past that you can communicate over great distances."

Desh nodded.

"Can others do this? I mean other sorcerers or apprentices?"

"There are a few, Merros." He allowed a small, tired smile. "We are hardly a vast army. I'd say there might be a hundred across the entire Empire."

"I need them. I need you."

"Whatever for?"

"I have couriers and I have a few trained storm crows. That is all. And I have a continent to protect."

"That's always been the case."

Merros nodded. "True, but we have a war now, and a large one."

Desh contemplated that. "Sorcery and war do not go well together, General Dulver. If we learned anything, ever, as a group, it is that."

"What do you mean?"

"It's extremely possible that the Blasted Lands are a result of sorcery that got out of control."

Merros looked his way with a dark expression.

"You think I jest?" Desh asked.

"No. I just didn't think anyone capable of that sort of power."

The sorcerer said nothing for a moment, but instead looked toward the window where Nachia could have easily looked down on them. He knew she was very likely listening to their words.

"There are only a few. I'm one of them." He shrugged. "More than one sorcerer working together can perform even greater feats. The City of Wonders was raised from ruination and moved from one place to anther. The Silent Army was raised at the same time and fought against invaders that would have taken control of the Empire otherwise."

Desh saw the changes in Merros's expression and curbed the thoughts before they could go too far. "Those feats are long past. Many of the most powerful among us died in the process of working those feats. I could, perhaps, rebuild a city, but as I have said before, there is a price to pay for sorcery and I fear you would not much like the cost."

The general looked at him differently from that moment on. It was a subtle thing, but Desh noticed.

"I'm not asking for any to get involved in the combat. I just need to have a better way to communicate between camps."

"Between camps?"

"Desh, we have one empire. They have seven kingdoms. I do not believe for a moment that those seven kings will be joining together to offer a single front." He sighed and shook his head. His arms moved behind is back and he clasped his hands there. "I have the First Lancers stationed at the Temmis Pass. No choice in that. It's the likeliest place for the Sa'ba Taalor to use to reach us."

Desh opened his mouth to speak and Merros silenced him with a gesture.

"I know. No one expected the bastards to attack Trecharch. That was an oversight caused because I thought they would have to come up through the Temmis Pass. They've found other ways, but I can't risk leaving the pass unguarded. If I did, if I do, I can guarantee they'll use it to their advantage."

He sighed and looked at Desh straight on, as few men would do willingly.

"Desh, I need to be able to organize my troops across several fronts. I have no doubt at all that they will attack from different areas. They have great black ships waiting for the chance to move up the Jeurgis and into the waters outside of Canhoon. I have a fleet of mercenaries heading in to deal with them, but no way to communicate with them. We've promised gold and that's a good motivator but not enough to guarantee any proper defense."

Merros took in another deep breath, ready to continue making his point.

It was Desh who silenced the general with a gesture this time around. "I'll arrange something. But, Merros, I mean what I said. None of them can aid you beyond speaking on your behalf. None of them will. I won't permit it."

"That is your decision to make. I will not question it."

"Be certain that your soldiers understand that as well."

Merros nodded his head. "I will. How soon can they be sent out?"

"Within two days I'll have them on their way. Make certain that you have the proper letters of introduction for them, please."

Merros offered a grim smile. "I'm grateful, Desh."

"You have a war to win and I've placed that burden squarely at your feet. The least I can do is offer a little help with keeping things organized, I suppose."

SIX

The ground came up very quickly and punched Andover Lashk in his right side. Since he was much smaller than the ground, and softer besides, he came off worst from the impact.

It was a long time before he dared move. Every part of his body seemed to ache and his head felt broken. He took a few experimental breaths and decided he could still manage to gulp in air, but breathing was all he could manage for several minutes.

Each of the mountains, each of the Hearts of the Gods was different. He'd known that, but somehow Wheklam seemed more determined than the other mountains he'd visited to make sure he never reached his goal.

How long had he been climbing? He could not say. He knew only that he was cold, and that the sun had set and risen a few times since he'd lost his hammer. He still had his axe – he had finished locking together the obsidian he had been given by Durhallem and the iron rings he'd been offered by Truska-Pren. The axe the pieces made was incredibly sharp, perfectly balanced and currently jamming into his side. Happily the thing was sheathed properly or he'd have been cut in half instead of merely beaten severely by his own weapon.

Andover very carefully rolled himself over and began the slow process of standing back up. There was a time he'd have stayed where he was for a while, but he knew better now. He suspected Delil might well come down and beat him senseless if he let himself remain in the same place for too long.

He looked up the side of the steep slope toward the distant spot from where he'd fallen. He found the spots where he had bounced before finally rolling to a stop.

"On the lighter side of this, nothing seems broken," he murmured to himself. Bruised and strained, yes. Broken? No.

Delil did not stop for him. He was on his journey, she was on her own. They were merely going in the same direction at the moment. Even so, part of him was almost certain that she might yet come down to beat on him if he waited too long. That alone was enough motivation. He started climbing.

Rather than let himself think of where he hurt or what lay ahead, he focused on putting one hand in front of the other. It was the distractions that kept getting him in trouble.

The ground was hard, and if he paid attention there were handholds. He had hands made of iron. They were more than capable of gripping the rock and supporting his weight. Delil did not have his advantages and yet she seemed to be managing well enough.

He started again, looking only as far ahead as the next potential area where fingers could find purchase.

The sun had almost set by the time he reached the top of the volcanic mountaintop.

The area was nearly as wide as the city of Tyrne, it seemed. The vast hollowed-out bowl of the great forge glowed with a warm light, but clouds of gasses rose from the depths stinking of molten metal and worse.

They were scents he knew well enough and in his way appreciated.

Far away from him, far enough that she was merely a speck in the distance, he thought he saw Delil sitting on the edge of the great pit. She had clearly decided not to concern herself with his condition after his fall.

He mirrored her action. He was not supposed to be with her. This was a personal quest, a private discussion between mortal and god.

Andover's body shook from exertion, and he drew in deep breaths of the foul air. He had endured worse in the Blasted Lands.

Below him the glow of Wheklam's Forge seemed to fluctuate. He looked down into the distant fire, and the smoke and gasses seethed, rising upward.

No. Andover frowned. Not smoke. Water. As he looked down into the heart of the forge he could still see the raging inferno that glowed below him, a literal lake of fire and molten stone, but above that, impossibly, water rose toward him, a greater body of water than he had ever seen before.

The waters seethed, forming waves that thrashed against the sides of the crater as if trying to escape. The scent changed; a potent odor came to him, and all he could think of was the stench of fish he'd smelled a few times at the river's edge. This was different, but close enough that he felt a sense of familiarity.

Then the waters rose up in a vast wave that caught Andover unawares, washing him into the depths before he could even catch a breath.

In his entire life, Andover Lashk had seen no body of water greater than the Freeholdt River and while that river was a substantial one, the most he had ever done was wade into the shallows and wash himself.

Put another way, he was not a swimmer. He thrashed madly for several moments, trying to find his way to any purchase at all. Ultimately he failed.

The water filled his lungs and he felt himself choking, fighting for breath.

He felt the darkness at the edges of his mind as surely as he saw the darkness stealing away his sight.

And then, beyond that dread, he felt the presence of a god.

He had already met with two gods, and in both cases the sheer power of those entities had overwhelmed his senses. This was no different. Wheklam moved through his body, a power impossible to deny. At that moment, as he was drowning in impossible waters, he had caught the attention of a deity.

He wasn't sure precisely how he would make his point with Wheklam. He had been told to offer himself to each of the gods and he had done so before by speaking his piece. That was impossible here so he held his arms wide apart and did his best to bow underwater, as his body was cast this way and that by the tides.

On the left side of his face, at the very edge of the jaw line, he felt a searing pain and forced himself not to scream. A finger's width of fire boiled across his skin. There was no light, no source for the pain, but it was real and he knew what it meant. Another god had accepted him.

Now all he had to do was live through the experience.

Far above him he could see the light from above the crater. Far below he could see the light of Wheklam's Heart.

In between there was water in endless supply and no air to breathe.

•••

The burden of leadership was a constant thing in her life. From the moment she'd accepted the crown placed on her brow, Queen Parlu had felt the weight of more than a few ounces of silver.

Trecharch was burning. Far in the distance she could see the light on the western horizon. The sun was above her, barely noticeable through the rain, but she saw the light as bright as the most magnificent of sunsets on the western horizon.

The view from her tower had always been spectacular. It allowed her an uninterrupted examination of the end of her world.

Trecharch had been her home since she was born, and that had been a very long time ago.

Trecharch was not like the other kingdoms. She allowed the citizens a say in how things were run. Not a large say, true, but still they had a voice that she listened to.

Now all she could hear, as the day grew older, was the sound of screams.

Her world burned.

There had been a time, when she was younger, when the citizens of the nation had considered overthrowing her rule. Not because she was a bad ruler – at least she tended to think she was not, but suspected many might disagree – but because they wanted change. They wanted less taxation and more freedom to decide for themselves how the world should work. Some had claimed that the forests were too full of trees and that cutting down a portion of them would make Trecharch a better place. That the wood from the trees had great monetary value was merely a coincidence, of course.

Frah Molen, one of her finest advisors, knocked politely before entering the chamber. In the past he had been her lover. Now he was much more than that. He was her friend.

He was beyond the age where the notion of rutting meant much to him. She was just as old, but her connection to the great forest had, as always, left her feeling invigorated.

"Frah." She sighed his name. "The fires are coming. I thought the rain might offer us salvation, but the fires are growing again and the Mother-Vine is sickened by whatever they have done to her."

Parlu was not a delicate woman, though many might have thought otherwise if they'd seen her. Her frame was thin, and her limbs were long. Her hair was graying from the deep browns it had been in her earlier years, but the gray only accented her mane these days. She was conscious that many men found her beautiful still. She saw the same beauty in her daughter, Lemilla, who would rule in her stead when she died – assuming there was anything left to rule.

"They come, Parlu. The invaders." Frah's voice was still as strong as ever. It was the rest of him that had weakened over the years. His back was bent by the decades and his magnificent red hair had first gone white and then fallen out completely. Still, she loved him.

He was one of the finest men she knew and it hurt her to think that he'd be dead before the day was over.

"I could hardly fail to notice them, Frah," she chided him softly. "I've never seen the likes of the creatures they ride. Are they Pra-Moresh?"

"No." He stepped closer. "They are smaller, but almost as deadly, and the people who ride them must surely be knights. I have never heard of fighters as brutal."

"Desh Krohan says they do not have knights. He says that all of them are like that. Deadly and filled with hatred for all of us."

"What a misery then."

She did not look away from the window. Far below her, she could see the first of the invaders crossing the Field of Remembrance, where the likenesses of each past ruler looked out toward the forest.

"I suppose it is time, then, yes?"

"Parlu…You don't have to do this." He placed one hand on her thin shoulder. His flesh was cold now, not as warm and lovely as it had been once, and she could feel the swelling in the joints of each finger.

"Of course I do, Frah." She settled her fine and strong hand over his gnarled paw and smiled softly. Far below, the archers fired volleys of arrows but the invaders kept coming. They wore armor, and they carried shields, and they sported heavy furs and helmets. The arrows struck but few seemed to do any real damage.

The people of Trecharch were renowned for their archery skills. For decades they had won archery competitions throughout the Twelve Kingdoms. When someone from a different country took the winning purse it was usually amid claims that they had cheated in one form or another, simply because the people of Trecharch were archers before they were soldiers.

The Sa'ba Taalor held their own with ease. The ones who were mounted rode with confidence and used great bows that had apparently been designed for use when riding. Most of the people in Trecharch could barely ride horses. They simply were not common among the great forest.

The enemy fired and nearly every one of their arrows found a home and maimed or killed.

"Parlu, please, don't do this."

"I accepted my crown, Frah. I knew the risks then, and I have long since reaped the benefits." Still, she thought back to her earlier days and the lovers she had known, the friends she had known. Many of the other nations claimed that marriage was a sacred thing. They swore by the notion that one man and one woman were required to make a life and that they should be together for all time. Trecharch had never held to that notion. There were exceptions, of course. Many chose one lover and stayed with them for life.

Perhaps that was for the best. In hindsight, she rather liked the idea of having someone she could hold onto one last time before she climbed the last steps in Orrander's Tower.

Frah was in the room with her. He had always been a wonderful friend. Ultimately he was enough.

"Watch over Lemilla. See her safely away, my friend. It is time."

He would not question her orders. It was not his way.

The wooden stairs barely creaked under her weight as she started up the final flights to the chamber of the Mother-Vine, but far below her, the great doors of the tower shook with the impact of whatever the invaders used to attempt access.

Pella woke in a small room, on the covers of a bed filled with goose down.

She did not wake slowly or gently, but rather all at once and with the knowledge that she was in danger.

The Sa'ba Taalor had come. They were below her and attacking the tower, she knew that as surely as she breathed. The knowledge came from outside of her, sent as a gift from Tataya.

Goriah was dead. She knew that, too.

Her stomach twisted on itself at the thought. Her Sister had been a beautiful person and she loved her and missed her and always would.

Her grief, however, would have to wait.

Pella closed her eyes for a moment and cast her senses outside of her body, taking in the whole of the tower with ease. She was near the base of the great tower, on the third level.

Parlu was ascending into the Mother-Vine, at the apex of the tower, where it was swallowed by the Mother-Vine. She had no choice but to reach Queen Parlu's personal chambers, where the final doorway into the Mother-Vine's sacred interior was located. Pella's abilities did not allow her to look into that final chamber. That was blocked from her by the power of the forest itself. All gods have their secrets, it seemed.

She had recently learned more of gods than she had ever wanted.

The guarding soldiers were preparing as best they could, setting barriers between the queen and the invaders. They understood exactly how bad the situation was.

Orrander's Tower was a great feat of architecture. The stones and mortar that built the place had been carefully sculpted along the side of the Mother-Vine over the decades and centuries, and might well have never lasted if not for the fact that the Mother-Vine had accommodated the addition. Seen from outside, the tower was only remarkable in its height, but from inside it was easy to see how much of the tower had been swallowed and protected by the great vine. Chambers that were far larger than they appeared had been absorbed by the vine and become a part of the whole. They were not crushed, they were not broken; they were simply made stronger and protected. Those chambers held a large portion of Trecharch's army. The soldiers had been called to protect their queen and the Mother-Vine alike and they were ready to die if necessary.

Fifty men with braces held the doors at the entrance. Thick logs had been cut and well seasoned, their bases shaped to fit slots in the stone floors. Metal gratings were pulled aside and the logs locked into those hidden slots, and then set against the great doors, bracing for any possible attack. A hundred men battering the doors would only be able to break through if they could shatter those logs, and the wood in question was carved from the Sentinels and as hard as stone.

Put simply, the Sa'ba Taalor would not gain access that way.

That didn't mean they weren't trying. A dozen or more of the brutes held on to a battering ram cut from one of the trees nearby and used it against the massive doors. The wood and metal of the door was damaged. Great gashes had been torn from the surface, and shreds of wood from both the ram and the doors fell to the ground as they continued the assault.

The doors would hold. The rest of the structure was a different case.

Pella could sense the other attackers. They were harder to find because they were so very high off the ground and she did not initially think to look for them there.

A dozen soldiers battered at the doors of the keep, with a gathering ready in case they got through. The rest climbed the walls, scaling the rough stone in some cases, climbing the Mother-Vine in others.

They were like ants, methodically swarming their way up the surfaces available to them and moving along similar lines. One or two found the pathways to climb and others followed after.

Far below, the battering ram knocked again and again, and a gathering of soldiers prepared for in case they got through. Most of the windows in the tower were small, and set high in

the walls. They were more for ventilation than for looking out
at the trees beyond. Most of the exceptions were high enough
up that few would consider using them and those that did
would not be able to see the attackers until it was far too late.
The angle of Orrander's Tower followed the curvature of the
Mother-Vine and did not allow for an easy examination of
the ground below.

Pella rose from the bed and moved toward the door, fully
aware that she was far too late to call the alarm. The invasion
had already begun.

The door to her chamber was unlocked. She would have
been surprised to find otherwise.

To her left a hallway turned slowly toward the center of
the tower, moving along a natural progression and deeper
into the Mother-Vine. To her right a stairway angled up and
down.

She took the stairs and moved upward, closer to the
domain of Queen Parlu, hoping she could reach the woman
in time to be of assistance.

Even as she moved she once more carefully spread her
senses, seeking information that could help her and others
deal with the attack of the Sa'ba Taalor. The people from
the Seven Forges were above her and below her as well.
As she climbed she saw the slender body of a young man
sliding through one of the narrower windows just ahead
of her.

She blew him back through the window with a thought. A
portion of the wall crumbled away as well, but his screaming
body sailed a great deal further from the tower. With luck his
death screams would warn others of their plight before it was
too late.

Pella called out to Desh and to Tataya alike, praying for

assistance. A brief flash of sorrow cored her soul as she instinctively started to call for Goriah as well before memory returned. How long had passed? How long had her Sister been dead? Where was the murderous bastard that had driven a blade through her skull? She would find him if she could. She would destroy him.

The stairs continued in their long spiral and she moved as quickly as she could, alert for any sounds around her.

There was nothing, no one that she could see, at least.

By the time she reached the queen's chambers her heart thudded at double the normal rate and her lungs burned with a demand for more air. None of that mattered as much as reaching Parlu before the Sa'ba Taalor.

The chambers were much as she remembered from previous visits. Parlu was a solitary woman at the best of times and she preferred to see visitors in private when she could. There had been several visits both formal and informal over the years. Once, long before she was apprenticed to Desh Krohan, she had come from the area and she had known Parlu better than most. She remembered the vast bed to the side of the chamber. She remembered the balcony that let Parlu see most of her kingdom with ease.

Frah Molen's corpse lay on the floor near that balcony. He had been cut in half by one savage stroke of a blade. His death had likely been very fast. A small blessing, to be sure, but a blessing just the same.

The heavy door that led to the only part of the tower Pella had never seen before lay open. The wood was wrecked, shattered by several powerful blows. An axe lay broken at the side of the door, bespeaking the force needed to hack through to the area where Parlu communicated with her god.

Just inside that doorway, the corpse of Lemilla, Parlu's only daughter, lay broken and bloody. Like Frah Molen, she had died quickly.

The stairway was narrow and barely allowed for one person to slide through easily. The wood of the Mother-Vine was exposed here, directly fused with the stone of the tower, and had swollen outward as if to seal the passage.

Bloodied footprints showed that whoever had passed had managed to get through easily enough, and that somebody was a very large figure.

Pella stared at the entranceway for a moment, uncertain if she should follow.

The laws of the people, of Trecharch, stated that none could enter the chamber save the queen. If she followed she was not certain if she would help or hinder the situation.

That hesitation very likely saved her life.

Viewed from outside, in the daylight, Orrander's Tower was an amazing sight. It climbed so very high into the air, mating with the Mother-Vine in the process.

On previous occasions, Cullen had stared at the structure with awe, oftentimes spending several minutes examining the minutiae of the fusion of manmade tower and nature at its very finest. The Mother-Vine enveloped the tower, sheltering the structure within her embrace.

According to legend. Orrander, the first modern queen of Trecharch, had offered herself as a sacrifice to the Mother-Vine to save them all from the Wellish Overlords. She had cut herself and offered her blood to the roots of the Mother-Vine, and in response the great vine had moved around her, embraced her, and healed her wounds before moving to force the Overlords from the area.

The Overlords were nightmares of the distant past. The

Mother-Vine was still here, still real, still pervasive in the lives of everyone in Trecharch.

And the Mother-Vine was dying. Madness lay where that thought wanted her to go.

Cullen stared at the massive trees around her, saw that they were still strong, and that the Mother-Vine was weakened and changing color as surely as autumn changed the trees. The leaves of the Mother-Vine were enormous here at her base. The shade from them was enough to cover wagons or, according to a few jests she'd heard in the past, large enough to work as the sails of ships in a crisis.

They were browning quickly, withering even as she watched. They were dying and the same death seemed to be creeping along the great vine itself, moving toward the heart of the Mother from several different strands that were all heading for the central core of the great plant.

The Mother-Vine was dying.

Cullen barely noticed on a conscious level any longer. She had run along the ground seeking to reach Orrander's Tower. She had fought her way past the devastation in Norhaun, all in the hopes of reaching the tower in time to offer some form of assistance.

Too late.

Cullen stared in horror, her heart frozen deep in her chest, and looked at the invaders as they climbed over the tower and the Mother-Vine alike. In the distance a gathering of the enemy battered at the Great Gate. They would fail, of course. That was inevitable. It also did not matter. The door held, but the enemy still found a way. As she watched a portion of the wall high up along the tower crumbled outward and spilled a body into the Field of Remembrance and crashed into the likeness of King Corranst, the last of the kings to ever rule the area. The body and the statue both shattered on impact.

In her soul she hoped it was one of the enemy that died that horribly. From her distance Cullen could not say with any certainty.

A handful of the enemies climbed into the tower. Most focused on the Mother-Vine, cutting and hacking with their weapons. Alone none of those wounds would have affected the great vine, but who could say what so many small wounds would do? Her father had told her stories of the Overlords and their countless tortures. Some had been long ways to kill a soul that would take days or even months. A few had involved cutting tiny pieces away.

From one location a horn sounded and then from others. Two of the horns came from the Mother.

Moments later the cutting stopped and the vermin who wounded the Mother-Vine descended from her sides. Cullen would have wept in relief at the notion if their sudden mercy didn't scare her so much. From what she had seen the grayskins did not believe in any form of kindness.

The notes from the horns had only started to fade away when the enemy stopped assaulting the Great Gate. Was it possible that all of them had decided to retreat? Had Queen Parlu managed to negotiate a peace with the enemy?

Cullen didn't know, but she moved back and into the woods without waiting for an answer.

The ground trembled. Or perhaps that was her legs. She could not say for certain.

Since she was twelve and took the crown, Parlu had climbed the stairs to the room where she now stood at least once every season to make her offering to the Mother-Vine. It was symbolic, of course, a mere drop of blood placed against the thick hide of the great, eternal protector. A remembrance of promises made and kept.

The sliver of a blade made the cut on her left palm as it had every season for decades, and she placed her bloodied hand against the Mother-Vine. Instantly she felt the connection that had revitalized her countless times before.

Life flowed into her. Not merely the life of the Mother-Vine but the life of everything connected to the Mother.

She felt the trees, the forest, and the animals. She touched the energies of the soil, the insects crawling on the trees and in the dirt. Every person in the whole of Trecharch was there for her to sense.

And, like a cancer, she felt the Sa'ba Taalor.

Her mother had once told her that everything in the universe was connected. She had felt that for herself the very first time she had shared herself with the Mother-Vine. That connection fed the Mother-Vine, fed Parlu, and colored every decision she had ever made. There had been peace in the area for a very long time because of that awareness of the lives around her and connected to her through the Mother.

The Sa'ba Taalor were not connected. There was no peace within them. They did not accept the world around them. Instead they were connected to something else. Something dark and powerful, and as alien to her as the notion of being left without the Mother's touch.

She could sense them, true enough, but they were a blight, a disease that moved among the strands of the Great Mother and killed her connection to everything else. Where the Sa'ba Taalor touched, there was a growing darkness that burned into her very soul.

She almost pulled her hand away from the Mother-Vine in an effort to escape the horrible chill left behind after each burning step the invaders took, but knew that to do so would be to abandon all she loved and cared for.

The Mother was injured and she had to guide the great plant in order to save them all.

Some of the horrid creatures must have sensed her, for they called to their brethren with horns and as a unit the vile presences started away, scurrying down from the Mother in an effort to escape the wrath she would cast upon them all.

The fingers of her left hand sank deep into the Mother-Vine as if into water, and she felt the potent energies of the Mother respond, filling her, offering her control of the Mother.

Parlu flexed her fingers and the world outside the tower moved, responded. The Mother-Vine shifted, but it moved slowly, without the usual liquid responses. For an instant she wondered if she had lost her connection to the Mother, but she knew better. It was the invaders. They had wounded the Mother and in so doing had weakened her as well.

Still, she would end them and the disease they brought with them.

Cullen felt the ground move again, and saw the great extensions of the Mother-Vine shift and break free of the earth. The ground shook, the dirt exploded, the vines seethed and whipped through the air, countless tendrils extending as they prepared to cut the enemies of Trecharch apart.

Cullen's heart soared. She had heard of the Mother-Vine moving, of course. She understood that the Walking Trees did not walk without her; still, this was a different thing, a far greater challenge.

Several of the grayskins jumped and ran as thick vines thrashed and whipped toward them. As she watched one of the bastards cleaved a tendril away as if cutting a snake in half. Another was not as lucky and grunted as the vine captured him and squeezed. Bones broke, flesh soon followed and the attacker died without uttering another noise.

The Mother-Vine moved again, and more of the earth broke as the roots slipped from where they had rested comfortably for centuries, spraying dirt and rocks and anything else in their way through the air.

Cullen allowed herself a moment to smile.

The Mother-Vine provides, indeed.

The rain of arrows that came down initially was impressive. Tusk felt them thud against his shield and bounce off his helmet in a clatter that nearly deafened him. Beneath him Brodem roared and growled and ran harder, faster, covering territory in leaps almost strong enough to unseat him.

Brodem was wise. He ran hard and soon they were away from the worst of the volleys of arrows. Tusk's arm was pierced in two separate spots where the shield was not enough. His helmet, made of bone and good steel, held up better.

Behind him his people returned fire, sending their own hail of arrows toward their enemies. That was what he commanded and that was what they did.

And through it all, his heart soared.

The Daxar Taalor had given him a command and he would obey or die trying. Durhallem said to kill a god and so he would go and kill a god. It was not for him to question how the deed would be done. He would take care of that when the time came.

He could see the god. The great "Mother-Vine" of the local people. He could also see that the vine was already dying. Glo'Hosht was a gifted murderer. The King in Mercury was moved on already, going toward the next stage of the Great

Wave, leaving Mother-Vine to Tusk. Tusk was not a merciful man any more than Durhallem was a merciful god.

When he approached the vast tower he saw the gates had been sealed. He did not have time to batter down the gates himself, and he did not much care for the odds. The trees here were on a scale he had never seen before and the wood was likely as hard as iron.

That left him only one option. He muttered a command in Brodem's ear and the great mount turned, charging toward the Mother-Vine and climbing quickly. Perhaps for the locals the notion of scaling a nearly sheer surface was something unheard of. Surely he saw no trails along the side of the mountainous column of green, but both Tuskandru and Brodem had scaled the side of Durhallem a thousand times, and while the texture was different, the climb itself was not so far from what they were used to. Brodem extended his claws and dug deep into the hard vine. Tusk clung to Brodem and called encouragement as the mount rose higher and higher into the heavy green foliage.

Further up he could see where the poisons were having their impact on the great vine. Here it still seemed healthy enough.

He would do what he could to handle that matter, though if he were completely honest Tusk had troubles deciding which of his weapons would serve him best.

Brodem let out a grunt and slid back a few paces. Tusk saw the arrow in his mount's shoulder and sneered. A cowardly attack. His eyes surveyed the area and he saw the archer easily enough. He was suspended on one of the branches above them, and had already drawn another arrow.

Tusk rolled from Brodem's back and caught himself on the angle of the vast plant's surface. "Go, Brodem! Kill him!"

Brodem did not hesitate, but instead charged, moving

faster than before now that he was unencumbered. The arrow the archer fired would have hit if Tusk had stayed with his friend, but unburdened, the mount was fast enough to dodge the bolt and, more importantly, clear the distance before the archer could draw again.

While the fool screamed and Brodem killed, Tusk looked at the stone wall not far away.

The Mother-Vine and the tower were mated. That was not an accident. He understood that instantly. In each of the Seven Forges the Daxar Taalor offered a place where their followers could join with them to communicate freely and feel the pure presence of the deities. That, too, was not an accident.

Tusk assessed the tower and the vine and moved, sliding sideways at first and then reaching the great tower itself. Where vine and stone met there were many footholds. He took advantage of them and began climbing in earnest.

Far below archers and warriors fought and died. Not far away Brodem killed and then ate and would have come to him if he'd called, but when a god makes demands it is often a personal challenge and best faced alone.

The climb was hard, but there were no challengers.

Below him his people climbed the tower and the vine alike and followed the orders they had been given. They cut the vine and made it bleed its clear sap. Then they descended again. He did not see Brodem. He did not look. The mount would do his part.

When Tusk climbed to the highest of the few balconies, he felt in his heart that this was the way, the right choice. It was not instinct alone that drove him, but the sure knowledge that Durhallem guided his actions. He was the King in Obsidian, Chosen of Durhallem. He was the divine sword of his god until such time as his god chose another.

He did not believe today would be the day his replacement was found.

The stone balcony held his weight with ease and he stepped inside a chamber filled with lovely decorations and exactly two people. There was an old man, who was currently aiming a spear at him, and a young girl who looked at him with terror in her eyes.

The situation was simple: the old man would die for the girl. He would fight and he would die in an effort to see her safe and protected.

Tusk moved quickly, drawing his heaviest axe in one swift motion and dancing past the spear thrust the man aimed toward him. It was a good attempt, but the man was old and unpracticed. He was soft in a way that Sa'ba Taalor had never been allowed to be soft and it cost him dearly.

The axe came down on the side of the man's face and through him as if he were a log to split. The spear fell from a lifeless hand and clattered across the ground.

The girl opened her mouth to scream and ran for an open doorway.

Tusk followed her and struck the back of her skull with his axe. The blow was not perfect, but it was enough She fell atop the stairs with a hole in the back of her head. Just to be certain, he drove one of his daggers through her neck.

After that he headed up the stairs.

Durhallem told him which way to go and he obeyed.

The view was not remarkable.

A woman in a white gown stood in the small room and shuddered; her body twitched and danced as if she were poisoned and dying of fits.

Her arm was lost in the wood of the Mother-Vine and Tusk understood all he needed to know in that moment. This was the god he was meant to slay. The vine and the woman were one, at least at this time. He felt vibrations moving through the ground beneath his feet and knew that his time was limited.

Durhallem spoke to him, made clear that the God-Vine was attacking, would kill his people if he did not strike.

When he spoke, it was not with his tongue. Durhallem said, "We end this now. You die as you should have so long ago."

The woman looked toward him. Her eyes were the same color green as the Mother-Vine's most perfect foliage. There had been a time when he was younger that Durhallem had awarded him with an obsidian blade. The sword he'd made with it had killed many foes and had even helped him kill a Mound Crawler in his youth. It was that blade he used to hack the woman apart. His first blow cut her arm away from the rest of her body. The rest of his strikes severed her head, her arms, her legs, and her torso.

Each cut was directed by Durhallem.

Tuskandru was the Chosen of the Forge of Durhallem and King in Obsidian. He was the instrument of his god's fury.

Durhallem was called the Wounder because of his lack of mercy.

Tusk was a perfect instrument.

Cullen felt the earth shake again and her smile fell away. This was not the same. This was so very different. The ground shook and seized and the great roots of the Mother-Vine tore free of the earth and shredded themselves in the process. Those roots had rested in the same spot for centuries, since before the fall of Korwa, since before the Cataclysm.

The mountains were constant. The rivers were eternal. The Mother-Vine was immortal.

And then, suddenly, the Mother-Vine was dead.

There could be no denying what she saw. The roots split as they came from the earth and pulled down structures and smaller trees alike. The other trees, the Sentinels, might well have fallen down, too, had they not been so deeply rooted themselves.

Above Cullen the trees screamed as the Mother-Vine that had fed them and provided, always provided, died. The great trunk blackened and rivers of sap flowed from the areas where the grayskins had cut her before.

The Mother-Vine died before her eyes.

Cullen watched it all with unseeing eyes. She stared at the impossible and her mind refused to accept it. A tree fell to her left and would have crushed her had it not rebounded off another tree instead.

The great storm clouds grew darker as the sun set and still Cullen did not move.

In the darkness of a night too impossible to believe, Cullen heard the sounds of the guards within Orrander's Tower screaming as they died. When the gateway was opened it was not the guards who came out, but the grayskins. A hundred of them spilled out, likely the very ones she had earlier seen scaling the sides of the tower.

She should have helped her people.

She should have tried to save them.

Instead Cullen had merely watched as her god died and her people followed suit.

She was still watching when the grayskins dragged barrels of oil from the tower's supplies to the base of the Mother-Vine. The fire did not take long to light.

She was still watching when the Mother burned.

She was not certain if she would ever move again.

SEVEN

When the sound came, it was worse than Tega had ever imagined possible. Above, in the ruins of the Mounds, the roaring note was enough to nearly deafen and to shake her teeth in their sockets. Here, deep within the endless night of whatever it was they were exploring, all possible thought was blown from her by the noise. It was everywhere and pervasive, a deep note that made her body feel like water and her bones like twigs resting under a boulder. She closed her eyes for fear that if she left them open her eyes would leak out of her skull.

How long did the note sound? There was simply no way to know for certain. There was no reference beyond the overpowering vibration.

When the noise finally faded away she knew it mostly because her insides no longer trembled. Her ears felt packed with mud and no sound seemed capable of reaching her.

The ledge they were walking along did not seem to notice the noise at all, for which she was very grateful. They'd traveled for... hours? A day? A week? Certainly for some time now, and while they were making progress toward the great light source below, it was still far enough away that they could not make out exactly what it was they were descending toward.

Still, the more they moved, the more certain Tega grew that this was, indeed, the remains of Korwa. There were structures here. Not merely occasional formations, but actual structures. They were broken, they were burnt, they were fused with the sand and the endless columns of glass and other items, but there were structures. Even if it was not Korwa, something vast had been here once and the specters of the people were still suspended in prisons of melted sand.

From time to time she saw one of the dead in their half-hidden, shadowy tombs and could almost believe that the frozen, ruined things were looking back at her, their eyes following as she moved along.

Desh Krohan had long since taught her the importance of a rational mind; still, the skin along her neck crawled when she looked at the frozen dead.

Not far ahead of her Vonders Orly was muttering and shaking his head. She suspected he was still in awe. He and his kind had long been treasure seekers and now, when there were treasures aplenty, he had little time to dig for them. Among the numerous dead there seemed an endless supply of gems and gold locked forever in the pillars of glass.

When the hand grabbed her shoulder Tega did not flinch. She had been trained better than that. Instead she focused her attention and prepared to unleash a defense if she needed to.

Nolan March was yelling. She could tell by the way his mouth contorted, the cords in his neck standing out, and she was able to make out what he said, but just barely. "Be careful! You're too close to the edge!"

Tega started. The man was right. She'd been looking at the columns, at the frozen dead, and had let herself get distracted.

Nolan gestured for her to move further from the edge and called for the others as well.

It was only then that she understood how dazed she was by the sound. It was like a physical beating. Her ears were ringing constantly, and her body ached.

Nolan gestured for all of them to sit and sorted through his bag until he found dried fruit for all of them to chew. The food was sweet and stuck to her teeth, but the act of eating seemed to help: her ears popped and her hearing was at least partially restored.

Tolpen worked his jaw a few times and seemed satisfied with whatever he was managing in the process. When he spoke it was too loud, but that was better than hearing nothing.

"This is madness. We've been traveling for... well, it's got to be more than a day, and I don't feel like we're getting anywhere."

"What else is there for it?" Nolan frowned. "We've orders and we need to follow through with them. Whatever is down there might be the only way to stop the Sa'ba Taalor."

"It might also be a brilliant way to get ourselves killed." Vonders spoke while using a small knife to worry at something stuck in the wall. Whatever it was shone with a dull metal glow in the dim light from below.

Tolpen sighed. "Same could be said of overburdening yourself with every shiny lump you find, and yet you keep going."

Vonders shrugged and then sighed when the lump popped free from the wall. "Whatever it is, it's gold. I'll take that when I can find it." He found a pocket in his cloak and hid his new nugget away.

"We have to continue on," Tega said as clearly as she could through the ringing in her head. "We have to find out what is down there and report back to Desh and the Empress, because that is what we've been told to do. If there's a chance we can find out what it is that so worries the Sa'ba Taalor, it'll be worth what we've been through."

She hoped that was true. There were deaths on her conscience. Three men were dead as a result of the expedition that she was in charge of.

"Even if we find the information, how will we get it to them?" Vonders eyed her warily. "Will you use your magic to contact them?"

There had been a few incidents with her sorcery. She would admit that easily; the result was that the men with her were understandably cautious about her attempting anything.

"I've communicated with Desh several times already. It's not a difficult thing and, well, speaking with him from a distance doesn't risk–"

"Causing anything to die a horrible, violent death?" Nolan's voice held an edge and also taunted. He was doing his best to deal with what had happened, but she knew well enough that he wasn't fond of sorcery. He'd made that point clear a few times already.

"Just so." She nodded her head.

"In any event, I think we are almost there," Nolan continued. "Another day and we'll find our way to the bottom of this chasm. Or at least we'll be close enough to know what it is we are looking at."

Tega thought she saw something from the corner of her eye and looked out toward the darkness beyond the ledge.

There was nothing to see but darkness and the dim light from below. She could almost make out the far side of the pit if she strained, but the illumination wasn't quite strong enough.

"You always talk like you're in charge here, Nolan. You're

not. You know that don't you?" Vonders spoke without any actual rancor, a smirk on his lips as he scrutinized another spot on the wall.

Nolan shook his head. "I never said I was. I'm just reminding you that we're here because the Empress and her advisors demanded it."

"Oh, I know, I just like giving you–"

Vonders stopped speaking and turned his head quickly, eyeing the darkness.

"Did you hear anything?"

Tolpen shook his head. "I can barely hear you blabbering on."

Tega still looked into the darkness. Something flitted past too fast to see clearly and she shook her head and raised one hand. "There's something moving out there."

"Certainly we're in an area where bats could be, I suppose." Vonders frowned as he spoke. "Don't know what time of day it is. If the sun's setting I would expect bats to leave from a cave this deep."

"There're no bats here," Nolan said. "If there were, we'd have seen them by now or at least heard them."

When the dirt and rocks fell from above they all caught the motion this time. It wasn't an avalanche, only a scattering of debris, but it was real, and they all saw it.

"Gods, what if this place collapses?" Vonders stood quickly, his little carving knife clenched in his hand like a sword.

Tega made herself stand up, and Nolan and Tolpen followed suit. Tolpen took the time to lock a bolt into his crossbow. He was, without a doubt, the best of them with a ranged weapon, but a standard bow would be of no use in the area where they stood.

A heavier collection of dirt and pebbles cascaded past them, and Vonders wandered closer to the ledge, looking up.

"Damn me!" He jumped back quickly and something roared as it moved toward them.

"Shoot it! Shoot it, Tolpen!"

"Shoot what? Get out of the way!"

Vonders backed toward them and Nolan had to step out of his way or risk getting knocked off his feet.

Tolpen raised his crossbow and sighted properly, but there was nothing to see.

Until the moment that there was. Whatever the thing might be it was immense, and it had a mouth full of teeth that looked like they should be used as the blades of swords.

The first thing they saw was a hand-like paw complete with several heavy claws. Tega stared at those thin fingers for a second and shook her head because they made no sense whatsoever. To be sure the claws looked impressive enough with their long hooked ends, but they were really rather on the small side. When the second hand showed up she frowned. It was a perfect duplicate of the first. Not a mirror, not a left mate to go with the right hand, but a perfect duplicate.

When the third showed up – this one missing a finger and a half in an old wound that had long since healed – she shook her head and started to ask if the others were seeing the same thing. The rattling of the great noise earlier might have shaken a few of her senses loose.

Then the head came into view. It was a massive thing, easily as long as her wagon had been, with barbs thrusting away from a scaly mouth filled with teeth of preposterous size.

After the teeth she didn't pay much attention to any other details, except that those teeth were bared and the mouth was making hungry noises.

Nothing that large should have been able to move at that speed. The entire head moved as fast as a freshly launched

arrow and narrowly missed eating Vonders. The only reason
the man lived was because Nolan hauled him backward as he
retreated himself. Vonders, like Tega herself, was staring with
wide eyes at the impossible sight.

Tolpen's crossbow bolt bounced off the side of the thing's
face and sailed into the darkness beyond.

Nolan cursed and pulled his axe free. The motion was
small, but enough to catch the beast's attention. More of
the immense thing crept into the resting area and Tega and
Vonders retreated while Tolpen pulled a curved blade from his
hip. He moved the opposite direction to Nolan and the head
of the thing swayed left and right, looking at both of them as
best it could. It had the eyes of a predator – two enormous
eyes to match the rest of the head – but Tega couldn't actually
tell if it could see with those eyes or if it was, in fact, blind
and was somehow registering their movements with another
sense. The eyes had no color at all. They were as dead white
as the rest of the thing.

A hideous rattling noise came from the throat of the beast
as it slithered forward. There were more hands, far too many,
and those hands sought out places to grip the stone as it
moved more of its bulk onto their ledge.

Nolan ran hard at the thing, screaming, and it whipped its
head toward him, opening that impossible maw. He brought
down his axe with all of his body in the swing and roared as
he chopped. The blade nearly bounced. For a second Tega
thought it would surely be knocked aside as easily as the
crossbow bolt had been, but the scaly hide bent a bit and then
the skin broke and blood welled out of the wound.

Nolan danced back as the thing flinched and then shrieked.
The noise seemed too loud to be real and too high-pitched for
a brute that size. Spittle painted Nolan's face and torso and his

hair whipped back from his face. He moved as fast as he could manage and then blocked with his axe when the mouth came for him. The second axe blow had little effect save to stop him from being eaten alive.

Tolpen's blade slashed across the neck of the thing and it let out another shriek as it was wounded.

Rather than retreat, however, the damned thing continued to spill onto their ledge from above.

Mound Crawler. She understood that intellectually, but Tega never expected to see one in reality. The arms of the thing were like the legs of a centipede. There were so many of them that they didn't make sense. The body was semiserpentine. It had a backbone that moved too easily for any mammal she had ever seen and it had folds of loose, scaled hide that reminded her of several different species of lizard – but it was built the wrong way, like everything in the Blasted Lands seemed to be malformed.

Tolpen swept his sword around a second time and backed away as the thing came for him. More of it landed on the ledge, and Tega genuinely feared that the ledge would collapse under them if it kept coming.

Nolan brought his axe down on one of the arms and severed it completely. The limb flopped to the dirt and the Mound Crawler let out another shriek and swept several of the arms on that side toward him.

Nolan backed up and hissed as one of the claws ripped into the meat of his thigh.

Tolpen cut at the oversized face again, drawing blood.

And then the Mound Crawler lunged toward him and bit his arm and his head and his torso in one massive bite. The sound of those teeth coming together was a noise Tega would never forget. Tolpen never had a chance to scream. He surely died instantly. The sword in his hand punched through the roof of the demon's mouth and through the nasal passage and it shook its head back and forth in an effort to escape the pain.

The first thrash of its head slapped the rest of Tolpen off the side of the ledge and spilled him toward the lights they had been seeking.

Nolan let out a shriek of his own and swung the axe again and again, hacking into the neck of the monster. Each blow opened a wound, but each wound seemed so damnably small. The thing kept coming and seemed like it would never stop.

Vonders stood next to Tega and looked at the Crawler, unable to draw his eyes from it. He did not move. He barely seemed to breathe.

Tega pushed at him. "Help Nolan!" her voice sounded too high, too tight in her throat.

Vonders nodded and moved forward, his hand still clutching his digging knife.

"Use your sword, man!"

Nolan was bleeding freely from his leg. He didn't seem to notice. His hands held to his axe and he brought it around in a hard arc, swinging once more with his entire body. The blow would surely have killed a man but the Mound Crawler merely flinched and kept moving onto the ledge, an endless run of arm-legs carrying the impossible shape. Each ended in a hand that seemed so small in comparison to the body. Had they not been close to death, Tega might have laughed. She felt an edge of mad giddiness trying to start her giggling. She refused to let that madness have her, and instead focused on trying to summon her power without blowing the whole lot of them into bloody mist.

The last two times she'd done this, she'd wounded her

own. That thought wrapped around her neck like a slaver's collar and crushed her down.

Nolan danced aside as the great head of the beast whipped around and it came for him.

That little digging blade of Vonders' punched through one of the great, colorless eyes of the Mound Crawler. Vile fluids blasted out from the wound and painted half of his body.

And the great beast slapped him aside as it screamed and did what it could to get free of the newest pain.

Vonders bounced across the floor of the ledge and clutched desperately at the edge, his eyes no longer wide, but closed in desperate prayer as the bulk of the monster moved toward him and the lower half of his body vanished over the edge, hanging into the darkness.

Drask watched the Mound Crawler as it moved, the seemingly infinite hands of the beast clutching at the wall and holding as well as a spider would.

The Fellein on the ledge reacted much as he would have expected, with screams and wild flailing swings of weapons.

It didn't look like the ones he'd seen in the past. Then again, the damned things were like the Broken: no two were the same.

He did nothing. It was not his place to do anything. The gods had told him to watch and nothing else. If the Daxar Taalor told him to kill the beast he would do all that he could. If they told him to kill the Fellein the response would be the same.

Instead he watched as the first of the men was cut into pieces and cast aside. He allowed himself a small smile when the sword of the man who died impaled the roof of the Crawler's mouth.

His head still ached from the last great noise. The air had shook before him. His eyes had grown blurry, as if he'd been watching vibrations in a previously still pond. There had been a moment when he'd thought his bones might grind themselves into powder and then Ydramil's voice had soothed him and a moment later the pain had gone away.

Just in time to let him avoid the Mound Crawler. It had been descending the side of the chasm and had stopped for the great sound. Once the noise had run its course the thing had started moving again. Drask had slipped sideways along the narrow lip of stone where he'd been perched and watched as it moved past him and straight for the fools chattering away on the ledge.

Tega was in there. He knew the girl, knew she was apprentice to the wizard, Desh Krohan, but she did nothing to stop the Mound Crawler though he had seen her do tremendous damage to one of the Broken.

The one who kept picking at the dirt was knocked halfway from the ledge after striking the first significant blow against the Crawler. He did not try to crawl back up the ledge, but instead held on and closed his eyes.

Perhaps he was praying to one of his gods. If so, Drask doubted the effort would do him much good. The Daxar Taalor would have ignored that sort of desperation. You took care of your challenges yourself or you died. That was the way of the Sa'ba Taalor and their gods.

The other man in the group let out another scream and jumped on top of the Mound Crawler's neck. He planted his feet wide apart and drove the axe's narrower blade into the top of the Crawler's head.

Then he got lucky, and as the Crawler reacted by driving its head upward in an effort to shake the pain loose, he fell to the side and rolled toward the distant wall instead of falling the other way and rolling off the ledge.

Lucky. There was no skill in the action. In fact the young man seemed less like a fighter and more like an animal. He was losing control of himself. Tuskandru and a few of his people would argue the advantage of going battle-mad, but Drask preferred to remain calm. Also, Tusk had the skill to carry off an occasional moment of berserk rage. This one? No. He was lucky.

Luck seldom lasts forever.

Drask watched on, assessing the skills of his enemies.

When the time came, if he had to, he would strike and he would kill using all that he learned by observing.

Assuming any of them were left to kill, of course.

Nolan felt no pain. He was too angry to feel much of anything.

His father, Wollis, had always warned him about losing control. All his life he had learned to use weapons on the rare occasions when his father was home and he'd practiced regularly, the better to show the man what he had learned when he came back to visit, and when they'd sparred, Wollis had easily beaten him again and again. There were words of encouragement and words of caution and the latter always focused on keeping his calm when he fought. It was a lesson Nolan had never really learned very well.

The problem was simple enough, really: there was no one to spar with on the farm, save his mother. And while Dretta March could hold a sword and fight well enough, she would always let her son win in their tests. She never quite had it in her to fight him with all she had.

So when Wollis came home, Nolan tended to expect an easy win and his father never let him win to soothe his ego.

His father fought as if his life depended on it.

Nolan was beginning to appreciate his father's philosophy. His axe was currently sticking from the scalp of the nightmare that had just thrown him. The handle, long enough to allow a proper two-handed swing, looked like a twig while sticking from the damned thing's scalp.

He drew the short sword at his side. There was no choice. He preferred the axe, but it seemed unlikely that the beast would let him take it back without trying to kill him.

Vonders was slowly pulling himself back to the ledge, his eyes once again open and wide. His face was a shade of white that might have been from the nasty paste from the monster's eye or simple shock from the combat, but either way the man was trying to gain his footing.

Nolan intended to help if he could.

He let out a battle cry and charged at the demon. It lunged and snapped at him with its bloodied maw.

Nolan managed a decent cut across the thing's brow and it turned its head to better see him with its remaining eye. His position didn't allow another effective sword stroke, so instead he drove his knee into the exposed eye of the thing as it moved toward him.

The thing let out a yowlp and he skipped back, swinging the sword. If he could blind it completely he might be able to do something with it.

Too fast, it was out of his way and that great head was coming for him again. Nolan dropped to the ground, his back slamming into the hard rock as the massive open mouth snapped shut where he had been standing.

A beard of heavy barbs ran under the chin, thick needles of cartilage and scales, and he rolled to the side rather than let himself get impaled on the points.

The thing let out a bellow of steaming hot air through its nostrils and blew a gout of bloodied mist out at the same time. Tolpen's sword was still jammed through the inside of its mouth causing harm. Good. Let it fester and kill the bastardly thing.

Only let it happen sooner rather than later.

He crawled to his hands and knees and scrambled toward the back wall of the ledge, as the thing started coughing and then looked for him with its one good, if watery, eye.

Nolan stared at the wounded beast. Perspective was a curse in this case, not a blessing. The monster was wounded, yes, but the wounds were tiny in comparison. Though it had lost use of one eye, and was bleeding in several locations, there was no danger of the damned thing dying any time soon.

He looked toward Tega.

"Will you kindly kill this thing?" It was as close as he could be to polite at the moment. In response to his voice the great head of the thing shifted and the one working eye scanned around him. The functioning eye was half-closed and watering heavily. Still, that teary orb focused on him and the great mouth under it opened again.

Behind the great beast, Vonders finally managed to pull himself back to the ledge and scrabbled away from the precipice, eyeing the beast warily and saying nothing. He had no weapons left on him that Nolan could see.

He was alive. That was something.

Tega moved her hands in a gesture that looked almost like she was brushing crumbs from her blouse. A moment later the monster let out another tremendous shriek and backed away, shaking its head. The flesh on the thing's muzzle was changing color, and parts of that altered skin were frozen, motionless despite the panicked expression on the rest of the vast face.

The thing backed further away and let out another loud noise as more of its bulk slipped from the ledge and it retreated, shaking its head from side to side in the narrow area. Vonders was knocked from his feet and sent stumbling but happily did not fall in the wrong direction this time.

Gravity might well have done the rest. The vast shape of the thing vanished from sight, and a cascade of rocks and dirt fell down again. Nolan couldn't tell if it had fallen or merely retreated.

He looked into the darkness beyond the ledge but did not follow.

"What did you do to it?" Vonders asked as he rose to his feet. Nolan could now see that his body was covered in whatever passed for blood and the fluids from the monster's eye.

Tega looked at him for a moment and shrugged. "The same thing I did to our rope anchor and arrow. I made it harder than it was."

Nolan shuddered at the very notion. She'd turned the damned thing to stone, or close enough at least.

Vonders was staring at Tega as if she had answered all of his prayers – and perhaps she had.

Nolan chose not to look at her for a while and instead focused on what might come at them from the darkness. He wasn't sure which scared him more, the girl or the unknown.

He wasn't completely certain there was a difference.

EIGHT

Desh Krohan looked around the chamber and struggled to remember why he was there.

Grief was a crippler, to be sure. He hadn't felt completely himself since Pathra's murder and now, with Pella gone, he felt drained of all vitality.

Mourning was a luxury he wasn't certain he could afford.

"Desh?" Nachia's voice cut through his clouded thought.

"Yes, Majesty?"

There were only a scattered few in the room. All of them were looking at him with expectant expressions.

"You were going to tell us of Trecharch?"

"Ah. Yes. The kingdom has fallen. Queen Parlu and Lemilla, her heir, are both dead. The Mother-Vine is gone. Destroyed. Pella is on her way back. She'll have more details. She observed the entire affair." His lips felt numb. He expected that was a bad thing, but couldn't seem to make himself care.

Goriah was dead.

He'd have to see if he could do anything about that.

All around him the people in the room stirred, shocked by the news. They'd known it was a possibility, but, really, no one had expected the Sa'ba Taalor to be so damnably efficient at overthrowing an entire nation.

"My troops are still three days out at the very least, and that's with a forced march." Merros Dulver looked around the room at the other military leaders under him. None of them were happy with the current situation. How could they be? The first major campaign of their military careers had just ended in a savage defeat.

Nachia spoke from her seat on the throne. "This is unacceptable." Her voice trembled with suppressed emotions. Rage, sorrow, shock. "Find the Sa'ba Taalor who did this. Destroy them."

Her anger was enough to drag Desh from the grief that was pulling at him.

"There are other considerations, Majesty. We will soon have more refugees coming here. They'll be running from the Sa'ba Taalor and they'll come this way seeking safety and shelter."

Merros spoke up. "They'll also be followed by the enemy. There's every reason to believe the war will come to us sooner rather than later."

"Are you sure about that, Merros?" Desh frowned. "Aren't there other areas they might consider?"

"They might very well, but why would they? Do they intend to cut off our food supplies? No. There are too many accesses to this city. They have black ships on the waters of the Freeholdt, according to the latest reports. I don't know if their ships can actually ride the Freeholdt all the way to the Jeurgis, but even if they can't, if those ships are carrying supplies, or even worse, troops, they'll be able to come at us from at least two different directions."

Merros stood up and spread his arms. "The nearest area we could draw reinforcements from was Tyrne, but those troops are already here. That would give us an advantage if I hadn't been obligated to send so many to Trecharch. Even if they turn around now, they'll only be a day or two ahead of the refugees and the enemy."

Desh nodded.

Nachia frowned. "So what do we do now? You're my advisors. Advise me."

Merros answered immediately. "We have to prevent them from reaching us from every possible angle. If they lay siege to us, we can hold out for a very long time, but the people in the areas outside the city walls will not last, and while we have food for the city proper, we can't feed refugees from three separate areas and the people of Canhoon, too."

Desh interrupted, "We have... surprising levels of food supplies. I shouldn't worry too much there. We are also doing what we can to prepare for extra people. A lot of extra people."

"The city is large, Desh, but it is not large enough to accommodate all of Trecharch."

Desh looked at the general for a while and suppressed a smile. "You'd be surprised, lad."

Merros, who looked as old as Desh but knew better than to think he was anywhere close to the same age, bit his tongue at being called a lad.

Desh gave him credit for that, and also reminded himself to afford the man the proper respect, especially in front of his peers. It was all right to be friendly in private, but in public Merros Dulver was in charge of the entire Imperial Army. That afforded him a great deal of respect.

Nachia stood up and started pacing. Her hair was loose and moved like a cloud around her head in the high humidity. She was, once again, dressed for comfort. Part of the sorcerer wanted to chide her about appearances but he was wise enough to keep his opinions to himself. This was neither the right place nor time for it.

"Desh, find the latest news. Use your Sooth or whatever they are called. Merros, take his advice into consideration and prepare for a siege. I would rather avoid a siege, but we will prepare for it nonetheless."

She skewered the general with her glance. "And while you are doing that, devise a good battle plan. If we're at war I have no intention of sitting here and waiting for the bastards to come to us. Find out where they are. Find out where they are going. Find out how to kill them."

She paced a few more small circuits in front of the throne and then looked at them. "Now. Do it now."

That ended the meeting. Desh left to head for his chambers and to call upon the Sooth, dreading the very idea.

Merros wandered down the streets between the palace and Dretta's place with his heart thumping too hard in his chest. The last time he'd been by to see her, he had not found her at home. He had no right to fret over such things. They had not made plans of any sort, and yet he found the idea of her not being home worrisome.

He found he thought about her far too often.

That was a problem.

He was supposed to be considering how best to repel the enemies of the Empire. He had armies to move and command and prepare for battle. The majority of the infantry he dealt with were hardly in any shape to fight and kill the Sa'ba Taalor. Most would more likely be cut down before they were old enough to grow full beards.

On that and a few other subjects he could not easily speak to Dretta. He had grown to trust her, of course, that was not the problem. The problem was that her son was one

of the young men under his command, and neither Nolan
March nor Tega had been reachable by any means, not even
sorcerous, for over two days.

He wanted to see Dretta.

He wanted to be honest with her.

He also did not like the idea of being in the same room
when she found out that she had effectively lost her only son.

The woman was enchanting – he pushed that thought
down roughly. She was Wollis's widow, after all – but she was
also a bit on the terrifying side. He could take her in a fight.
No worries there. After seeing Swech and Jost and Ehnole
and a few other women of the Sa'ba Taalor, he understood all
too well that the tendencies in Fellein to shelter women from
harm were probably not the wisest. The enemy had twice as
many soldiers automatically and their women fought as well
as their male counterparts.

Dretta could handle herself. He had no doubt of it. She'd been
with Wollis and he'd made his son learn to do so at an early age
and his wife, too. The northerners from his area were brutal.
Stonehaven raised only strong people, and when the army took
the younger men it wasn't uncommon for the women in the
area to work the quarries. Dretta was strong and capable.

The problem was not whether or not he could actually
handle her in a skirmish if she decided he had taken enough
from her with her husband. No, the problem was he didn't
think he could raise a hand against the woman no matter
what the circumstance.

That notion merely made him more uncomfortable.

The hairs on his neck rose.

The air was not precisely cold, but his flesh goosepimpled
just the same.

Likely he was being watched. First rule of surviving in a

war or a skirmish was simple: trust your instincts.

Instead of moving toward Dretta's house and checking on her, Merros moved on, his hand resting easily on the hilt of his sword.

It was possible that he was being paranoid. He might even be finding excuses for avoiding Dretta, though he doubted that.

It was just as likely that someone was waiting for a time when they could find the general alone and do him harm. There was a war going on and a lot of the people thought the war was his doing. They didn't say it to his face, but he'd heard about it just the same. Merros brought the Sa'ba Taalor to Tyrne. The same grayskinned foreigners assassinated Emperor Pathra Krous. They were destroying Trecharch (had destroyed it already, though few knew that yet) and the victims of the Sa'ba Taalor were already overflowing the streets in some parts of Canhoon.

Merros was not popular with everyone and he knew it.

There just wasn't much he could do about it.

He moved away from Dretta's place and felt his teeth grind together a bit. He'd planned to see her, to talk with her. The need to see her was almost as strong as the need to breathe. He tried not to notice that fact and instead moved a bit faster.

The slightest chance that someone would follow him and be led to her, putting her in danger, was unacceptable. It was his own desire to see her safe that kept him from her. He would not have anyone he cared for endangered because of his position. Better to keep away and be safe.

"Foolishness," he said and walked faster.

It was just as well. He needed to get sleep.

The walk home was uneventful, but it took a while before the feeling that he was being watched faded away.

•••

Swech watched Merros Dulver from the rooftops. There was an abundance of houses here, but few of them had much land. The city was old, and over time finances changed and people changed, too. Farmers no longer farmed here. Instead they sold off pieces of land and lived off the profits.

As a person who was now buying large pieces of property in the city herself, Swech had quickly come to understand the preposterous cost of a small hovel to call your own. The Fellein would need places to live while her people drove them from other areas. They would come here, at least according to the gods. The gods knew better than she. That was why they were gods.

Killing Merros would have been easy. Every time she saw him she was reminded of that fact. She remained thankful that the Daxar Taalor seemed to want him alive for now.

There were others, however, that they wanted dead. That was why she was moving along the roofs of the city long after the sun had set. Kallider came toward her. He was wise enough to make sure she spotted him. It was never in one's best interest to startle a Sa'ba Taalor.

"They are coming." He pointed with his chin toward the distant river.

"Our people? Or the ones we are supposed to kill?" Kallider seemed skilled enough in the ways of combat. He most assuredly would not have been chosen by the gods if he were not, but his ability to communicate concisely was questionable.

"What?" He frowned. "Oh. The ones we are supposed to kill."

"Well then, we should be about that. Lead the way."

One last glance down. Merros Dulver moved around a corner and faded from her view.

Kallider started along the roof, placing his feet carefully and stepping with the light grace of a natural hunter. Swech followed, very aware that a wrong move would topple her over the side of the four-story structure and down to the cobblestones below.

The jaunt was a short one and at the end of it Kallider scuttled down a corner of one of the buildings that had a preposterous amount of decorative work. She followed suit and made note of the location. It would make climbing easier if she had to reach the rooftops in the near future.

Initially Kallider had asked her why she chose to move along the rooftops but he understood quickly enough. No one else moved up there. No one else considered climbing to the tops of the angled roofs. The fall was deadly. There were advantages, however. With a little practice Swech had quickly learned the routes of several important figures that she was supposed to watch, and she had also learned the easiest access points to their homes.

She was rapidly becoming adept at walking where most of the Fellein would never consider going. There were exceptions, of course. One foolish man had spotted her and tried to sound an alarm. His body was found at the docks a few days later.

They moved quickly and as they moved the rains started again. That was a blessing and a curse alike, but one she took in her stride. The rains were cleansing. The rains also tended to make many of her targets run and hide as if they might melt were the water to strike them.

The men she was after this time would likely not care. They were cutthroats and scavengers. They were godless murderers who killed for profit.

In short, they were fighters.

She could respect that.

The rains came down harder, chilling the air and soaking her clothes to her body. The cloak she was wearing was light, but the water made it cumbersome. There were advantages to cloaks, but those were lost quickly if the fabric was sodden. The cloak came off and was set in the alleyway nearest their destination. Kallider kept his cloak on, shoving the watery wings of it back away from his arms.

Her skin was paler than his, and so she chose to hide most of it behind a thin veil. The fabric was little more than gauze, but hid her nose and mouth away. Shadows were a blessing of the gods, as were most things. Taking advantage of those blessings was part of a lifetime of training.

Kallider moved ahead of her and examined the ground carefully. While he did that she surveyed the alleys and streets along the edge of the docks. As expected, the rain had driven most people away.

The exceptions were the ones coming off the small ship that was currently unloading cargo and passengers alike.

A red-haired man with a predatory grin was holding court with the City Guard in the area. He had a hat in his left hand and she could see by the way he carried it that he was concealing something: very likely a small blade, to help him out of a mess if the negotiations failed. She had been among the Fellein long enough to understand that he was bargaining with the Guard. For the right amount of coin they would look the other way. She wasn't completely certain of all that was gained by the action until she accessed her host's memories. No taxes or levies paid on the materials brought into the city and no one learned of the passengers and what they were doing there.

She already knew about them. The gods had demanded

their deaths. That was enough for her.

Kallider stayed exactly where he was, waiting for her signal.

She made him wait for several long minutes while the man smiled and talked of how many coins he would have to give up.

Finally, after too long spent soaking in the rain and watching her targets gather and prepare to move on, the City Guard with the most rank on his shoulder held out his hand and watched while the negotiator offered several small silver pieces.

Time at last to do what the gods demanded.

The thought brought a smile to her face.

Captain Callan shook his head and avoided spitting with only the most meticulous self-control. He'd have been better off dealing with brigands on the road than the City Guard. At least the brigands were honest about their intentions.

Still, he was being paid handsomely enough, he supposed.

Seeing the attackers was purely an accident. His eyes drifted toward the alleys as he considered which way to a good pub. It was a walk, but the Broken Oak had excellent wine and clean beds. He wanted a clean bed in the worst way. Also, their whores were almost as clean as the beds.

The Brass Key was closer, but many of the sailors making deliveries went there first. As a result the place tended to be a bit filthier, much like his crew.

He was looking toward the Broken Oak when he saw shapes moving. They were dark and they were fast and if there had been any breeze at all he might have thought them shadows or even a bit of dust caught the right way, had it not been for the steady pelt of the rain.

A brave man might have called out a warning. A good man

might have done the same. A truly heroic soul might even have run to the aid of the passengers he had delivered to the port.

Callan walked back toward his ship and gestured at his lads, letting them know that trouble was heading their way.

The lads, being wise in the ways of their captain, continued their work.

Callan got himself back on the deck of his ship as quickly as he could without offering any sign that he had seen anything at all. His first mate, Vondum, was already preparing for any possible trouble.

The cargo had been delivered. That was all that was required of Callan. The rest was not his concern. The bodies of the men he'd delivered would still earn him the rest of his coin. Even if it did not, the goods his crew was currently moving and guarding would take away a portion of the sting. A small portion, granted, but still.

The shadows moved again and Callan watched them without looking in their direction. His father had told him the best way to observe the world was to never look directly at it. His father had been a very wise man when he wasn't drunk to the point of unconsciousness.

One of the men he'd dropped off looked toward the moving shadows and grabbed for his sword, letting out a cry of alarm.

The first of the dark shapes stepped in close to the swordsman, close as a lover, and then moved on. The sword fell from the man's hand and a moment later the man fell to his knees and then on his face.

By that point both of the shapes had engaged their enemies.

Callan had brought twenty men into the area. They were there for the sole purpose of working for his employer, who in turn worked for someone else. That was all he wanted or needed to know about them, aside from the fact that they were there in secrecy. He had kept his part of the bargain. No one had heard from him about their arrival and none of his lads had yet had a chance to get drunk and chat away.

Still, someone knew and that someone wanted the mercenaries dead.

The first shadow moved fast and stayed low, but managed to get cut just the same. The second man the shadow approached was dead in an instant, but the third struck with a small throwing blade that shimmered in the vague light before disappearing into the shadow's belly.

There was no noise from the one that got cut. The one that had thrown the blade, however, let out a powerful scream as his hand was cut away from his body.

That was enough to warn the rest. They turned quickly from their individual discussions and tasks and worked as a unit, backing toward each other in an effort to build a unified defense. No one would cut them from behind if they were careful.

They were not careful enough. The second shadow form was smaller and slipped inside their guarded area before they finished establishing it.

While they were fighting against the first dark shape, the second moved among them, slipping between bodies and striking with terrifying efficiency.

Callan had seen the Guntha in action. He had watched soldiers and sailors from nearly every port in the world. But he had never seen the level of efficient brutality that came upon his charges. While he watched on, they were chopped down, some from the larger shadow, others by complete surprise, as they were attacked from behind.

Callan put two fingers in his mouth and blew out a shrill

whistle. As one his men stopped their work and moved back to the ship. They moved quickly, while the shadows were otherwise engaged.

Vondum held his crossbow to his side and clutched at the small wooden carving of Lalos he wore around his neck. Callan did not believe in gods, but he threw his own prayer to the god of travelers, just in case it might help.

Twenty men died in short order, but not one of them belonged to Callan's crew. That was a victory in his eyes.

The shadows did not stay around, but ran back into the rain-soaked alleys and, if he were lucky, away from his existence forever.

Vondum stared at the bodies as the rain continued. Blood flowed from the corpses and into the waters soaking the docks. More of it ran between the boards and spilled into the river. It was too dark to study the rain for any possible portents, though he suspected a few of the lads were likely trying.

"What were those?" Vondum's voice was strained.

"From what the Lady Tataya told us, those might be the enemies we've been hearing about."

His first mate looked his way with a shocked expression. Finally he spoke. "Might I suggest we move to the other side of the continent? I don't think it's safe here any more."

Callan wished the man were joking. He also agreed with the sentiment.

"Finish unloading, then we disperse for the night. I have to talk to our employer about this one."

"Need someone watching your back?"

Callan nodded his head. The negotiation was likely to go poorly. He intended to walk away from it with his head still on his shoulders. "Aye, but I think I have someone in mind who can help me with this one."

Vondum didn't ask and Callan volunteered nothing. It was best sometimes to know as little as possible about a plan. Sometimes people got themselves caught and questioned and there was no doubt the City Guard would be calling on the Inquisitors about this one.

The Inquisitors were a problem, but only if they could link the bodies to his ship, or any of the illegal merchandise he'd just brought with him. That was why he needed to handle this particular situation as quickly as he could.

That, and there was a lady he wanted very much to see while he was in port.

They went their separate ways in a matter of moments and Swech looked back as Kallider began to falter. He was dying; there would be no saving him if she did not go back immediately and offer him aid.

She continued on.

Ultimately Kallider mattered no more or less than she did and the Daxar Taalor would decide his fate. If he better served them by living then he would live. If he better served them by dying, then he would die and the consequences of his death would have their impact as they surely must.

She recognized that he was of Imperial blood. There would be repercussions.

Swech closed her eyes and listened for the voices of the gods as she called to them with her prayers and told them what had happened and what she believed.

She opened her eyes quickly when she heard the sound of someone coming closer.

Swech did not strike. There was no need to kill anyone who approached her, only those who were a threat.

Jost was not a threat. She was a friend.

The younger woman was covered from head to toe in black. She was here for the same reason as Swech herself: to serve the Daxar Taalor.

"I have missed you," Jost said. She lowered her head for a moment, but never took her eyes from Swech.

"Later, when we have finished with the night's work, you and I shall discuss what has happened in my absence. For now I need your help with this." She pointed to Kallider, who still breathed, though barely. "For now, help me."

Swech looked down at Kallider and drove her dagger into his temple. His death was swift.

A moment later Jost gathered the man's feet and she captured him under the arms and they lifted his mass.

Getting him back to the place where she and Kallider had killed the assassins was easy enough. The people from the boat were moving crates and bags of supplies away from their ship in a hurry and did not take the time to look around. Even if they had, there would have been little to see as the rain continued to come down in a heavy cascade.

Leaving the body where they wanted it was easy enough.

He would be found. His death would serve the Daxar Taalor.

All was well with the world.

Jost waited until they were well away from the bodies before she spoke again, using only hand signals to convey her message. "I do not like the way you look. I prefer your true face."

Swech nodded and eyed her friend, responding in similar fashion. "I do what I must to please the gods."

Jost chuckled and moved with her, graceful and silent. They moved among the shadows and remained unseen by any save the occasional rodent.

It was good to have the girl with her again. Jost was a

reminder of home and she needed that. The gods must have sensed it, for surely they had answered her prayers. The Daxar Taalor could be so very kind.

The waves thundered around him and Andover Lashk did his best not to drown.

He could no longer be certain how long he had been in the waters, only that he was still alive, and had endured the crashing and beating that the water threw at him.

He was cold to his bones and his muscles ached. His eyes burned with the salt from the ocean waters. His head ached from the knowledge that Wheklam had filled his mind with. Though he had never been on the ocean or even to the edge of any of the great seas, he understood tidal currents and the location of the islands and continents that covered much of the world. There were other lands as vast as Fellein that had never been spoken of in his lifetime and he knew now that they existed and how best to get to them.

That was Wheklam's gift to him. He merely needed to survive it. The weight of his cloak had been too much and so he let it go. The weight of his weapons had been substantial, but he kept them. The hammer was long gone, but one did not cast aside the gifts of gods easily – at least he was fairly certain one did not. He was still working on understanding the proper way to deal with deities, and at the moment he was trying to understand how to deal with them when they threw him into waters without end.

A particularly large wave lifted him higher than he'd been in a while and Andover saw land ahead. The soil was dark and rocky and looked barren. He did not mind that notion in the least.

His first thought was to push for the land and so he did, but he did it carefully. He was not a skilled swimmer; in fact he barely understood how to tread the waters as he was doing now. Small strokes seemed the way to go and so he paddled with his arms and kicked with his aching legs.

There were several times when he was absolutely certain that the strip of land was coming no closer. When those times came on hard and fast he would stop for a moment and allow himself to simply float and breathe.

He heard a voice calling his name, or rather he thought he did. It was hard to hear much of anything over the sound of the surf as it ground itself into the sand and soil again and again. His eyes looked around but saw nothing but more water and a growing strip of land. And so he continued on until, finally, he felt the ground beneath his boots and he could once more stand on his exhausted legs.

The sun was like a furnace as it beat down on him and he welcomed it after the bitter cold of the ocean. He shivered and his breaths came in laboring gasps. He spit a dozen times in an effort to get the brine out of his mouths but there seemed to be more of the stuff.

Mouths. The one he was born with and now three Great Scars. The marks left on him by the gods were silent for the moment, but he knew they'd start talking again soon. Whispering, mostly, softly enough that only he could hear them. He found the sounds oddly comforting.

There was no one on the shoreline that he could see, no one who could have called to him or would have had a reason to do so.

Looking carefully, it only took him a moment to understand that he was on the other side of the volcano's pit. Here the ground sloped at a gentler angle. He looked behind him and was scarcely surprised to see that the ocean was gone.

A few hundred feet away a deep cavity led downward into the heart of Wheklam and even now he could feel the heat, what he had mistaken for the sun on his back before. Fumes and smoke rose from the crater and, even as he stared, he could feel the heat from the volcano drying the sodden fabrics he wore.

No ocean. No sea. Part of him was stunned. Most of him, however, was coming to accept that gods did not follow the same laws. If Wheklam wanted an ocean, then an ocean appeared.

Or perhaps it was all in his head and he was suffering a fever dream. He found he preferred the notion of gods.

There was no sign of Delil.

Just to be certain he called for her, his voice echoing off the sides of the volcano.

Because he didn't know how long he was supposed to stand inside the volcano, he let his instincts lead him toward the edge far above. Perhaps Delil was up there. He'd find out soon enough. Whether she was there or not, he knew he had to move on. There were time limits to consider.

If Delil was not there she would have to follow after him or go her own way. He wanted to be with her. He did not need to be with her. He had met with three gods and had four more to meet with before his promises were properly kept. A man was only as good as his word. He intended to be a good man.

Andover Lashk did not consider how he would have reacted to his current situation only a month before. There was a time that would have been foremost on his mind – that, and the image of the a young lady named Tega, who for a brief time was the center of his universe – but those times were gone. That Andover was gone.

Metal is forged in the heart of a furnace and tempered and shaped.

Drask Silver Hand would have been the very first to point out that there were seven forges in the Taalor Valley and that the Daxar Taalor were adept at shaping their weapons.

The City Guard handled many things. They could even, one assumed, handle an occasional murder. The story was different when the bodies numbered over a score and when one of them belonged to a member of the Imperial Family.

Callan watched the spectacle unfold from the comfort of his ship, and looked toward Tataya with a worried expression. "You can see why I called you, yes?"

The reason was obvious enough to Callan. Twenty of the bodies belonged to those who had traveled on his ship. The young man of imperial blood had apparently been killed by those twenty men. All of that might have been an inconvenience or a major dilemma, but none of it mattered to Callan as much as the man standing above their cooling bodies and ordering the City Guard to do his bidding.

"Honestly, Captain Callan, I don't begin to understand what any of this has to do with me." Tataya looked at the scene with moderate interest, but obviously felt none of his desperation. In fact she barely seemed to care at all about what was happening.

"I thought you might be able to help me clear up this mess." He tried not to sound as desperate as he felt.

"You are a captain who was delivering cargo. You were wise enough to report suspicious activity. If all of your papers are in order you have nothing to concern yourself over."

"Yes, well, it's the papers, you see…"

"Are they not in order?" She looked at him with cold eyes.

There was a challenge there and he knew it. She wanted him to defend himself properly before she would defend him to the man who had a dozen City Guard scrambling to obey him.

"Well, strictly speaking, I didn't actually have any cargo."

"Then lie."

"Excuse me?"

"Lie. You had no cargo. You were merely here looking for more work. You called on me because of past connections. I will not lie for you, Captain, but I will not expose your lie, either." She looked away from him and toward the Inquisitor on the docks.

"What's his name?"

"The Inquisitor?"

"Yes. Him." Callan swallowed though there was no moisture in his mouth or throat.

"That is Darsken Murdro. He is the third highest ranking Inquisitor in the city."

"Only third?"

Tataya smiled. "That means he's hungry. He would very much like to be the second Inquisitor. If he can manage that task, he will be in line to assume the head title in only a few years."

"Ah."

"Indeed. You should be extremely careful if you lie to him. He has been known to be very imaginative if he thinks someone is lying to him."

"'Imaginative?'"

"Oh yes. He can't actually torture you, of course. That luxury is denied him. But he can mete out punishments that are rather substantial."

Callan tried to decide if the redhead was toying with him. He could never quite tell if she was bluffing.

"Like what?"

"Well, he can decide where you will spend your time while he's waiting for a truthful answer from you."

"Where I'll spend my time? That hardly seems... Wait... As in where I actually get to wait? Can you offer examples?"

"Strapped to a post in the military barracks."

"A post?"

"The soldiers always need targets."

"Ah."

Tataya leaned against the railing of the ship and stared at the Inquisitor. "And here he comes. Prepare your words carefully, Captain Callan."

NINE

The refugees came, just as Merros had predicted. Well, Merros and nearly everyone else she had spoken to. As the Empress, Nachia did her best to make certain that they were taken care of.

There were a great number of landowners in the city, and many of them were outraged at the notion of having strangers coming into Canhoon and taking up residence.

The innkeepers and the owners of apartments, however, didn't seem to have as much trouble with the idea. They seemed quite pleased by the notion of increasing their prices.

Some things, she felt, you simply could not do anything about.

Adding to the interesting aspects of the situation was a large coalition of landowners who were currently arguing among themselves while she watched. They did not know she was watching, of course. She was hidden away in one of Desh's secret areas. She could see them but they could not see her. They also couldn't see the sorcerer, who was standing beside her.

"Why exactly are they fighting?" she asked him.

"Some of them think it's inappropriate to charge newcomers

more money than they would normally charge and others are determined to see the prices increased throughout the city." Desh crossed his arms and shook his head. "Nothing I haven't seen before, of course, but never on this scale."

"The ones who argue for keeping the prices the same, who are they?"

"Followers of Etrilla and Luhnsh, apparently. The priests have been busy trying to remind people that the gods are there and will help those who are good to their fellows." Desh frowned. "Which reminds me, Majesty. We are now receiving rumors from the east about a rather large gathering of the faithful led by a man called the Pilgrim. It seems he's gathering quite a following from the far east and heading in this direction."

"How far east?"

"Elda, Danaher and even Morwhen."

Nachia nodded her head. Morwhen was so far away that she had never been allowed to visit the place. Apparently barbarians ran the area, or at least they had in the past. It was hard to keep up with the areas of the Empire that were so very distant.

"Do you think these people are friends or foes, Desh?"

In the room they were looking into, a dark-haired woman raised her voice and stood up, causing several of those around her to look at her as if she had lost her mind. She pointed first at one of the men and then at another, a round-bellied man who had tried on several occasions to get the property taxes lowered, and who usually claimed that he was near poverty. For a desperate man he wore a great deal of finery.

"She looks familiar. Who is she?"

"That is the woman Merros is spending his time with. The widow of Wollis March. Dretta, I believe, is the name. You met her son and sent him off to the Mounds."

"No, no. *You* sent him to the Mounds. I merely approved your decision." She would not let the old fool rewrite the truth on her. That had been the folly of her cousin and not one she intended to mirror.

"Semantics." He waved a dismissive hand. "In any event, she was wise enough to buy up a few pieces of land before the worst started. She is likely going to make a good deal of coin in the coming months."

Nachia frowned. "What side does she argue for?"

"Leaving prices as they are and helping out the newcomers."

"Well. Then I suppose I like her."

"Why wouldn't you like her, Majesty?" Desh did not turn and look at her, but his eyes left the increasing agitation of the crowd on the other side of their hideaway. "Are you planning to choose the general's next romantic partner?"

"Hardly." She felt herself blush a bit and looked away, but she also saw the smile on Desh's face. He knew.

"Speaking of romantic partners, we still have to consider the viable candidates for you."

"Absolutely not. There is a war on and I have no time for looking at possible mates."

Desh said nothing to that and she continued looking away. "What will we do about this 'Pilgrim' and his followers?"

"We need to have a proper discussion with the church leaders. I know how little you want to risk their wrath, but we have to, and as much as I like Merros Dulver, I don't believe he's the right person to gather the elders together."

"Then perhaps you could?"

"At least half of the churches look at sorcery as an affront to their gods," Desh pointed out. "I should rather not risk being tortured or worse in the name of any deities."

"Well, then I suppose that leaves me."

"I'll make the arrangements."

Nachia sighed. "I will require the presence of my First Advisor."

"Naturally."

"Does the general's concubine have any preferred deities that we know of?"

"By all the gods, Nachia. I don't even believe they have that sort of relationship."

Nachia smiled. That question had successfully been answered.

She didn't know exactly why it was important that she know the details of Merros's love life, but she most definitely wanted to know.

He was a tall man, broad of shoulder and lean of waist. He walked with the confidence of a well-trained warrior, but he did not strut as so many did when they felt invincible. He had seen too much in his time and now he would see more.

There were gods to meet with and this was the place where he was most likely to find them. This was where the temples to the gods rose highest and where the greatest numbers of followers could be found.

He was a Pilgrim and his quest was a holy one.

He had much to discuss with the gods and time was growing short. He had to return to Canhoon as soon as he could if he were to help the gods with their sacred task.

Eyes that had seen the Empire before it was old looked upon the city of Goltha with an odd blend of pity and contempt.

They did not know. They could not know. The people ahead of him had been raised in ignorance. He intended to refresh their memories, though there was no reason to think they would thank him for the education.

The Pilgrim looked out across the valley ahead and frowned. He and his followers had a great deal of traveling to do yet, and he had not gathered enough of the faithful to take care of his appointed task.

Well to the east of the Blasted Lands, in an area of Fellein that had never once tasted the ashes of the ruined territory, several towns and cities gathered along the shores of the Empire's largest fresh water lake, Gerhaim.

Lake Gerhaim was spoken of many times by poets and scholars alike. Spanning an area large enough that the earliest settlers thought they had found a sea, the body of water had gathered thousands of people to its shores and in time those thousands had spread, building towns and finally cities.

The largest of those cities was Goltha, a place built largely from stone and fortified by walls that were legendary in their strength. Over the years Goltha had been attacked numerous times and repelled all comers.

In time the city of Goltha became the country of Goltha, and in turn that country became a part of the Fellein Empire. Goltha grew larger both as a city and as a country when the Empire came along. It was in Goltha, a city nearly at the center of the Empire, that the highest buildings had been raised. It was in Goltha that, according to the most common wisdom, all roads in the Empire met.

Goltha lay ahead of him and offered possibilities.

Behind him the faithful were moving on, heading toward Canhoon. He did not doubt that they would reach the city without him. They understood how important what they did was, and he had faith.

He had to have faith.

The sky ahead was dark with storm clouds.

"Sarmin."

The woman he called for moved to his side. She had been with him since he'd killed the men who were planning on harming her. Not because she had anything they needed, but simply because they were bored. He had followed a trail of bodies and come across them as they were attacking her farmhouse. Her husband was also alive as a result of his actions, but he was further back, hindered by the damage done to his leg.

Sarmin was strong in body and in faith. She was a devout follower of Plith and insisted that the Pilgrim's arrival was the answer to her prayers. So far he had not been able to dissuade her of that notion.

He had not tried very hard. The faithful were necessary.

"Keep them on track, please. I go to Goltha now. I believe we can finally gather enough of the faithful there. Time is short."

"We could go with you. We could show them the way."

"No. They must come willingly and they must not be intimidated into this. Had I come to you with four hundred people behind me, what would you have said?"

Sarmin looked down. "I'd have likely run away."

"The same is true anywhere. Strength in numbers is not the same as strength in faith."

"I will strive to keep the faithful on the right path." She lowered her head.

"Lemblo, Powl and Longrid should be able to help you in this." He paused for a moment. "Sarmin, I am grateful for all that you do."

"We all live to serve the gods." She looked at him with an uncomfortable level of affection and then moved away.

•••

The first blade came from his left, carried by a boy no older than ten if he had to guess. The second came from behind and that was the one meant to kill him. The boy was only a distraction.

His left hand reached out quickly and slapped the young arm that carried the dagger. The boy let out a squawk of surprise and pain as a bone in his forearm snapped. He fell to the ground quickly, the pain from the damage likely larger than anything he'd ever felt in his life before.

The sword was a different matter entirely.

The Pilgrim ducked and allowed himself to fall to the ground in the alleyway. The man had him. If he had not dodged aside, the blade would have cut deep and very likely killed him.

Though his assailant was taken by surprise by the maneuver, the advantage would not last long. His leg kicked out, striking the man in the knee. Something deep in the tissue of the man's leg cracked and he screamed, falling back, trying to keep his balance on a knee that no longer supported his weight.

The Pilgrim pushed himself into a standing position and drew his short sword from the worn scabbard.

"No! Wait! Please!" The man hopped backward on his one good leg, one hand out to ward off any blows, the other trying to hold his sword and support his injured leg at the same time.

The Pilgrim's sword cleaved through the mugger's jaw and throat with one swing. Satisfied that the man was dying and could no longer harm him he turned back to the boy.

On the ground now, lying in a puddle of muck, the lad looked his way with wide, terrified eyes.

"Is this how the people of Goltha welcome strangers?" The Pilgrim's voice was not tempered with kindness.

He had travelled far to the east of the Blasted Lands, to an area of Fellein that had never once tasted the ashes of the ruined territory. That had been a very long time ago, and now he was headed back to the west and places he had once sworn he would never see again. The gods had different plans for him.

"Get up, boy. I have places to go, and you will take me to them."

Though he whimpered as he rose, the boy did, indeed, stand. The Pilgrim was not the sort a smart boy disobeyed. Broken and scared, the boy knew enough to listen.

"I need you to take me to the Tower of Etrilla. Do this, and quickly, and I shall forgive your transgression."

The words seemed a bit of a struggle for the boy, but he nodded just the same. A moment later the lad was moving, holding his arm and whimpering as he moved through the streets. If there were any others with the boy, they chose not to come to his aid.

They moved down what seemed a nearly endless run of sidestreets and alleyways, until the Pilgrim began to wonder if his guide was trying to prepare another assault of some kind. He was considering asking exactly that when the boy stopped moving and pointed with his uninjured arm toward the vast marble structure ahead.

It was not a tower, really, but the building was tall enough to be impressive. Etrilla was the God of the Cities and as such most of the monuments to his glory were like fingers pointing toward the sky. There had likely been a time when the temple had been the largest structure around, but it had been overshadowed by others as time went on.

Seventy feet in height, the Tower of Etrilla was festooned with the images of hundreds of faces, each different and likely sculpted in the likeness of a person living back when the entire structure was being finished. Each visage wore an expression as unique as the people they were modeled after, and though there was truly no time for such luxuries, the Pilgrim spent a few minutes absorbing the details. Few of the manmade structures he had seen this far east were as breathtaking.

The boy did not wait around. As soon as the Pilgrim lost himself in staring his guide slipped away into the stream of people moving through the great city.

That was just as well. He had served the Pilgrim's needs and was no longer of any significance.

The Pilgrim entered the greatest of the temples in the city and strode with purpose through the marble hallway leading to the center of the structure. As with the exterior of the temple, the interior was filled with endless likenesses of people both common and extraordinary.

At the very center was a large table carved from a dark wood that had been polished meticulously. Sculpted into the center of the table was a likeness of Etrilla, a stout figure with arms heavy from years of labor, carrying a massive block upon one shoulder. Unlike many of the images of gods, Etrilla remained unchanged.

Four stood before the table, though there was certainly room for many more. There were no benches or chairs within the structure: Etrilla believed that work came before rest and offering places for the latter did not inspire the former.

The people all wore robes. That had changed. Etrilla was a laborer. Robes were not designed to aid in strenuous efforts.

The gathering smiled their welcome – though the oldest among them eyed the sword at the Pilgrim's side.

"Do you seek solace here?" The oldest spoke carefully, his

eyes leaving the hilt of the Pilgrim's sword reluctantly.

When he spoke, the voice was not his own, but belonged to the being for which the tower had been built. "Do you know me?"

They were devout, the four who stood before the Pilgrim. They knew who spoke to them.

When the Pilgrim spoke, the followers of Etrilla listened.

The Inquisitors were, as a rule, very scary individuals.

Darsken Murdro was one of the scariest. He knew that and used it to his advantage. He was not extraordinary in height, though he was bulkier than most. His skin was the color of dark mahogany and his long hair was coiled into several braids that ran halfway down his back. The people of Louron were much darker than the average person in Canhoon, and that led to a great deal of unease for many of the people he dealt with.

Louron was known for many things and few of those things were considered pleasant in the eyes of most. One of the things the swampy area was best known for was dark sorcery. The other point that attracted most people's attention – and more so even than the claims of sorcery – was that Inquisitors were trained there to handle their tasks.

The man before him was doubtless guilty of numerous sins. He could see the pulse in his neck, the sweat on his skin and the way he looked everywhere but directly into the Inquisitor's eyes and know that.

According to his masters back in Louron, there were three primary skills required of any Inquisitor: Empathy, Observation and Patience. Empathy let an Inquisitor read the intentions and conscience of a subject. Observation allowed for all of the small details that could learn the truth of any circumstance. Patience allowed for terrorizing a subject properly. An angry man could be scary. A patient man who gave away nothing in his expression was usually worse in Darsken's experience.

He knew, without any real consideration, that the man calling himself Captain Callan was not a murderer. Would he kill if cornered? Most would. Would he kill if his life depended on it or if someone were trying to take from him? Very likely. Would he kill twenty-one men, including a cousin of the Empress?

He doubted the man was capable. His crew could have helped, but there was still a great deal of niggling doubt involved in the notion.

"What did you see, exactly, when the men died?"

"I saw nothing. I wasn't here."

Darsken smiled thinly and stared hard into the man's eyes. He made absolutely certain he was the center of the captain's attention by tapping the edge of his stick on the deck of the ship. "I doubt that. Think very carefully and answer me again. What did you see when those men were killed?"

Callan looked from him to the stick and frowned. All of the inquisitors carried a short staff of one form or another and most were personalized. In this case there were deeply detailed engravings circling the wooden staff from the foot to the crown. Darsken knew each of them intimately as he had carved them during his lifetime of training.

Callan looked away from the stick, more unsettled than before.

"There were two people that attacked them. They were in the shadows. I didn't see them clearly. I think one was a woman but I couldn't say for sure."

Darsken took one step closer, his eyes locked furiously on Callan's. His smile faded, and his voice lowered by a full octave. "Why did you lie to me, Captain Callan?"

"Because…" Callan looked away again, trying hard to find the right words that would save him from the Inquisitor's wrath. "I was scared. I was paid to bring those men here."

"Who paid you?"

Callan looked away, desperate now, and his eyes sought Tataya. Darsken knew her, of course. They had been associates on several investigations in the past. She shook her head, offering no help.

"I give you a name and that name comes for me. He hires twenty more just like the ones on the dock, only this time around he's paying them to kill me."

"Did you know you were bringing assassins into the seat of the Empire?"

"Assassins? I was told they were mercenaries! Bodyguards!"

Had he the time and the patience Darsken knew he could have broken the captain. Instead he nodded his head. "You tell me the name. If you do not tell me what I want to know, I will look more closely at why a ship the size of yours only brought twenty men into the port instead of unloading a great deal more."

"I–"

Three sharp taps of the stick on the deck and the captain stopped speaking. "I have more important affairs to investigate than your deliveries. Keep it that way. Tell me what I need to know."

The man looked once more toward Tataya. She nodded almost imperceptibly.

"He said his name was Foster. Losla Foster." Callan's skin was paler than ever and his pulse was singing in the veins of his neck.

"I am done with you. I appreciate your honesty."

Callan did not speak, but he nodded and backed away.

Darsken made a small gesture to Tataya, asking without words if she would walk with him.

As she passed the captain she placed a consoling hand on his shoulder and moved to follow Darsken.

Where Darsken walked, the crew from the ship and the City Guard parted to let him pass. Two wagons had been loaded with the corpses from the docks and were already moving away, their cargo hidden under baskets and blankets. People would talk, but the exact scene of the crime was already cleared, courtesy of the guard and the rain.

When they had walked far enough away to suit him Darsken looked to Tataya and smiled mischievously. "Was he sufficiently scared, do you suppose?"

Tataya smiled back and let out a small laugh before she caught herself. "I think he came close to wetting his breeches."

"He is not the killer. You already knew that, of course." Darsken paused a moment. "He is also guilty of many crimes, but none I am concerned about."

"Callan has done favors for the Empire."

"Which is why I do not care about his many crimes." Tataya looked at him carefully and he offered nothing but his usual placid smile. The sorcerers never could quite decide what to do about the Inquisitors. The feeling was reciprocated. According to the laws of many areas within the Empire, sorcery was against the law. According to the Empress it was not. Also, and this was important, wizards were extremely dangerous when cornered.

That might have dissuaded almost any City Guard from dealing with the sorcerers, but the Inquisitors, some of them at least, were trained to handle the risks that wizardry offered. Some, including Darsken, used sorcery of their own in cases. There were rumors that the Inquisitors even used necromancy. Darsken did nothing to dissuade such rumors.

"Darsken, we have known each other for a long time."

"I dare say yes." He smiled and waited for her questions.

"Do you know anything of necromancy?"

His smile did not change. "If I say yes?"

"I might ask for your assistance with an unusual case presented by the enemies of our Empress."

"The corpses of the soldiers returned from the Blasted Lands?"

"How do you know about that?" She seemed genuinely s urprised.

"I tend to hear many forms of confession, Tataya."

She nodded her head. "Would you be able to help?"

"Are the bodies here?"

"Some samples, nothing more. Most were in Tyrne, and they were burned even before the city."

"That is the best way to handle dead things." He nodded.

"I know you don't raise the dead, but can you or any of your people talk to the dead?"

Darsken looked away from her, knowing what she would ask next.

"There are ways, Tataya."

"My sister… Goriah…."

"What is forbidden for you is also forbidden for me." He walked again, slowly, and she followed.

"So you cannot?"

"That is not what I said. I said it is forbidden. We have ways. Sometimes the need to learn who killed someone requires more than questioning those who might have seen the crime."

She didn't actually ask. She didn't dare.

"We will talk soon, Tataya. If you feel the need. For now, I must find out more about a man who was paid by the Imperial Family to kill at least one member of the same bloodline."

"Who?" He had surprised her a second time. That was a rare feat.

Losla Foster was the personal assistant to Laister Krous. If what the captain had said was true, the Krous family was very likely to be at war with itself in the near future.

He could have told her. She might have appreciated the information. She might also have run to the man he was about to hunt and warned him and Darsken could not allow that.

"Soon, perhaps. Before I mention more I must confirm certain details."

She didn't question him. She knew better.

"Tataya?"

"Yes, Darsken?"

"I am truly sorry for your loss. Goriah was an extraordinary lady."

No more words were spoken. None were needed.

Despite the incredibly early hour, Nachia Krous agreed to see the Inquisitor.

He was a dark man, wearing dark clothes, with a square face and a body that most closely resembled an effigy made of tree trunks and a large barrel for ale. She had seen larger men, but few who looked so unsettlingly solid. She could easily understand how he would prove intimidating to most people.

Having been raised in a family of royals, she was not easily intimidated and being tutored by a sorcerer had guaranteed that few could make her uneasy.

The Inquisitor – she had already forgotten the man's name, but knew that Desh, standing to her right, had not – smiled and his face brightened with the expression.

"I am grateful, Majesty, that you agreed to see me. I am afraid I bring unfortunate tidings."

She suppressed a shudder. Her mind immediately went to invading armies and the dread that they had moved on to another target so quickly. Still she managed to keep her expression blank of any worries, a skill Desh had taught her long ago.

"What has happened, Inquisitor?"

"Majesty, I was asked to investigate an attack this morning. Over twenty men were killed in the night, near the docks. I am so sorry, but one of them was a relative of yours, Windhar Krous." He paused a moment while she looked at him and for the first time the man looked uncomfortable in her presence. "He is your second cousin, I believe."

"Was. He was." She paused a moment and swallowed. She knew Windhar, of course, but aside from being another courtesan in the family crowd she could not have told anyone much about him. Pleasant enough to look at, but not really much of a conversationalist and hardly the most significant member of her family. Brolley would be upset, however. They had been much closer. "Do you know who killed these men?"

"It is my understanding that these men were brought here by a man named Losla Foster, though I cannot say why they were brought here, I do know that a man with the same name has been employed for several years by Laister Krous. I could not currently say if that is the same man, or if it is merely a coincidence."

She liked the Inquisitor. He had a way of carefully avoiding making accusations he could not back up.

"I would like very much to know the absolute truth of this, Inquisitor. Until you have an answer for me I must ask that you work only on this investigation."

The man looked at her for a moment and lowered his head. "I cannot promise discretion in this investigation, Majesty."

Nachia smiled at the man. "Not at all, Inquisitor. I would not ask that of you. By all means, let it be known that you are investigating the murder of one of my family and that I intend to bring the full might of the Empire down on the heads of everyone involved."

When the Inquisitor smiled again it was a cold thing, a smile that allowed for no hope of happiness or peace for those who managed to block his path.

"As you wish, Majesty."

The Inquisitor left the room and Nachia looked toward her First Advisor. "Do you think Laister could actually be that foolish?"

Desh pulled down the hood that had, once again, hidden his face and sighed. "I think Laister is fairly convinced that he is invincible. So, yes."

Nachia leaned back in her throne, ignoring the way it made her back and side ache.

She stared at the distant wall and shook her head. "Danieca will not be happy."

"Considering that she has made her support of Laister well known, you might consider getting the information to her by one means or another." For the first time since Goriah's death, there was a tone of amusement in Desh's voice.

"Oh, I plan to. Just as soon as I can."

Desh nodded his head. "Merros has begun moving troops."

"Where?"

"He's clearing a pathway between here and Trecharch for the refugees. He is also planning a few surprises for those who follow them."

"Will they be followed?"

"I believe it's already happening, though proving it is difficult. The Sa'ba Taalor don't quite follow the normal rules of engagement. Their troops move as they will. They do not seem to have supply trains or established routes."

"How are they managing that, Desh? How are they getting where they need to be without forming proper columns?"

"Here's the thing, Majesty. They are adept at moving through the Blasted Lands and surviving there. As I understand it the main sources of meat for the Sa'ba Taalor have always been hunted in that wasteland. They hunt and kill and live off the meat of the Pra-Moresh." He paused to make sure she understood how insane that concept was. She did.

"After that, finding food to eat in virtually any part of the Empire must be the easiest thing in the world for them."

Nachia remained quiet for a long while, her brow knitted in thought and her mouth working silently at what words she might need to say.

Finally she responded, "What can your magics do to make that more challenging for them?"

Desh looked at her hard for a moment, his expression almost tempestuous, and then he laughed. "I had never thought of that. Not a once."

Nachia smiled. Her smile was exactly as warm as that of the Inquisitor before he left her presence. "Give it a great deal of thought, Desh Krohan. I want to make their lives more difficult as soon as possible."

Desh nodded his head and started across the chamber. "With your permission I wish to speak to a few of my associates. Corin is more of a specialist in these matters than me, but I suspect we can come up with something... appropriate to your needs, Majesty."

Nachia waited until he left the vast room and then got off the throne. She preferred walking when she was thinking and she had so very much to think about if she wanted to save her Empire from the Sa'ba Taalor.

TEN

The town of Jorhuan was fortified. Many of the larger cities had forgotten about the previous wars, but Jorhuan was not among them. Surrounding the actual town were two walls. The first was made of stones and rose a staggering thirty-five feet into the air. There were two gates, both of which were currently being guarded against any strangers. The North Gate faced Trecharch and had been sealed, because if there was to be a siege the last thing needed were people asking for assistance. They would have no food and would be of absolutely no use to Jorhuan.

It was a harsh life lesson, to be sure, but better that strangers stay out and move on than that they clog the streets.

The South Gate remained open, but was guarded against any enemies. Members of Jorhuan's City Guard were currently spaced along the walkway for the outer wall, carrying loaded crossbows to discourage anyone foolish enough to try attacking, and they were alert for anyone attempting to come their way from the north or the west.

The nine followers of Wrommish came from the south. They walked, and not one of them carried an obvious weapon.

That they were Sa'ba Taalor would have been obvious

to anyone looking carefully. They did nothing to hide their appearance. They had light gray skin and they were dressed in common enough fashion.

Because they approached on foot and bore no weapons, the guards on the walls paid them little attention.

The guards at the gates were a different matter. The first of them was bored. He had been on duty for over four hours and there had been nothing out of the ordinary, not even anyone coming from the north trying to gain entry. They had been warned, of course. The birds had been sent out with messages notifying all that Trecharch was fallen and to expect refugees and to offer them aid.

That aid would not be forthcoming and the guards all understood why. The Imperial Army was on the way and would soon be engaging the enemy, but Jorhuan was not a large city and they could expect remarkably little by way of assistance, though they were on the made pathway from Trecharch to Canhoon. First look to yourselves, then to your brothers. Offer aid when you can, but anyone who would risk their own lives to help strangers was surely addled.

It was a philosophy that had always suited the temperament of the people of Jorhuan.

The second guard was younger and dreamed of fighting the enemy. He had no idea what the enemy might look like, but Sherea was young and beautiful and she liked the notion that he might save them all from the enemy. In order to impress her he would gladly kill a hundred men.

All men are young once, and even those who are older are often made foolish when a woman smiles.

He was thinking of Sherea's smile when the strangers approached. That meant he was ready for trouble.

"Lem. Look at these ones." He felt his blood surge as they

came closer. The Sa'ba Taalor were supposed to have gray flesh and these folks looked gray to him. Though not as gray as he'd have expected. He had thought their flesh would surely be the same color as granite, but no.

Lem looked his way and stifled a yawn. He knew of the younger man's affections for Sherea – and she was worthy of a few stray thoughts, though his own wife was much more to his liking – and he shook his head.

"What am I looking at then, Kell? More tradesmen? More mercenaries?"

"I think it's them. The enemies."

Lem's eyes wandered toward the strangers. There were nine of them. Hardly an invading army. He was about to say as much when he looked more closely at the one leading them. The man was lean, but hard. His body seemed nearly sculpted and his tunic showed a series of scars on gray flesh. The scars seemed to make a design, but he could not see it clearly. The man's face was equally lean and another deep scar ran across his left cheek. He had a thick braid of hair running down his back.

He carried no weapons, but the way he moved was predatory. Cats moved that way when they were stalking birds or butterflies to torture. He hated cats. They were nasty creatures, but he had to tolerate them as his wife loved the damned things.

Despite the fact that Kell had made a dozen inaccurate claims regarding the invaders earlier, Lem now stood tall and reached for his club. Lem was a very large man and most people upon seeing the stout club he'd carried for years decided it was best to remain calm, lest he decide to bounce it off their skulls.

"How can I help you this fine day?" Lem kept the words

pleasant, but swept the air around his legs with his club and locked his eyes with the first of the strangers. Beside him Kell was hastily pulling his axe from his belt. If he moved with his regular grace, the situation would be resolved before Kell was ready.

N'Heelis, Chosen of the Forge of Wrommish and King in Gold, smiled with both of his mouths. The effect was unsettling for Lem and Kell alike, and while Lem was trying to recover from the oddity, N'Heelis broke his skull with a single palm strike.

Kell was trying to understand exactly what had happened to the larger guard when N'Heelis ruptured his airway with a follow-up maneuver that the young guard never even saw.

N'Heelis did not speak the tongue common to the Fellein. He did not care. He was here for a reason.

"Kill them all. Every last one. We offer no mercy this day."

Once through the gate the Sa'ba Taalor moved quickly, becoming individuals instead of a crowd. Three of them moved up the two separate stairs leading to the walkway on the first wall.

There was no time to celebrate. The followers of Wrommish had been given a mission and they intended to see it through. Wrommish wanted Jorhuan by the end of the day. N'Heelis was glad to provide whatever his god demanded.

The eight with him were younger and not as fully experienced in war as many of his followers, but that was not a concern. They could fight. They now had a chance to prove themselves.

The gates remained open after them. Two stood at the open gates and looked inward, prepared to kill any who tried to flee.

Grath and Delon went up the stairs on the left side and

Larrister took the flight on the right. They moved gracefully and quickly, all of them wearing heavy guards on their forearms to allow for some protection.

The first City Guards went down without a protest. They didn't question the people coming toward them because there had been no alarm sounded. Delon managed to break the neck of her opponent soundlessly and he slumped to the walkway. Larrister was not as fortunate and the body of his target fell from the walkway and crashed into a stall below where the fight occurred.

That was enough to alert the rest of the guards. Weapons were drawn and soldiers charged, prepared to fight for the safety of their people.

Grath stood aside and let Delon go first. Delon did not disappoint. She moved quickly and as the first guard came for her she blocked his attempt at swordplay and broke his arm at the elbow. He screamed and dropped his weapon. She moved on and let Grath finish the task.

On the other side Larrister moved like a thrown blade, cutting down the first and then the second opponent without even changing expression. He swept the legs of the first guard and forced the man's face into the wall hard enough to shatter it. The second came for him and was thrown over the wall, but not before his body was bent into a new shape. Larrister was not subtle, but he was powerful.

The others moved forward, charging past their king and attacking. There were no weapons. This was a test of their unarmed skills. An axe came down and was deflected; a hand broke the wrist of the axe-wielder and the weapon was taken away and thrown at another opponent.

N'heelis watched and judged.

When the City-Guard came from their barracks on their

horses, he stood prepared for them. Just as his followers had their parts, so too did their king.

Men on horseback have many advantages. They have speed, they have mass. They have weapons meant to impale or kill with ease.

N'Heelis had training and faith.

The first horseman came at him swinging a long flail. Moving aside was an easy enough task. As the rider charged past, surprised to have missed, the king broke the horse's hind leg with a brutal kick. Horse and rider both fell, and in so doing created an obstacle for the rest of the horsemen.

Horses veered. Riders tried to compensate for the sudden changes. N'Heelis took advantage of every delay, striking again and again and often killing or maiming with a single blow.

When a weapon came to him, which was not uncommon as they fell from the hands of his enemies, he used them. A spear dropped from a rider's grip and N'Heelis used it to block a sword and impale a rider.

The men fighting him quickly learned to keep their distance and it was only a matter of minutes before the first crossbow was leveled at him.

Their gods chose the kings of the Sa'ba Taalor because they exemplified all that the individual gods wanted from their followers. N'Heelis was no exception. Throughout his long life he had fought with few weapons and relied on his body as the main offense and defense.

The crossbow bolt was aimed at his heart. He saw the archer aiming for him and moved, sliding sideways. The bolt that should have killed him slipped past and grazed his forearm instead.

When four more of the guards aimed at him, he knew dodging alone would no longer take care of the matter. One arrow was a very different consideration.

While the King in Gold was keeping the attention of most of the people near the southern gate, his followers took care of their own business. None of the Sa'ba Taalor paid the least bit of attention to the spectacle. Instead they followed his commands and eliminated the guards along the wall and moved quickly to the northern gate.

The guards did not continue to ignore them. The first few fell quickly before N'Heelis distracted the locals but the rest did not stare down into the center of the area. Instead they took note of their enemies along the wall and did their best to kill the intruders.

Grath took a crossbow bolt through his left eye and roared his pain for all to hear. He was a fighter and a skilled warrior but the pain was immense and he fell to his hands and knees, defenseless.

Delon considered Grath a friend but her duty was not to protect a weak ally. She served the King in Gold and Wrommish. The axe of the closest guard served to cripple the archer who had fired before another bolt could be set in the crossbow. Four long strides later she shattered his jaw and shoved the man aside on her way to the northern gate.

Larrister fared better. His sheer size and ferocity unsettled his opponents. They had never seen a grayskinned man before, nor had most of them ever been in a serious fight beyond a moderate amount of training.

Jorhuan was fortified, yes, and as with all of the people in Fellein, the City Guard had all spent their time in the armies of the Empire, but none of them had ever seen combat. It is one thing to practice war games and another entirely to engage in war.

The City Guard hesitated when Larrister roared and came

for them. Larrister did not hesitate. He charged like a bull, grabbing any item that was of the right size and hurling it at the closest target, the better to confuse and disorient. Where Delon had to engage all her enemies, fully half of the City Guard facing Larrister panicked and ran before considering their actions.

Larrister's choice of tactics failed him when the guards on the lower level, beside the northern gate, aimed crossbows at him and fired. A bolt plunged into his calf. The wound was not serious enough to stop the man, but it slowed him substantially.

Delon won the race for the gate, taking out the last of the soldiers in her path before moving down the walkway and attacking the two men who were looking toward Larrister and reloading their crossbows.

She did not give them time to change targets.

While Delon and Larrister made their charge, the rest of the Sa'Ba Taalor with them systematically killed anyone in their path, regardless of age or gender. They had their orders and they followed them.

The entire affair might have ended with none of the invaders killed if not for the actions of Branfer Hollis, a hunter who took one look at the invaders and promptly released his dogs.

The animals were well trained and had been employed on numerous occasions to help the hunter take down big game. They moved for the strangers when Branfer pointed and they came in low and fast enough to catch the Sa'ba Taalor off guard.

N'Heelis watched a boy he'd seen raised from infancy move the wrong way to defend himself and die in an instant. The dog ripped open his throat and tore at his face.

He did not have time to do anything about it, even if he'd had the inclination. Men with crossbows were trying to kill him and staying alive was taking all of his concentration.

Another of his followers went down, struggling with the dog, and came back up after breaking the animal's back. He came back up bloodied and missing three fingers.

The situation might have only grown worse from there. The dogs were fast and they were savage. The opening of the north gate changed everything when Tusk and his riders came through.

The dogs were vicious. The mounts were worse.

Tusk came with seventeen of his people. Most of them were on mounts and pulling wagons loaded with corpses.

Tusk did not interfere with the actual taking of the town. That was not his purpose. He delivered the dead and nothing more, but he watched and he smiled as N'heelis and his followers finished the work they had started.

Tusk looked to N'Heelis when he was done and smiled. "A good day's work!"

N'Heelis looked to his people, the wounded, the unscathed and the dead, and agreed.

Then he began the work the Wrommish demanded. There were bodies that had to be moved, and more of his people came through the open gates to assist.

What the gods demanded he was glad to do.

The Temmis Pass was not a well-known point on the map. It was mentioned, as was the town of Hallis, the very small collection of buildings that made up the most western point in the whole of the Fellein Empire. The population was usually a bit under a dozen.

Currently Hallis was home to a much larger gathering:

the tents and supplies for the First Lancers Division. A city of canvas and wagons surrounded the tiny gathering of buildings. To say the people of Hallis were unsettled would be a vast understatement.

Colonel Lockner Horast had every intention of following the orders given to him by General Merros Dulver. To that end the men were ready for war. Each of the Lancers remained prepared and armed at all times and within easy walking distance of their steeds. They wore light armor and sported great shields, hand-to-hand weapons and, of course, their lances.

The Sa'ba Taalor came up the only easy access point for the area, moving en masse up the Temmis Pass, ready for whatever might come their way. First up were foot soldiers, and they came armed and wearing armor. No two were alike, and most of the people in the small town would have been hard pressed to say which was the most terrifying.

The Sa'ba Taalor were not giants. They were not monsters, but they were almost as alien as any of the nightmares from legend. All of the people in the town had heard of the Pra-Moresh. None had ever seen one. All had heard of the invaders, and they had been witness previously when the King in Iron spoke with the Empress Nachia Krous. They had surely never expected to see a greater spectacle in their lives and that was their mistake.

The Sa'ba Taalor came in formation, moving in lines thirty soldiers wide and carrying various weapons and shields. As they walked they tapped the edge of whatever weapons they carried on the edge of the shields and did so in perfect step with their strides. The end result was a sound rather like thunder. If it was designed to unsettle the locals it worked very well.

The entire population of Hallis – all twelve of them - took it upon themselves to get away while they could, and moved between tents and past wagons as they ran from the newcomers.

As soon as they had cleared the way, the First Lancers Division charged in.

The Sa'ba Taalor struck an impressive sight as they marched in formation up the trail from the Blasted Lands.

The first rank of horsemen made an impressive sight as they impaled a dozen of the men who could not break formation fast enough to avoid being run through. The lances did their jobs and their targets died or were maimed. The charges continued forward into the ranks of the Sa'ba Taalor while their riders drew short swords and swept their blades into the flesh of their enemies.

The reaction was immediate and violent. The formations fell apart into a seething mass of conflict. Horsemen tried to move forward and their enemies did their best to cut them down where they stood. Both had moderate success. The first of the horsemen was pulled from his saddle and thrown to the ground even as his ride was nearly beheaded by an axe chop to the neck.

The Sa'ba Taalor broke ranks and moved around the first chargers, heading for the rest of the enemies they saw waiting for them. The second rank of lancers moved into them at a hard run, first using lances and then switching to flails, bashing in skulls and denting shields as they charged past.

The First Lancers were among the best that Fellein had, and they proved it that day.

The fighting started brutally and did not slow down.

Through the first assault only two hundred of the Lancers were sent in. The rest waited as patiently as they could, knowing that to charge in any sooner would only add to the congestion and chaos of the moment.

The enemy was proficient at fighting, but hardly seemed ready for handling the soldiers on horses.

That changed the moment the first rank of mounted Sa'ba Taalor showed themselves. The fighting had been going on for several minutes and the foot soldiers had done their very best to clear a path. What had seemed initially to be a panic on the part of the brutes from the Blasted Lands was, in fact, merely a clearing of the way. The mounts were not horses. They were larger, and they were carnivores. The chargers were trained to fight against other horses and riders. They were not prepared for the ferocity of the nightmares the grayskins rode.

Horses and riders alike attempted to retreat, but it wasn't meant to be. The mounts pulled horses down as they tried to get away, rending flesh from the animals' flanks and tearing them to the ground. Their riders were equally brutal, using weapons familiar and completely foreign to the Fellein alike.

Still the lancers continued on until, at last, the first groups sent in had been taken down by the enemy.

And while they were in the process of being slain by the Sa'ba Taalor, the rest of the lancers waited.

While they waited, a solid wall of horses and men, the Archers Division moved into position and began firing arrows into the ranks of the enemy. Some were ready with shields, but the combat had weakened the proper formations and far larger numbers were taken by surprise. The hail of arrows did the job it was designed to do and sent the grayskins scattering, reaching for shields and trying to prepare themselves. The second volley did almost as much damage, but by the time the third came the Sa'ba Taalor were once again ready for the attack.

By that point over a hundred from each side were either dead or dying.

The sounds of horns calling from lower on the Temmis Pass caused an instant ripple among the Sa'ba Taalor. The formations came back together, this time with the mounted riders to the front. They sported spears in some cases but few, it seemed, had ever used a lance.

Sadly for the lancers they seemed perfectly willing to learn. Worse still, they were excellent at adapting to new situations. Spears and stolen lances alike came into play and the mounts charged at the horses and riders. The horses charged back but even from a distance Lockner could see that the training was only barely holding. It was one thing to expect an animal to charge at a soldier, another to expect even welltrained horses to charge a predatory nightmare.

While the two groups were engaging, the Sa'ba Taalor moved their archers forward.

The First Lancers Division had excellent training. Their enemy had numbers, and four times as many archers. In the end there was only one possible conclusion.

Delil was waiting for Andover in the valley past Wheklam. The land there was rocky and the waters that trickled through the area ran hot and steamed up the air. By the time they ran across each other both had stripped down to the bare essentials and were sweating profusely.

There was no food to be had, so they went hungry.

"You look different, Andover." Delil sipped at a flask of water and moved carefully over the ground. The earth here was dark, broken and tended to slip out from under unwary feet. He began to understand why so many of the Sa'ba Taalor walked softly instead of merely stomping their way across the landscape.

"How do I look different?" He touched the third of his Great Scars, momentarily selfconscious. If Delil saw the gesture, she did not say anything.

"Your skin is more like ours. And your eyes have the proper shine to them."

He frowned as he contemplated that. "Do you suppose I am becoming one of your people?"

"Would that bother you?" She looked at him carefully, her feet seeming to know exactly where they should move.

"I don't think so." He shook his head. "No. I am already no longer who I was. I have hands, and I have…" He shook his head at a loss for words.

"You have what?"

"I'm not sure. I have never been good with words, Delil."

She laughed. "Liar. You are very good with words. You've used them to make a hundred excuses in the time I've known you." She did not understand the nature of the gesture he offered. That was just as well. She'd have likely broken his skull if she had.

"I have hands. I have spoken to gods. I'm supposed to speak to more. I never expected any of this."

"The gods have chosen you, Andover Lashk."

"Yes, but what have they chosen me for?"

She rolled her head, working to stretch the tension from her body. "Who can say the will of the gods before they let their will be known? Only fools, that is who. Gods do not always explain themselves until they are ready."

Andover nodded his head and looked toward the next mountain. It was, as they all were, a vast thing. "Which mountain do I look upon, Delil?"

"You stand before great Ordna, the Bronze Mountain."

He considered that and nodded. "What does Ordna do?"

Delil looked his way and snickered. "Whatever Ordna wants. Ordna is a god."

"You're not as funny as you think." The words were spoken without malice.

"Ordna teaches the way of great weapons. Ordna teaches us to break walls and crush armies with ease."

As she spoke she started up the rough edge of the mountain. There were easy handholds, but it was going to be a very long climb. The side of the mountain rose like a column, towering and straight, unlike the last mountain which had been rounder and had fewer decent places to place a foot. Still, Wheklam and Ordna had one thing in common: they were meant to be challenges that had to be faced.

"'Break walls and crush armies?'" He shook his head as he started ascending. The climb was easy enough, but he had to pull his body upward with his hands as often as not and the strain was easy to feel as it grew inside his body.

Delil looked down at him over her shoulder. From this angle he could see most of her body and the scars that ran across her, detailing every struggle she'd experienced. The scars told a story. Someday he hoped to learn all of the tales that made the whole of the woman.

"Do you have siege weapons in Fellein, Andover?"

"I have no idea what a siege is. What do the weapons do?"

She shook her head and smiled. "You will soon discover the answer to that question, I suspect."

The ground was soft and sandy and wet.

Lored, Chosen of the Forge of Ordna and King in Bronze led his mount across the damp sand with a smile on his face. He was not smiling because his mount, Pre'ru, was making unhappy noises about the moisture on his paws, but because he was now off the ship that had been transporting him and his people.

He scanned the shoreline with both his flesh eye and his bronze one and nodded his satisfaction.

He did not like the ships. They swayed and rocked and left him feeling restless.

Night covered the world. The sky was clouded and few stars shone through the veil of storm clouds. The keep ahead of them was a massive affair, with heavy stone walls and reinforced gates. It would be a good challenge and one they looked forward to overcoming in the name of the Daxar Taalor.

Donaie Swarl, the King in Lead, had done her part and transported them to the far eastern side of the Fellein Empire. Now he and his would do their part and seed the fury of the gods in virgin territory, as ordered by Ordna and the other Daxar Taalor.

Donaie walked down the gangway from her ship and moved over to where he rode Pre'ru. The mount made no noise as she put her hand into his thick mane. They were positively old friends after their time together on the vast black ship.

The air was hot here. Ordna was used to the sort of heat he encountered, but there was also a breeze and that was a pleasant change.

"We go our own ways now, Lored."

He nodded and looked at the king before him. She was a tall woman, and heavily muscled. He wondered idly what their children would look like if the Daxar Taalor decided they should have any.

"Do you stay here, Donaie? Or will you move on?"

"I'm finished here. I go back toward the west. To the south. There are ships massing. They wish to engage us in combat."

She looked in that direction and then back to him, here eyes aglow with the thrill of the coming battles. "They do not understand the Great Tide or that it is now upon them, Lored. We must both teach them lessons."

He slapped her shoulder with companionable affection and she smiled. "Go teach the water riders about the tide, Donaie Swarl, and I will teach them about the land."

"Keep Pre'ru safe. He's the better part of you." Her voice held a teasing note.

"I would say the same about your ship, but it reeks of dead fish."

"Less so now that you are off of it." She waved one hand in farewell and he nodded to her even as she walked away.

Then he rode forward and bellowed to his people, "We ride! There's blood in the air!"

They roared their agreement and began to move, heading for swamplands in the distance.

There were people there that needed killing and he was in a mood to help them along the paths of their destinies.

His people moved quickly and efficiently. They had practiced their maneuvers over every sort of terrain for most of their lives and now, finally, they would have a chance to use them properly. It was one thing to war against the other kings of the Seven Forges and something entirely different to work against the enemies of the gods.

Praxus walked closer and nodded to Lored and Pre'ru alike. "This is Elda?"

Lored nodded and eyed the closest wall of the keep. "One small part. Elda is a kingdom. Elda is a large part of the entire Empire and has many soldiers." He pointed to the stone barrier. "Elda also likes walls almost as much as Tarag Paedori." The King in Iron loved walls. Lored loved knocking walls down. They had been friendly rivals for a very long time.

"Where is Blane?" Blane had traveled to Fellein before and met with the previous Emperor and their sorcerer, too. He was a ferocious fighter, but it wasn't his skill with a sword that was needed just then.

Praxus frowned. "Working on one of the catapults, my king."

"Find him for me. I want to make sure I word the demand for surrender properly."

"You are going to write a demand for surrender?" The man's broad mouth frowned in bewilderment.

"Of course," he smiled. "I will strap it to the very first stone we send through their wall."

Praxus chuckled and nodded. "I will find Blane."

By the time the siege engines had been assembled Blane had written down five copies of the articles demanding surrender and the sun was starting to rise.

The sound of horns came from the keep ahead of them and Lored nodded his head. "They call to arms! Listen to them! Break their walls!"

The first missile ripped through the air and struck true, smashing into one of the stone walls and sending a rain of debris falling into the interior of the keep. Before the dust had settled, fourteen more volleys blasted the wall and collapsed the entire barrier.

Lored stared at the ruin of the first defense and scowled. He had hoped for a greater challenge. The wall was not built to withstand the sort of weapons he had brought with him. Against a gathering of soldiers with ladders it would suffice, but he and his did not climb walls, they destroyed them.

"Gather your shields! Raise the battering rams! Bring them down in Ordna's name!"

"Ordna!" the name echoed across the shattered wall. "Ordna!" Horns called from both sides as if there could be any doubt that the battle had been started.

The soldiers who spilled from the ruined barrier came fast and hard, prepared for battle. Men with heavy armor and shields came toward them from above, moving down trails that had once led to gates that had been sealed against any possible attackers.

Lored raised his longbow and reached for a handful of arrows. The fools came toward them wearing armor and sporting shields. The armor was hastily slapped in place and the shields were carried at the oddest angles, where they could do remarkably little good. Most of the troopers were not wearing helmets.

His first arrow punched through his target's forehead and dropped the man where he stood. That single arrow had been a signal to the rest of his archers and they paid attention.

The advancing wave of soldiers promptly retreated back to their shattered wall, and Lored grinned. In his own tongue, one that the locals likely would not understand, he called out, "Reload! I see towers along the remaining walls and I want them knocked down!"

He called to Blane and Praxus and had them pass on the message: the rest of the keep would be surrounded by troops and cut off. The message went out quickly and the riders set out to follow his commands.

As he watched through the vast holes in the wall before him, the soldiers inside the keep prepared themselves properly, gathering their armor more completely and taking the time to put on their helmets and position their shields.

Once again he waved for Praxus and the man came forward. "Take down the rest of the wall. I don't want them thinking they can hide behind it."

Before the order could be completed a coalition of men from within the keep came out, unarmed and heading toward Lored where he sat upon Pre'ru. He slid down from the mount's back and patted his old friend on the shoulder. He rested one hand on the handle of his mace and waited calmly.

The man at the front was older, but in good shape. He did not wear armor, but his uniform was covered with buttons and cords and many decorations. His hair was pulled back into a thick braid.

Lored did not speak. He kept his expression neutral and waited for the man to come to him. He watched the old man's eyes look him over, from his scaled armor to the metallic sculpture that had replaced a portion of his face, a gift from Ordna. The bronze flesh moved and felt. The bronze eye moved and saw.

"Why have you attacked us?" There should have been rage in that voice. There should, at the very least, have been indignation. Instead there was only fear. Lored did not change his expression, but he was disappointed.

"You are part of Fellein. We are at war with Fellein."

"But what did we do? How do we sue for peace?"

"Surrender your keep. Offer us your troops as ours, and we will consider your request for peace."

"I cannot. I have a king I answer to. I have made oaths and sworn my fealty." He was nervous as he spoke. They were words he did not want to say, but felt he had to say just the same. He had made vows to kings, after all.

Lored nodded his head in the way of the Fellein and then he brought his mace around in an arc and shattered the man's face. The soldiers behind the man let out noises and he looked at them and sneered.

"You will surrender to me or you will die!"

Three of them retreated. One of them stood his ground and reached for his sword. It was a very pretty sword, with gems and gold wire around the hilt. Despite the ornamentation the man pulled it with ease and dropped into a proper stance.

"You have killed a good man today and you will die for your troubles!" The voice shook with rage.

"I have killed a weak man. It was meant as a mercy." Lored bared his teeth in a grin as he spoke.

The swordsman lunged forward with his sword in position and Lored blocked with the handle of his mace. He shoved the man backward with his full body weight and the man fell back exactly far enough to let Lored hit him with the heavy end of his weapon.

Depending on who you speak with, a sword is a gentleman's weapon. It requires skill and demands respect. Lored had several swords. He used them regularly. Now and then he preferred the way a mace felt when it was crushing a skull.

The other three men tried to run back to the keep and Lored whistled to Pre'ru. His mount took them down easily, clawing two of them to the ground and beheading the third with one bite of powerful jaws.

Lored laughed and several others joined him. If this were the best the Fellein had to offer, the war would be a short one.

"Take down the walls!" He waved his mace and his followers obeyed. The volleys from the catapults obliterated the remaining wall facing the ocean, killing at least a dozen who stood too close to the damaged structure.

"Take them all! Take this place in the name of Ordna!"

"Ordna!" they roared as one. "Ordna!" they prayed to their

god, offering sacrifices in the name of the deity.

Lored joined them in the offering to the Daxar Taalor. Their offerings were many that day and their god was pleased.

The entrance into Ordna's heart was not at the top of the mountain. Instead it came upon Andover as a nearly complete surprise. One moment he was concentrating on where he would place his hand and the next his fingers found purchase on a ledge that he was sure had not been there before.

He did not question this. He understood now that the gods had their ways.

The walk to the center of the mountain was uneventful. Delil walked beside him and looked only ahead. He returned the favor. Delil meant a great deal to him, but he also knew that she was not why he was in the heart of Ordna. He was here instead to meet with a god.

So the last thing he expected when walking around a bend in the tunnel was to find his mother waiting for him.

At fourteen, roughly the same time he decided he knew how best to handle his world, his mother and father sent him on his way with instructions to stay away or face the scarred knuckles of his father's fists.

"Mother?" His voice broke as if he were just starting puberty and he felt himself blush.

"No. Not your mother. I have merely chosen her face for dealing with you." He felt the presence then. That vast, overwhelming power that he had now felt three times before. This was Ordna. A god.

His mother stood before him and shook her head.

He dropped to one knee before the god and offered his hands before him as he had with Truska-Pren. The axe he had been given by the gods rested in his open palms.

His mother reached for the weapon, but it was Drask Silver Hand who plucked it from his grasp.

Drask loomed above him, his eyes burning beneath a furrowed brow. Though he no longer wore a veil, Andover recognized him. The Great Scars on Drask's face were different. There were seven of them, one for each of the Daxar Taalor, and they ran in perfect lines from just below his nose to just above his chin. The man's dark hair flowed loosely around his broad shoulders.

Silvery eyes regarded the weapon before handing it back.

"Why are you here, Andover Lashk of Fellein?" The voice was Drask's, but the words seemed impossibly heavy, as if they might crush him. The attention of gods was not an easy burden.

"I am here to make myself known to you, Ordna."

"Stand. Walk with me."

Andover obeyed, quickly settling his axe back at his hip and moving next to the larger man. As they walked, the walls shifted until they were standing in a chamber carved from warm, brown rock. The ground beneath them was a mosaic, meticulously laid out from small tiles that depicted seven different symbols. He recognized Truska-Pren's visage among them. A face carved from obsidian scowled in the detailed illustration: Durhallem. In the exact center of the mosaic a face made of bronze tiles rested. Ordna glared up toward the ceiling, a face shaped from endless angles of metal. The rest of them were lost in shadows and distance.

"What is war, Andover Lashk?"

He stopped examining the artwork on the floor and looked at the god wearing Drask's face.

"I don't know how to answer that."

"Honestly. It is always best to be honest when talking with

gods." There was a hint of humor in that comment and for brief instant Andover realized how much he missed Drask. The man was had not always been kind, but he had always been honest.

"I think war is a conflict between two people."

Drask's silver hand tilted left and right, making clumsy waves in the air. "Yes. No. Give more details."

"War is a conflict between two people that cannot be resolved with words and promises."

"Better." Drask did not smile, but he tilted his head into a nod in that way Drask did sometimes.

"Now, what is the purpose of war?"

"To settle matters once and for all?"

Drask/Ordna nodded. "Resolution. A final decision. That is the purpose of war." The god turned and looked toward the distant wall. Only where the wall should have been there was now a view into the distance. "War has many purposes, Andover Lashk. Resolution is a part of that, yes, but there is more."

Drask walked toward the image on the wall and Andover followed. The air felt different where the image was and Andover smelled the scent of a river, the odors of familiar spices in the air. As he approached the image he saw a collection of stands and small tents, set up near a riverside. This might not be Tyrne he looked at, but it was close enough. He could just about reach out and touch the world he had left behind. As if to prove his point a breeze caressed his brow as he came closer still to the moving image.

"Is that Tyrne?"

"You already know that it is not. It is Freeholdt, at the banks of the Freeholdt River. Tyrne no longer exists. Durhallem now stands at the spot where Tyrne once stood. This was done to make a point. This was done to explain to the people of Fellein that war is here and they will fall before us."

Andover nodded his head slowly. "Durhallem is in two places?"

"Yes. Durhallem stands here and there. Just as this mountain, Ordna, will soon stand here and in a different part of Fellein."

"Why?"

"We are at war, my people and yours."

The muscles in his mouths pulled in different ways. They were foreign as yet. He was not used to having different mouths and the feeling was uncomfortable.

"Tell me what you are thinking, Andover."

It wasn't a request.

"I'm not certain if they are my people any longer. I am not certain of anything."

Drask nodded. "Good. Then you are learning the greatest truth of war." The god made flesh turned and faced him and that massive silver hand rested on his shoulder. "Fellein is old and has grown stagnant. There has been no change for too long. There must always be change, Andover."

Andover tilted his head, absolutely unaware that he was mirroring both Drask and Delil in the way they asked questions without words.

"There are Seven Forges here, Andover Lashk. Just as the forges in a blacksmith's are used to shape and strengthen, so too are the forges here used to the same end. Durhallem demanded that you walk the Blasted Lands and learn to fight before you were allowed to meet. Truska-Pren gave you new hands, yes, but you were made to endure great pain in the giving. That was not a mistake or an oversight. As Drask Silver Hand told you then, life is pain."

Drask/Ordna stepped closer, until he was inches from Andover's face. He was bigger than Andover, but not as big as the man remembered. "Metal must be heated and shaped. So, too, with people. You have been heated and shaped, but you are not yet complete. Do you understand?"

Andover continued to frown. "Not entirely."

"Good enough." Drask nodded. "When you were with Wheklam what did you learn?"

"How to build a boat. How to judge the winds on the water. How to swim. How not to drown. How to fish if I need food." The words came freely and Andover felt an unsettling sense of awe. He was not aware that he had learned these things, not on a conscious level, but now that he spoke, the comprehension was there. He had never sailed, never built a boat, never fished, but the knowledge was there as surely as he understood how to walk.

"Wheklam held you under the waters. You were tempered by the touch of a god. Now you must be heated again and shaped again."

"What do you mean?"

"Andover. You have worked as a blacksmith. You understand the process of making a tool or a weapon. You have forged your own weapon and killed with it, yes?"

"Yes. My hammer." The hammer was gone now, of course, but he'd made it and used it well.

"Your hammer. The first of many weapons you will make in your life. You have the skills to make more. You will do so before you leave here. Metal will be shaped and formed and you will carry a new weapon, whatever you decide to make."

Andover nodded. If the gods wanted him to make weapons he would. It was the least he could do in exchange for all they had given him.

"Gods make tools and weapons, too, Andover. You are one such weapon. Each and every one of the Sa'ba Taalor is a weapon of the gods. We have shaped them, as we are now shaping you, do you understand this?"

Andover considered those words carefully before nodding.

"Are you… Am I Sa'ba Taalor now?"

"That is for you to decide." Drask looked at him and then moved his arms away from Andover. "You can leave here and go back to your people. Step through that spot…" He pointed to the image on the wall. The image that moved, where water lapped at the edge of the river, and the scent of cooking meats brought a rumble to Andover's stomach and a flutter of familiarity to his heart. "Three steps, and you are in Freeholdt, never to return here."

Drask crossed his thick arms and continued to look at him. "Freeholdt is not yet touched by the Sa'ba Taalor, though it will be soon. You would have time to get away before that happened and you have the skills to survive should you wish to avoid my people. Your life will not be easy, but it will be yours."

The Silver Hand walked a few paces now and gestured to the ground, where seven faces of seven deities glowered toward the ceiling. "Or you can stay here and finish what you have willingly started. You can be shaped by the gods, forged into a different being. Your life here will not be easy, either, but you will be accepted by the Sa'ba Taalor and you will have a purpose in this world beyond finding your next meal."

"What will I learn from you, Ordna? If I stay, what will you teach me?"

"Do not ask what I will give you, Andover Lashk. Merely know that you will learn and be shaped. You will be prepared for war."

Life is pain. War is change. The raw materials of life hammered and shaped into something with a purpose.

He did not ask if he had to choose now. He already knew the answer. He was in the presence of a god and gods did not wait on the whims of mortals. He could only guess how rare it was for a god to give a mortal options.

Andover turned his back on the land where he had been born and walked toward the image of Drask Silver Hand.

ELEVEN

"Why are you still here, Cullen? Everything is gone already. Everything is dead." Deltrea's voice harped at her. Deltrea was dead, of course, but it seemed not even death could shut the woman's mouth.

"I told you before, I'm waiting for something."

If she looked in the direction of Deltrea's voice she could almost see her friend, long and lean and smiling that lazy, lusty smile of hers. She missed Deltrea more than she would have thought possible. Enough, it seemed, to let herself wallow in the madness of fantasies.

She'd have thought she could do better when it came to spectral companions, but apparently her mind wanted Deltrea and she had to accept that.

"Does this make you our new queen?"

"What?" She looked toward the voice but there was no face this time. "No. Why would it?"

"You told me once you were related to the queen, didn't you?"

"No. That was my grandmother." She waved the question away. Or maybe she waved at a fly. It was hard to say sometimes.

Cullen had watched the grayskins move on and the people of Trecharch stumble past her, though she could not have told anyone which came first. Days moved past her with no true recollection beyond the end of everything she had ever believed in. She might never have moved again if hunger hadn't finally snuck past her shock and bitten hard enough for her to notice.

In exchange for her vigilance, she had gotten Deltrea's voice in her head. A blessing, perhaps, or a way for the Mother-Vine to make her suffer even more.

The Mother-Vine lay dead before her, burned and hacked and destroyed. That fact sat as well with her as the notion that sun would never shine again or that the Great Star would fly away and find a new home somewhere far away. None of the concepts made sense in her eyes.

She spent a week foraging in the woods around the ruins of the tower and circling the ruin of the Mother-Vine. What she touched failed to feel real under her fingertips. Her skin was numb and she could not escape the horror of what her world had become.

Sections of the great vine fell from the trees and shattered to the ground at random intervals and Cullen watched. It was all she could do. In time she found a decent bow and gathered arrows. Neither were hard to find. The grayskins had not claimed anything but the bodies of the fallen and most of her people who had gone past wouldn't have known how to use a bow or were too weak to use one. Those she saw were not the sort to fight. The old, the diseased, the young. The rest were gone along with the Mother-Vine.

On the ninth day Cullen climbed to the remains of the Mother-Vine and slowly scaled the great husk. She wasn't quite sure why, except that she seemed to have a need.

That was the only reason she had stayed this long anyway.

"What are you going to do, Cullen? Whittle your name in the remains?"

"You're very rude, Deltrea."

"Well, death has made me like manners less."

"Nothing could make you like manners less. Shouldn't you be off fucking Lurne's ghost?"

"Now who's lost her manners?" There was a pause and Cullen scaled the remains, pulling herself up the vast trunk of her dead god with ease. "Besides, I haven't found any other ghosts to speak with."

"Just as well. I'd be bored without you."

"That's why I stay, you know. To save you from boredom."

"I have lost my mind and you are an echo of that loss."

"You have lost your way, Cullen. There's a difference."

"Well, should you happen to know the way I should go, please feel free to tell me. Otherwise I'm just staying here until the winter comes around again."

Deltrea's voice stayed silent, but that was just as well. Cullen would have never noticed. She was too busy looking at the brilliant slice of green hiding in the ruined trunk of the Mother-Vine.

Had anyone told her that she would reach for that sliver of green in a vast field of dead, gray ruin, she would have laughed at the notion. Cullen was simply not that brave and would have been the first to tell anyone as much.

Still, her fingers reached, and touched, and burned with the vitality of the treasure she found hidden in the depths of a dead god.

Deltrea no longer spoke to her. Instead she screamed. Cullen screamed, too.

•••

Drask moved as carefully as he had for days now. He could have made noise and he had no doubt he would not have been heard over the sound of complaints coming from below. Tega was quiet. The larger of the men was quiet as well, but the small one, the one he thought of as the digger, continued to bemoan the lack of food.

He reached into his pouch and took out a logga nut. Most people required a knife or a rock to open one of the hard nuts. Drask had a silver hand. He found it very useful for just such situations.

They had made surprisingly good time. Despite the constant complaints, the digger led them well enough, careful to avoid the more obvious pitfalls.

Drask merely followed, as he had been ordered.

Until they reached level ground.

Everything that he had already seen in the depths of the Mounds was here as well, only more so.

There were columns of crystalline rock that held hidden things within the murky depths; half-seen bodies and remnants of other forms. Near his left hand he could see a human head, burnt and blistered and torn, suspended in the stone and staring with one wide eye in his direction. He did not fear such things, but they made him uncomfortable.

When Ydramil spoke it was with Ganem's voice. Ganem was the King in Silver and so this was not at all surprising to Drask. Her voice was smoky and sultry and Drask closed his eyes, delighted to hear the familiar tones.

"It is time, Drask Silver Hand. You will soon learn secrets never meant for the Sa'ba Taalor."

Drask nodded his head, fully aware that the god knew and could see all that he did.

"There are places forbidden to your people for your

protection. This is one such place. But there are also secrets here, for even gods have their secrets. You are trusted as none of your kind have been trusted before in this. Think carefully before you react. Know that your actions and words will have consequences."

Drask spoke softly, but he spoke. "Ydramil, I have served all of the Daxar Taalor. I have lived in each land and studied the ways of every king and every god. Yours is the path of reflection and consideration. I have chosen to follow your ways. I will not disappoint you."

"The Fellein will soon find what they have sought. Here there is a weapon that can be used against us. It is also a weapon that can be used by us and for us. Look upon their discovery when the moment comes and if you would honor me, take up that weapon in my name."

"How will I know this weapon, Ydramil?"

"You are a warrior, Drask. You will know it as you have always known weapons. You will see it for what it is."

The voice faded, but the presence did not. For this moment in time Ydramil kept close watch on Drask and that by itself was enough to make him understand the gravity of the matter ahead.

Drask watched the Fellein as they moved across the flat surface of the ground and closer to the source of the light they had been seeking for so many days.

"By the gods, Vonders! Do you ever stop complaining?" His voice was louder than he'd meant it to be, but the sentiment was sincere and Nolan glared at the source of his frustration.

"No, not often." Vonders looked back at him and smiled. It was the first time Nolan had seen the man look remotely cheerful in the last two days.

"You've enough of your trinkets to buy a castle when we get home. You should be celebrating, not pissing about how hard your existence is."

Vonders shrugged and patted the pouch he'd sewn into his cloak. "Can't spend a fortune here. It isn't worth a fortune here, and even if it were, I've still got to finish this nonsense."

Nolan knew that Orly was only complaining to hide the fact that he was terrified. The nightmare that had killed Tolpen had been unsettling enough, but when they found Tolpen's corpse far below them several truths became evident. First that the thing Tega called a Mound Crawler was not dead. There was no sign of the vast body. Second that other things were alive down here. Hart's body had been chewed on a great deal. Most of his face was gone and the droppings of whatever had fed on him were nearby.

Tega reached into her cloak and pulled out three pieces of pabba fruit that should not have been there. They were fresh and smelled as perfect as a sunrise over the mountains looked.

"Eat," she said. He could see the strain on her face. Though she had explained little, he understood from her words that sorcery of any sort had a cost. Getting fresh fruit from another part of the world might have seemed like a parlor trick to some, but there were no fruit stands here and however she had managed the feat she had to reach a very great distance to gather the feast.

Vonders snatched the fruit and sniffed it eagerly.

"Gods, Tega. Now if you could just manage a bit of bread and a good cheese."

Nolan looked carefully at Tega. "Thank you, but do you need this more than me?"

"I can manage on one fruit, same as you." She smiled and he felt his stomach flutter. He had seen her kill with a gesture, had watched her quite literally make a monster explode before his eyes, but she was still capable of smiling and making him forget all of that. She was lovely, true enough, but that wasn't it. She was also kind when she did not have to be and that forgave many sins in his eyes.

"I think the glow is stronger here." Vonders's voice had lost some of its waspish edge now that he was eating.

"It is," Tega agreed. "I think we have almost reached our destination."

"Then why have we stopped here?"

Tega smiled in his direction. "Because we are tired. We are thirsty and we are hungry. Better to allay those troubles before we face whatever comes next, I think."

Nolan nodded his head. There was wisdom in the notion and he was certainly tired enough.

The fruit was perfect, fresh and sweet and juicy. He made himself savor it instead of wolfing the food down. Vonders did not follow the same philosophy.

Nolan looked away from the other man and scanned the area above them. There was a lot of darkness up that way and he could only guess that they had descended close to a thousand feet. He was wrong. Drask would have pointed out that they were closer to five thousand feet down.

"I hope that if we find a weapon against the Sa'ba Taalor that it is light."

Tega frowned and pulled a section of pabba fruit from the whole. "Why?"

"I will do what must be done, of course, but I have no desire to carry a great weight all the way back up there."

A second later they were all looking at the vast distance they had covered.

Vonders sighed. "The problem isn't the weight so much as

the entire thing will be uphill."

Tega laughed at that, the sound echoing away from them and bouncing back. The look of horror on her face when the sound started was enough to make both of the men with her smile.

It was as close as Nolan could remember to being genuinely relaxed in days. He finished his food and licked the juices from his fingers, relishing the taste. By the time he had finished the others were long done.

"We should go." Vonders spoke almost too loudly and Nolan looked at the other man. He gestured with his hand, pointing in the direction that they'd come from. Nolan looked that way but only after starting to collect his belongings. The move hid his taking the time to look where Vonders pointed.

He barely managed to keep his face calm when he saw the giant moving carefully down the path.

The man was enormous, but moved with the grace of a cat.

Before any more time had passed, Vonders had a throwing blade in his hand and Nolan tried to get his attention and stop him before he could throw. The challenge was to do so without being noticed himself.

He was too late. Vonders Orly was a clown half the time and he was greedy to a fault, but he was also a trained soldier and he had moved through the periphery of the Blasted Lands a hundred times or more. He knew how to handle his weapons and he knew how to aim at a target.

The blade cut the air silently and moved for the shadowy form. If the blow was not perfect, if the enemy did not get injured, but instead merely noticed the attack, they were going to suffer for Vonders' actions.

The blade sailed flawlessly into the darkness and the man moved, stepped to the side and swept his hand at the spot where the blade should have buried itself into him.

The man's head turned and his eyes flashed with a light all their own.

He made no sound as he moved, but instead came in fast, charging toward Vonders. If the scavenger had thought to escape before he was struck, he failed in his efforts. The man came out of the semi-dark and drove his fist into Vonders' chest with a hard, wet noise. Vonders let out a grunt and fell back, his face twisted with pain.

As Vonders fell backward the man moved in closer again and drove his knee into the muscles of his attacker's thigh. The thick bone snapped. Nolan watched the way Vonders' leg bulged unexpectedly and then saw the bone rip free of the muscles around it. Vonders never even screamed. He got lucky and passed out before the pain could fully register.

The man turned, his entire body lowered into a crouch, and his right hand glimmering oddly in the faint light. His left hand held a blade of some sort, but from his current distance and in the dim light, Nolan couldn't quite make it out.

The fight was over before Tega even noticed it was happening. That was hardly her fault. She was not trained in fighting situations and besides, the entire thing had happened in two heartbeats.

"Drask Silver Hand!" Tega stepped forward, her hands held out at her sides, showing clearly that she held no weapons.

The giant nodded, but his attention remained firmly focused on Nolan. "Put down the weapon. Do not make me hurt you."

It was only then that Nolan realized he'd drawn his axe. His grip on the handle was tight enough to make his fingers hurt.

It wasn't conscious, but he calculated his chances of taking the man down before the situation could get worse. The odds were not in his favor. He put the axe away.

Vonders coughed and groaned, drifting slowly back toward consciousness. Nolan knew he would wake properly soon enough and that the pain of his leg would come down on him like a felled tree.

"You're following us?" Nolan could think of nothing else to say.

"I am." There was an odd tone to the man's voice. A sibilance that made Nolan's flesh shiver.

"Why?"

"My gods wish me to know what you do down here. I obey the desires of the Daxar Taalor."

Nolan nodded. He wanted to stall for time but could think of nothing to say.

"You've broken his leg." Tega had moved forward to examine Vonders where he lay on the ground.

"He attacked me."

"Well, yes, you were following us."

"Had I wanted you dead, you would be dead." Drask looked down at her. The man's face was broad, his jaw was strong and squared and his longish hair tied back away from his face. His skin was gray and looked lifeless, but he lived and moved and breathed. His eyes glowed, much like a cat's in the right light. It was an unsettling effect and Nolan found himself wondering if the stranger could see as well in the dark as a feline. His face was mostly hidden in the darkness but Nolan could see that something was off about the way his mouth moved.

When Drask came closer he saw and understood what that something was. The lips of the man's mouth were sealed into a scar. At regular intervals along that scar slits ran from his chin to just under his nose. Each of those slits moved as he spoke. Each revealed a hint of teeth and gums.

Nolan looked away and forced himself to breathe. This was an abomination. Not as severe as the dead things that had moved and attacked when he was on his way to Tyrne a few weeks earlier, but just as unsettling and offensive to his senses.

Drask said, "You are Tega. The apprentice to Desh Krohan." He moved around her, his unsettling eyes scanning the area.

"I am. We are here. We are here to find a way to end the war between our peoples."

"You seek a weapon that will stop the war." Drask nodded. He moved his hands and Nolan saw the metal appendage that took the place of a real hand. He saw the fingers move, the hand flex, and bit down on his own lip to stop from screaming. He was not a cowardly man, but the unnatural things he ran across unsettled him.

"Do you seek a weapon, Drask?"

"I seek what my gods ask of me."

"That's not a no."

"Neither is it a yes."

"Why are we at war, Drask? Why did one of your people kill the Emperor?"

Drask shook his head. "I do not know. I traveled with Andover Lashk and others, and I heard about the murder only after I returned to the Taalor Valley."

"I can't mend this. You've broken his leg and his chest is bleeding." Tega spoke softly, but there was little else to hear.

"He should not have attacked me."

"You should not have followed us." Nolan spoke without thinking. He knew the situation was tense and yet he opened his mouth and made comments that would not ease the problems. His father would have disapproved and he felt shamed as a result of that knowledge.

"I am here. You are here. This is either a peaceful situation from here on out, or we fight and I kill you." Drask spoke calmly and looked directly at him. Nolan did not know how skilled Drask was – though the evidence of his abilities was currently bleeding and broken on the ground – but the stranger had enough confidence for a dozen men.

Nolan took a step toward him and Tega shook her head. "Stop. Do not provoke him, Nolan."

There it was. He clamped down with his jaw and stopped himself from saying something foolish. This girl was in charge of what he did here. He did not have to like it, but he had to accept it.

Of course, the girl was also a sorcerer and had killed monsters that slapped him aside with ease. It would be best if he didn't think of her as weak.

Drask turned away from him as if he didn't matter, and Nolan felt himself bristle at the notion.

Best not to say anything foolish. Best not to do anything to escalate the situation. He didn't know enough about his enemy aside from the fact that he looked monstrous.

Still, he desperately wanted to beat the man down.

Drask started walking, heading toward the very thing they had been traveling to reach for the gods knew how long.

"Where are you going?" Tega spoke before Nolan could.

"I intend to find the source of the light."

"What about Vonders?"

Drask frowned, puzzled for a second. The expression was doubly unsettling as it pulled the muscles in his mouth – mouths?! – in strange ways. "Your man is not my concern."

"You cannot go on without us."

"I can." Drask looked at her. Studied her. Perhaps weighing

his chances of surviving her powers. Did he know what she was capable of? Nolan was unsure. "I will."

"We cannot leave him here." She sounded frustrated.

"Have your man carry him." He spoke slowly now, as if to a person of dubious capacities. "He is not my concern."

Without another word Drask was moving on, heading toward the potent illumination in the near distance. It was no longer a matter of hours or days, but of minutes to reach that spot.

Nolan looked at Tega. He looked at Vonders, broken and bleeding on the ground.

There was a mission to consider.

He followed Drask.

After only a moment, he heard Tega following and he damned himself for his lack of compassion.

Half a continent away the Pilgrim marched, and behind him a growing column of people moved along and kept pace. They were tired, but they understood that this was a mission of the gods themselves.

They knew this because the Pilgrim's closest followers told them as much. They knew this because they had seen his actions on their own, or heard of his amazing deeds. They knew this because though none of them had brought much by way of supplies, still they did not go hungry and they did not go thirsty.

In Goltha the Pilgrim had stopped and approached the greatest of the temples to Etrilla armed with only a simple sword and his faith, and come away with two hundred followers. Each of those followers had enough supplies to stop the hundred already following from going hungry, and when their food ran out, there were others who offered food and clean water.

He was a quiet man, but he answered questions when asked. He spoke with conviction and he spoke with a deep knowledge of the past that was haunting to those who listened to his answers.

That was all the news that Merros Dulver had received of the man so far and he was not comfortable with the information as it stood.

Desh nodded when they looked over the pages of written descriptions. "Well, it's different."

"Yes it is. I also have to wonder where this man is coming from and what he's doing."

"As well you should." Desh looked toward him. "He's a part of the greater sum of parts, isn't he?"

"You're being cryptic. It suits you well enough, but now is not the time."

Desh waved his hand, dismissing the notion. "It's always a good time to be cryptic. Comes with the territory. But in this case I'm being accurate. He's up to something. We have no idea what. He could be coming here to help. He could be coming here to lead a small gathering of people who believe that they must be here to seek protection or to volunteer themselves for some obscure purpose."

"It's not really a small gathering, Desh. There are over a thousand of them."

Again he waved a dismissive hand. "It's a matter of perspective, really. We have fifty times that number trying to find homes in the city already."

Merros rubbed at his temples. His headache was back and growing exponentially the longer he spoke to the First Advisor. "Yes, and that's a problem."

"Not your problem, Merros. We have a head of the City

Watch here. He has to deal with the overflow."

"All of us have to deal with it, Desh. I've already had to chase off several squatters from my own home."

"Hardly an issue I'd think. You're normally not there but for a few hours."

"You see? Right there. You think you're being witty, but really, it's only annoying."

"No, really it's funny. You're just too close to appreciate the humor of the situation. If Nachia were here she'd agree with me."

"Where is the Empress?"

"She's dealing with her family. More precisely, she's having them dealt with. The Inquisitor. What's his name?"

"Murdro, I think."

"Darsken Murdro, that's right. He's investigating who, exactly, was behind the murder of her cousin. All signs lead to another of her cousins. She's not taking it very well."

"Shouldn't one of us be with her?" He felt his guts tighten. "What if someone tries something foolish?"

Desh smiled at him. "You have obviously never dealt with Darsken Murdro. The only thing anyone will do around him is behave and pray he does not notice them."

"I've only seen him from a distance but he seemed pleasant enough."

"Oh, he is," Desh nodded. "So is a murder rose until you decide to hold the blossom in your hand and sniff it. Perfectly inviting and even charming until the poisons burn your skull open."

"By the gods, man, where do you hear about these things?"

"I was the one who advised Empress Detelia to outlaw the farming of the things. Foolish sort of thing to cultivate in the first place, but they were very popular eighty years ago."

There had been a time when Merros was absolutely convinced that Desh Krohan was a charlatan and spread rumors of his power strictly to make sure everyone thought he could perform sorcerous acts. He had no doubt in his mind that Desh worked on the rumors and convinced as many as he could. He also had no doubt the man could truly work sorcery though he had never actually seen Desh himself do anything at all that qualified as mystical aside from wear his robes.

"So the Empress is safe?"

"She has a dozen armed guards and an Inquisitor. Not even her worst blood relatives are foolish enough to try anything right now."

That was one less thing for him to worry about and Merros was grateful for it. "Back to where we were. What are we supposed to do about this Pilgrim fellow?"

"Absolutely nothing. Let him continue on his way. If he is a threat and he and his followers reach the city, the City Guard will handle him. You have more pressing matters to attend to. Like Elda. How are we going to handle that matter?"

Merros shook his head. "We're not. Elda did not deliver their conscribed allotment of soldiers. They fell short despite the threat of levies and fines and a lack of protection from the Empire. So now they face levies, fines and an attack from the Sa'ba Taalor. Should the invaders move past Elda, they will find that we have amassed a few surprises for them."

"Levies and fines?" Desh frowned. "Aren't they the same thing?"

"Technically, I suppose. In my case the levies are the number of soldiers I will take by force from any would-be refugees from the battlefront. The fines will be monetary. Wars cost money. Failure to offer the proper levies will add to the fines."

"You are a cruel man, Merros Dulver."

"I prefer to think of myself as practical." His head hurt.

"That expression right there. The way you rub at your temples when you think of how much you have to do? That is why I made you a general."

"Nice of you to confess. And you're saying my pain is beneficial to my career?"

"It means you're the right person for the task. If you didn't mind using Elda as an example I'd think you heartless. An army should have a heart."

"Hearts don't win wars."

"I disagree."

"I'm telling Nachia that you confessed to manipulating me into being a general of the Imperial Army and that it was not, in fact, her cousin."

"I never denied it. I merely clarified. I suggested. He signed the papers."

"Are you sure Nachia's safe?"

"She's still in the castle. She's as safe as she's likely to get."

Swech watched the Empress as she moved across her court, her arms behind her back clasped together as if she feared letting them free of each other, where they could lash out.

She was hidden, of course. Dressed in her black clothes and wearing her veils, to hide away hair and face alike, despite her hiding place, because caution required not being seen or recognized. The crawlspace where she hid herself was concealed in the very wall of the large room. There was a reason that she'd taken the key from around the neck of Libari Welliso when she'd killed him. Access to several hidden chambers had gained her access to several different keys before Tyrne burned. No one looked for the keys now, because they were assumed destroyed with the city.

The gods were wise.

The Empress of the Fellein Empire was in a bad mood. Even if she had not heard the words spoken, Swech would have understood the body language. Tension in muscles throughout the woman's body. Her hands not still, but clenched with each other as if fighting for dominance. Her posture stiff and her teeth grinding against each other.

She was not the same carefree creature she had been before ascending to the throne of her Empire. That made her at least moderately wise.

"My cousin, my blood and yours, is dead! He was murdered two nights ago in the company of cutthroats fresh from a boat that delivered them to the city. What I want to know is *why* he was murdered. The investigation so far has led to a very real possibility that one of the members of our family is responsible. One of the people in this room."

There were twenty or more members of the same family, the royal bloodline, apparently, all in the room with her. If she understood correctly, they were all in line for the throne if Nachia died. Blood was what mattered in Fellein, not skills or faith. And wealth. She was learning that quickly enough. If one had money one could open any number of doors.

She shook off her reverie as the family members present went through their motions. They nearly crawled over each other in an effort to declare their innocence. She knew which of them was involved, of course, though he was not responsible for the death in this case. His hired blades were supposed to kill the Empress. That was why she had killed them.

The gods wanted the Empress alive. She did not know why and she did not need to know. Was she curious? Of course.

But the certain knowledge was not required and not knowing did not cause her to suffer. The gods had wanted the Emperor dead. They wanted the Empress alive. That was all she needed to know.

The guiltiest of the parties, Laister Krous, crossed his thick arms and scoffed. "What possible purpose could any of the family have for murdering Windhar? Who is served by such foolish notions?"

Nachia Krous turned on her cousin with a smile on her face that would have made most enemies hesitate.

"Who indeed, Laister? The most solid connection we have to the brigands found with Windhar lead to Losla Foster."

He was good. Laister Krous barely even twitched.

"Darsken Murdro." Nachia gestured with her left hand to a dark-skinned man with a powerful build and long black hair that exploded into tails of differing lengths. He was dressed unremarkably, and carried a short staff. "Inquisitor Darsken Murdro is here to speak with each of you. You will answer his questions to his satisfaction and only after you have done so will you be allowed to leave this chamber."

Once again the protests started. Not everyone raised their voices. A few looked toward the dark man with nervous expressions. One of the older women in the group leaned back in her seat and looked coldly toward Laister. Her smile rivaled that of the Empress. It was a promise of pain and suffering on an epic level.

When Nachia Krous continued her voice snapped. "You will do this thing! You will stay here. You will answer his questions! We will know, all of us, exactly what has happened to our kin. Should any of you attempt to leave before Inquisitor Murdro has allowed it, the guards in this room will see you punished."

She moved toward the doors to her private chamber, which meant that she headed straight for the hidden access point above those doors, where Swech was currently waiting. Swech did not move. She did not fear discovery. She was well and truly hidden within walls that were several feet thick.

Her surprise when she saw the Inquisitor looking directly at her could not have been more complete. There was no mistaking it. He was not looking in her general direction. His eyes were on her.

The Inquisitor made a gesture to one of the guards and the man moved closer. Those dark eyes never left her. He spoke softly and the guard looked toward the chamber the Empress had entered.

Swech did not stay around to contemplate how she had been seen. She merely moved, as quickly and quietly as she could, fully accepting that her hiding spot had just been discovered.

The guards entered the chamber of the Empress at the same time Swech was dropping down behind one of the heavy curtains that surrounded the windows of the room.

The guard that grabbed at the curtain to move it aside managed to handle that task and to offer Swech her chance to strike at the same time. His body was exposed as the heavy fabric was pulled away and she drove a blade into his neck without hesitation.

He fell back, choking on his own blood, and Swech helped him along, sending the dying man stumbling across the room to knock aside a small table.

Nachia Krous saw her and her face dropped with shock. She had not expected to find anyone in the room. She should have been prepared – her predecessor had been assassinated after all – but she remained surprised enough to let Swech move past her at a dead run.

By the time the dying guard had collapsed and the Empress had let out a call of alarm, Swech was out of the room and moving down the hallway toward the next wing of the vast structure.

One unfortunate guard came out from a side door as the alarm was sounded. He stared at her and started to draw his short sword. She was already moving faster than he could draw the weapon, but she shifted position and then broke his neck with an elbow strike as she moved past.

Within ten minutes she had vacated the palace. There were other tasks she needed to attend to, and there was little time to dwell on the unexpected discovery. Still, she marked the Inquisitor in her memory as someone to be aware of.

TWELVE

The sun had set and the Imperial Highway was overflowing with the people who followed the Pilgrim.

He stood at the head of the massive entourage and nodded his head in satisfaction. The sky was already dark with perpetual clouds. The volcanic activity in the distance and the burning of Trecharch were enough to guarantee that the stars would soon be hidden behind a thick layer of clouds, but here, for the moment, the Great Star and a few others were still visible.

Sarmin and Lemblo stood on his left. Longrid and Powl on his right. There had been a time when all four of them had been soft. The walking had changed that. Their muscles had hardened as surely as their skin had grown dark with the sun's treatment.

Sarmin smiled at him and he nodded back. His face was not designed for smiling and that was something they had come to understand about him.

"How much farther, do you think?" Powl looked his way as he spoke. Like so many of his followers the man seemed to believe that every word from his mouth came from the gods themselves. He had surrendered the notion that he could convince them otherwise. He spoke with experience, he spoke with the sure knowledge that they needed to reach Canhoon as quickly as possible, but he did not speak with the voice of the gods, not in this instance.

"We have several days' hard walking ahead of us."

"Will we make it to the city in time?"

The Pilgrim looked at Powl and frowned. "We must and so we will."

Powl frowned, too. "There are some who say they cannot walk any further."

"Then some will not make the journey. We must ensure that enough do."

The Pilgrim grew tired of the doubt coming from his follower and looked away from him. He saw the expression on Powl's face. The man wanted words to soothe him and comfort his doubts.

"Believe this, Powl. The gods wish us to succeed. They have given us all we need to prosper in this. We merely have to continue on the proper path. Ours is a sacred path and the way will be cleared of heavy obstacles as has been the case all along."

It seemed enough for the man.

Later, after everyone had settled in for the night – as much as anyone could settle themselves comfortably on a road designed to be traveled by wagons and horses – the Pilgrim saw Sarmin staring at him in the darkness.

"What bothers you, Sarmin?"

"You know what we travel to. Does it concern you at all?" Her brow was knotted with tensions and doubt.

"I was born for this. I slept for a very long time waiting for this event. It was ordained. I am not bothered by what will happen, child. I look forward to it."

"I am scared." She looked away, her face still troubled.

"The weather has been kind to us. We have found the food we need and no one has come up lame, despite Powl's worries. That is because the gods favor us in our mission. We do the will of the gods. We are the instruments of their desires. Do you understand this?"

She listened to his words and slowly the tension left her face. "You are kind to listen to my worries."

"You follow me into the unknown, Sarmin. How can I do less than prepare you for what we know must happen?"

Sarmin closed her eyes and smiled and slowly drifted to sleep.

The Pilgrim did not join her; his mind was filled with the endless possibilities of what could go wrong and how to prevent disasters from stopping them.

The gods had need of the people who followed him. He would see this through. He had no choice in the matter.

His was a sacred mission.

Tarag Paedori looked upon the corpses of his enemies and nodded his satisfaction. The First Lancers had fought well and employed surprising strategies. The archers with them had done their jobs well and over a hundred of the Sa'ba Taalor were dead or maimed as a result. The dead were being taken care of. The injured were being tended to.

The small town that had been an outpost of the Fellein was now gone, crushed under the armies of the Sa'ba Taalor.

To the south and east he could see the smoke from Durhallem's second home. The newly formed volcano roared and spit ashes and flame into the air. Almost directly east of where he and his forces were gathering, Canhoon waited.

There was no rage in his heart. He had offered his anger to

the Empress of the Fellein only because the message he had to convey was made clear to him by Truska-Pren. He needed only look to the skies to know that he did well in the eyes of his god. The clouds that gathered were a sign of his success.

Ehnole stood nearby, her eyes scanning the whole of the eastern horizon. She offered no opinions. She made no statements. She followed orders and even now supervised the removal of the dead.

The Daxar Taalor said to place the dead within a pit and leave them behind. This had already been done. The last of the dead – both Sa'ba Taalor and Fellein alike – rested together now. In death they were no longer enemies. They were merely meat.

At home, in the Taalor Valley, the bodies would have been treated differently. They'd have been offered to the gods by those who killed them. Here they were offered as one in the names of all the gods.

Tarag looked upon the dead and nodded.

"You have done well, Ehnole."

She offered a formal bow and nothing else. She was a proper soldier and that was why she moved up the ranks of the King in Iron with ease. There were no decorations upon her to denote rank. None were needed.

"We offer the dead to the Daxar Taalor." Tarag spoke clearly and as he spoke, all of the people who followed him stomped one foot in unison. At a distance of one hundred feet, those he had appointed earlier repeated his words and again, the Sa'ba Taalor responded by stomping the ground. The ground fairly shook, as it should when the gods demanded.

"We offer our lives to the Daxar Taalor!" Ehnole and all of the others within range of his voice repeated his words and again the ground shook with the feet of the Sa'ba Taalor.

Tarag Paedori raised his arms to the heavens and roared his words for all to hear. "We offer our enemies to the Daxar Taalor!"

As one they raised their arms above their heads. As one they stomped one foot into the ground. As one they repeated his words. Tarag Paedori's blood surged and he looked at his armies. They ranged in age from ten years into their fifties and higher. They served the gods of the Seven Forges as he served the same deities. They obeyed his words but only because the gods demanded it. There was no ego in his words. There was only praise for the gods they had all been raised to serve until their dying days and beyond.

Even Kallir Lundt, the Fellein who now followed their ways, raised his voice and his arms to the gods of war.

"The enemies of our gods will fall before us!"

Oh, how they roared their approval then.

"It is time! Now is the time of the Daxar Taalor!" Without another word he walked forward, heading for his mount and the call to war. A hundred horns sounded their ululations, though they were surely unnecessary. A hundred more responded.

Tarag Paedori knew that the Fellein thought they were great warriors. They also thought that the Sa'ba Taalor were small in numbers. They were wrong. Fifty thousand warriors rode or walked behind Tarag Paedori at that moment and they were but a portion of a much greater army.

"We offer the dead to the Daxar Taalor!" He gestured to the vast pit they had spent over a day digging and then filling with corpses. He marched on, and his forces followed.

And behind them, left to fester in their shallow grave, the dead began to move.

All must answer to the gods of war.

•••

Cullen walked through the ruin of Trecharch and into the lands beyond, where trees did not rise toward the clouds and once upon a time, the open spaces would have terrified her. The road she followed was well traveled and the proof of that could be found in what had been left behind.

Many of the escapees from the Sa'ba Taalor had tried to take their possessions with them and a good number discarded those goods when the grayskins came after them. It was a simple lesson to learn: a favored vase is not worth dying for at the hands of a merciless enemy. The road and the areas around it were littered with the items thrown aside or dropped when the enemy came through on a killing rampage. There were no bodies, though there were many areas where it was obvious people had died. Blood painted the dry soil and the places where the dead had fallen still showed signs of the weight of those bodies.

"Where are you going now, Cullen?"

Deltrea continued her tirade of questions and complaints. Sometimes Cullen did not know if she should be grateful or if she should kill herself just to make the noise stop. Still, if Deltrea talked she did not have to think so much, and thinking hurt.

"I'm following the road. I have to get to Canhoon. I have to let them know that Trecharch is dead."

"I should think they already know. They can probably see the smoke." Deltrea's voice sounded hurt. To be fair, she had died somewhere back there. She had every reason to feel hurt.

"That doesn't matter. They need me. I have something for them." Somewhere within her she felt it stir, the life she had snatched from the dead Mother-Vine. She needed to see it safely to the City of Wonders. There was a man there who needed to know about it. She could not see a face, she did not know a name, but she could sense him. He needed to know. It was of the utmost urgency.

The road ahead of her was different. There were people up there. Not a lot, but enough to make her aware of more than the life that burned inside of her.

For a moment she feared it was the grayskins, but no. These were people with flesh that resembled life instead of decay. They were active, and they were moving and speaking the same language that she did.

There were more than ten, but she couldn't have given an exact number. They moved along the road and gathered the salvage that others had left for them to find.

They were destitute, the lot of them. They picked at anything that might have value and carefully placed their treasures in the wagon they brought with them, dragged by two of the saddest-looking horses she had ever seen. She had not seen many, true, but these were old and withered and swaybacked. Cullen wondered if they could have supported the weight of even a small man on a saddle without collapsing. She had her doubts.

Most of them saw her, decided she was harmless and nodded before moving on, but one of the men kept staring, his eyes focused on her arm with an unsettling intensity. It only took her a moment to understand he wasn't looking at her, but at the bow she carried.

She shook her head to warn him away and he frowned, likely trying to decide if it was worth the trouble to try to take from her.

Just to make sure he stayed dissuaded, she notched an arrow and tapped her finger along the fletching to make sure he got the point. Eventually he looked away, muttering under his breath. Cullen decided to keep an ear on the lot of them as she walked past. If he chose to try his luck she'd kill him for his troubles. They were little better than grave robbers in her estimation. Not that she and her stolen bow had any right to judge.

The skies were darker here. The winds stank of ash and worse. There was an aroma of death that came from the south and west, the direction of Jorhuan. She had never been to the town before and knew that she would not be going there now. The stench alone would have deterred her, but that roiling heat in her guts, the Mother-Vine's mark inside of her, told her that it would be a bad choice and she chose to listen to it.

There were others on the road, but as a whole they were broken remnants. There were no soldiers here, only a scattering of scavengers. Of course, some scavengers still had teeth.

The five men who came at her were not overly large, nor were they dressed with any particular adornments that made them threatening. It was the way they walked, the way they looked around that let her know.

One of them nodded an acknowledgment of her. The others did not. All of them moved with too much bounce in their step and she could clearly see the way their hands twitched. It wasn't nerves. They were signaling each other. She didn't know what the signals meant, but she doubted they were of benefit to her situation.

Deltrea agreed. "They mean you harm. I can smell it on them."

Cullen didn't answer. Instead she took the arrow she had already notched and fired it into the first of the men. Her aim was nearly perfect and he staggered back with a new hole punched clean through his throat.

The next arrow was out, drawn and airborne before the scavengers had a chance to react. The first man was painting the road with his blood, his hands trying to staunch the flow and failing. A second let out a long, warbling scream, the arrow sticking out of the side of his face. She could see that the arrowhead was embedded deep into bone. He would live, but there'd be no fight in him.

Two of the others froze, the third and the last of them took a few strides in her direction and finally stopped when she aimed at him and shook her head. "I lost to the grays. Doesn't mean I'm not trained. Gather yours and back away, or you'll all die right at this spot."

The one she'd skewered in the face was still screaming. She couldn't blame him. He was trying to speak but his words were lost in the gasping, wailing bellows that came from him. He could have been mistaken for a Pra-Moresh.

The cockiness they'd had before was gone. The brave one, the one that had got closer, was still considering his options, but she could see the other two had already grown wiser from the encounter.

"Keep looking at me, and I'll split your eye open. You doubt me, you take one more step this way and test my skills."

For several seconds she thought she might have to carry through but he finally backed down, looking at his fallen friends and letting common sense prevail. He had no weapons. She had a bow and enough arrows to whittle him down to half his size.

She waited several minutes for them to gather their wounded and dying and leave before she continued on.

"You should have killed him, Cullen."

"I know."

"Then why did you let him live?"

"There's enough death here. I can smell it on the wind."

"What if they come back for you?"

"I guess you'll just have to warn me, Deltrea."

"You know I'm dead, right?"

"And yet here you are, still talking to me."

Because part of her saw the wisdom in Deltrea's concerns, Cullen walked faster and, when the road took her past a collection of trees that hid where she had been and she was certain no one could take it as a weakness, she started to run.

She ran for a long while, moving at a pace that should have left her gasping for breath after only a few minutes but didn't. She ran until the sun began to descend, and she did so effortlessly.

Cullen did not consider the impossibility of that any more than she considered the burning ache that the Mother-Vine left inside of her. Possibly she was slightly mad by that point, as those who suffer great loss can become if they think too much. Cullen did not think that was the case. She simply accepted that the fire the Mother-Vine had lit inside of her wanted to be in Canhoon and that she needed to get it there before it could burn her away completely and leave nothing but ashes.

She could not have said how far she would have to go to reach the city, but she knew she was heading in the right direction by the trail of discards cast along the sides of the road.

Inquisitor Darsken Murdro stood before the assembled members of the Imperial Family and smiled pleasantly. He had been doing exactly that for over an hour, not speaking but merely looking from one to the next while they fussed and straightened their immaculate clothes, very likely considering the best way to get out from under his gaze without being punished for their actions.

He was not in a hurry.

Silence can tell a great deal about a person. Most people fail to see that. They think that words are the end of all that a person can learn. Darsken knew better.

Darsken learned as much from what was not said as he did from what was.

He finally walked forward and looked at Brolley Krous. The Empress's brother was a boy, but he was working toward being a man. It had taken remarkably little to find out about his misadventures with the Sa'ba Taalor. His actions since then had been exemplary.

"You are Brolley, yes?"

The young man looked up from his hands and nodded. He had deeply wounded eyes. It took no real effort to see that he tortured himself mercilessly over his past actions.

"I am sorry for your loss. Please, go now, and mourn properly."

The young man rose, nodded once more and then looked at his kin before leaving the chamber.

Several of the family members had thought to leave the room when the earlier disruption had occurred. The guards took care of that very quickly. Darsken had handpicked them, because they had worked with him in the past. They knew what he expected and they were quick to follow his orders.

His knuckles creaked and cracked as he worked his thick fingers over his staff. Most of the Krous family looked at him, hoping that they, too, would be released from his presence.

He looked to Danieca Krous and frowned softly. "You as well, Milady. I am filled with sorrow for your loss."

She smiled but did not move.

"I am fine here for now. I wish to know what you discover."

He'd have bet coins on that being her answer.

Darsken lowered his head momentarily in a sign of respect. One by one he offered his condolences to a great number of the family. This was the town where the Krous clan held the most sway and that was saying a great deal. Even the lowliest of them had wealth and power. They were the ones he released first. He knew exactly who he wanted. He knew precisely who Losla Foster worked for and currently he was the only man who knew exactly where Laister Krous's assistant was resting his head.

He also knew that Laister wanted that information himself.

The catch when dealing with powerful people is that they must never be allowed to see you grow nervous. That was one of the many things that was driven into the Inquisitors. Like patience, it was a very significant part of the examination process.

He smiled softly and looked at the remaining people. "I will leave you now. I will return soon. In the meantime, food and wine will be provided for you."

It was Laister who stood and shook his head. "This is unacceptable! What if I need to relieve myself?"

Bluff and bluster. The man needed to show Darsken who was in charge. Unfortunately for him, the Inquisitor already knew the answer to that question.

"There is a chamber pot in the corner. I made that arrangement earlier."

Laister Krous puffed out his chest and fairly swelled with righteous indignation.

Darsken smiled calmly in the face of the man's outrage. He locked eyes with the man he knew had ambitions for the throne. Eventually Laister looked away, uncertain how to react to a man who stood up to him without even breaking a sweat.

Empathy, Observation and Patience. It would not take much longer.

The weather in Louron remained unchanged by the volcanic eruptions. The swampy region was hot, humid and still.

To hear the Roathians speak of Louron was to hear of a green hell. The land was half submerged; the waters stank; the people were savages, cowards and very likely guilty of sorcery. What land there was teemed with massive trees that dripped a heavy moss, and the insects in the area seemed to have a special love of human blood.

Whatever the people of Louron might think of the Roathians remained a mystery. Very few of the locals willingly left the area for long, and those that did tended to be the sort that wiser people actively avoided.

The stories of the sort of sorcery that the Louron performed were dredged up from the worst kind of nightmares. To hear a good number of the religious leaders speak, Louron dealt with demons (no one could say exactly what a demon was, but they all agreed the things had to be bad), raised the dead with great regularity, and could tear the soul out of a person with a single word and a drop of blood.

Desh Krohan would have been the first to admit that at least two of the rumors had a foundation in truth. As he had never in his long life encountered a demon he was willing to concede that there might be some exaggeration in that category.

The great black ships of the Sa'ba Taalor were allegedly peopled by demons. Grayskinned monstrosities with ferocious bloodlust and a penchant for death. Desh Krohan might have allowed a certain truth to that, too, but would have pointed out that "demon" was excessive.

When the three ships came for Louron they floundered in the shallow waters. The vast structures could move through rivers if the waters were deep enough, a fact that Fellein had recently learned, but the shallow depths of the coastal flats surrounding Louron were too much. After several aborted attempts, the Sa'ba Taalor were obligated to lower smaller boats to work their way toward the shore.

There was little consideration about whether or not leaving their ships abandoned was a wise thing to do. They were at war and the Sa'ba Taalor were warriors.

Fully three days later, when no communication had come from the followers of Wheklam that had made their way to the shore, five more ships were sent.

Understandably, they proceeded with much more caution.

After first examining the three abandoned ships, the captains consulted and decided to proceed together under the leadership of the most seasoned of their group.

The head of the second invading party was a woman named Truatha. She was an excellent tracker – having hunted a great deal of prey through the Blasted Lands over the span of her life, a task that few would willingly undertake – and noticed the signs long before she would have moved forward.

Truatha called a halt and those behind her obeyed. She summoned the other captains to her and they consulted together about what she saw.

"Look there." She pointed to an area where the footsteps of the previous Sa'ba Taalor could clearly be seen. So, too, the tracks of their mounts. The area was a broad, sandy expanse and, after consideration, two of the Sa'ba Taalor walked slowly and carefully across that area, looking for any signs of struggle or traps. There was nothing. The land was solid under their feet and the tracks of their predecessors moved across the terrain in an orderly fashion before disappearing. There were no dropped weapons. There were no telltale signs of bloodshed or even attacks from the closest copse of trees.

The tracks of over a hundred Sa'ba Taalor and a dozen or more mounts simply vanished.

"How is this possible?" The speaker was Lor, who was sometimes Truatha's lover and always a trusted ally. She crouched low to the ground and examined the tracks carefully. "The weather has been good. No rain. The wind has blown some of the sand but not much. They have either vanished from the world or someone has brushed the sand so perfectly that I cannot see a single trace."

Truatha looked at her friend and walked closer, moving with the same caution. Curiosity was an excellent way to get killed if one did not apply the necessary observational skills.

They took their time and studied the area. There was no indication of what had happened to their predecessors.

Truatha asked for ten volunteers. She then picked from the hundred and seventy-three that offered themselves.

Ten hard, skilled warriors walked across that sandy plain and continued on unchallenged. They struck the ground with spears, they fired arrows into the closest copse of trees, but nothing happened beyond what one would expect in those situations.

The ten continued on until they reached the other side of the sandbar and the waters began to fill in the low areas again, all of them puzzled and ready for combat.

"What is this then? Where is the enemy we would fight?"

The only answer came in the form of one old man, stoop shouldered and carrying a small net filled with fish in one hand and a short staff in the other.

None of the Sa'ba Taalor with them spoke the language of the Fellein. They had not expected to encounter anyone. They had been waiting for a battle on the seas, not for an expedition across salt flats and marshlands. They would adapt, of course, but communication would be a challenge.

Still, one had to try.

"Old man!" Truatha called out to him and pointed to him, lest he be confused about the matter.

He looked her way with a puzzled expression and after a moment shrugged his shoulders and moved toward her.

Despite the heat and humidity he was dressed in a cloak over his baggy pants and open-toed shoes.

As he approached he tapped his stick against the sands occasionally. Finally he made his way past the ten, who watched him without acting, and stopped in front of Truatha. He was a short man, as seemed the case with many of the Fellein. He was also thin and older than any man she had ever met in her life. The Sa'ba Taalor who could no longer fight did not live for long.

When he smiled he bared a total of four teeth. His facial hair and the hair on the top of his head was a light gray with occasional darker hairs to remind anyone seeing him that the lighter colors were signs of age.

When he spoke it was in her tongue, though with an accent. "How may I help you this day?"

Truatha managed to hide her surprise. Several others did not.

"We seek some of our people who came here a few days ago. They have disappeared."

"Oh, yes. They were here." He nodded and continued to smile.

"Where are they now?"

The old man looked around and scratched at the scruff of beard on his chin. "They are not here any longer."

"Yes, I see that. Where did they go? Do you know?"

"Ah. I believe they tried to attack some of the people here. That is forbidden." He nodded his head, his smile continuing. Truatha wondered if she had come across a simpleton. There were a few among her people who were not very bright but could fight well enough to live through that flaw.

"What do you mean? Why is it forbidden?"

"The rulers here. The Council of the Wise, they do not permit invasion by force."

"How do they stop it?"

"I am not a member of the council. I could not say." He shook his head. "I must be on my way. My dinner will spoil if I don't cook it soon." He waved the fish to make his point.

He waved one hand and started on his way and Lor came closer, looking on as he resumed his trek.

"He is so old…"

"Yes."

"Do you intend to let him go?"

"Yes."

"What are we to do now, Truatha?"

"He says that fighting is forbidden."

She gestured to one of the ten, a young boy she had never met before. He was eager to show his worth.

With a simple hand signal she sent him to kill the old man.

Either he would succeed, or she would know why.

As is often the case with the young the boy tried to prove his worth with as much flair as he could manage. The knife he threw cut the air flawlessly and passed through the old man as if he were made of shadows.

The old man turned back to look at his would-be attacker and smiled. "You see? Forbidden."

Truatha had followed the blade's progression. When she looked back to the young attacker he was gone.

"Where did he go?" She couldn't have told you exactly who that question was directed at, but it was Lor who answered.

"He faded away." Her voice was strained.

"What do you mean?"

"He was there. I saw him throw the knife and as it left his hand, he faded. Like mist."

Truatha gestured to another of the ten. This one was older and possibly more cautious. She moved toward the old man and drew her sword, a long, sharp affair with a curved blade.

The old man looked at her as she came closer and shook his head. "I would not."

The girl's name was Hrua. She was a skilled fighter and moved in quickly, aiming a blow that should have severed the old man's head. The blow never reached him. Truatha saw it this time: as Hrua attacked, her body blurred out of focus and then vanished completely.

"What did you do?" The words were roared at the old man, who continued on his way, a soft and sad smile on his wrinkled features.

"You cannot attack us. The Council of the Wise does not permit it." He tapped his stick in the sand and water of a low spot. "There is no way around this law. If any of you attack, you will fade away."

"Where have they gone?"

"There is a place." His smiled slowly changed into a frown. "It is not a place you want to go. There is no way back from it."

After only a few moments' consideration, Truatha called back her forces and headed for the ships.

"Where are we going?" asked Lor.

"We cannot fight this."

"We are surrendering?"

"No." Truatha shook her head. "There is no one here to surrender to. We are simply not going to fight this."

"I don't understand." Sometimes she wondered about how smart Lor was. She often overlooked the times when the woman had trouble with thinking things through because she was a brilliant fighter and fun in bed, but now and then it hurt her to admit her friend was not stubborn, merely stupid.

"There is no point in fighting someone we cannot hurt or attack without hurting ourselves. I will fight a warrior. I will not fight a rock. I will fight an army, but I cannot fight the winds of the Blasted Lands. I will fight a ship of enemies, but I will not fight a wave that will crush my crew."

She paused a moment. "Should we attack these people, we become as smoke in a hard breeze. I saw this with my eyes and you did, too. And so we will no longer fight them."

Lor nodded her head. There were plenty of sailors and warriors among the Sa'ba Taalor. Though the crews would be working longer hours they divided their forces and regained control of the other three ships.

Truatha was wise enough to know that she was not the king. Donaie Swarl would decide what happened next. Had Wheklam spoken to her at that moment she would have obeyed her god, of course, but barring that, she deferred to her king.

There are many reasons that people are afraid of the Louron. The Sa'ba Taalor learned one of them that day.

"We haven't spoken much of late." Nachia's voice was soft and bordered on cautious. That meant she was worried about him, so Desh put on his brightest voice and smiled reassuringly.

"No, we haven't. That pesky business with the Sa'ba Taalor keeps getting in the way."

She smiled obligingly. The problem with people who are close to you is that they can often tell when you're lying, whether or not that lie is made with words. She could tell. There was nothing he could do about that.

Rather than dwell on the obvious, Desh deflected the worry with a question. "Has your Inquisitor discovered the guilty party yet?"

"Oh, he knows. He's known for quite some time. He just wants to give my dear cousin every chance to confess before turning him over to me."

"And what do you intend to do about the situation?"

"Laister was planning to have me assassinated. I know that's a traditional manner of handling the internal problems in my family, but I don't particularly appreciate it in this case." She walked around Desh's private chambers as if she owned the place, which to be fair, was technically true.

Nachia plucked an apple from a bowl of fruit and commenced eating it. "I believe I'll have him executed properly."

"Really? What a novel idea."

"Do you disagree?"

Desh smiled. It was the sort of smile that had made more than one person pale when dealing with him.

"You have an interesting quandary. On the one hand, you have every reason to have Laister executed. Doing so could, depending on who you talk to, even cement your position as a ruler who will tolerate no nonsense. On the other side of this debate, many would argue that solidarity within the Imperial Family is a must in times of war."

The expression she fired his way was pure venom. "And

what would you have me do, old man? Should I promote him to First Advisor?"

"Look carefully at my contract. You don't have the right." He smiled.

"I can't very well let him go free."

"Of course you can. He is guilty and you know it and I know it and he knows it – and more importantly he knows that we are very well aware of his actions. The likelihood is that he'll be worrying over every little sound he hears for the next year. You already have his man in custody and can certainly make an example of him if you feel the need."

"I don't like it and I don't trust Laister. He'll try again."

"Strip him of all that he owns and he'll never do anything of the sort again. Remove him from the family by Imperial Decree. No name. No title. No property."

Nachia chewed at the apple for a moment, obviously intrigued. She was not known for her kindness. She could be kind, she was ruling as well as he'd hoped she would, but she was not always the kindest of souls.

She shook her head. "He still has information and influence. Too much of both. Even if he is stripped of everything, he has enough knowledge to cripple half the family. Not me, of course. I never quite got the nerve to dabble the way that he did."

Desh shook his head and grinned. She said that last as if it were a thing to regret.

"If you take everything from him he has nothing. More importantly he also has no name and no protection."

"Who would he need protection from?"

"Without giving the matter much consideration there's Brolley, Towdra, Endon and, of course, Danieca."

"Danieca?"

"Windhar was her grandson, after all."

Nachia looked at him for a moment, the juice from the apple glistening on her lips, the latest bite half-ruminated in her mouth. After a moment she spoke around the morsel, something she would have never considered in public. "Strip him of all he has and his name, you say?"

"I think that's the best way to honor the wishes of all involved, really, and you also take back the holdings that he has owned and misused over the years."

"How much of the Krous fortune rests in Laister's hands?"

"Enough that he can afford to hire twenty cutthroats and attempt to assassinate the Empress without fearing the consequences."

"And are there papers that have to be signed on this sort of situation? I have never actually written out an Imperial Decree before."

Desh walked over to his desk and plucked a freshly written document making the appropriate proclamation from a small stack of papers he had been working on. Nachia read it carefully and nodded.

A moment later she had signed the copy and marked it with her seal.

"You know I used to mock Pathra for listening to your advice constantly."

"You also used to mock me for offering my advice constantly."

"You are an amazing man, Desh."

"I'm an advisor. It's what I'm supposed to do. I advise, nothing more."

"You are a liar, sir."

Desh moved across the room and poured a small glass of sweet wine for each of them.

"I am a liar in that I have not consulted the Sooth. Instead I have one of my associates handling that for me. The last time was... draining."

Nachia suppressed a shudder at the way she'd seen him the last time, drenched in what seemed to be blood and exhausted.

"On matters sorcerous I leave the where and why to you, Desh."

He nodded his head. "I have Jeron working on finding all that we need. He searches now for information regarding what is north of the Seven Forges, on the location of Tega and her escort, on where the different armies of the Sa'ba Taalor are gathering. The news is not all grim, but most of it leans in that direction."

"You cannot reach Tega?"

"She might be too busy to communicate. Something might be stopping her." He took a small sip of his wine. The potency of the stuff was not to be overlooked. "She might well be dead. It's hard to say."

Nachia took a small sip of her own wine and then consumed the last bite of her apple. "Goriah... I'm so very sorry about her death, Desh."

He looked out the window toward the endless gray sky and the distant, seething column of smoke where Tyrne should have been. "Some things are inescapable, Nachia. Death is one of them. We will all achieve that state eventually, even me, and I have been alive for a very long time and have no plans of changing that status in the foreseeable future."

"Your people exploring the world for us." Nachia looked ready to flinch as she asked her next question. "How goes the war against the Sa'ba Taalor?"

"We are currently being attacked from four separate directions, my Empress, and they seem determined to meet here." He walked to the map he had pasted to the wall with wax and pointed. First, far to the east. "Elda is suffering. Merros's plans have worked so far. He let them take one small corner of Elda and has held them off from going any further, but there are doubts he can hold them there. They have machines that can hurl boulders through the air. Not much survives when those rocks land." He poked another spot to the far south, closer to home. "The Louran are holding their own. Reports are that the invaders attacked and then decided to depart. I have no idea as to why, exactly, but they left quickly."

"Can you find out why? It could be of benefit."

"Yes, it could, and I suspect the answer is that Louron has its own sorcerers. Their sorcery is different from mine. Subtler a lot of times. Perhaps your Inquisitor can offer enlightenment." He did his best to keep the edge out of his voice. The Louron were an unsettling people.

"The Sa'ba Taalor have moved to the east of Louron and are attacking along the shores of Corinta. The Brellar have been alerted and should be on their way to the area to work on our behalf."

"Can the Brellar be trusted?"

"There's gold involved. They can be trusted as long as we pay." He looked toward Nachia and saw the sour expression on her face. "It's not a perfect solution, Nachia, but it's all we have. Pathra let the naval forces of Fellein waste away. He trusted the lies and I'm partially responsible for that. I didn't think we would have troubles like this."

"I don't understand this." She took back her wine in one gulp and then gasped. Having done the same a few times he could understand the reaction. When she had recovered from the drink she shook her head and looked at him again. "You have your Sooth or whatever it is and you never knew that this was coming?"

"I've told you before, Nachia, that magic has a cost. Dealing with the Sooth takes more than just a few hours of my life. It takes preparations that can span months. Years, no, decades of effort have gone into learning what I have in the last few months. That is why I have someone else looking right now. My resources have been severely limited. The preparations I had for dealing with the Sooth were in Tyrne. It will be months before I can properly contact them again without having to steal the power I would need from other people."

She shook her head, frustrated. "I have seen a few of the powers you have, Desh. I know that they exist, but sometimes I swear I feel you are deliberately avoiding using them."

"I absolutely am." He looked at her hard then, as he had looked at her when she was younger and reckless and prone to mischief. "I absolutely am avoiding using my abilities."

"What are you afraid of?"

"Losing control." He shrugged and settled back, while she looked him in the eyes, not the least concerned about his stern expression. That had not changed over the years.

"Explain that to me. Losing control of what?"

He held out his hand and spread his fingers wide. The opened hand was lowered until it was only a foot or so from Nachia's face and he focused his will. "Look carefully, my Empress."

It was a trick, really, the sort that apprentices used when they felt the need to show their powers. He created a small electrical charge and held it in the palm of his hand. The glowing bolt jumped from one finger to another, slithering around his hand like a hyperactive serpent. Even if she had touched it, the worst she'd have managed was a tingle and a few hairs standing on end.

"I have seen this trick before, Desh."

"Yes, I remember, you wanted to study. You would have if I hadn't caught you in the act."

It was a bitter point between them from time to time, but the past was the past.

"This is an easy thing, Nachia. This is a sparkle in the air. I could hold this for a dozen days and never grow tired. But as you have already said, it's a trick and little more. What you want, what everyone seems to want, is for me to end this war before it can get any larger."

"Yes. That's exactly it."

He nodded. "Would you have me cast lightning from the sky and burn our enemies into ashes?"

"Could you do that?"

"Very likely. I could obliterate an entire army of them. I would be sore when it was finished, and I would surely be weak for some time, but I could do it."

"Then why won't you?"

"What happens if I miss?"

"I don't understand." She frowned, her lower lip jutting out in a specter of the child she was not that long ago.

"Let's say I aim that lightning storm at Tuskandru. I understand he's the one who destroyed Trecharch. If I aim at him and I make my preparations I have to be careful to aim at the right location. If he moves, if I miscalculate and he is one valley away from where I think he is, then the lightning I send will hit something else."

"Then you send it again and again until you hit him."

"It's not a sword, or an arrow, Nachia. It's lightning. A single stroke can destroy a forest. One blast can kill a dozen people. A dozen of *your* people. Understand me on this, if I cast lightning to kill a living being it will *find* a living being. I can no more control it after it has been cast than an archer can control an arrow after he has let it loose."

She was weighing the possibilities. He hated that fact more than he could say.

The bolt that danced around his hand moved and grew as he willed it, and now it arched around his entire arm, crawling, hissing, releasing tiny tongues of electric outrage that burned the very air. That it was a deadly thing was undeniable.

"I can burn a man with what I hold now, Nachia. I can kill with one touch. But once released it is no longer mine. No more than that arrow I discussed. If I cast this away, it finds a target and destroys it. If I am lucky it only strikes that one target. Perhaps I cast it toward the window and aim for a bird, but the bird moves so my lightning moves on and reaches the river and strikes a boat and burns the cargo and the sailors and the boat and the very water."

"Then you don't miss, Desh."

Desh shook his hand and the lightning grew bolder, writhing around his arm and moving to his other hand, a massive snake of electricity now.

Nachia stepped back a bit. He would have never let her be hurt by it, of course, but she did not know that.

"I could cast a lightning storm to destroy the Sa'ba Taalor in Elda. I can look on a map and see where it is. But there is a great deal of distance between here and Elda and there are mountains, there are birds and rivers and cities. And if the map is poorly drawn, instead of striking the Sa'ba Taalor I have just burned away a thousand people and leveled the town of Rethmar. Or, worse, I am off by a greater amount and Danaher burns."

"You have made your point, Desh."

He threw the lightning and let it strike his map. The paper crackled and burned in an instant. The wax that held it in place melted and the entire affair crumbled in a smoldering mass.

"I can kill one man from a thousand miles away. I have done so. I can create waves that will sink their ships, but I cannot stop those waves from destroying anything else that is nearby when that happens. I can call to the Sooth and ask them to tell me when and where to strike, but what have I said about the Sooth on countless occasions?"

She sighed. "The Sooth lie."

"That is correct."

"You could strike at the Seven Forges."

"I cannot hit what I cannot see and the gods of those mountains, or whatever sorceries they use, have always made it impossible for me to see what lies beyond the Blasted Lands. You know this."

Nachia Krous did not like being outargued. It went against her nature to concede defeat.

"Do you doubt that they have gods, Desh?"

"No. We have seen the things they can do. I couldn't hope to mimic the hands they made for Andover Lashk..." He paused a moment there and swallowed. The boy was gone and it bothered him that he hadn't even considered him for weeks on end. "...or any of the rest of their people. You saw what they did to Merros's soldier, the one with the metal mask for a face. I cannot work that sort of sorcery and I have never heard of it being worked elsewhere, so no. I just don't like the notion of gods being involved."

"Why not?"

"Because it's always possible that gods can do what I cannot and properly aim. If that's the case, what's to stop them from dropping another of their damnable volcanoes right on top of this city?"

Nachia paled at that possibility.

"Remain calm. There are many reasons that Canhoon is called the City of Wonders, my Empress. We are safer here than in almost any other spot in the world."

He hoped that was still true. He hated that he might be lying.

THIRTEEN

Andover Lashk left Ordna with still more knowledge in his head, calculations and equations the likes of which he had never conceived of before. He also left with two short spears and a new bow, complete with a score of arrows.

How much time had passed? He no longer knew.

It did not matter. The gods would do as they pleased and though he knew he was walking and climbing and living as he had to, he also knew that time was not moving the same for him and Delil as it did for others. A fourth Great Scar cut across his mouth like a slash from right to left. As with the previous three, he accepted the blessing of the god Ordna and knew he would do all he could to live up to that blessing.

When he reached the base of Paedle he saw a temple waiting before he even set foot on the sacred ground.

Delil stopped outside the temple and crossed her legs. "Paedle is one of my chosen gods. We have a long understanding. This journey is yours alone, Andover."

The temple was an elaborate affair. The entranceway billowed with a dozen gaudy, diaphanous veils that snapped and fluttered in a breeze coming from inside.

Andover looked carefully at the sharp angles and the

quartet of faceless stone statues at each corner. One statue was of a young girl. Another of an old man. The third of a woman heavy with child, and the final of a male in his prime. All were naked and carved from a glossy black stone flecked with silver. Each head was featureless. No face at all, and only a hint of where ears should be.

Delil pulled out her weapons and began methodically checking all of them again. He did not have to ask if she felt it was necessary. He already knew the answer.

Andover set down his new weapons before he entered the temple of Paedle.

There were walls, he knew that, but upon entering they seemed to stretch away for eternity. There was no horizon for his eyes to rest on.

At first there was nothing but the endless distance of the temple and the breeze but eventually he noticed the movement from the corner of his eye.

The veils he had seen before moved, separate from the doorway where he had assumed they were anchored.

They shifted and danced in the air and as he looked at them they made forms in the wind: here a withered shape crouching; next a tall, thin man reaching toward him.

There had been a time in his life when Andover would have seen a spectacle like that and applauded the street performer likely responsible for such chicanery even as he tried to understand how it was done.

These days he was wiser. As the veils formed another shape and reached for him, he dodged the cloth that tried to touch his body. There was no consideration, merely automatic response.

"You have learned well, Andover Lashk." The voice seemed to come from the shifting veils, but it also filled his head. "Not every weapon is a blade or a hammer."

A moment earlier there had been a dozen cloths of different colors but they merged, shifting into one form. That shape was long and thin and could have been male or female. It was impossible to guess.

Andover bowed before Paedle, arms held out to his sides, his head lowered.

"What is war, Andover Lashk?"

"War is a conflict between two people that cannot be resolved with words and promises." He remembered that one. It was easy.

He never saw the form move, but it was gone. "No." The voice came from behind him and Andover turned quickly, but there was nothing to see.

The figure was next to him, moving around him, a shifting shadow too fast to be seen. His eyes ached from trying to keep up. "War is one way to end a conflict between two people. There are others."

"I don't understand. Aren't you a god of war?"

"What is the best way to win a war, Andover Lashk?" Paedle – and there was no doubt that this was the deity. He could feel the overwhelming presence of a god even if in this case it was almost completely hidden – ignored the question and moved again, drifting away from the area and settling in the distance. Range did not seem to matter. The voice was as clear as ever.

"I don't know. I would think with greater skills and forces?"

"If a thousand solders must move between two mountains to reach their destination, what is the best way to stop them?"

"You could have an army waiting on the other side, where they cannot see their enemies until it is too late." He nodded, pleased with his answer.

"Would it not be easier to block the passage between the mountains?"

"I suppose. If the mountains are close enough together."

"You have spoken with Wheklam and learned of the sea." It was not a question. "If one hundred ships are crossing the ocean to fight against an enemy, what is the best way to stop the invaders?"

"I don't know."

Paedle was there again, next to him, the voice neither male nor female, young nor old. "If the ships burn, or if there are holes in each of them, how will the invaders find their way to distant shores?"

"I–" A shiver tore through his body and Andover dodged to the side as the shape came closer again. Fading from one side and appearing on the other. His iron hand moved and caught at the wrist of the shape. He found nothing to capture but a delicate, needle-thin blade. Had it struck he'd have barely noticed. The blade dripped with a thick, clear syrup.

"If a king seeks war, and orders his people to fight, what happens if that king dies?"

"The war is stopped?"

"Perhaps. It might also be delayed. It might also continue with a different leader, but the new leader might not be as strong, or as capable. If you were to strike at me with a sword, right here and now, how best would I avoid that blade?"

Andover shook his head again.

"I could fight you with another sword. I might have a bow and kill you before you come for me. I could threaten to kill someone dear to you…" For a moment the shape shifted, changed and looked suspiciously like Delil before once again hiding in a cloak of semidarkness. "If I knew of your intentions, I could poison your food, or choke you to death in your sleep. There are a thousand ways I could kill you before you ever drew a sword. There are just as many ways to stop an army or kill a king."

When Paedle moved closer this time the cloak was cast aside and the figure that moved forward was featureless. There was no face, there was no sex, instead the shape continued to change and shift, a column of liquid silver that was almost humanoid, but not quite. The voice came from everywhere even as the image flowed and melted into the ground of the temple.

"The best way to end a war is to make certain that it never happens. The best way to win a war is to change the shape of the battles to suit your needs."

Andover considered those words as he looked around the interior of the temple. It was smaller now, he could actually see the walls in the distance where before there had been nothing, though still larger than even the palace in Tyrne.

"Sit, Andover Lashk, and learn the ways of a silent warrior."

Andover settled himself on the cold, marble floor.

"If I had let this blade cut me?" He set the dagger on the ground and carefully wiped the wetness from his iron hand.

"You would be in great pain and possibly near death. There are many ways in which you must prove yourself. Expect several lessons throughout your time here. None of mine can long survive unless they are aware of all that surrounds them."

The lessons began a moment later.

"How can you stand being in a different body?" Jost leaned against the wall of Swech's bedroom chamber and looked around the room. The bed was large and comfortable. The floor was tiled in dark wood.

"You know the answer to that, little one. The gods make demands and I obey."

"Does it hurt?"

Swech smiled and brushed her hair. "No. Sometimes. This shape is not as well conditioned as my body. There are muscles that I use that this body does not seem to have ever needed. Sometimes I wake up sore." She shook her head and rose from the bench where she prepared herself for the day. She was dressed well enough, but anyone who looked at her before she was completely clothed would have been astonished by the places where she could hide a blade.

"They are soft." Jost's voice held a thin edge to it.

"Not all of them. Never forget that. It is too easy to assume that they are weak, but some of them are very deadly. Some of them are worthy warriors." Again her mind shifted to Merros Dulver. He had seemed soft back when she'd first met him, but she had seen him only the previous day as he walked down the street, and she had heard him speaking with several of his followers. He was a skilled tactician. Had he known she was there he would likely have ordered her death.

It would not have resulted in her death, but he'd have ordered it just the same. He was loyal to his people as she was loyal to her gods. Nothing would change that. If he were weaker, she would not find him attractive despite his pink skin and his godless ways.

No. Not godless. He worshipped the same god she did. That all of her people did. He just called his god by a different name. He called his god by a different name, even if he did not know it.

"Duty."

"Eh? What duty?" Jost tilted her head.

"Never mind. I am thinking aloud."

"What are we to do next?"

"We have caused suspicion in the family. We have saved the Empress not once, but twice, and we have prepared the city."

"Prepared the city for what?" Jost frowned, her arms crossed over her chest. She, too, bristled with weapons, but hers were more obvious.

"The Great Tide rolls to Canhoon from all directions, Jost. We will soon have armies coming here to take this city. They are overcrowded and already cannot support the weight of their own people. When we add the Sa'ba Taalor, they will falter and then crumble."

"How will we prepare the city?"

Swech quickly tied her hair back and covered it with a shawl, as many of the fishmongers and elderly did. The fabrics were dark and helped hide her distinguishing features.

"We will remove the methods they have for escaping when the Great Tide comes."

Jost frowned.

Swech smiled.

"There are three others who left Taalor with me, Jost. There were four but one is dead. The other three have been busy as well, and one of them has prepared something to help us capture our enemies."

Jost craned her head to the side again, but Swech did not answer the silent question. She had no idea as to how she possibly could.

The Pilgrim stared at the foothills ahead of him and nodded his head, satisfied. Three days at most and they would reach Canhoon.

Behind him close to three thousand followers continued to

move. In every town they had crossed, in every city, he had stopped at temples and spoken to the leaders of the different churches. He had spoken and they had listened, drawn to his voice and to the conviction of his words.

The four who were closest to him continued to give him updates, continued to let him know when someone grew too sick to continue or simply changed their mind and tried to sneak away in the night. There was no punishment for fleeing. If their faith in the gods was so weak that they feared doing as the gods asked, then he had no need of them.

This was a sacred quest, a call to arms from the gods themselves, a last chance to fight against the forces sent to destroy everything that the people of Fellein believed in, and the Pilgrim would see it through one way or another, but he would not punish those who lacked the faith to join him.

The gods would see to their punishment instead.

Three days. The sun was setting but they continued on for another hour before he was satisfied that they had traveled far enough.

Once again, no one wanted for food or a place to rest their weary bodies.

The gods provided what was necessary.

Drask looked down at the patterns of light as he had for the last few days, and studied them, fascinated. There were endless patterns, it seemed.

Not far away the Fellein were doing something similar. Tega was, at least. The young man with her paced instead, often scowling toward Drask as if he were the cause of the difficulties they faced.

The lights below them burned, flowing and shifting and whirling, an endless maelstrom of illumination that refused to be categorized. The light was not cold, but it gave off no heat that he could feel. There seemed to be nothing between them and the lights, but currently his backside was planted on that nothing and while he could feel a pressure there, he could not see any reason for him to not be allowed to touch the very lights he was looking at so intently. However, so far, his best efforts had been denied.

He had struck at the solid air with his hand, with his boot, with his axe and even had started a fire with his meager supplies in an effort to understand what it was that kept him from his goal.

There was nothing.

Ydramil said only that he would know when the time was right what he had to do. He would know the weapon when the time was right. He had no doubt that the lights he stood over were that weapon. The challenge of getting to them remained a mystery.

The only good news was that the Fellein had similar luck.

He broke the shell of a logga nut between two of his fingers and slipped the meat into one of his mouths, chewing slowly and methodically.

The young man stared at him, mouth open, and even from a distance Drask could hear the rumble of his stomach. Perhaps if he waited long enough they would simply starve to death and save him from any grief. He had doubts.

There were times when Drask Silver Hand was polite to a fault, especially in comparison to most of his people, but there were also times when boredom did him in. "If you want it, boy, come take it from me."

The lad was large for a Fellein, but that he was young was also obvious. He was gangly and too thin and also he had very few noticeable scars.

He balled his fists and came for Drask. Maybe it was hunger. Perhaps, he, too, was tired of trying to solve the puzzle of how to reach their prize after waiting for far too long.

As the boy came toward him Drask rose to his feet, grateful for a distraction after too long lost in contemplation. The boy did not draw a weapon and Drask held to that standard.

Tega called out, "Nolan! No!" but it was too late. The youth charged, one balled fist curled back and ready to launch at Drask.

Drask slipped to the side and drove his elbow into the side of the boy's head. Not hard enough to take him down, but certainly with enough force to make him foggy in the brain.

Nolan staggered and came around faster than Drask would have expected, his face twisted into the same sort of rage he'd shown when dealing with the Mound Crawler. He let anger ride him. That was a strength and a weakness both.

Drask exploited the weakness.

"Come! Come get your meal, boy! Come teach me how well you fight!"

Nolan charged, reaching for his weapons as he moved.

Drask could not suppress his smile.

His silver hand caught the axe blade that came for him with a scream of metal on metal. Nolan was strong, especially for his size, and he was furious, which helped him feel even stronger, but Drask plucked the axe from his grasp with ease and bent the boy's wrist back in the doing.

The weapon clattered across the barrier that stopped them from falling toward their prize.

The scream that came from Nolan was pure and savage and while Drask could admire that, he could not forgive that the youth was too angry to focus.

Not far away, Tega paced, eyes wide, contemplating the outcome. She expected her compatriot to die.

Drask's leg swept down and kicked the lad's ankle out from under him as he started to move. Nolan let out a grunt and dropped to the ground. He caught himself on one knee and both hands, the other leg sprawled out behind him by the force of Drask's strike.

The boy looked up at Drask and snarled again, struggling to stand.

Drask brought his knee up fast and smashed it into the side of the boy's head.

Nolan flopped bonelessly to the ground.

Drask considered his enemy.

Tega considered Drask.

Drask looked her way. "A wise man would eliminate a threat."

"He is not a threat to you. You know this and so do I."

"He has weapons. He tried to kill me with an axe."

"He was hungry."

Drask shrugged. "I tire of games."

"We seek the same thing. We want to understand what is below us."

The boy was clever, but not clever enough. While Drask spoke with the wizard's student, the youth reached for a dagger up his sleeve and then lunged.

Drask caught the hand with the blade under his heel and stomped down. Bones broke and Nolan screamed. Not one to leave a fool unpunished, Drask ground the hand under his foot a second time and watched the boy thrash, his face stretched into a mask of agony.

"Enough!" Tega's voice broke.

Drask looked at her and felt the air around him shift. There was a pressure that had not been there before and he could feel his hair moving.

"If you do anything at all, Tega, I will kill him and you."

She stayed where she was and focused only on him.

Without hesitation he stomped on Nolan's hand again, breaking more of the small bones and driving the blade of the dagger into soft, pink flesh.

Blood flowed from the wound.

"I have seen what you can do! I will kill him! I will kill you if you do not stop your sorcery!"

Just as quickly as it had manifested the pressure around him evaporated.

"Stop hurting him!"

She had taken strides toward them but he could tell by her body language and her expression that she was more worried about the boy than about retribution. Drask stepped back from him and eased three of his throwing blades into his hand. If the air around him changed again, he would kill her before she could blink.

As she started to reach for Nolan, the air under her softened and Tega fell.

Drask had exactly enough time to make the connection between cause and effect before he, too, was falling. The boy's blood had broken whatever seal held them away from the ever-changing streams of lights.

There was nowhere to run. He had grown too comfortable with the impossible situation and now he paid the price.

The lights he had seen from a distance came closer and Drask studied them as impassively as he could. The boy fell with him, his eyes once more looking toward Drask with an unrelenting hatred.

The blades were still in his hand. He threw one at the boy. It was simple, really. Sooner or later Nolan would try to kill him. He could see it in the mad expression on the young man's face.

The blade sank into Nolan's throat and vibrated there as blood spilled freely from the new opening in his flesh.

Drask focused again on the lights below and watched as Tega hit them and sank with a splash. Whatever it was they were here to find was not solid at all, but flowed like water.

Drask Silver Hand had always been curious. He kept his eyes open as he fell into the endless, shifting lights.

Above the liquid that swallowed Drask and the Fellein, the air screamed again, louder than it had before. So loudly, in fact, that stone shattered and flesh was pulped and the vast crystalline formations of the Mounds visibly vibrated with the sound.

Within the towers of crystal the bodies of the long dead moved and gasped, and the frozen flotsam and jetsam of a city in perpetual ruin shimmered and danced.

In the Blasted Lands, the Mounds themselves shuddered as the sound escalated, forcing dust and ice and even the winds to move, pushing everything away from the ground as the skin of the Mounds split. Light crept through the perpetual twilight of the Blasted Lands, and from as far away as the Seven Forges that light could be seen painting the skies first a brilliant shade of blue and then red and finally white.

Sitting in the protection of a cluster of boulders and feasting in the remains of a Broken wretch, Drask's mount Brackka died violently when the lights touched his body and incinerated his flesh. His shadow burned itself into the stone, the only sign that he had been there at all.

There were creatures that lived in the Blasted Lands. Like Brackka, they were destroyed, ripped asunder by winds and light and sound that shattered bones.

Along the Edge, the great wall that marked the end of the

Blasted Lands, the worn stone was undamaged, but only a hundred yards away, the ground was suddenly glazed with a new layer of glass. That glaze cracked and in some cases shattered a moment later as the perpetual ice and snow in the area heated to near boiling point, billowing up as clouds of steam and drowning a few of the creatures that remained.

At the Seven Forges, Durhallem shuddered under the force of the blast, but, as had been the case for a thousand years, the sentinel of the Taalor Valley withstood the brutal assault. Beyond the mountain the valley was unscathed and the great entrance into the valley was nowhere to be seen. With the Sa'ba Taalor gone there was no reason for the doorway to remain open and Durhallem had sealed it.

The bodies of the dead surrounded Andover Lashk.

His iron hands were dyed crimson with the blood of his fallen enemies.

At first they had come one at a time, and then they came in twos and threes, and even as he brought them down more came, a slowly gathering procession that meant to see him destroyed by their hands.

At first he had known fear, but then the presence of Wrommish filled him. He had felt the gods around him before, had felt their powerful scrutiny and been overwhelmed by the raw potency of their shapeless forms.

This was different. As he fought, the god climbed within his skin, managed to fit within him and speak to him at the same time.

He felt his body change as the god used him. He fought the enemies that came for him and felt the direction of Wrommish. He stood upon the crystalline bridge of Boratha-Lo'ar and felt at peace as his fists crushed flesh and his body was bruised and battered again and again.

They were his fights. Wrommish offered guidance but did not strike a single blow.

The ones he fought were the faithful of Wrommish. Over the centuries the bodies of the faithful had been offered to the furnace beneath him, where they burned and became one with their god. The Sa'ba Taalor were no longer present, but their dead were here and they served their god even centuries later. They fought against Andover Lashk and beat upon him again and again. Sometimes he won, but even with the wisdom of Wrommish to guide his moves, he often failed.

There was no rest. There was no food. He did not die though he was delivered a thousand fatal blows.

What he did was learn. A lifetime of lessons in unarmed combat were given to him and then a dozen more lifetimes were offered him as well.

Time does not move the same way for gods, and when in their presence time moved differently for Andover as well.

He had been in the heart of Wrommish for only a few hours according to Delil, but when he came out he could barely remember her name. She had been a part of his world a very long while back and recalling how to speak was a challenge when he first left the cave.

Within the Heart of Wrommish, Andover Lashk dealt with his trials unaware of any change in the Blasted Lands. As mighty as the explosion was, the gods had their ways of defending against incidental catastrophes.

Deep within the Mounds, neither Drask, nor Nolan nor Tega was aware of the violent transformation.

They had other, stranger things to consider.

FOURTEEN

The black ships rode steadily up the Freeholdt River and stopped at the town that bore its name. A majority of the people had already fled to Canhoon or points east in an effort to escape the inevitable, but not everyone left. Those that stayed did not believe that the ships would stop, or that the attackers could possibly be as fearsome as the claims stated.

The ships did not go further up the river. Beyond Freeholdt the waters were too shallow and the waters too treacherous. To the south the fires of the second Durhallem spat smoke and worse into the air, and the heat from that eruption was oppressive in the extreme. Refugees had come to Freeholdt and quickly moved on, fearing that the Sa'ba Taalor would come for them.

The refugees were wise in their way. The army disgorged by the ships was large, and each of the shapes that waded in from the shallows of the river came carrying all that they needed to bring death and mayhem with them.

The City Guard of Freeholdt was heavily depleted. Threats of a lashing meant remarkably little to the guards who wanted to see their families to safety, and promises of extra coin held little appeal when the winds shifted and the stench of decay came spilling in from the south.

If the Sa'ba Taalor came expecting a glorious battle they were disappointed. The City Guard quickly surrendered when they saw the size of the army coming for them, and the officials within the town were front and center when the surrender occurred.

The followers of Durhallem, often called the Wounder or the Unforgiving, offered exactly the same mercy as they had always offered. Those that surrendered, those that chose to fight and those who tried to flee were killed. The town itself was constructed mostly of wood and as a result of that simple fact was razed as the sun set and the Sa'ba Taalor moved up the riverside. The Imperial Highway ran along the river here and the Sa'ba Taalor did not hesitate to take advantage of that well paved pathway. Nor were they foolish enough to expect that no traps had been laid for them.

Long before the heavily armored troops of Durhallem's followers moved along that stretch, the followers of Ydramil, Paedle and Wrommish moved through the woods and scouted the paths leading to Canhoon.

Not all of the Sa'ba Taalor followed the same philosophies as Durhallem's brood, but for the present time they made exceptions. Most they encountered were slaughtered quickly and efficiently. Those that were not, soon wished that they had been. Ydramil's King, Ganem, often sought the answers to life's riddles. Sometimes that required calm reflection and other times it demanded other forms of information-gathering.

Those who asked the questions could have taught the average Inquisitor a few new methods of gleaning the truth.

They were three days away from Canhoon when the Mounds exploded and the Blasted Lands shook and flashed with an unspeakable brilliance.

•••

Cullen never even slipped her bow from her shoulder. She just ran.

She was walking with a small group of other survivors, traveling together toward Canhoon, when the nightmares came for them.

The mounts of the Sa'ba Taalor had terrified her when she'd seen them in the woods, but here, without riders, on the ground and hunting, they were so much worse.

One moment a man named Tomlo was explaining what he could about Canhoon – he had been there several times, which was several times more than Cullen – and the next they were running as a beast came for them, roaring and bulling through the low brush along the side of the road.

There should have been no way for the things to hide in the scrub and yet they came from nowhere. Tomlo saw them first, and tried to run. She saw his eyes widen in fear and then the man was turning, his long legs bunched and muscles tensing and the paws came into her sight and caught him at his shoulders and ripped downward, peeling the flesh from his arms and driving him down to his knees in one savage blow.

Cullen screamed. Tomlo screamed. The great predatory beast roared and then there was madness.

The bow never once crossed her mind. Cullen ran, bolting from the road and charging through the woods. Here she was closer to comfortable. The road offered no cover, no protection of any kind, but the woods? The woods were home and always had been.

The problem was that there was no way to negotiate with the hellish beasts coming after them. They were an unknown. When she was a little girl, her parents had traveled to Canhoon on behalf of the Queen. She did not understand the reasons and couldn't remember if she ever had known them, but the end result was that she stayed in the house of her grandparents for almost a month. Her grandfather had taught her that there were predators in the Trecharch, bears and others. He had also explained that some of the beasts could be negotiated with.

"Bears don't want you. They want either food or to be left in peace. Give them what they want and they will leave you alone."

Whatever madness the beasts were that the enemies rode, they wanted only one thing: blood.

By the time she had scrambled up a tree with enough low-lying branches to accommodate her, the worst was over. The slaughter was done.

Cullen waited as patiently as she could, doing her best not to focus on the creatures that ate the people she had been talking with only minutes before. There was no way of moving from where she was until they were finished. By then the sun had set and she had to venture out in the darkness.

Before his death Tomlo had stated that they were only three or so days away from Canhoon. She decided to make it in two. Sleep was not going to come to her that night in any event.

Deltrea kept her company, often by providing graphic descriptions of how each of her friends had died while Cullen cowered in the trees.

Despite Deltrea's best efforts, Cullen felt no shame. It was not only a matter of self-preservation. She was also on a mission. The Mother-Vine had plans for her and she had to keep those plans.

Tuskandru sat among his followers and listened to their cheers and conversations. The war was going well. Trecharch had fallen and the people who ran from them were closer to death than most could have imagined.

Around him the fires blazed and his people feasted as well they should. Some of what they roasted and ate had once carried swords, but most were fourleggers: horses and cows and small, screaming things called sheep. There were a variety of meats and Tusk tried them all. Universally he found them interesting.

When the feasting was mostly done he called out to Halrus, one of the men he'd set to guard duty earlier.

Halrus came forward with a grin on his face.

Tuskandru, king of the followers of Durhallem, struck the smile from the man's features with one hand. Halrus staggered back, shaking his head and drawing his sword in the same motion. King or no king, he was a follower of Durhallem himself and no one would strike him without fearing the consequences.

It was Tusk who grinned now.

"Come for me! Come for me, Halrus, and while you come tell me why nine humans got past you on the road this day!"

Halrus eyed his king and moved his sword in a circle around his wrist. It was a pretty move, but meaningless. The very act of sweeping the sword in a short circle required that he let the weapon move too loosely to be effective. That aside, Tusk was smart enough not to get cocky. Sword patterns were meant to distract and he would not let himself be distracted.

"I let no one get past me!"

"Brodem and Loarhun both fed on their corpses after killing them!" Tusk's voice was loud only because he wanted all to know why he had challenged one of his own in the middle of a war. "I have feasted on the meat of one of them, as Brodem was feeling generous enough to share." He gestured with one hand to where very distinctly humanoid remains continued to roast on a spit above a nearby fire. "You may call Brodem a liar if you feel the need, but he will defend his honor the same as anyone here."

Brodem let out a growl that shook the woods nearby and sent small animals scurrying for better hiding places.

"Why did nine Fellein walk down the road you were guarding this day, Halrus? Explain yourself!"

"My king…" There was nothing Halrus could say. He was caught and he knew it.

Tusk continued to grin, challenging with his eyes until Halrus had no choice but to either attack or retreat.

That was no choice at all. The followers of Durhallem do not retreat, and Tusk had struck him a brutal blow first.

The swordplay stopped and Halrus came for him, using the caution of a wise man, for Tuskandru was king for a reason and combat prowess was a large portion.

He brought the sword around in a low sweeping arc, hoping to cut Tusk's legs out from under him but Tusk danced to the side, the teeth around his neck clacking and chattering as he moved.

Halrus came in a second time, feinting for Tusk's head. For one moment he was off-balance, leaning too far forward. Tusk shattered his knee with a hard kick.

Halrus winced as he lifted the ruined leg. He did not have the luxury of stopping. He did not dare. His face was pale from the pain of the blow but that did not matter. Tuskandru might have let him live, might have been satisfied with humiliating him, but he had attacked his king with a sword when his king carried no weapons.

The sword Halrus had forged with his own hands was beautifully balanced and held an edge that could cut thick hides and leather with ease. The tip was keen and could and had pierced metal on more than one occasion.

The blade never got near Tusk. When Halrus swept it toward the king again, Tusk swatted it aside with his helmet. While Halrus had been finding his balance on one good leg, the king had pulled the great helm free and the large teeth of the helmet caught the blade and deflected it easily.

Helmet and sword were cast aside and Tusk came in hard, driving his thick fist into Halrus's stomach, and then his chest, and then ramming his elbow into his enemy's clavicle as he staggered back. The collarbone broke and just that quickly one arm was useless.

Halrus tried to defend himself but it was no good. The king struck again and broke the other collarbone. In an instant Halrus had one leg to stand on and three useless limbs. He could rant and roar all he wanted but the king had crippled him.

Before he could recover from the damage, before he could even fall down, Tuskandru grabbed Halrus in both of his thick arms and raised him over his head.

"Brodem! A treat for you!"

Halrus screamed as he sailed through the air.

Brodem roared again and took his new plaything. He was kind enough to kill Halrus quickly. Because he was a generous spirit, Brodem shared him with the other mounts.

All around him Tusk's followers cheered.

He held up one hand and called for silence and they listened.

"Fail me and you fail Durhallem. Fail Durhallem and know our god's mercy! I don't care if you need to shit in the woods or sharpen your knives; do not turn away from your guard duties when called. Do you understand me?"

His followers answered, screaming his name and Durhallem's. He gave them a moment and then nodded his head.

"Eat! Feast! We are almost to the capital of the Fellein! Our battle will be glorious!"

Tusk moved back to his spot and settled on the ground. Stastha smiled at him as he reached for a piece of meat.

Sometimes the gods were kind.

Merros Dulver's day started well enough. In the morning he met with Dretta March and they broke the fast together, discussing the current state of Canhoon and its preparations for the inevitable conflict coming their way.

According to the latest reports Stonehaven had fallen to the Sa'ba Taalor. The place where Dretta had lived and raised her son and waited for her husband on countless occasions was gone. He was so very grateful that she had decided to come to Canhoon instead of returning there.

Of course, Canhoon looked to be lined up for invasion next. The Sa'ba Taalor were coming from several different directions and they looked to be meeting in the next few days at the gates of Canhoon.

"How will you stop them, Merros?" Her dark eyes looked into his, trying to read the future, perhaps. Whenever she stared too intently he was made uncomfortable; he prayed she would never stop.

"We have gates, Dretta, and walls that are over fifty feet in height. They will at least slow the bastards down."

"I was out shopping yesterday and saw you talking to several of the newcomers. What were you saying to them?"

"Near the wall at the northern gate?"

"Yes."

He shook his head and felt his lips press together even as he spread a blend of fresh fruit and honey onto the hearty bread she'd prepared.

"Ever since Tyrne we've had a great deal of people coming in, naturally, and now with Trecharch there are more. It seems that everyone wants to place their belongings along the outside of the wall and start building their homes in that spot." He shook his head and waved the bread around as he warmed up to his subject. "It's not a particularly safe location. They are setting their tents on the *outside* of the walls. Of course I can't allow that. I've tried to explain a dozen times to the people who showed up there and now I've posted proclamations explaining."

"Explaining what, exactly?"

"If their possessions and people are on the outside of the wall they will not have the protection of the wall. Also, they'll be the equivalent of an invitation to the Sa'ba Taalor. They'll literally be a stepping stone to help our enemies get over the wall with more ease."

"How do you mean?" She still stared, but she listened, studied his words, paid attention in ways so few women seemed capable of in his experience. That was not fair. Others listened as well. It just seemed to matter more that Dretta paid heed.

"You have not seen the great beasts they ride. I have. Those creatures can scale nearly sheer surfaces and can pounce like cats. I think with even a little advantage that the creatures will find a way to climb the walls and if they manage that, the deaths they cause will be hellish."

He took a moment to chew at his food and eyed the sweet cheese she had cut in advance. "In any event, I have the guards clearing the walls today and every day from now on. No one will add to the risk of the Sa'ba Taalor taking us by surprise."

"Surely you'll have sentinels."

"Of course. They're already in place and staying alert. But better to avoid giving the enemy an open invitation."

"If the Sa'ba Taalor come here, if they lay siege to the city, how long can the city hold? Are there supplies enough with all of the refugees coming in?"

Merros smiled at her. He was fully aware that she had purchased a lot of land, that she had set up places that would work as housing for people if it came to that. He also knew that she had stocked many supplies away, ordering them from both up and down river. She was wealthy, just as he was. Both he and her husband had made a great deal of money while they explored the Blasted Lands.

"At the very least we have enough supplies to handle at least two months. They would be lean weeks, to be sure, but enough to handle a substantial siege should it come to that." He shrugged. "It would have been more, but the fall of Tyrne took a lot of supplies that had not yet reached us here."

Dretta nodded at that and poured a tiny glass of the potent wine she managed to find in the market. The only other person Merros knew who was willing to pay for the stuff was Desh Krohan. It was delicious and only to be consumed in small doses.

They talked of training the new soldiers, of how best to get rid of the cursed vines that kept creeping up the walls of Dretta's place, of how best to prepare a boar caught in the wild, something both of them knew a surprising amount about. While Merros did not often cook he'd requested recipes from several cooks on the road and had come up with what would, in theory, be a wonderful preparation. They agreed that they should try to cook one of the beasts as soon as time permitted.

They did not dwell on the approaching armies. They did not speak of the reports that something horrible had happened in the Blasted Lands. Some subjects were simply too large to consider.

Instead, they spoke of the growing tide of people coming from the east, people who were citizens of the Empire and not more grayskins. It seemed likely that volunteers were coming to help the citizens. That, or a small army of people were coming to demand better protection from the army.

The one point of positive news on the war front was simply that the Sa'ba Taalor in the far east had not managed to gain much footing. The soldiers were managing to keep them locked down around one fort that had been taken quickly.

While they discussed the ranged weapons of the Sa'ba Taalor – weapons the likes of which Merros had never seen and which he wanted to examine up close – they rose from the breakfast table and moved around the room where Dretta did most of the cooking. There were days when she had help, but this was not one of them. Fruit spreads and bread did not take as much effort as a roasted calf or the occasional meat pies.

Looking back later, Merros remained uncertain exactly what happened. They were standing one moment and the next thing he clearly recalled was holding her naked body in his arms and kissing her amazing mouth urgently.

There was a moment of brilliant, scintillating panic, and then she did something with her hands to make him forget all about the fact that he was laying with Wollis March's widow.

He did things with his hands, too, things that had her making the most fascinating noises. When it was done he was exhausted in the best possible way. She must have been, too, because both of them slept half the afternoon away.

He could always blame the wine, of course. It was a potent blend and he knew that before he sipped, but the simple fact remained that if he'd been asked, he'd have admitted their encounter was virtually inevitable. The attraction he'd felt for Dretta was as strong as any he'd felt for a woman in a long while.

It was later, after they made love a second and third time, sated and sore and wonderfully exhausted, that the guilt came for him and settled on his chest.

Wollis's wife.

Dretta March, the amazing woman he'd spent an unforgettable day with, was Wollis's wife.

Wollis, who had been his finest friend and confidant.

She lay unclothed on the bed beside him, her face slightly turned away, her eyes closed and her breaths coming steadily. He took the chance that she was asleep to study her.

The guilt was bad.

But not bad enough. Despite his misgivings, he smiled at her sleeping form.

She was amazing. There was a very real chance that what he felt for her was love.

And that notion terrified him.

The world was ending and Teagus sat in a cell, very nearly forgotten.

It was a clean cell, true enough, but it was not at all what he was used to.

There had been a time when he was respected. He had spent a great deal of time in this cell wondering exactly when that changed.

He knew the answer, or course. He was far from a stupid man. He just didn't like admitting that he had done things of a questionable nature with girls who were barely more than children. That dark part of him that answered his urges whispered in the recesses of his mind that there were no laws against talking to girls and making suggestions. He had never forced the issue with anyone in his life.

His station in Tyrne had kept him safe from repercussions. He knew that. But Tyrne no longer existed and he had struck at the highest-ranking member of the Imperial Army in a fit of grief and rage. The price he paid for his outrage was a beating, followed by walking in leg irons from the edge of the Empire back to Canhoon. By the time the walk was done his ankles were bloodied and the meat under the irons was infected.

He had learned a lesson. Do not cross the military.

There were members of the Church of Etrilla who came and cleaned his wounds. They fed him. They cared for him. They barely knew him, but the head of the church in Canhoon had shared many correspondences with him over the years. They may never have become friends, but they were at least friendly.

Of course, the very reason he was locked in a cell was preventing that friendship from ever blooming into a reality.

In the cell closest to his, a man was bellowing endlessly. He knew his name. Laister Krous. They had met more than once, and they had been associates on several deals over the years. Power and money are often attracted to like.

While he looked at his healing ankles, picking at the wrappings and peering at the cleaned scabs, Teagus listened to the conversation in the adjoining room.

"Why are you here?" Despite being locked in a cell, Laister Krous's voice dripped contempt.

The voice that answered was also known to Teagus. It took him a moment to recognize the older woman. Her words were softly spoken, but the waspish quality of her words carried easily enough. Danieca Krous was not happy.

"Did you think you could kill any member of this family without consequences? Did you think you could kill my grandson without me finding out?"

"Frankly, I never much cared." There was a long, dramatic sigh. "I've been stripped of my money, my title and even my name, you toad. What else do you think you can take from me?"

He could hear the purr in the old woman's voice. "Your dignity. Your life."

"Do your worst! There are guards outside the door! And I am not without my influence!" He did not speak or merely yell. He roared his words.

Her voice did not change in the least as she responded. "Do you know what the best part of still having my fortune is, Laister? I can pay enough to reach past your influence. And I can pay these fine men to take care of the rest of my desires, too."

The sounds of a scuffle were clear. Though he had never been one to indulge in fisticuffs, the priest knew the sounds clearly enough. Laister made a few inarticulate growls that were surrounded by and eventually overwhelmed by the noises made when fists and boots meet soft flesh.

It was a long fight, but ultimately the end result was inevitable. The whispery noises that came his way were those of a man being dragged and then carried away.

Teagus considered the noises and worried at his lower lip while he clenched and unclenched his hands nervously. It was appalling to think that someone could be taken away so easily.

He had almost calmed down when he heard Danieca's voice addressing him. "I haven't forgotten about you, either, Teagus. You are a vile man with disgusting habits. Had I not trained my blood to know better than to answer to your type, I'd have killed you a long time ago. Or possibly just nailed your manly parts to a bench. I'm still considering that possibility."

That was all she said. It was all she needed to say. He could not tell when she left or if she left, so he did his best to cry silently.

Inquisitor Darsken Murdro looked at the cloth-covered body as it was pulled from the water of the docks, and stopped the City Guard long enough to take a long and hard look at the corpse.

Laister Krous was dead. Darsken was not the least surprised. His flesh had been beaten until it was a deep combination of colors. Several of his teeth were broken or missing. His knuckles showed signs that he had fought hard for his life, but, ultimately, there had never been any doubt about the way his life would end.

The City Guard were well compensated to protect the upper echelons of society in Old Canhoon. They knew the faces of the powerful and they also knew when the powerful fell. Laister Krous could not have fallen much further.

Tataya was nearby, lurking in the shadows. She did not lurk often, but when she did it was an impressive feat. Her hair alone normally stood out enough to guarantee that she would be noticed and her clothes, usually designed to catch a man's eye, were now replaced with subdued colors and a cloak that hid away all of the assets she usually used to make certain she was not easily forgotten.

When he had finished examining the body he waved a hand at the guards to continue their work. He had what he needed. There would be no further punishment, for now.

"I know what you want, Lady Tataya. I do not believe that I can help you."

Tataya frowned from the shadows.

"There are laws, you see? And if I am to enforce them, I must also follow them. To do otherwise sets a bad precedent."

"I never asked you to resurrect my Sister. I asked if you could let me talk to her." She stepped toward him, her eyes looking toward him with the sort of intensity that very likely withered lesser men.

"It is the same thing. It requires the use of abilities that I have sworn would only be employed in answering the question of who has committed a crime and even then only under the most dire of circumstances." He kept his smile in place. Remarkably little made him lose his smile.

"I–"

"Ultimately you know that the only person who can give me permission in this case is the Empress. I would likely accept the word of Desh Krohan, but I am not likely to listen to anyone else. I am very sorry, Tataya. I would help you if I could."

The simple fact was that necromancy took a lot of effort and the dead themselves often suffered for the actions of the necromancer. Pulling a spirit back from the realms beyond the living took effort and often caused a torturous amount of pain for the spirits. Why else would they scream so much when he summoned them?

"I understand, and I thank you."

Someone else sighed. Darsken felt his skin crawl. It was seldom that anyone could surprise him, but the sorcerer had managed.

"I need to speak to Goriah, Darsken." Desh Krohan's voice was immediately recognizable.

Darsken lowered his head and nodded. "Then you shall, but understand I accept no responsibility for any pain she suffers as a result of the summoning."

The sorcerer came out of the shadows, seeming to pour from them like water from a spilled jug. "What must be must be."

"Not here. I need to see her body."

"Then come with us. She is waiting."

Darsken felt the smile slip on his face. They were prepared for his request.

The palace was a solid distance from the docks. He made sure to take his time on the walk.

"You have employed necromancy in your past, Desh Krohan?"

The sorcerer looked at him for a moment and nodded. "You know I have."

"It is true I know that you were one of the reasons that necromancy was forbidden. That said, why do you not handle this matter yourself and avoid the chance of indiscretion?"

"I do not believe there's threat of that." The wizard paused and sighed. "And I have forgotten more of necromancy than I now know." The wizard looked toward the palace and his lips pulled down in a quick scowl before he caught himself. "Also, I suspect I will be called on to defend this city soon and I need to conserve my energies."

"Have you?" Darsken frowned at that thought.

"I am old, Darsken Murdro. I am very, very old." The sorcerer considered him carefully. "Are you saying you would not willingly forget necromancy?"

"Not while it is a tool I must use."

"Then I pity you."

"But without it, how would you get your answers, Desh Krohan?"

The wizard nodded his head.

FIFTEEN

"Would you explain how this is even possible?" Merros's voice held an edge that would not go away. The man had been smiling when he showed up, but now he stared around him with a brow that was heavy with tension and one hand resting on the hilt of his sword. Desh made it a point to study people. Whatever had relaxed the man so thoroughly was now a thing of the past.

The general was not addressing him. He was actually speaking to the stable master, a man who currently was looking around the room as calmly as he could for a method of escape. To be fair, Merros Dulver could be a bit intimidating. He also had earned a reputation when he started punishing the occasional deserter or soldier who simply would not follow orders.

"I swear to you, General Dulver, that I or one of my men have been here at all times." The stable master was trying to put on a good face, but he was shaking and his brow was pimpled by fat drops of sweat that the weather was not responsible for generating.

Merros Dulver looked at the dead horses throughout the long stables and cursed under his breath.

Desh and the general had been taking one of their fairly regular walks and keeping each other posted on what had occurred in the last few days. They had passed communications back and forth but mostly had been far too busy to consider an actual meeting. Now, frankly, there wasn't much time to spend on anything else. The armies of the Sa'ba Taalor were on their way. There was simply no way to avoid that unpleasant fact.

While Merros looked at the dead animals, Desh considered what they had in common and made a deduction.

"Poison."

Merros turned his way, scowling. "What did you say?"

"Poison. We should check the feed and the water. I'd guess poison. And a good one, too. That sort of thing is not inexpensive."

"And do you have a list of poisoners and how much inventory they carry? Can we query them and find answers?"

Desh ignored the sarcasm in the question and smiled tightly. "I have just the man to help us with this."

"Oh, really?" He had Merros's undivided attention.

"I have seen him work near-miracles. He is responsible for the recent change of events in the life of Laister Krous."

Merros nodded. "I like him already." He then looked back at the stable master. "I want samples of the water and the feed set aside. Keep them safe." The look he skewered the poor bastard with was exactly why Desh had wanted him for a general in the forces.

"Who in the name of all the gods would poison a stable full of horses?"

"Who has the most to gain from killing them, Merros?"

Merros looked at him and scowled. It seemed the only expression he was capable of generating. "You think the Sa'ba

Taalor murdered every horse in the royal stables?"

"I think you need to find out if the horses at your military stables are well."

"Oh, by the gods!" Merros looked around for his personal aide. Taurn Durst was watching from easily a hundred feet distant and started in their direction before the general could call his name. The man was a bull, pure and simple. He had somehow managed to fit a human skin over his preposterous body, but Desh had a powerful suspicion that Durst was actually a very large bull. It explained why his face looked so heavy and his body shook the ground when he walked.

"Aye! Ho, sir!"

Merros closed his eyes for a moment, a look of long suffering moving across his features.

"Taurn, I need you to alert the stables. Have all of the horses checked, and have the feed and water checked for poisons. Set samples aside. Get fresh water drawn from the river for the horses."

"Aye! Ho, sir!" The man turned and stalked away. He didn't just walk, but seemed to actually generate an air of menace that moved with him. Desh was suitably impressed. It had taken him lifetimes to manage what the man accomplished simply by existing.

"I keep asking him not to bellow," Merros said. "He keeps explaining to me that he has to lead the troops around me by example. I'd like to yell at him. I would, but he has a point."

"You chose him for a reason. Allow that he has the right idea and worry about other things instead."

"Aye. You're as right as he is, I suppose. Still, the way he's always there and always waiting for my commands…"

"That's his duty."

"I know. But, your Sisters never seem so bloody eager."

"They have plenty to be eager about, Merros. Mostly they enjoy the finer things in life, like tormenting the men around them with their looks."

"They are rather… spectacular."

"They should be. They use sorcery to make certain they are noticed."

"Really?" Merros shook his head. "I'd have never noticed."

"If you could notice, they'd be doing the work the wrong way."

"What do you mean?"

"What do you see when you look at the Sisters?"

Merros grinned. "I tend to see them and little else."

"That's the idea. They are gifted at keeping people offguard."

"To what end?"

"The exact same end that your Taurn Durst manages so easily. When people are looking at them, they are not looking at me. When he comes stomping up the street, most eyes are on him, and that allows you a modicum of freedom."

Merros looked at him for a long moment and shook his head. "You have a strange way about you."

"How do you mean?"

"I mean if I take off my uniform no one looks at me. I know. I've done it."

"I doubt that is true any longer."

"How do you mean?"

"You tried this before, back when you were Captain Dulver?"

"Yes."

"You're *General* Dulver now. You are in charge of the entire Imperial Army."

"Yes, but it's rather like that cloak of yours, Desh. With it you are a presence to be feared, the powerful advisor to the Empress and a sorcerer of unknown skills. Without it, you're rather nondescript."

"I'm not sure if I should feel insulted by that."

"You're not one of the Sisters. Without their robes, there would be mass chaos."

"Fair enough."

Merros changed the subject back to more important matters. "They're here sooner, not later, Desh." He looked around the area, his eyes scanning every access point. It was an automatic thing and the sorcerer knew that, but it was still interesting to note that the last group he'd seen who had the same tendency was the enemy they now faced.

"They are very likely already here. I have a few of my people trying to find any of their sort in town, but so far no luck."

"For how long?"

"Since we arrived. They believe in war, Merros. Not every war I've been in involved swords and horses and shields."

"But you have found no sign?"

Desh looked around very carefully for a moment and then shook his head. "I know they are here. However they are hiding, be it sorcery or something else, they are very good at it."

"What? You think their gods are helping them?"

Desh felt a grin he couldn't quite suppress. "You don't?"

"No." The general shook his head.

"You are a brilliant man. I've seen what you have accomplished getting a very weakened army in shape, and I've watched your work fortifying the defenses of first Tyrne and now Canhoon – and yet, Merros Dulver, you are sometimes powerfully stupid."

"Say again?"

That made Desh's smile grow a bit more. Merros was offended. So offended that he forgot who he was dealing with.

"I spoke clearly. You have actually seen the actions of their gods in play and yet you deny them."

"What do you mean?"

"By all the gods, Merros!" He was actually laughing a bit. Really, he'd had less frustrating conversations with Nachia when she was eleven and those particular discussions had often led to him ranting for hours. "*You watched a man summon a volcano with a sword strike.* That wasn't sorcery of any kind I know. That was divine intervention. A god literally forced a mountain from stable ground. What else do you need to understand the power involved here? We are lucky they haven't simply eradicated us completely."

"Yes, well, when you say it like that…" Merros frowned, lost in thought, then shook his head and blushed. "I am daft."

"Or very optimistic."

"How can we possibly win this, Desh?"

"You are working on your side of that equation and I am working on mine. You wanted faster communications and I managed it. You want answers on the horses and I'll work on that as well. You wanted to know where the enemy is coming from and, well, I have accomplished that, too, though the answer is not a pleasant one."

"I am still trying to understand the idea of the Mother-Vine being gone."

"Aye. I'm finding that challenging, too." He looked away from the general, lost in memories of when the Mother-Vine had been a different sort of entity entirely.

"I know people who think you should be able to end all of this, Desh." Merros wasn't accusing him; he was making conversation. Desh was wise enough to know the difference.

"We've already discussed that."

"I know. I'm just trying to find the right words to avoid

having you boil me in my own skin."

Desh grimaced inwardly; there was a very real possibility that he would never live that incident down and it had occurred over three hundred years earlier. "Speak directly. I like you, Merros. I'll try to avoid killing you."

"You said it yourself. They have gods. They have shown us their strength. You doing the same might well work to deter them."

Desh nodded his head. "I've thought about that. The problem here is that it's about fear."

"Well, yes, that was rather my point."

"So now we come to a different question. Do they fear me more than they fear their gods?"

"I don't understand."

"I can threaten them. I can make them suffer. They have been raised to believe that their gods are all-powerful and all-important. Unless I can be those things, I have no hope of convincing them that I am anything remarkable."

Before Merros could answer, a young soldier ran up to them calling the general's name.

Dulver took the message the boy handed him and dismissed the lad immediately. Whatever had to be done, he had no intention of passing the information back to the same messenger. Too many chances of things going astray, Desh supposed.

Merros read quickly and shook his head. "Every last horse. Every single horse within the Imperial palace and through the whole of the military stables."

"General Dulver!" They turned to see another young runner coming, holding another folded, sealed note.

"Well, this bodes poorly."

The boy was sent on his way and the note was read and

this time Merros Dulver grew pale. "It would seem the First Lancer Division is returning to Canhoon."

Desh frowned. "I though you reported them all slain."

"Well, yes, that was the problem. Still, they and the archers they took with them are on their way back here as we speak."

"General Dulver!" This runner came from the northern gate's direction. He was older and he looked utterly terrified. Refugees had been coming in steadily from that direction since Trecharch fell. That the man could get through the press of people was impressive.

"What is it?"

"The enemy is coming, General. There is an army of the grayskins coming down the Imperial Road."

"How far out are they?" Desh interrupted, looking to the messenger and breaking protocol without the least concern.

The man looked at Merros for a moment and then answered Desh. "They are two days out at the most. But they do not stop. They continue walking even in the dark and I think they will be here sooner than that."

Merros shook his head and cursed under his breath. Desh looked at Merros for only a moment and then gestured toward the chambers where Nachia kept her residence.

"Come along, General. I fear you might get your wish."

"What wish is that?"

"You may yet get your display of power from me."

Nachia Krous looked down from the top of the very highest tower in the palace. The view it afforded her was one that most would never see. She wished she could appreciate it more than she was able to at that moment.

From where she stood in the tower it was possible to see for a great distance. Far off, she could see them gathering, the armies of her enemies moving into place, settling before a final march would put them at the edges of Canhoon. The way between where they were and Trecharch was mountainous, but not this close in. A field of dark shapes impossible not to notice. She could not make out individual forms, but she could most certainly see the gathering, like a massive swarm of distant ants, if the ants had learned to light campfires.

This was war then: a crawling, endless panic; a fear that the world would not end well. How many people would die in the next few days as the Sa'ba Taalor came for her, to take her head and her crown and claim the entire world for their own?

She thought of the King in Iron, the behemoth of a man she had faced off against with her heart hammering in her chest. She had stared him in the face, but she'd had to crane her neck into a very uncomfortable position to achieve that task. He was leading his forces to her, and he could destroy cities with a gesture.

She was breathing hard and trying not to panic by the time Desh and Merros made it to her chambers.

"Majesty." Desh moved into the room and she felt the panic abate. He had that effect on her. He always had. He was a strong, soothing presence even at the worst of times.

She pointed to the window facing north. "There. Look, Desh. You can see them from here."

He walked past her without a sound and looked. "They come from several directions, Milady, as we knew they would."

Nachia took in a deep breath and faced her First Advisor. "And what can we do about them?"

"We have our forces gathered, Nachia. But we have been struck a blow. The horses are gone. All of the stables. Someone poisoned them."

She cursed under her breath. "So we have no cavalry at all?"

"We have no lancers. We have no horses. We still have a very large army waiting here to defend us."

"And they have those damnable beasts of theirs. That gives them a rather substantial advantage, Desh."

The man looked past her, studied one window and then the next.

Merros Dulver was oddly quiet. She looked his way and he stared at Desh.

"I think we might have reached the time when I ask you to use sorcery, Desh."

The First Advisor nodded. "That is why I am here, Majesty. You know that this will exhaust me. I will be tired to the point where there is little I can do for a day or more. Still, I will make an example of one target. You have but to choose one."

Nachia looked at the latest maps, moved from one window to the next and finally decided. "Let the forces in the north know that the Fellein Empire is unforgiving. They have destroyed Trecharch. They should pay for their actions."

Merros stepped closer and looked at her maps. He used his finger to indicate where the greatest gathering of the Sa'ba Taalor were, according to the latest reports. It was one thing to see distant forces gathered and another to know which areas would have the greatest concentration of the enemies.

"How many of our people will be hurt in the process?"

Desh looked at her after she'd asked the question and the expression on his face was as revealing as a stone wall. "I suppose we can find out in the final body count. As I warned you before, I can aim this. I cannot control what happens once I let it go."

"Aim what, exactly?" Merros sounded worried. Nachia knew how he felt.

Desh Krohan did not answer with words. Instead he walked to the window that faced north and raised his hands into the air. There was a balcony outside the window. It was narrow and Nachia had never quite had the nerve to walk outside on it. Heights did not scare her nearly as much as the notion of falling did. It was one thing to look and another to risk losing her balance.

Desh Krohan stood on that narrow balcony and concentrated. His face was set, his brow furrowed with tension. His hands were steady, however, and he moved them as he muttered to himself.

When he was finally ready he pointed with his fingers widespread and hissed a word beneath his breath. She could not hear the phrase, but the sounds that she did hear made her feel queasy.

In her entire life she had never seen magic used in a display of force.

She prayed fervently that she never would again.

Tuskandru looked around the area and nodded. Durhallem had told him where to stand, where to wait with his people, and that was exactly what he intended to do.

His army was vast, yes, but he knew firsthand that there were powers well beyond those offered by a good sword, and he had seen what the sorcerers of the Fellein were capable of. They could fly! They could move from one place to another at speeds that seemed impossible. He had never seen them attack and according to his god they only did so sparingly.

Durhallem said an attack was coming. He had no reason to doubt his god.

His forces waited patiently while the other army moved forward, shuffling along on dead feet. The gods had their ways. A city was cleared and the corpses of the enemies were placed as the gods demanded and then those corpses rose and walked. A gift to the Fellein. They would have their dead back.

In the far distance he could almost make out the city of Canhoon. It was the goal of all the kings for the moment. They would reach that goal soon, but first he was to wait where he was while the wizard of the Fellein showed his power.

He would wait.

He was patient.

Cullen felt the power building.

She did not question the sensation, but instead allowed instinct to guide her and ran hard and fast, her legs pumping furiously. She was a full day ahead of the Sa'ba Taalor, getting closer to Canhoon all the time.

"Run, Cullen! Run as hard as you can!" Deltrea's voice cracked with raw panic and the sensation was contagious. Cullen sprinted harder still, her vision shaking as she hurled herself downhill along the Imperial Highway. The woods were fine when dealing with the grayskins, but now that she was well ahead of them the road was better.

She ran until she felt her sides burning and then she slowed, still moving but no longer as quickly. There were limits to what she could accomplish. She could climb a tree with ease, scale a hill or run along vines, but she had never covered long distances before and her legs burned and her chest and sides ached. She had run miles farther than she knew, pushed on by the power that nested inside her.

The presence inside of her, the last remnant of the Mother-Vine, urged her on and she moved, gaining new vitality from that odd presence. She did not run, she couldn't have any longer, but she moved forward and she looked toward her destination, Canhoon.

Deltrea's voice became a wordless scream of panic and Cullen fell to her knees and then curled into a ball on the ground. The fine hairs on her arms and neck rose into the air; so too the hair on her head. She covered her ears and closed her eyes, but the light still came and the sound followed.

Ahead of her the heat that came her way crisped her hair and dried her throat. Behind her, the world boiled.

She would have boiled as well, but the presence she held inside deflected the blast.

Swech was looking at the palace when the world went mad.

She was contemplating the reactions to all that was happening in Canhoon. The people who ran the stables were moving in a fury of activity, and soldiers crawled over the palace grounds like ants on a corpse.

She had seen Merros Dulver walking earlier with the wizard, Desh Krohan, and she had made certain not to be seen. He was a handsome buck and she admired him.

The general and the sorcerer had been in a hurry and they'd headed into the heart of the palace, barely bothering to look around at all.

She was expecting news from Jost, but so far nothing had been forthcoming.

The younger girl had been sent to find one of the sorcerers. Not Desh Krohan, but another, a man named Jeron. Until Krohan came back to Canhoon, Jeron had been in charge of the city in many ways. Now he did the elder sorcerer's bidding and sent his mind out to find the secrets of the Sa'ba Taalor. The wizards had an array of their members moving through the Empire and communicating together. They spoke of the

Sa'ba Taalor and shared secrets that the gods did not want shared. It was time to end the problem.

Jeron was to be killed or converted. Jost was the one to handle the matter in either event. That decision came from Paedle, not from Swech. There was no discussion necessary.

She pondered the fate of the sorcerer even as Desh Krohan stood upon a balcony so high above her that even her finest bow and arrow could not have hoped to reach him. The only reason she recognized him at all was because of his robes, which moved and shimmered and seemed so very alive.

The sun was gone and the world was moving toward proper night. There was a glimmer of color at the edge of the world and beyond it the darkness and the stars. Her eyes were not prepared for what happened next.

The sorcerer moved his arms and threw them outward as if he might be hurling rocks from his hands.

Instead of rocks it was lightning that spilled forth. A great, potent stream of liquid light ripped across the darkening skies and turned the world white. Stark shadows snapped into focus, but the tongues of liquid blue fire that ripped from his hands took away all other colors and made those shadows dance madly.

Had she been in her own flesh her eyes would have adjusted instantly. A second set of eyelids would have moved, and protected her from the glare as surely as they protected her eyes from the dust of the Blasted Lands. She was not in her body, however. She wore a different woman's flesh.

The light blinded her for a moment, leaving her seeing phantom shapes in blue.

The sound came next, a roar as pure and potent as the screams of the Mounds. The noise rippled through the air and echoed off buildings, sending throaty vibrations through her entire body.

Swech closed her eyes and waited, while all around her people reacted to the unexpected sound and sight as if the world itself were ending.

Swech knew better, of course. The Daxar Taalor were not yet ready for the world to end. Though they were surely fine with certain parts falling into ruination.

Trecharch burned once more. What the Sa'ba Taalor had failed to do was taken care of by Fellein's greatest sorcerer. That the land was already in ruin was a given, but the trees that remained, the animals foolish enough to come back to the area after the Pra-Moresh came through, all found out what magic could do.

Lightning ripped down from the heavens in a thousand brilliant tongues, stroking the earth, the trees, the rocks with fires so potent that wood exploded into flames, the ground boiled and rocks were shattered. Birds and insects startled from their rest fell, stunned or cooked where they waited. The few humans left in the area – and there were only a few, as most had either been killed or long since had fled the area – died just as quickly, their bodies burnt into husks in a moment.

Along the path of destruction the army of corpses meant as a perverse gift to the Fellein were destroyed. Flesh fried, bones burned, metal and cloth disintegrated in a pyrotechnic display. Water evaporated or boiled, and for a dozen miles the world was scarred.

Less than a mile from the massive detonation, Tuskandru watched and experienced a new sensation. He was not familiar with fear. He had been startled many times, but never had he been afraid.

He did not like it. The unfamiliar emotion was burned out of him, replaced by anger.

All around him his people stared, shocked by the unexpected ruination.

When the lights had finished bathing the sky, and the sounds had completed their roaring reminder that some things were beyond mortal understanding, Tusk looked at his people and observed their reactions.

Most of them did as he did. They looked around and assessed the end results of the attack. A few trembled.

He marked the ones who were afraid. They would be watched.

"Durhallem warned us to wait and so we did!" He had no choice but to yell. Even then he was uncertain how many could hear him. It did not matter. What was important was that his people understood that he was not afraid, and that he and they should be ready for war.

Some turned toward him. Others stared around. Tusk nodded and reached into the satchel attached to Brodem's saddle. The horn was easy to find. It was all that filled that particular bag.

That noise got the attention of all of them. The note was sharp and clear as he called them to war. It was time to ride. They would not stand still and cower in the darkness. The Sa'ba Taalor were warriors. Any who forgot that would suffer the wrath of their king, the wrath of their god.

"We ride! We have a people to conquer!"

Tusk could barely hear their responses, but he felt them in his flesh. The roar of his followers was as loud as the thunder itself.

In minutes they were mounted and riding or walking as befit their abilities.

Fear was for lesser beings. The Sa'ba Taalor had nothing to fear. Their gods were with them.

•••

Merros Dulver watched on as Desh Krohan rained destruction down on a land that was days away. It started as a lick of light from his fingertips and exploded outward from there.

There was no way to escape the sight.

He squinted against the light coming from the skies and spewing forth across the distant area, and watched the fires burning. The sun set, but the glow from the north matched the dusk's fading light.

The air stank with the discharge of power.

Nachia stood at his side and looked at the ruination.

She turned to look at her First Advisor with wide, genuinely shocked eyes.

"What if you'd missed?" Her voice was small, barely a whisper.

Desh sighed. "And how many times have I offered you that exact argument."

The sorcerer walked away from them heading, Merros supposed, for his private chambers. "I am tired now," Desh muttered. He did not look back.

From the north Tuskandru gathered his armies and moved, slipping among the trees and advancing with more stealth than many would have thought him capable of managing. The simple fact was that after the earlier display of power it was best to let the enemy think that he and his were gone until it was too late to do anything about it.

To the east, the movement of the army was more direct. The Imperial Highway was occupied with the movement of troops in numbers that would have had most of Canhoon trembling if they could see that far, but the army of King Tarag Paedori was still over a day away and moving at a steady pace. The rear echelons of that army stopped when the sun set. The forward wave did not stop but continued, moving slowly but deliberately in the direction of Canhoon.

In the direction of home.

As with Tuskandru, the King in Iron brought with him a gift of the dead. Lancers and archers alike moved along the path, bearing little by way of weapons but not needing any, either.

Kallir Lundt, once of Fellein and now of Prydiria, stood next to his king and stared after the moving dead.

"I don't completely understand. Why send them back if they are unarmed?"

Tarag Paedori looked down upon him. The man was well over a head and shoulders taller. He was, without doubt, the largest man that Kallir had ever met.

"The dead are a reminder. They let the Fellein know that the gods favor us. Should any have lived long enough or have written a record of the past, they are a reminder that the Fellein once used armies of the dead to fight their wars."

Kallir nodded his head. "None will remember, but they will be scared senseless by the very notion." He spoke a complete truth there and he knew it. When he saw the dead rising it was all he could do not to run away. He was not easily frightened, but dead things should stay dead.

The King in Iron looked at him for a long, silent moment and then looked back toward the distant Canhoon. "Are you uncertain, Kallir Lundt? These were your people before you joined us."

"No. I have accepted the gifts of Truska-Pren and I have been given so many gifts." Still he spoke the truth. The maps that the Sa'ba Taalor had of Canhoon were drawn by memory, and they were remarkably accurate. There were discrepancies, to be sure, but fewer than most would have imagined. "I know that what must come next is inevitable."

The king nodded. "That is good. I want you with us for this. I want you to bear witness to what happens to Canhoon and the rest of the Empire."

Kallir nodded his head and did not speak. He had seen the power of the gods of Taalor and yet, he felt doubts. They had mended his face. They had punished others before him, and he had watched as one of the arrogant, youthful fools who sometimes must beat their chests to prove themselves had fallen to the ground before him and been transformed. He had learned in a moment where the mounts came from. They were the humbled, those who lacked the faith needed to follow the Daxar Taalor. He knew the Daxar Taalor had power.

Still, his faith was strained. He had never seen any action on the part of the gods of Fellein but still he found himself wondering if the army he sided with would be strong enough to take on the vast forces of an empire at least a hundred times the size.

He wondered if the gods of Fellein were truly absent.

One gauntleted hand rested on his shoulder for a moment and he looked up toward his friend, ally and king. The eyes of the man glowed with their own light in the semidarkness. All around him the Sa'ba Taalor lit the area with faint starlight wherever he looked. "Rest, Kallir. We ride at dawn and we ride until we reach Canhoon."

Kallir nodded and moved toward his tent, still feeling a sense of unease.

He would pray and soon enough he would know if his prayers were answered.

SIXTEEN

In his dreams the stranger before Teagus was dour and hard and spoke for the gods. "Etrilla steps aside now. It is time for Kanheer to come forward and save his children."

He should have felt fear at the idea that war had come, and yet there was a savage joy in his breast.

"How can this be when Kanheer has slept for so long?"

The Pilgrim stood before him with the dust of a thousand miles of walking on his clothes. He was gritty and he was grim and he carried his sword drawn and ready for combat. He was hard where Teagus was soft. He was hardened and tested in combat. The only time Teagus had attempted to fight in the last decade had resulted in a beating and being locked in chains.

"Kanheer was preparing for this time, as gods do. There were people to place just so, and forces to gather in the right places." Despite his harsh features and the cruel set of his mouth, the man spoke calmly and patiently. His voice soothed the worries in Teagus's soul. "You are where you are because Kanheer needed you to be in this place at this time. I am where I am because the god of war summoned me from my sleep and told me to gather an army."

"You have an army? You'll fight these Sa'ba Taalor?" Was it possible that a few words from a man he'd never met before could make Teagus so optimistic? No. It wasn't the words, but who said them. He could not have said exactly why the Pilgrim filled him with hope, but there was something about the weathered features and rough strength of the figure that did just that. Here was a man who spoke with the authority of the gods themselves. Here was a man whose purpose was righteous. "What must I do?"

"Prepare yourself. Say your prayers to Etrilla. Say more prayers to Kanheer. It is time for us to save the faithful. It is what we were created to do, Teagus of Tyrne. We must remember the dead and protect the living. It is what our gods want of us."

"But I am in a cell. How can I help from a locked room?"

"There are no prisons for the faithful. When the time is right, come to the Eastern Gate and wait for me. We will meet in the flesh soon enough."

Teagus opened his eyes in the darkness. There was light, yes, in the distance. The flickering light from the guard's lantern down the corridor. He looked toward that light, his eyes drawn to any form of illumination as he contemplated the dream. The exact same dream he'd had the night before. At least he believed it was the same. The sleep was over; the dream was fading and left little beyond a strong sense of hope.

His eyes studied the light for a moment before he realized that he should not have been able to see the light at all from his cell. There was normally a door in the way. The door was missing. Not open. Gone. Missing.

Teagus considered that for several seconds and then rose from his narrow cot and moved toward the hallway.

Faith means believing in miracles, especially when they

happen before your very eyes.

An army came to Canhoon, led by a Pilgrim and summoned by gods. Here, at last, there was hope.

The passage was clear. Leaving was unsettlingly easy.

The day broke clear and sunny, with a gentle breeze from the east and a low enough temperature to keep the bugs slow and sluggish. That by itself was a start for a good day in the eyes of most.

Still, war was upon the land and new orders had been given. The great gates leading to Canhoon were shut and barred, and guards were placed at the smaller entrances near each of the gates. The City Guard reigned within the city, but at the walls the soldiers were picked and carefully instructed by Merros Dulver himself. There would be no mistakes.

The northern gates were closed after Cullen made her way into the city. The sight of the great wood and steel barriers being shut and then barricaded with heavy oak arms caused a great deal of whispered discussion.

A vast river offered fresh waters to Canhoon. The waters ran deep and wide and flowed along a series of docks set just outside of the massive wall that surrounded the city. One area allowed greater access. A section of the barrier had been cut away to permit boats greater access, but as she looked on she could see the soldiers fortifying that spot with massive wooden barriers that had apparently been cared for over the years. The wooden walls were slipped into place and locked together. She might have doubted that they could hold off the grayskins but she could also see the massive iron bands that helped keep the shapes in place. Guards bellowed and a hundred men or more hauled the barriers along a series of rails that looked freshly greased. She wondered idly why they did not have animals pulling the massive structures. There was not a horse to be seen anywhere and she'd expected a great number of them from the tales she'd heard growing up.

"Have you ever seen such a town, Cullen?" Deltrea's ghostly voice sounded as overwhelmed as Cullen felt.

The buildings started low, mostly hidden behind the vast walls around the city. Each wall was of a different era and while all had been kept in good repair, the styles were as different as the times. The first was made of massive stones that had been placed together close to the heart of the city. Each stone was cut and polished until the whole of the thing looked like one piece, save only for the differences in the color of each enormous stone. She could not begin to understand how they had been assembled. It would take armies of men just to slide one piece, let alone to raise them on top of each other.

"Sorcery," Deltrea said. "It must be."

Further out the second wall was slightly lower and made of bricks cast from the clay of the river. Time had not been kind, but the wall still stood, and even from a great distance she could see how thick the structure was, how very solid.

The wall that surrounded the entirety of the city was made from smaller stones and not as perfectly put together. She could see handholds all along the thing. The outer lip of the wall, however, rose at a sharp angle and offered shelter from the sun for a dozen feet or more. Anyone attempting to scale that wall would be stopped by the massive outcropping. At over sixty feet in height she had doubts that anyone could scale it easily. There were a few, survivors of Trecharch who were used to scaling rough surfaces, but even the most inventive would have to hang like a spider scaling a ceiling to manage the underside of the angled walkway at the top of the wall.

Guards walked that wall, a dozen or more in plain view and she assumed many more besides. Cullen studied them for several moments and then moved on.

Hunger was a new force inside of her and she dug around her clothes until she found her small satchel of coins. It had belonged to someone else on the road, but that someone had died holding it. She suspected they tried to barter with the grayskins and died for the attempt. In any case one of the coins bought her several pieces of fruit and a slice of fresh roasted beef on a slap of hard bread.

Cullen chewed slowly but took big bites. Her stomach demanded no less.

While she ate she stared at the men building their wooden wall and watched the people trying to get past it as quickly as they could. Most seemed calm but a few were eager to get past and locked within the confines of the city.

One of the City Guard looked at her for a moment, saw the bow and arrows, the food at her side and nodded before moving on.

Deltrea said, "He wants to know if you can use a bow, I bet."

Cullen shrugged and ate.

"I hear that only a few women in this area can fight for themselves. Most are pampered and kept safe from any possible harm."

Cullen managed not to laugh pabba fruit out of her nose, but it was an effort. "Do you see anyone here who looks pampered, Deltrea?"

She looked around herself to prove her point. There were too many people. That was the first thing worth noting. Many were dirty from days on the road, and most wore expressions of exhaustion and desperation. She knew, because she had seen the same look on her own face when she was cleaning herself at the river earlier in the day. "They are hungry and they are scared."

"Of course they are, because they cannot fight and they cannot hunt." Deltrea's voice sounded petulant. "They come from places where they've never had to survive a fight with enemies that wanted them dead."

Despite knowing better, Cullen took the bait. "Have you lost your senses? Look at them!" She tossed aside the remains of her pabba fruit and waved her hands to encompass everyone. "These are our people, and more besides! There are Roathians here, and the remains of Tyrne! They have nothing! They have less than nothing!"

In her guts the heat from the Mother-Vine roiled and curled and stretched and she grunted. The heat wanted food and so she shut her mouth and grabbed up her slab of beef, chewing on the meat and the hard baked bread under it. It stopped her from making more of a fool of herself. She could see the people around her still eyeing her warily, this girl who talked to the air and argued besides.

The men who walked past were dressed in military finery. She did not know the ranks, but she could see they were in the upper echelons. They had too many shiny buttons and cords of gold on their clothes to be otherwise. The leader of them was a man who walked with the confidence of a killer. He pointed and spoke, and the others around him nodded and obeyed his orders.

"General Dulver, a moment if you would, sir." A man had come from where they worked on constructing the barrier against the river and what lay beyond it. He practically simpered.

The man she was watching nodded and listened as the

details were laid out. There were problems with the tracks that the wall was supposed to slide along. Too much debris had built up over the years and even with the grease they ran into obstructions.

"Durst, please walk with Kermon here and show him how to clear the tracks." Durst looked like he should have been on the team moving the sections of the wall, or just possibly as if he should have been a section of that wall himself. He scowled at the interloper and nodded. Kermon looked like he wished he were anywhere else, or possibly as if he should have considered fixing the issue without asking for assistance.

Life in the military did not change. She had spent years listening to orders fall from lead tongues onto lead ears.

The general looked her way and nodded politely, then quickly looked a second time, examining the bow and arrows at her side. She looked at them herself. The bow was standard enough. The arrows were whatever she could find on the road and some were from the enemy.

"You are coming from the north? From Trecharch?'

She squinted up at him, and nodded, even as she swallowed the lump of chewed beef. She had not been expecting conversation.

"I am sorry for your losses. We were not fast enough."

Cullen shook her head. "They came with Pra-Moresh and stranger things. They came in great numbers. There would have been nothing to do, especially after they killed the Mother-Vine."

"We are looking for soldiers if you need employment and can use that bow."

"My friend Deltrea was saying how the likes of people from Canhoon don't much need female soldiers."

The general smiled. "I am not from Canhoon. And I need

every soldier I can find who is willing to fight."

"I'm to find a wizard first. A man named Krohan."

The general looked at her for a long moment with a half-smile on his face. He was handsome in his way, but aged by the mantle of his duties. The smile made him seem younger again.

"You seek Desh Krohan?"

"He's the one. You know him?"

"Oh, aye, everyone knows him or at least of him. In my case I've met him several times and will be seeing him within the hour."

"Can you get me to him?"

"Possibly, but he's busy and not likely to see a woman with a weapon aimed his way. I might have to take that from you until after the meeting." He kept a light tone in his voice. She liked that. Too many people seemed to find it important to make demands instead of simply explaining themselves.

"I expect I can approach without a weapon."

He stayed where he was expectantly and after a moment Cullen realized he was waiting on her to join him. Flustered, she grabbed her food and slipped it into a fold of her oversized blouse, then grabbed her weapons.

As they walked he asked her questions about what had happened in Trecharch and she answered them truthfully. There was no point in lying.

She spoke of the deaths of her friends, including Deltrea, but he made no worrisome noises as she'd feared he might. He was a soldier. He had been in combat. He very likely had a few ghosts of his own he spoke to when the time was right. Or who spoke to him, for that matter. She could tell that by the way he moved and the way he looked around. He did not strut like so many of the younger soldiers. He did not puff out his chest or scowl at the people around. As they spoke they moved across the streets and hills of the city and Cullen ate her food. By the time they reached the gates of the palace – and had there ever been a city with so many walls? So many gates? She had her doubts – he had likely gleaned as much information as he had hoped.

The general smiled at her. "In all of this I've forgotten to ask you your name. Who is it I'm to say wishes to see Desh Krohan, the First Advisor to the Empress?" His tone had not changed and Cullen wondered idly if she was supposed to be impressed by the title he offered.

"My name is Cullen." Her hand moved over her abdomen to where the endless heat moved and pulsed inside of her. "My message for Desh Krohan comes from Moale Deneshi. He will know the name."

Truer words had seldom, if ever, been uttered.

Captain Callan did not enter the city. He stayed with his ship and watched on as the great wall was assembled. He had been given passage to leave as he pleased or to enter, but he doubted that he would stay.

In addition to the offer of safe passage he had also been given a commission and if Callan could be said to have any god it was the coin of the realm, regardless of which realm he was in.

Vondum chewed at a sliver of dried beef that was likely as hard as steel. He did so without bothering to taste the stuff, but merely so that he would have something to do as he watched the laborers build their wall.

"It's not that I'm not enjoying watching a herd of men try to replace horses, because I have coin on at least one being crushed before this day is done and I like my coin – but why are we still here, Callan?"

Callan's face had a heavy growth of beard on it at the moment and he was contemplating scraping it away. His skin itched and he hated that feeling.

Along the docks he could see heavy gratings that ran under the wooden platforms. He knew from past experience that those grates filtered the water going into the city and stopped anything larger than a mouse from creeping in.

There were other boats and ships around him. Most were readying for leaving the area.

He frowned. "There were four boats due in from Freeholdt. None of them have come round."

"And they won't and you know it. We've all heard the stories. The black ships are on the water and waiting for their signal to come in." Vondum shrugged. "We stay here, and half the crew goes into the city and we remain here. We leave now, we might have a chance to slip past them. Or we go round the city and take the river east."

Callan nodded. "East is sounding like a fine notion to me, lad. How about you?"

"East is a destination I can find some good thoughts about. West and south do not bode a good day." Vondum switched the dried beef to the other side of his mouth and looked toward the water. "Today, Callan. If it's not today, I'll take my chances in the city."

"You'd leave?"

"Coin only spends if you are alive to spend it. I've heard the stories. You've heard them too. Time to leave or tuck ourselves in a safe place. The Sa'ba Taalor are coming."

"We go south, we can meet up with the Brellar." Callan rose and dusted off the seat of his pants and walked to the edge of the deck , looking down into the waters. "We get more coin and an army of savages to fight against the black ships."

"Really, it's much the same answer. We can't spend the coin if we're dead."

Callan sighed. "Off the ship with you then. I'll find new bodies to take with me. I think it's time to fight against these bastards. They've killed half the ports we sail from and they're aiming to kill this one, too. They keep it up we have nowhere left to sell our wares."

Vondum considered that for a moment and then spat his dried beef into the water. An instant later a fish snapped at the meat. Callan hoped it enjoyed the meal.

"It makes me grouchy when you're right, Captain. So let's go the way you want, but let's do it quickly, before I change my mind."

"What about the lads?"

"They'll mind, long as there's coin involved."

"I thought you couldn't spend if you were dead."

Vondum looked at him and smirked. "Aye. But the lads don't think that far ahead."

"Fair enough."

Half an hour later the ship was on its way. They took a wide turn and headed back out toward the waters of the south, toward dead, ruined Freeholdt and the waters beyond, where black ships sailed and demons waited.

He should have been terrified, but Callan felt alive. He always felt best when he was heading to the sea.

The horns would sound soon. Swech nodded her head. There were hours at most before the war came to Canhoon and when it did she would be ready. The time to wait had never really come to pass. She had been far too busy. That was the advantage of staying busy.

Jost would likely be back soon to report on the activities of the others.

There was little left to be done for the moment and so Swech took a bath, rinsing the grit from her body. Grit was everywhere these days, as the storms from Durhallem and distant Wheklam continued to vomit toxic filth into the air. The next mountain would move soon, though at a far enough distance that she would not even be likely to feel the great eruption when it occurred.

Once she was cleaned and dressed she left the small apartment where she had met with the others and moved back toward her home deeper in the city.

There were things to be done. There were appearances to keep. She felt a flutter in her chest at the thought.

The meal would be a quick one of necessity and she was not sure it would even be one that she shared, but she could not afford to take that chance.

The servants had done their work and the oven was warm. The roast had been finished and the fruit and cheese had been laid out. It only took a matter of a few minutes to pull the cooking bird from the oven and place the dough into the heat to finish baking.

By the time everything had been laid out properly the sun was rising.

She checked to make sure her clothes were proper and that her hair looked as good as it could after cooking and then she went out to the porch and waited in the early morning breeze.

When Merros Dulver came through the open gate into her private estate she stayed where she was. The general came to her, as he always did, and he smiled an apology. "I cannot stay but for a moment, Dretta. The armies of the Sa'ba Taalor are gathering."

Swech smiled warmly and nodded her head. "Then you should eat. You will have a busy day saving us from the savages."

He smiled gratefully and sat across from her at the table. "You are wise, Dretta March." He poured himself a cup of cold water and then watched as she set up a plate with a collection of his favorites. "I worry, Dretta. Will you be safe?"

"I will not leave my home, Merros. I will be safe here until you return to me."

He ate his fill and then she led him inside and away from prying eyes. He would be going to war soon. The thought of war, of combat and bloodshed, always left her aroused.

The horns sounded from outside Canhoon and were answered immediately from well within the wall.

The first wave of grayskins did not look as intimidating as many had expected as they moved toward the closed Western Gate. They had numbers, to be sure, but they did not march in unison and few of them seemed to have any weapons.

The gates were closed just the same and the guards waited, gathering together to watch the figures, a dozen of them all told before the first horn sounded. Most retreated back to their posts, shamefaced by their lack of proper behavior. A few continued to stare until the watch captain roared his orders. Captain Tinner was not known for his gentle touch with a lash. They moved quickly to get to the proper places after that.

Tinner was a good man, seasoned and trained and well used to making sure that the city was kept safe. It didn't matter that no one had attacked in over a century. Tinner was a career soldier and knew the value of discipline. He was one of a dozen or so men who'd made absolutely certain that the walls of the city stayed in good shape and was the first to send men out to clear the tents and supplies from those who wanted to use those walls as a lean-to.

He was also smart enough to know when something wasn't right. He ordered that the group traveling toward them be hailed and so they were. He watched as they continued on, making no sign that they had heard the hail. After the second and third attempts failed he called for one of his guards to hand him a bow and took careful aim.

The arrow sailed true and slammed into the thigh of the leader of the group, a solitary man wearing the colors of the Imperial Army and acting not at all a part of the same.

That the arrow struck true was a given. He could see it where it stuck, watch it shift with each step the man took.

Tinner called for the alarm to sound and was rewarded with a blast from the horn closest to him and several others as well.

As the sound issued again and again from around the outer wall, the gates were doublechecked and tested for security. Canhoon was sealed from traffic in all directions and the smaller doors near the gates were sealed and barricaded with stout wooden supports.

Behind the walls, safely locked away from the invasion, the people of Canhoon and the refugees who swelled that city's population stared uneasily at the walls meant to protect them. They were here now, trapped, whether or not they wanted to go anywhere at all.

Tinner watched as the marching shapes moved to the doors and pressed against them, moving to force their way through barriers that would have withstood nearly any force known to the Empire.

He gave the signals and the archers along the wall took aim, firing into the crowd that pushed forward. Arrow after arrow struck flesh and the shapes that should have screamed or made noises did nothing at all save continue on as they had.

He gestured to one of the runners, a lad of twelve, too young to fight but fast enough to work conveying messages. While the boy waited he wrote a quick note and ordered it taken to the office of General Dulver.

The message was simple: *The dead have returned, as you said they might.*

He kept his calm. There would be no panic on his watch. Sorcery was almost inevitable and after the display of the day before it was also no longer surprising.

Merros looked upon the dead things battering at the Western Gate and felt his stomach turn. They were dead. They certainly looked dead and they most decidedly smelled dead. They were also his soldiers, or had been in life.

Desh Krohan stood next to him on the high wall and looked down. His face was somber and his demeanor was worse. He was not a happy man.

"They're very dead. I wouldn't waste any more arrows on them."

"Yes, well, it took a few volleys before the watch captain decided exactly that." He looked at the wizard and then down into the moving collection of the dead and shook his head. "What do you propose we do about them?"

"Well, you could burn them but you risk burning your doors at the same time. They're mostly metal, granted, but the heat it takes to burn a body is substantial and the structural damage if they don't stop moving might well be enough to cause troubles." Desh looked down and shook his head. "That's why we outlawed necromancy in the first place."

"Necromancy?"

"That." He gestured. Below him the dead kept pushing against the doors, which stubbornly refused to be pushed open, for which Merros was exceedingly grateful. "Any sorcery that deals with the dead or their spirits."

He bit his tongue, fully aware that the man he was dealing with had brought back Goriah's body when she was killed and that the body had not been buried or burned.

"My suggestion is leave them where they are."

"Leave them?"

"It's that or burn them. I mean I suppose you could send someone out to cut them down, but it won't go well." Desh shook his head. "It never does."

"Well then. That's that. We'll leave them until I can think of a better way. The guards won't be happy about it."

"The first one that complains, give him a sword and suggest he cut them all down to smaller pieces that are more easily scattered and burned. That should calm down the discontent."

"You are wonderfully mad, Desh Krohan."

"'Be a part of the resolution of the difficulties, not a portion of the complaint about the same.' That's what Theurasa Sallis always said."

"Who?"

"My teacher a long, long time ago."

"Did you speak with the young woman, Cullen?" He wouldn't have asked, but ever since the woman had been introduced to him Desh had seemed unsettled, even more than he'd been after destroying a small army.

"I did." Desh frowned, worrying his lower lip. "She has been... enlightening."

"Who is Moale Deneshi?" He asked because he felt it might be important. He had no desire to pry into the sorcerer's life. It wasn't healthy to do so, but the man's reaction to the name had been as strong as if he'd been bitten in his privates by an angry goat.

"She was my lifemate a long time ago. She gave her life to preserve the Mother-Vine. It's complicated and nothing you need to worry about."

Merros nodded his head and took the hint, but he also knew the man was lying. Whatever had occurred the situation wasn't over yet. He could sense it. That, however, was the least of his concerns.

"They're coming from all directions, Desh. This is going to be a long and bloody siege."

The sorcerer looked at him. "I admire your optimism."

"I'm sorry?"

"The Sa'ba Taalor are going to destroy us in short order, Merros. If they continue to raise the dead to fight on their side then we will surely be overrun within a few weeks at the most. The corpses will bring sickness. Plague winds, at the very least. If they decide to place one of their volcanoes on this city we're all dead anyway."

"Do they plan to do that?"

"No. Corin has looked into the matter. The next of their mountains will rise far to the east. Likely where they are fighting now."

"Desh, I've got a lot of troops in that area." The sorcerer nodded. "Advance notice might save a few of them."

"I'm letting you know what I know. There's likely going to be an eruption in the far east. That is all that I know. Everything else is guesswork."

"What makes you think it will happen in Elda?"

"It's a stronghold for your military over there. They've successfully been holding off the Sa'ba Taalor. It's what you'd do in the same situation with a similar weapon. It's what I'd do."

Merros stared furiously at the man with no idea of how to respond. He hated that the man was right.

"They're coming. The real enemy. They're almost here." Desh pointed. The army was impossible to miss. A thousand people moving on the Imperial Highway had seemed impressive. This, however, was much more than that.

Merros looked on and felt his stomach fall away into the very bowels of the planet. They did not wear matching armor. They did not carry identical banners, or swing weapons that looked alike, but there was no doubt that the moving river of flesh that filled the highway was an army.

Helmets of every imaginable type, shields great and small. Swords and maces and chains and bows and odder items he could not hope to fathom were carried in the ready hands of the Sa'ba Taalor as they came forward.

There were tens of thousands of them. They continued on toward the Blasted Lands for as far as his eyes could see, and they moved in perfect unison. Thousands of feet rose and fell together, sending out a synchronized thunder with each step forward. At regular intervals bannermen carried vast red flags emblazoned with the black face of an iron god. That face was familiar to him. He had seen it once on an iron box that offered a crippled young man a chance to use his hands again. That had been a few months ago but it felt like a lifetime.

"These are the forces of the King in Iron," Merros said. "This is only one portion of their army."

Desh Krohan nodded his head. In the distance, a great distance off, actually, they could just make out the shapes of the mounted soldiers. It was hard to say for certain, but there seemed a good number of them as well. "It might take them less time to take the city than I originally thought."

•••

Nachia Krous looked out from her tower and tapped the sword against her hip. The armor was not comfortable, but she wore it. If her army were prepared to fight she would be prepared as well. Her brother, Brolley, stood nearby. He, too, was dressed in armor. He seemed far less calm than she did.

Brolley was currently staring at the gigantic black mark on the land where Desh had cast his destructive spell. He'd been staring at that spot a great deal.

"There are soldiers down there," he said.

"Yes, Brolley. I'm currently looking at them. There are a very large number of them, really."

"No. I mean to the north. There are more soldiers. They aren't all moving together but they're there and they are forming up. I don't think there are as many as you're looking at, but it still seems a lot of them."

Nachia sighed and walked over to look where her brother was staring. He was correct. There were a great deal of them and they were gathering, falling into a loose formation.

She had already looked to the south and seen more of them. The only point that seemed unimpeded was the east, and that was likely an illusion. It was only a matter of time before they were well and truly surrounded on all sides.

There was a temptation to call for Desh Krohan. It was strong, but she ignored it.

He would come when he was ready and would likely not be long in heading in her direction. There was a war to fight and she had chosen her commanders. She had to trust in them a bit, and for now she would watch and observe.

Nachia looked to the east, just in case an army might be hiding.

There was no army, but there were a great number of people.

They were entering the city in an orderly fashion and even from as far away as she currently was she thought she could feel them looking toward her in her tower.

This was the Pilgrim, perhaps. The man they claimed gathered the faithful to his side and planned to help the Empire.

She hoped the claims were true. They needed all the help they could get.

The mass of soldiers stopped at what had to be a carefully considered distance. They were just out of range of the crossbows, which meant they were beyond the range of the archers as well. The dead did not care either way, but continued to push and batter at the doors with no noticeable effect.

Desh Krohan looked at Merros and shook his head. "You should go to the palace, General."

"I'm needed here."

"No, actually, you are not. The watch captain seems quite competent and you are needed where you can best strategize and prepare for a multitiered attack on the city."

The First Advisor was not joking. He meant it, and Merros could see that, but he wasn't at all pleased by the notion.

"I didn't come out here to investigate and run."

"Were you planning to throw open the gates and strike down the dead? After that, were you going to singlehandedly kill the entire force of invaders waiting out there?"

"Desh–"

"No." Desh cut him off, speared him through with a dark stare. "It's not a request of you, Merros. Get to the palace. I need you where you can do the most good and that's not here."

"I'm a soldier, damn it."

"You're the commander of the entire army! I have four hundred swords on the way here and a thousand more being rallied. Go to where you can do me the most good and prepare for the siege, Merros!"

He hated to leave. He hated even more that the damned fool sorcerer was right. Had he known then, back before the madness started properly, all that he knew now, Merros Dulver wasn't completely sure he would have accepted the commission into the military at a higher rank. Command was a necessary evil, but not one that sat well with him in this circumstance.

He looked out over the wall again as rank after rank of the Sa'ba Taalor moved to the sides of the road and formed into precise lines.

They did not speak. They did not shuffle impatiently. They simply stared at the massive doors of the Western Gate as more of their people moved forward and slid into position.

Merros turned and walked away, his fists clenched in cold fury.

The men at the Eastern Gate had planned to bar the smaller doors, but the Pilgrim stopped them.

He walked to the heavy, reinforced door and walked through the threshold with one hand bracing the door open and the other on his sword hilt. His countenance was harsh and the guards hesitated for only a moment but that was enough. It was only a matter of moments before the faithful began spilling into the courtyard closest to the gate, and they moved quickly, not taking the time to linger.

They were a large gathering, dirtied by their time on the road, lean and hungry and universally as somber as the man who led them. Had there been a dozen the City Guard would likely have contained them and locked the doors. But they were not a dozen or even a hundred. They were literally an army. They kept walking across the threshold and moving to the side allowing the next person through as their leader held the door and gestured for them to move to the appropriate place.

Hendil, the captain of the watch for the Eastern Gate shook his head and let them enter. They were not the Sa'ba Taalor. They were citizens of Fellein and his orders said nothing of killing their own in an effort to close a door. Better to let them in and recruit them as far as he was concerned.

By the time the last of them had come through the doors it was a calm, sweating tide of people who closed and barred the doors for him. Without another word the man who led them walked on and headed deeper into the city. He marched as a man with a mission in mind, and his people followed the same way.

As he moved toward the second wall of the great city he was joined by a scattering of others.

One such was Teagus, the priest of Etrilla, who looked to the Pilgrim and smiled. "I dreamed of you."

"No. You dreamed what the gods want you to do."

"Yes, but I dreamed that you would lead me."

The Pilgrim looked at him for a moment. "Will you follow me and do the bidding of the gods, Teagus?"

"You know my name?"

A woman answered for him. She was lovely and dark and there had been a time when Teagus would have done all that he could to convince her that sleeping with him was the will of the gods.

She said, "The Pilgrim has known the name of every last person to follow him. He has walked this path before."

"I don't understand."

She smiled. "You will. Soon. Very soon."

The Pilgrim answered as well. "Etrilla has called me from my resting place and summoned me back to the City of Wonders, here to do the will of all the gods as they follow Kanheer into a time of war. We who have sought peace and the comfort of a simple life are now called to do battle for our Lord of the Blood. We who have harvested grains and hunted game must now defend all that we have loved and all that we could hope to love against an enemy that wishes an end to everything we would see kept whole, Teagus of Tyrne. Just as they struck down your city, they would strike down all that matters to us."

Teagus saw other faces that were familiar as they joined in the migration. They came from different places, walking at a calm but brisk pace to keep up with the man who led them all. Many walked with calm acceptance. Some wept, for their lot was not going to be an easy one and they knew it.

Teagus might have run. Once upon a time he surely would have attempted to barter for his safety, but he knew better now. He had acted poorly in his time. He had used his authority for his own carnal satisfactions and he had lived comfortably while many suffered. That was not what Etrilla asked of his followers. There was a time for rest and a time for work. There was a time to reap the rewards of labor and a time to offer sacrifices in the names of the gods.

He had never sacrificed before.

He had blamed Merros Dulver for the fall of Tyrne, but he was the chosen of the City God and he was the one who failed to protect that city.

He would redeem himself now.

It was time.

He was given a second chance and he was so very grateful.

There were many stairs along the second wall. The inside wall had to be guarded and though there were a few soldiers currently in position there were not enough to even consider stopping them.

They climbed the stairs as they moved along the wall, maneuvering past buildings in some cases and in others walking past recently cleared fields where the newly formed towns of the refugees had been raised and then razed in preparation for the coming assault.

The guards along the wall stood in place and watched them, often with open mouths and a deep, abiding sense of shock. There were a hundred guards spread over the whole of a wall that could hold ten times that many soldiers. There were over two thousand of the Pilgrim's followers. The math was very easy. Best to let them alone as they seemed intent on doing no harm.

In all it took over an hour for the followers of the Pilgrim to take their positions along the wall.

It took Merros Dulver fifteen minutes to find the Pilgrim.

"You!" he called from below and pointed directly at the Pilgrim.

The Pilgrim nodded his head and stared back, his face set and grim.

"Why are you here?"

The Pilgrim looked at him for a moment and breathed out. "We are here to protect the city of Canhoon. To protect the Empress of Fellein and to raise the Silent Army."

"The Silent Army?" Merros shook his head. "What is a Silent Army?"

"Long ago Desh Krohan and the sorcerers of Canhoon summoned the Silent Army to defend against the enemies of the Empire. They were summoned and they served and when they had finished serving, they lay themselves down to rest until they were needed again."

General Dulver looked at the Pilgrim and then looked toward Teagus. "And aren't you supposed to be locked away?"

"Etrilla has forgiven my transgressions and yours as well, General Dulver. We are here to help you in your hour of need."

"You might consider buckets of water near the Western Gate. We're likely going to need them to put out the fire."

He had no idea what the man was prattling on about. Teagus would help to save the Empire but forgiven or not, he doubted that he would ever care for the general's company.

"We are here to save the city, Merros Dulver. That is enough. That is all you need to know."

Dulver listened to the Pilgrim's words and shook his head. "Just don't leave a mess along my wall. I'll be sending soldiers here soon and they'll need you out of the way."

"Merros?" For a second he almost failed to ask, but he had to, he needed to make amends. "I'd ask you to beg Empress Nachia's forgiveness on my behalf. I was not as good a man as I should have been in my younger years."

"Mention her name again and I'll come up there and kill you where you stand."

Teagus nodded. That was fair enough under the circumstances.

"It is time." The words were spoken softly enough, but around the entire wall the followers of the Pilgrim stood straighter.

To Merros Dulver the Pilgrim said, "The Silent Army comes. Do not stand in their way."

The Mid Wall around the heart of Canhoon stood over

fifty feet in height and was surrounded by cobblestones in all directions. A drop from the top would likely kill, but there was always that chance of failing.

"I have no blade," said Teagus, and the Pilgrim nodded and obligingly slit his throat for him. The sword's tip was sharp and cut through meat and tendons with ease. The pain was brief, but not unbearable.

Teagus gurgled a bit as he stepped forward from the edge of the wall and plummeted straight toward the cobblestones below.

"By the gods!" Merros stepped back quickly and avoided the blood splatter that followed. The next body fell a moment later and then the next and the next. Most of them had blades. Those that did not either asked help from a neighbor or, if they were desperate enough and short on time, bit through the meat of their own wrists.

Merros Dulver looked on, horrified as one after the next the followers of the Pilgrim bled themselves and then fell to their certain dooms. Their blood ran thick and hot between the stones and their bodies shuddered and twitched.

Teagus, the child-loving priest, looked his way as he died, a beautiful smile on his fat face.

"Why? What have you done?" He looked up to the Pilgrim who remained standing above him on the second wall.

"Have you forgotten along with the rest, Merros Dulver? The gods always demand a sacrifice."

The Pilgrim did not cut himself, nor did he plummet to his death. Instead he spread his arms far and wide, a sword held in one hand, and he called out in the old tongue, reciting the names of the gods, one after the other.

With each name he was transformed.

•••

Merros looked at the dead bodies around him and shook his head.

"Madness." The closest guard was standing still, staring at the bodies and blood. "You!"

The man flinched.

"Get to the barracks. Find anyone off duty and get them to help you with this." He waved an arm to indicate the bodies. "Go. Now."

The need to get back to the palace grew in him. It was a sense of dread that he refused to ignore.

"What if there's no one in the barracks?"

"Grab people off the street. I don't care how you do it, just get it done!"

Far above him on the second great wall, the Pilgrim stood still, looking down upon his dead followers.

It was time.

Maybe the sun was merely in the wrong spot. Perhaps the sight of two thousand or more people throwing themselves to their deaths had, understandably, rattled Merros Dulver more than he wanted to admit.

Whatever the reason, he took no notice of the Pilgrim where he still stood on the wall. He paid no heed as the color of the man began to change.

When he had awoken he was transformed, altered by the needs of the gods. He was made flesh and blood and lived after a long, deathless time at the bottom of a slow moving river.

Now he was transformed again. The needs of the gods were different and so he responded to them.

The gods demanded sacrifice and so he had gathered the faithful to him and asked that they offer themselves to the gods they served. A few had crept away in the night. A few others died before they could reach Canhoon as the trek across the land was not a gentle one and he had kept a hard, steady pace.

Below him the bodies of the faithful shifted and the one guard who was supposed to find enough assistance to move their bodies looked on and then ran, biting his lower lip in an effort not to scream. He broke flesh and bled a crimson beard down to his neck as he ran for the barracks. He did not look back, he did not dare.

There were no witnesses to see the transformation. The Pilgrim's skin hardened and darkened. His clothes changed too, taking on the form that he had worn for hundreds of years.

When he had first been created he and his brethren rose from the soil of Canhoon to defend the city against the enemies sent to destroy or control the fledgling empire. They were born for war, to defend, to protect and to kill as needed. In time they served their purpose and all of them faded, falling back into the stone and earth from which they rose.

The people of Canhoon had called them the Silent Army, for they were born without tongues and had no need of speech. They could move together, they could fight together with the skills bred into them.

There were secrets then. Great sorceries were used to forge their bodies, blood was shed and the bodies of those crushed within the earth of Canhoon as the city fell into ruin and shook itself apart were mixed with those sorceries. The Silent Army was born of pain and sacrifice and raised to serve.

The Silent Army was born again in much the same way.

The Pilgrim lowered his head and looked down at the stone wall beneath his feet. He had stood here once before when he was raised the first time. His feet had been where they were now.

Below him, along the entire range of the second great wall, the bodies of the faithful melted. They flowed into the spaces between the cobblestones, following the very path their blood had already taken.

The Pilgrim spoke the words that had summoned him the first time and added to those words of power the names of the gods who had resurrected him for this very purpose. He made his prayers, he commanded the power that the gods of Fellein afforded him, the gods remembered and forgotten alike.

The hardbaked clay of the second wall moved and danced, rising in columns all along its length.

The pillars of clay shifted more, and took form, mirroring the very shape of the Pilgrim where he stood, looking down upon the edge of the city he had sworn to protect from the moment of his creation.

Beyond the barrier where he stood was the area called New Canhoon, the places that had risen over the course of centuries. He contemplated those changes as his flesh continued its transformation from soft skin to living stone.

Seconds, minutes, hours. None of them mattered. To the naked eye the Silent Army seemed to rise in a heartbeat. To the Pilgrim the process seemed slow, and nearly as painful as a real childbirth. He ached with each transformation and felt the pain of his brethren as they were reborn from the bodies of the sacrificed.

Etrilla had kept sentinels in the City of Wonders, though few had ever considered them and none in many a decade. When the Silent Army had served its purpose many fell into ruin and were absorbed back into the city that birthed them but others climbed the towers and rooftops of the city and stayed where they chose to rest, frozen in position as they watched over Canhoon. They did not live, and they felt no need to move, but they had been there for as long as anyone, even the oldest of the sorcerers, could remember. Canhoon had its statues, true enough, but remarkably few of them had ever been sculpted by human hands, at least among those that stood above the city.

Those long silent sentinels moved at last, breaking free of the places where dust and time had long coated their bodies. Across the city the birds that had roosted along the statues broke into panicked flight while the oldest of the Silent Army moved to join their newly reborn brethren.

The Silent Army rose again. The Silent Army lived again.

Canhoon would be saved if they had any say in the matter and for a collection of beings that did not speak, they had a great deal to say.

How does one face a god?

Andover Lashk was learning quickly. He had stood before six gods and now he walked the final steps to face a seventh. So far the experience had never managed to become more comfortable.

Ydramil was the easiest mountain to climb, and oddly that only added to his discomfort. No, not discomfort. Fear.

He had scaled mountains, faced floods, fought literal armies to be where he was and the thought that he merely had to walk through an opening in a gentle slope rather terrified him.

There was a growing dread in his stomach that the final god he faced would be the worst.

In appearance he was no longer the same man he had been once upon a time. He knew that the moment he entered Ydramil's domain. The walls around him were silver, smooth and polished to an incredible sheen. He could see himself for the first time in a while, truly see himself and all of the changes that had taken place in his body.

He was taller, he was broader, he was… well, he was older. How much older? He could not say, but at a guess it had to be at least a decade's worth of transformation in his shape. He had been redefined by the gods. He had been, was being, reshaped.

Forged.

His hands were larger. That made no sense to him but they, too, had grown. Hard, living iron, forged by Truska-Pren. He had never considered that it could truly be alive and yet, the evidence was in front of him. A part of him. His body had changed because it had to. Hard work made muscle and he had been working very hard indeed.

The very things he had grown to admire in the Sa'ba Taalor now stood out on his flesh. A series of gray scars on gray skin told the tales of the combats he'd experienced. Not all of them. The battles he'd had in Wheklam's heart had not left physical marks. They had instead marked his mind. He had fought so many foes that it seemed to him the fear had been pounded from his body. The idea of facing ten men did nothing to make him nervous, merely wary.

The images in the silver walls around him moved of their own volition. They were images of him, to be sure, but he was standing still and they were not. The eyes that looked at him burned with an inner light he was very familiar with. The mouths on his reflected face moved and whispered, but there were no sounds. They were images, not solid beings.

The presence of Ydramil was with him.

One by one the multiple reflections of his body shifted. They took their time and settled in the gray dust that covered the floors of the vast cavern. It only took a moment for Andover to follow their example.

"I offer myself to you, Ydramil, as I have offered myself to all of the Daxar Taalor."

All of his reflections spoke and this time the words were clear. "You are welcome here, Andover Iron Hands. You and I have much to discuss."

When the god reached for him Andover fell back and closed his eyes. The impact was greater than he imagined possible.

The Blasted Lands were calm. The storms no longer raged and the ground was hidden beneath waters that slowly thawed after centuries of constant freezing.

The Mounds were no longer as they had been. Many had fallen completely and collapsed into the crust of the earth though a few still stood in the placid waters.

Three shapes crawled from the tunnel they had all used to gain entrance to the depths of hidden power locked away in the Mounds.

What had been Drask Silver Hand looked toward the Seven Forges for only a moment before turning and heading for the Temmis Pass. The others followed in silence.

Where they walked, the waters boiled.

For seven hours the Sa'ba Taalor gathered. At each of the sealed gates the armies grew until Canhoon was surrounded by an army as large as any seen in a dozen lifetimes.

At the end of that time the King in Iron made a gesture and the ranks closest to him called out with their horns – long, ululating notes that echoed from the distant foothills and bounced back to crash along the solemn stone barrier that held the armies at bay.

From all sides the other gathered armies made their calls, until the sound was very nearly as loud as thunder pealing across the whole of the city.

And then the noise stopped.

Desh Krohan watched and felt a shiver run through him.

There were so many of the enemy and he could not do what he had done before from this range. It was likely that if he tried he could eliminate most of the army, but not without a cost that he was not willing to pay.

He had eventually made his way back to Nachia's side as she stood in her tower and looked out on the vast armies gathered at the edge of the city, unwilling to rest for now. Instead she paced slowly around the cylindrical room and absorbed the sheer volume of enemies ranked together and held back by little more than a series of walls she knew would fall before their collected might.

Desh knew she considered asking him to strike against the enemy again. She considered it, but did not ask.

He was grateful for that small blessing. His answer would have been the same and that might well have ended the friendship and trust he had spent years cultivating with the new Empress.

Merros Dulver wrote messages and handed them to runners. The runners returned with other messages. Some reports were inconsequential. No one had attacked yet, but they would.

"Should we destroy the bridges between the first and second walls?" Merros sounded so very tired. Desh understood all too well.

Nachia shook her head. "No. There are too many of my people who need those bridges. Have soldiers ready to defend them. Have archers waiting."

Desh looked up. "I have seven sorcerers ready to destroy

the bridges if the command is given, Majesty. They await only your command and nothing less."

She nodded her head. Stone walls and brick roads could be destroyed with far more ease than a troop of soldiers that moved. He had explained the reasons to her before. Preparation made a difference. The bridges could be marked, and had been. Each sorcerer would only attack a single bridge if it came to that. Each bridge would be shattered and anything standing on it or near it would be destroyed as well.

"Desh, what do you know of a Silent Army?"

He looked to the general with a surprised expression. "The Silent Army? They were raised once upon a time to stop the enemies of Fellein. It took more power than you could understand, Merros. More than the remaining sorcerers could muster, I think. And it required sacrifices."

Merros scowled and walked to the window closest to him. After a moment he moved to the next window and studied the ground far below.

"What sort of sacrifices?"

"Power has to come from somewhere. The events that led to raising the Silent Army included a good number of deaths, and the use of necromancy to focus that power. I have told you before that necromancy is forbidden. There is a reason."

"Desh, earlier today I saw a gathering of madmen throw themselves off the Mid Wall. They cut their own throats and dropped to the ground before my eyes, and they claimed that they were offering themselves to the gods."

Desh frowned at him.

"Desh, they said the Silent Army was coming and not to stand in their way."

"That seems a rather significant thing to overlook telling me, Merros."

"I'm telling you now."

"Why didn't you mention this earlier, General?" There was frost in his voice that he could not prevent.

Merros shook his head. "I've been a bit busy today, First Advisor." There was heat in the general's voice.

Nachia calmed them both. "Enough. War. We have a war to win."

"Why are you mentioning the Silent Army?" Desh moved past the general and looked out the window. At the closest wall, the Great Wall as it was often called, the situation looked unchanged. At the New Wall, the barrier that currently kept the Sa'ba Taalor at bay, the same was true. But at the Mid Wall, something was different. The wall was a great distance away, but Desh Krohan's eyes were still as sharp as ever.

In perfect formation shapes stood atop the wall and looked out toward the New Wall or possibly beyond.

"By the gods, could we be that fortunate?" His voice cracked like a young boy's.

Nachia shook her head. "What are you prattling on about, old man?"

Desh's smile grew. "The Silent Army! Nachia! The Silent Army is here! I don't even begin to know how that's possible but they are here as they were before. I can't say they'll win against the Sa'ba Taalor, but they could damned well change the tide of the coming battle."

Nachia did not speak, but instead moved to the window and squinted down toward the city below. Desh pointed until she saw them and she studied the shapes.

"Why don't they move?"

"I don't know. I would think they'd protect Canhoon as they did in the past."

It was Nachia who thought of it first. "How long in the past, Desh?"

"Five hundred years, at least. Longer, probably. I can't remember that far back." He waved the question aside as if it were a house fly buzzing by his face.

"Desh, Canhoon was smaller then. So much smaller. The Mid Wall was raised when the city nearly fell. You're the one that told me that."

"Well, that could be an issue."

"What do you mean?"

"They might not understand that what is beyond that wall should be defended."

Nachia looked out the window again and then shook her head. "Maybe you could explain that to them?"

"I don't know that they'll much care to talk to me, actually."

"What do you mean? Didn't you say that you made them?"

"Well, yes, but I didn't exactly ask their permission." He looked out the window at the unmoving forms along the Mid Wall. "They might still be holding a grudge."

"Still? What do you mean?"

Before he could answer the horns sounded again. One short burst and then two more and in fast succession.

And as the last note sounded, the Sa'ba Taalor attacked.

On the first note the dead stopped their endless pounding at the doors, as if suddenly understanding that they had no impact. Several had broken, battered limbs but could feel no pain and suffered not at all.

On the second note the dead moved into position. Those closest to the wall took a dozen strides away from the wall and fell to the ground, lying prone. Those closest to them fell atop their bodies, covering them with their mass. Layer after layer, the dead at the Western Gate fell upon their brethren, until the corpses had to climb to find a new resting place.

On the third note, the dead that could do so clutched at the bodies closest to them and held tight.

Tarag Paedori looked upon the mountainous hill of the dead and nodded, satisfied.

Kallir Lundt, next to him, nodded as well and felt his blood roar.

The King in Iron wore a great suit of iron armor and a helmet that covered all of his head. His face was uncovered most times, but now he lowered the great mask of Truska-Pren over his visage. The god's face glowered at all who saw the king, and deep within the sockets of the mask the glow of Tarag Paedori's eyes was clear.

With a single wave of his hand the Sa'ba Taalor who rode their mounts moved forward. The great beasts ran, building up speed, and the foot soldiers before them hastily moved out of their way. Several hundred bodies lay before them, a ramp to help them gain access to the top of the wall meant to deter them.

The King in Iron was the first to make the walkway at the crest. The great beast under him clawed at the edge of the stone lip and found purchase, pulling both its own bulk and that of its giant rider to the top with ease. As soon as he had regained his balance Tarag Paedori started looking for his access to the ground on the other side.

There were guards upon the wall. They'd been watching as the dead fell to the ground and they'd been watching as the King in Iron and his riders climbed that mountain of flesh.

Most of them stayed to fight as Tarag Paedori came for them. The sword he drew was a brutal thing, heavy enough to crush bone and bend armor with ease. He carried it the same way and used it without hesitation, sweeping the foolish aside with each strike. Some died and others merely broke, but none of them mattered.

His sole concern was gaining the ground on the far side of the stone barrier and getting to the gate.

The guards before him fought. Archers grabbed bows and tried to place arrows in his body, but the armor he wore was thick, solid and well crafted by his own hand and the missiles could find no purchase there. Those that found his blood-red cloak and black tunic made it no further, but the sight of them sticking though the heavy fabric left more than one archer doubting that the man was killable.

He let them worry instead about his ability to kill. Pordra, his mount, roared and charged and tore into anything before them. Tarag smiled grimly under his helmet and cut down anything the beast could not reach, until, finally, the great gate stood before him. A series of pulleys and levers were needed to close the monstrous barrier. Once sealed it was simple to lock the barrier into a sealed position. The mechanism was old but well-tended and Tarag admired its craftsmanship for a moment before unlocking the heavy chains from where they were anchored.

Coils of metallic chains sang as they unrolled back to their usual position. The vast doors, sealed and locked for the first time in decades, groaned and rumbled as they pulled apart and slid away into the tracks that had been designed to accommodate them.

Once the task was finished, Tarag Paedori drew the heavy hammer from his side and destroyed the antique tracks and pulleys, ensuring they would never work again.

"To me! Come to me and kill them all!" He roared his command and was rewarded with a hundred battle cries as his people came forward.

As he turned to charge one man stood before him.

He was dressed in full armor of his own and had even managed a helmet.

"Face me, King in Iron!"

Tarag lifted his faceplate for a moment to study the man. He was of average size and he carried a sword with skilled hands. He was also trembling, terrified, but he stood his ground before the king.

He challenged the king.

"What is your name and who are you to challenge me?"

The man lifted the plate on his helmet and revealed a weathered, sweating face. "I am Captain Mendre Tinner of the Imperial Guard. This is my gate and you'll not pass beyond this point without facing me."

The man's voice shook. Still, he stood his ground.

"What weapons do you choose, Captain Mendre Tinner?" Tarag spoke calmly, while his soldiers formed behind him and slowly, carefully, the ranks of the soldiers serving the Fellein gathered behind their captain.

"Come again?"

"What weapons? Sword? Axe? Bare hands? What weapon would you use to face me in singular combat?"

He looked from his sword to the monstrous blade in Tarag's hand. "Any weapon?"

"I am Tarag Paedori, the King in Iron and Chosen of the Forge of Truska-Pren. You have challenged me to singular combat, yes?"

The man looked around, nervous, but hopeful. Here, he understood, was a chance to save his people.

"Yes, that's right."

"If I win this combat, you die and forfeit your claim to this gate. If you win this combat, my people turn from your city and do not return." He paused. "Agreed?"

"Yes, by all the gods, yes!" The fear was less now. Hope was a powerful weapon in its own right.

"By all the gods? No. By Truska-Pren. You have challenged. I offer you the choice of weapons. What will you choose?"

Around them, behind the king, the Sa'ba Taalor moved along the wall, their mounts spreading out for a substantial distance, all of the riders looking down on the challenger and the challenged.

"Fists!"

Tarag nodded his head. "Do you wish to wear armor? Or will we go bare fleshed?"

The man considered carefully, as well he should. Without armor he could move faster. So, too, could the king. Without armor, his blows would do more damage. So, too, the king. Armor would let him absorb some of the blows the king offered and would protect the king from him as well.

"Armored!"

Tarag Paedori nodded. "You have offered honorable combat. I accept. Should any of your followers attack during this time, my people will return the favor. So long as your followers remain outside the fight, my people will as well. Do you understand?"

"Yes."

Tarag Paedori climbed down from his mount and moved to stand in front of the captain of the guard.

Tinner stared at him, gaped, took in his full size and realized that he would be fighting a man who outweighed him by at least a hundred pounds, likely more.

"You are reconsidering the use of weapons?"

Tinner looked him up and down and nodded, likely not

even aware of the action. "I am reconsidering my challenge. You are... large."

"You may choose a weapon and I will follow suit."

Several of the Fellein were following him, their eyes on his body and a few had crossbows aimed at him.

He spoke up. "Should any Fellein fire a weapon at me or mine this truce is done and I'll see all here dead. Do you understand me?"

The crossbows lowered a bit. Some still stayed aimed his way, but without the same focus.

"I... Swords. I choose swords." Tinner's voice shook again.

"That is wise. A good sword could kill me."

Tarag Paedori walked back to Pordra and considered several different swords. He finally decided the one he carried would suffice.

His faceplate was placed back over his face. Truska-Pren once more glared down at his enemies.

Captain Mendre Tinner looked at him for a moment and took a combat stance. He was substantially smaller than Tarag, but the King in Iron had long since learned that size was not the only strength in a warrior. His armor was lighter, he was possibly faster, his skills were untested and might prove substantial.

"When you are ready, Captain Mendre Tinner, come for me."

The captain came in hard, swinging his sword to aim for the throat. A wise choice as many people left their necks vulnerable.

The sword in his right hand swept to block the captain's blow, knocking the weapon to the side, and he drove his left fist into his enemy's helmeted head, knocking the helmet askew.

Tarag Paedori had forged his own armor, his own helmet, and had designed them to fit perfectly. They were not loose, because armor that moved in the wrong ways offered no protection.

The helmet on Tinner's head was not designed for him. Whether it was a trophy or simply belonged to another the king could not say, but it was loose and the impact rattled the captain's head inside it.

He had accepted a formal challenge and had no intention of playing kindly with his enemy.

Tarag Paedori pivoted on his hip and, as Tinner tried to adjust the helmet, he drove his elbow into the man's head and face and sent him staggering back.

His blade cut through the captain's chest and the armor over it. The blow was meant to kill but the armor was good enough to slow it. Tinner grunted and fell to his knees, his helmet nearly sideways on his head and a great rend in his chest plate and his chest alike. Blood flowed heavily.

Tarag kicked the man in his chest and knocked him sprawling.

The second sword stroke succeeded where the first failed and Tinner died quickly.

The face of Truska-Pren looked up from the death of a good man and an adequate warrior and scowled at the masses of the Fellein who watched on, their faces pale, their bodies sagging in defeat.

Tarag Paedori was disappointed. He had hoped more might come forward to fight for their people.

"Kill them! All of them!"

To emphasize his point the King in Iron drove the tip of his sword through the closest guard's face and pushed onward.

Fifty thousand of his followers moved at his command, ready to seize the city.

•••

Nachia Krous stepped back and shook her head.

"The Western Gate is open." Her voice was broken and her spirit wasn't far behind. The gates should have held for days and as soon as the Sa'ba Taalor attacked they were opened and the enemy came through.

"What?" Merros and Desh both moved to the window and saw that she was right. The movement of the Sa'ba Taalor from this range made them tiny, but they swarmed quickly through the opening in the gate and spilled across the cleared area around the first defense, attacking anything foolish enough to stand in their way.

Desh stared hard, his face tight with tension and she could see him calculating the odds that he could do something about the problem.

"No, Desh. Not yet."

"If I don't do something now it will be too late."

She remembered the blistering arcs of light and the thunder that shattered the peace for as far as she could see. She could look even now and see the vast wasteland where he had done as she asked and leveled a portion of their enemies' forces.

"And if you miss? How much of Canhoon could you destroy?"

He withered. From the lines on his face to the posture he offered, he looked closer to his actual age than she had ever seen before.

Merros looked down toward the wave of enemies filling the area. "We've got to seal the Mid Gate. Now."

"There are still people–"

Merros shook his head. "Doesn't matter. Save some or lose all."

Nachia moved closer, shaking her head, prepared to argue though she knew he was in the right.

"There has to be something!" How many people? How many hundreds and thousands would die if they acted now?

How many would survive if they waited? Trecharch had already taught a lesson, to be sure.

The cell where Cullen waited was comfortable. It had been dressed with fine silks, there were pillows aplenty and a thick, luxurious fur to keep her warm. But it was still a cell.

She stared at the bars. They were not well decorated.

There was a crisis. She knew without being told what it was. The grayskins had made it to Canhoon and surely were attacking like the animals they were.

Deltrea sat next to her, shaking her head. "Hardly seems the way he should greet you."

"I'm nothing to him. It's the thing in me he wants."

"What is it, anyway?" Her friend leaned down and placed a spectral hand on her stomach. There was no pressure to feel. "What does it do?"

"Mostly it burns in me. I know it does something, but maybe it's not time to know yet."

"They're coming. If they find you here, with that thing inside you, they'll cut you open to get to it."

"You don't know that."

"I can't see them just ignoring it." Deltrea shrugged. "Least they don't seem interested in having their way with anyone. They just flat out killed me. Not a one of them tried to put any man parts inside my body."

"Well, you were dead."

"Be wiser than that. Wouldn't have stopped a few I knew."

Cullen's look of disgust changed into a mask of agony, as the thing inside her uncoiled and its power flared.

"Ahhhh!"

"Come now, I've said worse before about Tremm."

"Ah. No. Not."

She stopped speaking and fell to her side, the pain too big to contain. Whatever was in her was moving, and though she didn't think it wanted out just yet, she expected it would not be long. Sure as the dead screamed, it was changing its position inside of her and getting ready for something.

There were no corpses to use as a foothill on Tuskandru's side.

There were, however, trees. The trees were good enough to fall when they were hit with enough axes.

After that it was just a matter of strength to see them put in the right position and the followers of Durhallem were strong, let no one say otherwise. Because they needed to earn the right to fight for their god he had the children move the trees into place.

After the first volley of arrows killed those foolish enough to get too close they listened to his words and raised the trees by hastily cut tips that held the earth and by use of ropes that pulled the vast trunks higher. When the trees fell the second time – the first when they were cut down, the second when they were aimed at the wall – their weight was enough to break the wall's edge. It was a matter of moments for the mounts to climb their new entry points. It was only minutes later that Stastha and Loarhun tore the last of the guards down to the ground and then her mount pulled the gears and chains of the door until they finally opened.

Durhallem surely smiled down as Tusk rode through the opened gates and gestured for the children who had earned the right to make their first kills. Some of them were surely his seed and others were not, but they were all children of Durhallem and they were killers. He smiled as grown men fled from his young followers or tried to fight back and died.

A gesture to Stastha had the horn sounding and the armies of Durhallem followed again, driving back the foolish and the brave alike.

Mendt, all of nine and still pink in the skin, drove her

spear though a pregnant woman's belly and then turned and rammed the same point through the neck of a man screaming his grief even as he tried to kill her.

She did not waste her time smiling. There were more people to kill.

Tusk adjusted his helmet and pulled sword and axe alike. He allowed them the first kills. He would not allow them the last.

Durhallem was generous and Tusk could be no less.

In a chamber far beneath the main palace, a place known to fewer than five living souls, Goriah's body writhed; her hands clutched at the shroud that had covered her and pulled it away.

Tataya looked on, her face nearly expressionless, but her heart hammering wildly in her chest. What they did here was forbidden for a reason.

Pella stood on the other side of the marble table where Goriah's form shuddered and moaned.

At the head of that table Darsken Murdro slipped his fingers into the fine blonde hair of the dead Sister's head and looked down at her, his face surprisingly calm when one considered the powers he wielded.

Goriah's eyes opened. There should have been a caul of pale, milky white over her eyes and it was there for a moment, but as they watched on her Sisters saw that film fade away, saw her eyes stare first at the ceiling above and then roll into the back of her head as she screamed.

Both Tataya and Pella flinched.

Darsken looked to Tataya and shook his head. "Now is not the time for you to feel fear. Now is the time for you to ask your questions."

Tataya thought carefully before she spoke.

•••

Too far away for anyone in Canhoon to notice, Lored, Chosen of the Forge of Ordna and King in Bronze, roared his approval as the siege engines finally shattered the massive wall around the center of Elda.

His people roared too, and then smiled.

Elda would have fallen either way, but he wanted them to understand the power of Ordna's ways. They believed as he did, yes, but to see their beliefs made real, that was what all of the faithful desired.

The people of Elda spent three days doing their very best to defend against Lored and his people. The walls were heavy and the soldiers well trained, but they also preened and strutted and talked to each other until he tired of waiting and started the siege before they had been ready.

War was never meant to be discussed to the point of futility. War was meant to be handled quickly and with much bloodshed. Lored showed them the error of their ways.

After the walls fell, he and his people moved into the city quickly.

What the King in Iron lamented was not found by Lored. The people of Elda were trained in war, and they fought well, even if they lacked discipline and cohesive leadership.

Lored wanted to strike himself, but the patience of his followers must first be rewarded. They were allowed to fight and to kill as they saw fit.

For two days Elda burned and streets stank of blood and death.

On the third day, Lored and his people left the city, riding north and west, heading to join the rest of the Sa'ba Taalor, but only after they had killed as many Fellein as they could stomach with their endless appetites.

On the fourth day Lored woke early and stretched and praised Ordna for his many spectacular gifts.

"As you have asked, Great Ordna, I have done. All that I have and all that I am is yours."

He raised the bronze spear he had crafted for his god and hurled it into the air, aiming for Elda.

His god took it from there. The spear rose higher than should have been possible and arced toward the very center of the city. When it reached its destination the tip of the spear drove down into the ground and immediately shattered.

Seconds later, the ground exploded. From a full day's ride away, Lored felt the ground shake and his blood boil. The Daxar Taalor offered miracles every day to the faithful but few of them were so very direct.

Ordna's people roared their approval and called to their god as the mountain rose in the distance. Fire clawed at the sky. Lightning ripped down the heavens in celebration of the god's rebirth.

Ordna rejoiced and his people rejoiced with him.

Somewhere in Canhoon, Glo'Hosht walked unseen. Many were the people chosen by the gods to die. Glo'Hosht and his chosen worked to kill a select few. Some tides are stopped by mountains. Others are freed by the removal of a single obstacle. The Great Tide was upon Canhoon.

The time to open the gates was here.

At the Southern Gate Swech and Jost carefully aimed and struck again and again, the fine, poisoned darts working to kill before those they stabbed could even feel the sting of death.

The gate opened quietly to the waiting forces.

The army that spilled through the gate was not quiet. They did not need to be. The reason for silence had already been killed by the time they could enter.

They came prepared for war and found dead guards waiting for them. Not the sort to let a delay in the celebrations slow them down, the Sa'ba Taalor rode into Canhoon anyway and sought new enemies to kill.

•••

The forces at the Eastern Gate were not yet inside when Canhoon struck back.

There are those who have never quite understood why Canhoon is called the City of Wonders.

There are tales, to be sure, but stories for a dozen lifetimes back or more seldom hold much sway with the living. They are fables and notions and tales to scare children into behaving and seldom much more.

Canhoon had rested well, it was time to awaken.

The Silent Army stood facing the outer wall of the city and watched, expressionless, as the Sa'ba Taalor broke through and threatened all that they had died to protect.

As one, the vast army of statues shifted, placing their sword tips against the wall beneath them. It was a small thing, but this time people noticed.

If they were concerned about the odd action, they did not have time to respond. As soon as the blades touched down energies unseen spilled from the sentinels and lashed out across the land.

Roughly one thousand yards in from the edge of the outer wall the ground shook across all of Canhoon.

The Sa'ba Taalor were in motion, but they were not foolish. Training sometimes pays off where common sense might not prevail. The warriors stopped their forward motion almost as one and looked carefully at their surroundings.

At the Northern Gate Tusk shook his head, spat and for the first time in his life demanded that his followers retreat. He was not amused, but he was also not foolish enough to argue when Durhallem told him what must be done.

At the Western Gate Tarag Paedori did the same, immediately wheeling around and reversing the charge.

At the Eastern Gate the attacking forces stopped their advance and left the unbroken gate in peace.

At the Southern Gate those who had already gained entrance continued on and those who had not retreated.

The timing was important. Those who failed to listen died quickly.

The ground shook a second time and then the whole of the city shook.

The permanent structures in the city were almost unaffected. They had been built to withstand amazing trauma, and the sorcerers who had rebuilt the city had been in their prime and eager to prove themselves.

The walls of the palace did not shift, though a great deal of furniture moved and shuddered and danced. Merros Dulver managed to pull Nachia from the window where she was still staring before an errant marble bench could crush her against it.

Throughout the area called Old Canhoon and a distance beyond it as well, the buildings stood and the possessions within them shuddered and the people screamed as if the world were ending.

Maybe they were right.

The ground shook again and the city groaned. The bridges over the river that ran between the First Wall and the Mid Wall bucked and roared and screamed as they were torn asunder. The stones had rested there for centuries and been tended as necessary, but they could not withstand the force of the ground itself rising.

All of the ground. There was a line, surprisingly even, that ran around the entire circumference of Old Canhoon, and along that line everything toward the center lifted at once. The ground shivered and moaned but did not collapse. The great stone roads were not destroyed. The very buildings that had once rebuilt themselves from the ruins of first a great earthquake and then an invading army did not falter or fall.

The Sa'ba Taalor who had retreated, even Tusk, all nodded with understanding even as they backed away in dread. This was not the work of their gods. This was something different and unknown.

They had been saved from the madness by their gods and they rejoiced in their hearts, but to see the city begin to rise was unsettling just the same.

Old Canhoon groaned as it continued to rise, the whole of the city and a deep wedge of stone and dirt and the heart of the earth came with it, lifting higher and higher into the air as every last soul who could prayed to gods or contemplated the end of their lives.

In the highest tower of the palace a spot from which numerous rulers had looked down over generations on all that they had sworn to protect, the Empress and her closest advisors stood and held tightly to the edges of the walls as they looked out and watched the city rise.

There was a very strong possibility that Merros Dulver screamed. It was equally likely that Nachia Krous made sounds that did not normally come from the most powerful ruler in the known world.

Desh Krohan did not scream. Desh Krohan first gasped and then started laughing with joy. He clapped his hands and jumped up and down with the enthusiasm of a very happy toddler, he bellowed his excitement. "By all the gods I never thought I'd see the like again!"

Merros managed to swallow his fear and looked at the madman laughing as the world floated away below them.

"See what? This? What in all the world is happening?"

"This!" he gestured madly. "I forgot that Old Canhoon can do this!"

"What is it doing?" Nachia jabbed a finger in his direction. "What did you do to my city?"

"I didn't do this, my dear! Old Canhoon did this! This is why she is called the City of Wonders! She's escaping!"

Nachia tried hard to look through all of the windows at once and failed and finally focused on her First Advisor again. "Well? Where is it going?"

Desh stopped laughing and looked at her, his face suddenly worried all over again.

"Do you know, I have absolutely no idea. I just know that it is going and we have a chance to regroup and prepare all over again."

"What's different this time, Desh Krohan?" Merros looked at him and shook his head. "What could possibly make a difference? No matter where we go, I can promise you the Sa'ba Taalor will follow."

Desh smiled again. "This time we have them."

The wizard pointed to the window. They had continued to rise and currently a substantial flock of birds was moving around the palace wall, exploring their new, unexpected neighbor in the sky.

"Who? The birds? What will they do, shit on their armor?" Merros was close to hysteria. He had never much liked sorcery and even using it a little made him uncomfortable. Moving cities was well beyond his usual horizon for calm.

"No, Merros!" Desh walked over and gripped the general's shoulder. He spun him toward the window and pointed toward the Mid Wall. "Them! The Silent Army! They're here to protect us. It's the only possible reason for the city moving, because I promise you, I had nothing to do with it this time around. Not the city and not the army."

Merros and Desh and Nachia were all looking out the window when the next miracle occurred.

As one the Silent Army raised their swords and dissolved into the wall they stood on. Only seconds later they walked out of the wall as if passing through a curtain and stood around the wall, now facing outward, toward the edge of a city that continued to rise higher into the air.

Merros frowned for several seconds and then did something he had never truly done before in his life.

He thanked the gods.

ABOUT THE AUTHOR

James A Moore is the author of over twenty novels, including the critically acclaimed *Fireworks, Under The Overtree, Blood Red, Deeper,* the Serenity Falls trilogy (featuring his recurring anti-hero, Jonathan Crowley) and his most recent novels *Blind Shadows* and *The Blasted Lands*. He has twice been nominated for the Bram Stoker Award, and spent three years as an officer in the Horror Writers Association, first as Secretary and later as Vice President. He lives in Massachusetts, USA, where he is putting the finishing touches to *The Silent Army*.

genrefied.blogspot.com • *twitter.com/jamesamoore*

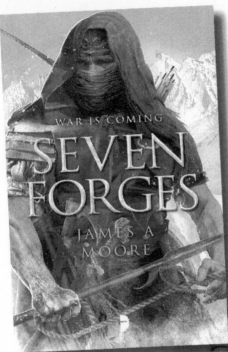

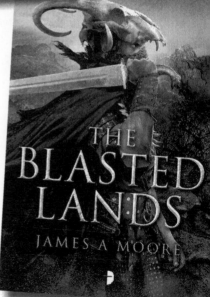

~ I ~
**SEVEN
FORGES**

War is coming

~ II ~
**THE BLASTED
LANDS**

*War has
come*